THE FANTASTIC WORLDS OF MALCOLM JAMESON

by

Malcolm Jameson

THUNDERCHILD PUBLISHING
Huntsville, Alabama

THE FANTASTIC WORLDS OF MALCOLM JAMESON

Copyright © 1939-46 by Malcolm Jameson

Published by arrangement with the Jameson estate

This Edition Copyright © 2019 by Thunderchild Publishing

This collection includes:
- Blind Alley – June 1943
- Fighters Never Quit – August 1942
- The Giftie Gien – April 1943
- Chariots of San Fernando – January 1946
- Vengeance In Her Bones – May 1942
- Heaven Is What You Make It – August 1943
- The Old Ones Hear – June 1942
- Not According to Dante – June 1941
- Train for Flushing – March 1940
- The Goddess' Legacy – October 1942
- Doubled and Redoubled – February 1941
- Catalyst Poison – April 1939
- Transients Only [only as by Mary MacGregor] – December 1942
- Children of the Betsy B – March 1939

Edited by Dan Thompson

ISBN: 9781695882065

Published by Thunderchild Publishing. Find us at
https://ourworlds.net/thunderchild_cms/

Cover by Dan Thompson

Foreword

I've titled this volume of Malcolm Jameson's work *Fantastic Worlds* because that's exactly what it is about. Jameson is best known for his straight science fiction such as the Bullard and Anachron stories (already published in previous collections), but he was also adept at more fantastic flights of imagination. The stories presented here are a mix of fantasy and science fiction that feature ghosts, demons and monsters; some supernatural, some natural and some the creation of science gone wrong. Magic in various forms appears, generally to the detriment of the characters involved. Old fashioned ghost stories are given unexpected twists, often darkly humorous. And the extremes of evolution are explored in "Chariots of San Fernando."

Since most of these stories were written in the years that World War II raged around the globe, it is not surprising that the war shows up in many of them. Sometimes it is directly as in "Fighters Never Quit" or "Vengeance in Her Bones." Sometimes it is less obvious but still evident in the background of stories like "Transients Only," in which the housing shortage in Washington, D.C. during the war plays an important part. Jameson had been a Naval officer who experienced combat during World War I and that understanding of what war is like is evident in his work.

Certainly the best known story in this collection is the novella "Blind Alley" but it is not known by that name. Rather, it achieved recognition as the *Twilight Zone* episode "Of Late I Think of Cliffordville" which was originally broadcast on April 11, 1963. Starring Albert Salmi, John Anderson, and Julie Newmar, Jameson's story was turned into one of the rare hour-long episodes in the series' fourth season.

A pleasant surprise for me in assembling this collection was the discovery of Jameson's story "Doubled and Redoubled." It's a fine story in its own right but what struck me was the similarity of the plot to that of the movie *Groundhog Day* (1993). I have no doubt this is just coincidence, but it is a strong one.

It is a real pleasure for me to bring these stories back into "print." Most have not been available since their original appearances in the pulp magazines of the 1940's. I hope you enjoy them as much as I have.

Dan Thompson
1 November 2013

Blind Alley

He was rich and old, and he longed for the good old days, and the good old ways of his youth. So he made a bargain by which he got back to those days, and those ways, and —

Nothing was further from Mr. Feathersmith's mind that dealings with streamlined, mid-twentieth-century witches or dickerings with the Devil. But something *had* to be done. The world was fast going to the bowwows, and he suffered from an overwhelming nostalgia for the days of his youth. His thoughts constantly turned to Cliffordsville and the good old-days when men were men and God was in His heaven and all was right with the world. He hated modern • women, the blatancy of the radio, That Man in the White House, the war —

Mr. Feathersmith did not feel well. His customary grouch — which was a byword throughout all the many properties of Pyramidal Enterprises, Inc. — had hit an all-time high. The weather was rotten, the room too hot, business awful, and everybody around him a dope. He loathed all mention of the war, which in his estimation had been bungled from the start. He writhed and cursed whenever he thought of priorities, quotas and taxes; he frothed at the mouth at every new government regulation. His plants were working night and day on colossal contracts that under any reasonable regime would double his wealth every six months, but what could he expect but a few paltry millions?

He jabbed savagely at a button on his desk, and before even the swiftest-footed of messengers could have responded, he was irritably rattling the hook of his telephone.

"Well?" he snarled, as a tired, harassed voice answered. "Where's Paulson? Wake him up! I want him."

Paulson popped into the room with an inquiring. "Yes, sir?" Mr. Paulson was his private secretary and to his mind stupid, clumsy and unambitious. But he was a male. For Mr. Feathersmith could not abide the type of woman that cluttered up offices in these decadent days. Everything about them was distasteful — their bold, assured manner; their calm assumption of efficiency, their persistent invasion of fields sacred to the stronger and wiser sex. He abhorred their short skirts, their painted faces and their varnished nails, the hussies! And the nonchalance with which they would throw a job in an employer's face if he undertook to drive them was nothing short of maddening. Hence Mr. Paulson.

"I'm roasting," growled Mr. Feathersmith. "This place is an oven."

"Yes, sir," said the meek Paulson, and went to the window where an expensive air-conditioning unit stood. It regulated the air, heating it in winter, cooling it in summer. It was cold and blustery out and snow was in the air; Mr. Feathersmith should have been grateful. But he was not. It was a modern gadget, and though a touch of the hand was all that was needed to regulate it, he would have nothing to do with it. All Paulson did was move a knob one notch.

"What about the Phoenix Development Shares?" barked the testy old man. "Hasn't Ulrich unloaded those yet? He's had time enough."

"The S. E. C. hasn't approved them yet," said Paulson, apologetically. He might have added, but thought best not to, that Mr. Farquhar over there had said the prospectus stank and that the whole proposition looked like a bid for a long-term lease on a choice cell in a Federal penitentiary.

"*Aw-r-rk*," went Mr. Feathersmith, "a lot of Communists, that's what they are. What are we coming to? Send Clive in."

"Mr. Clive is in court, sir. And so is Mr. Blakeslee. It's about the reorganization plan for the Duluth, Moline & Southern — the bondholders protective committee —"

"*Aw-r-rk*," choked Mr. Feathersmith. Yes, those accursed bondholders — always yelping and starting things. "Get out. I want to think."

His thoughts were bitter ones. Never in all his long and busy life had things been as tough as now. When he had been simply Jack Feathersmith, the promoter, it had been possible to make a fortune overnight. You could lose at the same rate, too, but still a man had a chance. There were no starry-eyed reformers always meddling with him. Then he had become the more dignified "entrepreneur," but the pickings were still good. After that he had styled himself "investment banker" and had done well, though a certain district attorney raised some nasty questions about it and forced some refunds and adjustments. But that had been in the '30s when times were hard for everybody. Now, with a war on and everything, a man of ability and brains ought to mop up. But would they let him? *Aw-r-rk!*

Suddenly he realized he was panting and heaving and felt very, very weak. He must be dying. But that couldn't be right. No man of any age kept better fit. Yet his heart was pounding and he had to gasp for every breath. His trembling hand fumbled for the button twice before he found it. Then, as Paulson came back, he managed a faint, "Get a doctor — I must be sick."

For the next little while things were vague. A couple of the hated females from the outer office were fluttering and cooing about the room, and one offered him a glass of water which he spurned. Then he was aware of a pleasant-faced young chap bending over him listening to his chest through a stethoscope. He discovered also that one of those tight, blood-pressure contraptions was wrapped around his arm. He felt the prick of a needle. Then he was lifted to a sitting position and given a couple of pills.

"A little stroke, eh?" beamed the young doctor, cheerily. "Well, you'll' be all right in a few minutes. The ephedrine did the trick."

Mr. Feathersmith ground his teeth. If there was anything in this topsy-turvy modern age he liked less than anything else it was the kind of doctors they had. A little stroke, eh? The young whippersnapper! A fresh kid, no more. Now take old Dr. Simpson, back at Cliffordsville. There was a doctor for you — a sober, grave man who wore a beard and a proper Prince Albert coat. There was no folderol about him — newfangled balderdash about basal metabolism, X rays, electrocardiograms, blood counts and all that

7

rot. He simply looked at a patient's tongue, asked him about his bowels, and then wrote a prescription. And he charged accordingly.

"Do you have these spells often?" asked the young doctor. He was so damn cheerful about it, it hurt.

"Never," blared Mr. Feathersmith, "never was sick a day in my life. Three of you fellows pawed me over for three days, but couldn't find a thing wrong. Consolidated Mutual wrote me a million straight life on the strength of that and tried their damnedest to sell me another million. That's how good I am."

"Pretty good," agreed the doctor with a laugh. "When was that?"

"Oh, lately — fifteen years ago, about."

"Back in '28, huh? That was when even life insurance companies didn't mind taking a chance now and then. You were still in your fifties then, I take it?"

"I'm fit as a fiddle yet," asserted the old man doggedly. He wanted to pay this upstart off and be rid of him.

"Maybe," agreed the doctor, commencing to put his gear away, "but you didn't look it a little while ago. If I hadn't got here when I did —"

"Look here, young man," defied Mr. Feathersmith, "you can't scare me."

"I'm not trying to," said the young man, easily. "If a heart block can't scare you, nothing can. Just the same, you've got to make arrangements. Either with a doctor or an undertaker. Take your choice. My car's downstairs if you think I'll do."

"*Aw-r-rk,*" sputtered Mr. Feathersmith, but when he tried to get up he realized how terribly weak he was. He let them escort him to the elevator, supporting him on either side, and a moment later was being snugged down on the back seat of the doctor's automobile.

The drive uptown from Wall Street was as unpleasant as usual. More so, for Mr. Feathersmith had been secretly dreading the inevitable day when he would fall into doctors' hands, and now that it had happened, he looked out on the passing scene in search of diversion.

The earlier snow had turned to rain, but there were myriads of men and lots of equipment clearing up the accumulation of muck and ice. He gazed at them sourly — *scrape, scrape, scrape* — noise, clamor and dirt, all symptomatic of the modern city. He yearned for Cliffordsville where it rarely snowed, and when it did it lay for weeks in unsullied whiteness on the ground. He listened to the gentle swishing of the whirling tires on the smooth, wet pavement, disgusted at the monotony of it. One street was like another, one city like another — smooth, endless concrete walled in by brick and plate glass and dreary rows of light poles. No one but a fool would live in a modern city. Or a modern town, for that matter, since they were but unabashed tiny imitations of their swollen sisters. He sighed. The good old days were gone beyond recapture.

It was that sigh and that forlorn thought that turned his mind to Forfin. Forfin was a shady fellow he knew and once or twice had employed. He was a broker of a sort, for the lack of better designation. He hung out in a dive near Chatham Square and was altogether a disreputable person, yet he could accomplish strange things. Such as dig up information known only to the dead, or produce prophecies that could actually be relied on. The beauty of dealing with him was that so long as the fee was adequate — and it had to be that — he delivered the goods and asked no questions. His only explanation of his peculiar powers was that he had contacts — gifted astrologers and numerologists, unprincipled demonologists and their ilk. He was only a go-between, he insisted, and invariably required a signed waiver before undertaking any assignment. Mr. Feathersmith recalled now that once when he had complained of a twinge of rheumatism that Forfin had hinted darkly at being able to produce some of the water of the Fountain of Youth. At a price, of course. And when the price was mentioned, Mr. Feathersmith had haughtily ordered him out of the office.

The doctor's office was the chamber of horrors he had feared. There were many rooms and cubbyholes filled with shiny adjustable enameled torture chairs and glassy cabinets in which rows of cruel instruments were laid. There were fever machines and other expensive-looking apparatus, and a laboratory full of mysterious tubes and jars. White-smocked nurses and assistants flitted noiselessly about like helpful ghosts. They stripped him and weighed

9

him and jabbed needles in him and took his blood. They fed him messy concoctions and searched his innards with a fluoroscope; they sat him in a chair and snapped electrodes on his wrists and ankle to record the pounding of his heart on a film. And after other thumpings, listenings and measurings, they left him weary and quivering to dress himself alone.

Naked as he was, and fresh from the critical probing of the doctor and his gang, he was unhappily conscious of how harshly age had dealt with him after all. He was pink and lumpy now where he had once been firm and tanned. His spindly shanks seemed hardly adequate for the excess load he now carried about his middle. Until now he had valued the prestige and power that goes with post-maturity, but now, for the first time in his life, he found himself hankering after youth again. Yes, youth would be desirable on any terms. It was a thoughtful Mr. Feathersmith who finished dressing that afternoon.

The doctor was waiting for him in his study, as infernally cheerful as ever. He motioned the old man to a chair.

"You are a man of the world," he began, "so I guess you can take it. There is nothing to be alarmed over — immediately. But you've got to take care of yourself. If you do, there are probably a good many years left in you yet. You've got a cardiac condition that has to be watched, some gastric impairments, your kidneys are pretty well shot, there are signs of senile arthritis, and some glandular failure and vitamin deficiency. Otherwise, you are in good shape."

"Go on." Now Mr. Feathersmith knew he would have' to get in touch with Forfin.

"You've got to cut out all work, avoid irritation and excitement, and see me at least weekly. No more tobacco, no liquor, no spicy or greasy foods, no late hours. I'm giving you a diet and some prescriptions as to pills and tablets you will need —"

The doctor talked on, laying down the law in precise detail. His patient listened dumbly, resolving steadfastly that he would do nothing of the sort. Not so long as he had a broker on the string who could contact magicians.

That night Mr. Feathersmith tried to locate Forfin, but Forfin could not be found. The days rolled by and the financier felt better.

He was his old testy self again and promptly disregarded all his doctor's orders. Then he had his second heart attack, and that one nearly took him off. After that he ate the vile diet, swallowed his vitamin and gland-extract pills, and duly went to have his heart examined. He began liquidating his many business interests. Sooner or later his scouts would locate Forfin. After that he would need cash, and lots of it. Youth, he realized now, was worth whatever it could be bought for.

The day he met with his lawyers and the buyers' lawyers to complete the sale of Pyramidal Enterprises, Inc., Mr. Blakeslee leaned over and whispered that Forfin was back in town. He would be up to see Mr. Feathersmith that night. A gleam came into the old man's eye and he nodded. He was ready. By tomorrow all his net worth would be contained in cash and negotiable securities. It was slightly over thirty-two million dollars altogether, an ample bribe for the most squeamish demonologist and enough left over for the satisfaction of whatever dark powers his incantations might raise. He was confident money would do the trick. It always had, for him, and was not the love of it said to be the root of all evil?

Mr. Feathersmith was elated. Under ordinary circumstances he would have conducted a transaction of the magnitude of selling Pyramidal with the maximum of quibbling and last-minute haggling. But today he signed all papers with alacrity. He even let Polaris Petroleum & Pipeline go without a qualm, though the main Polaris producing field was only a few miles south of his beloved Cliffordsville. He often shuddered to think of what an oil development would do to a fine old town like that, but it made him money and, anyhow, he had not been back to the place since he left it years ago to go and make his fortune.

After the lawyers had collected their papers and gone, he took one last look around. In his office, as in his apartment, there was no trace of garish chromium and red leather. It was richly finished in quiet walnut paneling with a single fine landscape on one wall. A bookcase, a big desk, two chairs and a Persian rug completed the furnishings. The only ultramodern feature was the stock ticker and the news teletype. Mr. Feathersmith liked his news neat and hot off the griddle. He couldn't abide the radio version, for it was adorned and embellished with the opinions and interpretations of various commentators and self-styled experts.

It was early when he got home. By chance it was raining again, and as he stepped from his limousine under the marquee canopy that hung out over the sidewalk, the doorman rushed forward with an umbrella lest a stray drop wet his financial highness. Mr. Feathersmith brushed by the man angrily — he did not relish sycophantism, he thought. Flunkies, pah! He went up in the elevator and out into the softly lit corridor that led to his apartment. Inside he found his houseboy, Felipe, listening raptly to a swing version of a classic, playing it on his combination FM radio and Victrola.

"Shut that damn thing off!" roared Mr. Feathersmith. Symphonic music he liked, when he was in the mood for it, but nothing less.

Then he proceeded to undress and have his bath. It was the one bit of ritual in his day that he really enjoyed. His bathroom was a marvel of beauty and craftsmanship — in green and gold tile with a sunken tub. There was a needle bath, too, a glass-enclosed shower, and a sweat chamber. He reveled for a long time in the steamy water. Then, remembering that Forfin might come at any time, he hurried out.

His dinner was ready. Mr. Feathersmith glowered at the table as he sat down. It was a good table to look at, but that was not the way he felt about it. The cloth was cream-colored damask and the service exquisitely tooled sterling; in the: center sat a vase of roses with sprays of ferns. But the crystal pitcher beside his plate held certified milk, a poor substitute for the vintage Pommard he was accustomed to. Near it lay a little saucer containing the abominable pills — six of them, two red, two brown, one black, and one white.

He ate his blue points. After that came broiled pompano, for the doctor said he could not get too much fish. Then there was fresh asparagus and creamed new potatoes. He topped it off with fresh strawberries and cream. No coffee, no liqueur.

He swallowed the stuff mechanically, thinking all the while of Chub's place, back in Cliffordsville. There a man could get an honest-to-goodness beef- steak, two inches thick and reeking with fat, fresh cut from a steer killed that very day in Chub's back yard. He thought, too, of Pablo, the tamale man. His stand was on the corner by the Opera House, and he kept his sizzling product in a huge lard can wrapped in an old red tablecloth. The can sat on a small charcoal stove so as to keep warm, and the whole was in a basket. Pablo dished out the greasy, shuck-wrapped morsels onto scraps of torn newspaper and one sat down on the curb and ate them with his fingers. They may have been made of fragments of dog — as some of his detractors alleged — but they were good. Ten cents a dozen, they were. Mr. Feathersmith sighed another mournful sigh. He would give ten thousand dollars for a dozen of them right now — and the ability to eat them.

Feathersmith waited impatiently for Forfin to come. He called the operator and instructed her to block all calls except that announcing his expected guest. Damn that phone, anyway. All that any Tom, Dick or Harry who wanted to intrude had to do was dial a number. The old man had an unlisted phone, but people who knew where he lived called through the house switchboard notwithstanding.

At length the shifty little broker came. Mr. Feathersmith lost no time in approaches or sparring. Forfin was a practical man like himself. You could get down to cases with him without blush or apology.

"I want," Mr. Feathersmith said, baldly. "to turn the hand of the clock back forty years. I want to go to the town of Cliffordsville, where I was born and raised, and find it just as I left it. I propose to start life all over again. Can you contact the right people for the job?"

"*Phew!*" commented Mr. Forfin, mopping his head. "That's a big order. It scares me. That'll involve Old Nick himself —"

He looked uneasily about, as if the utterance of the name was a sort of inverted blasphemy.

"Why not?" snapped the financier, bristling. "I always deal with principals. They can act. Skip the hirelings, demons, or whatever they are."

"I know," said Forfin, shaking his head disapprovingly, "but he's a slick bargainer. Oh, he keeps his pacts — to the dot. But he'll slip a fast one over just the same. It's his habit. He gets a kick out of it — outsmarting people. And it'll cost. Cost like hell."

"I'll be the judge of the cost," said the old man, stiffly, thinking of the scant term of suffering, circumscribed years that was the best hope the doctor had held out to him, "and as to bargaining, I'm not a pure sucker. How do you think I got where I am?"

"O. K.," said Forfin, with a shrug. "It's your funeral. But it'll take some doing. When do we start?"

"Now."

"He sees mortals only by appointment, and I can't make 'em. I'll arrange for you to meet Madame Hecate. You'll have to build yourself up with her. After that you're on your own. You'd better have plenty of ready dough. You'll need it."

"I've got it," said Mr. Feathersmith shortly. "And yours?"

"Forget it. I get my cut from *them*."

That night sleep was slow in coming. He reviewed his decision and did not regret it. He had chosen the figure of forty deliberately. Forty from seventy left thirty — in his estimation the ideal age. If he were much younger, he would be pushed around by his seniors; if he were much older, he wouldn't gain so much by the jump back. But at thirty he would be in the prime of physical condition, old enough to be thought of as mature by the youngsters, and young enough to command the envy of the oldsters. And, as he remembered it, the raw frontier days were past, the effete modernism yet to come.

He slept. He dreamed. He dreamed of old Cliffordsville, with its tree-lined streets and sturdy houses sitting way back, each in its own yard and behind its own picket fence. He remembered the soft clay streets and how good the dust felt between the toes when he ran barefoot in the summertime. Memories of good things to eat came to him — the old spring house and watermelons hung in bags in the well, chickens running the yard, and eggs an hour old. There was Sarah, the cow, and old Aunt Anna, the cook. And then there were the wide-open business opportunities of those days. A man could start a bank or float a stock company and there were no snooping inspectors to tell him what he could and couldn't do. There were no blaring radios, or rumbling, stinking trucks or raucous auto horns. People stayed healthy because they led the good life. Mr. Feathersmith rolled over in bed and smiled. It wouldn't be long now!

14

The next afternoon Forfin called him. Madame Hecate would see him at five; and he gave a Fifth Avenue address. That was all.

Mr. Feathersmith was really surprised when he entered the building. He had thought a witch would hang out in some dubious district where there was grime and cobwebs. But this was one of the swankiest buildings in a swanky street. It was filled with high-grade jewelers and diamond merchants, for the most part. He wondered if he had heard the address wrong.

At first he was sure he had, for when he came to examine the directory board he could find no Hecate under the H's or any witches under the W's. He stepped over to the elevator starter and asked him whether there was a tenant by that name.

"If she's on the board, there is," said that worthy, looking Mr. Feathersmith up and down in a disconcerting fashion. He went meekly back to the board. He rubbed his eyes. There was her name — in both places: "Madame Hecate, Consultant Witch. Suite 1313."

He went back to the elevators, then noticed that the telltale arcs over the doors were numbered 10, 11, 12, 14, 15, and so on. There was no thirteenth floor. He was about to turn to the starter again when he noticed a small car down at the end of the hall. Over its door was the label, "Express to 13th Floor." He walked down to it and stepped inside. An insolent little guy in a red monkey jacket lounged against the starting lever. He leered up at Mr. Feathersmith and said:

"Are you *sure* you want to go up, pop?"

Mr. Feathersmith gave him the icy stare he had used so often to quell previous impertinences, and then stood rigidly looking out the door. The little hellion slid the door to with a shrug and started the cab.

When it stopped he got off in a small foyer that led to but a single door. The sign on the door said merely "Enter," so Mr. Feathersmith turned the knob and went in. The room looked like any other midtown reception room. There was a desk presided over by a lanky, sour woman of uncertain age, whose only noteworthy feature was her extreme pallor and haggard eyes. The walls were done in a flat blue-green pastel color that somehow hinted at iridescence, and were relieved at the top by a frieze of interlaced pentagons of gold and black. A single etching hung on the wall, depicting a

15

conventionalized witch astride a broomstick silhouetted against a full moon, accompanied by a flock of bats. A pair of chairs and a sofa completed the furnishings. On the sofa a huge black cat slept on a red velvet pillow.

"Madame Hecate is expecting you," said the cadaverous receptionist in a harsh, metallic voice. "Please be seated."

"Ah, a zombi," thought Mr. Feathersmith, trying to get into the mood of his environment. Then as a gesture of good will, though he had no love for any animal, he bent over and stroked the cat. It lifted its head with magnificent deliberation, regarded him venomously for a moment through baleful green eyes; then, with the most studied contempt, spat. After that it promptly tucked its head back in its bosom as if that disposed of the matter for all eternity.

"Lucifer doesn't like people," remarked the zombi, powdering her already snowy face. Just then a buzzer sounded faintly, three times.

"The credit man is ready for you," said the ghostly receptionist. "You'll have to pass him first. This way, please."

For some reason that did not astonish Mr. Feathersmith as much as some other features of the place. After all, he was a businessman, and even in dealing with the myrmidons of Hell, business was business. He followed her through the inner door and down a side passage to a little office. The fellow who received him was an affable, thin young man, with brooding, dark-brown eyes, and an errant black lock that kept falling down and getting in his eyes.

"A statement of your net worth, please," asked the young man, indicating a chair. He turned and waved a hand about the room. It was lined with fat books, shelf after shelf of them, and there were filing cases stuffed with loose papers and photographs. "I should warn you in advance that we have already made an independent audit and know the answer. It is a formality, as it were. Thought you ought to know."

Mr. Feathersmith gazed upon the books with wonderment. Then his blood ran chill and he felt the gooseflesh rise on him and a queer bristly feeling among the short hairs on the back of his neck. The books were all about him! There were two rows of thick

16

volumes neatly titled in gold leaf, such as "J. Feathersmith —
Private Life — Volume IX." There was one whole side of the room
lined with other books, in sets. One set was labeled "Business
Transactions," another "Subconscious Thoughts and Dreams," and
then other volumes on various related aspects of their subject. One
that shocked him immensely bore the horrid title of "Indirect
Murders, Et Cetera." For an instant he did not grasp its import, until
he recalled the aftermath of the crash of Trans-Mississippi
Debentures. It was a company he had bought into only to find it
mostly water. He had done the only thing to do and get out with a
profit — he blew the water up into vapor, then pulled the plug. A
number of suicides resulted. He supposed the book was about that
and similar fiascoes.

He turned to face the Credit Man and was further dismayed
to see that gentleman scrutinizing a copy of the contract of sale of
the Pyramidal company. So he knew the terms exactly! Worse, on
the blotter in plain sight was a photostat copy of a will that he had
made out that very morning. It was an attempt on Mr. Feathersmith's
part to hedge. He had left all his money to the Simonist Brotherhood
for the propagation of religion, thinking to use it as a bargaining
point with whatever demon showed up to negotiate with him. Mr.
Feathersmith scratched his neck — a gesture of annoyance at being
forestalled that he had not used for years. It was all the more
irritating that the Credit Man was purring softly and smiling to
himself.

"Well?" said the Credit Man.

Mr. Feathersmith had lost the first round and knew it. He had
come in to arrange a deal and to dictate, more or less, his own terms.
Now he was at a distinct disadvantage. There was only one thing to
do if he wanted to go on; that was to come clean. He reached into his
pocket and pulled out a slip of paper. There was one scribbled line
on it. "Net worth — $32,673,251.03, plus personal effects."

"As of noon, today," added Mr. Feathersmith, handing the
paper across the desk.

The Credit Man glanced at it, then shoved it into a drawer
with the comment that it appeared to be substantially correct. Then
he announced that that was all. He could see Madame Hecate now.

* * *

Madame Hecate turned out to be the greatest surprise so far. Mr. Feathersmith had become rather dubious as to his ability to previse these strange people he was dealing with, but he was quite sure the witch would be a hideous creature with an outjutting chin meeting a down-hanging beak and with the proverbial hairy warts for facial embellishments. She was not like that at all. Madame Hecate was as cute a little trick as could be found in all the city. She was a vivacious, tiny brunette with sparkling eyes and a gay, carefree manner, and was dressed in a print housedress covered by a tan smock.

"You're a lucky man, Mr. Feathersmith," she gurgled, wiping her hands on a linen towel and tossing it into a handy container. "The audience with His Nibs is arranged for about an hour from now. Ordinarily he only comes at midnight, but lately he has had to spend so much time on Earth he works on a catch-as-catch-can basis. At the moment he is in Germany — it is midnight there now, you know — giving advice to one of his most trusted mortal aids. No doubt you could guess the name, but for reasons you will appreciate, our clientele is regarded as confidential. But he'll be along shortly."

"Splendid," said Mr. Feathersmith. For a long time it had been a saying of his that he wouldn't wait an hour for and appointment with the Devil himself. But circumstances had altered. He was glad that he had *only* an hour to wait.

"Now," said the witch, shooting him a coy, sidelong glance, "let's get the preliminaries over with. A contract will have to be drawn up, of course, and that takes time. Give me the main facts as to what you want, and I'll send them along to the Chief Fiend in the Bureau of Covenants. By the time His Nibs gets here, the scribes will have everything ready."

She produced a pad and a pencil and waited, smiling sweetly at him.

"Well,' uh," he said, a trifle embarrassed because he did not feel like telling her *quite* all that was in his mind — she seemed such an innocent to be in the witch business, "I had an idea it would be nice to go back to the town of my boyhood to spend the rest of my life —"

"Yes?" she said eagerly. "And then —"

"Well," he finished lamely, "I guess that's about all. Just put me back in Cliffordsville as of forty years ago — that's all I want."

"How unique!" she exclaimed, delightedly. "You know, most men want power and wealth and success in love and all that sort of thing. I'm sure His Nibs will grant this request instantly."

Mr. Feathersmith grunted. He was thinking that he had already acquired all those things from an uninformed, untrained start in that same Cliffordsville just forty years ago. Knowing what he did now about men and affairs and the subsequent history of the world, what he would accomplish on the second lap would astonish the world. But the thought suggested an addendum.

"It should be understood," he appended, "that I am to retain my present . . . uh . . . wisdom, unimpaired, and complete memory —"

"A trifle, Mr. Feathersmith," she bubbled; "a trifle, I assure you."

He noticed that she had noted the specifications on separate sheets of paper, and since he indicated that was all, she advanced to a nearby brazier that stood on a tripod and lit them with a burning candle she borrowed from a sconce. The papers sizzled smartly into greenish flame, curled and disappeared without leaving any ash.

"They are there now," she said. "Would you like to see our plant while you wait?"

"With pleasure," he said, with great dignity. Indeed, he was most curious about the layout, for the room they were in was a tiny cubicle containing only a high desk and a stool and the brazier. He had expected more demoniac paraphernalia.

She led the way out and he found the place was far more extensive than he thought. It must cover the entire floor of the building. There was a long hall, and off it many doors.

"This is the Alchemical Department," she said, turning into the first one. "I was working in here when you came. That is why my hands were so gummy. Dragon fat is vile stuff, don't you think?"

She flashed those glowing black eyes on him and a dazzling smile.

"I can well imagine," he replied.

19

He glanced into the room. At first sight it had all the appearance of a modern chemical laboratory, though many of the vessels were queerly shaped. The queerest of all were the alchemiots, of whom about a dozen sat about on high stools. They were men of incalculable age, bearded and wearing heavy-rimmed octagonal-lensed eyeglasses. All wore black smocks spattered with silvery crescents, sunbursts, stars, and such symbols. All were intent on their work. The bottles on the tables bore fantastic labels, such as "asp venom," "dried cameleopard blood," and "powdered unicorn horn."

"The man at the alembic," explained the witch, sweetly, "is compounding a modified love philter. You'd be surprised how many star salesmen depend on it. It makes them virtually irresistible. We let them have it on a commission basis."

. She pointed out some other things, such as the two men adjusting the rheostat on an electric athanor, all of which struck Mr. Feathersmith as being extremely incongruous. Then they passed on.

The next room was the Voodoo Department, where a black sculptress was hard at work fashioning wax dolls from profile and front-view photographs of her clients most hated enemies. An assistant was studying a number of the finished products and occasionally thrusting pins into certain vital parts. These were other unpleasant things to be seen there and Mr. Feathersmith shuddered and suggested they pass on.

"If it affects you that way," said the witch, with her most beguiling smile, "maybe we had better skip the next."

The next section was devoted to Demonology and Mr.Feathersmith was willing to pass it by, having heard something of the practices of that sect. Moreover, the hideous moans and suppressed shrieks that leaked through the wall were sufficient to make him lose any residual interest in the orgies. But it was not to be. A door was flung open and an old hag tottered out, holding triumphantly aloft a vial of glowing violet vapor.

"Look," she cackled with hellish glee, "I caught it! The anguish of a dying hen! He! He!"

Mr. Feathersmith suffered a twinge of nausea and a bit of fright, but the witch paused long enough to coo a few words of praise.

She popped her head into the door beyond where a senile practitioner could be seen sitting in a black robe and dunce's cap spangled with stars and the signs of the zodiac. He was in the midst of a weird planetarium.

This is the phoniest racket in the shop," she murmured, "but the customers love it. The old guy is a shrewd guesser. That's why he gets by. Of course, his horoscopes and all these props are just so much hogwash — custom, you know."

Mr. Feathersmith flicked a glance at the astrologer, then followed her into the next room. A class of neophytes appeared to be undergoing instruction in the art of Vampirism. A demon with a pointer was holding forth before a set of wall charts depicting the human circulatory system and emphasizing the importance of knowing just how to reach the carotid artery and jugular vein. The section just beyond was similar. It housed the Department of Lycanthropy and a tough-looking middle-aged witch was lecturing on the habits of predatory animals. As Mr. Feathersmith and his guide looked in, she was just concluding some remarks on the value of prior injections of aqua regia as a resistant to possible silver bullets.

He never knew what other departments were in the place, for the witch happened to glance up at one of the curious clocks that adorned the walls. She said it kept Infernal time. At any rate, His Nibs was due shortly. They must hurry to the Apparition Chamber.

That awesome place was in a class by itself. Murals showing the torments of Hell covered the long walls. At one end was a throne, at the other a full length portrait of His Nibs himself, surrounded by numerous photographs. The portrait was the conventional one of the vermilion anthropoid modified by barbed tail, cloven hoofs, horns, and a wonderfully sardonic leer. The rest of the pictures were of ordinary people — some vaguely familiar to Mr. Feathersmith.

"His Vileness always appears to mortals as one of their own kind," explained the witch, seeing Mr. Feathersmith's interest in the gallery. "It works out better that way."

Two imps were bustling about, arranging candles and bowls of incense about a golden pentagon embedded in the black composition floor. There were other cabalistic designs worked into the floor by means of metallic strips set edgewise, but apparently they were for lesser demons or jinn. The one receiving attention at the moment was immediately before the throne. The witch produced a pair of ear plugs and inserted them into Mr. Feathersmith's ears. Then she blindfolded him, patted him soothingly and told him to take it easy — it was always a little startling the first time.

It was. He heard the spewing of some type of fireworks, and the monotone of the witch's chant. Then there was a splitting peal of thunder, a blaze of light, and a suffocating sulphurous atmosphere. In a moment that cleared and he found his bandage wisked off. Sitting comfortably on the throne before hiin was a chubby little man wearing a gray pinstriped business suit and smoking a cigar. He had large blue eyes, several chins, and a jovial, back-slapping expression. He might have been a Rotarian and proprietor of a moderate-sized business anywhere.

"Good morning," he said affably. "I understand you want transportation to Cliffordsville of four decades ago. My Executive Committee has approved it, and here it is —"

Satan snapped his fingers. There was a dull plop and an explosion of some sort overhead. Then a documentfluttered downward. The witch caught it deftly and handed it to His Nibs, who glanced at it and presented it to Mr. Feathersmith.

Whether the paper was parchment or fine-grained asbestos mat, that gentleman could not say. But it was covered with leaping, dazzling letters of fire that were exceedingly hard to read, especially in the many paragraphs of fine print that made up the bulk of the document. Its heading was:

COMPACT

between His Infernal Highness Satan, known hereinafter as The Party of the First Part, and one J. Feathersmith, a loyal and deserving servant, known as The Party of the Second Part. To wit:

The perusal of such a contract would have been child's play for the experienced Mr. Feathersmith, had it not been for the elusive nature of the dancing letters, since only the part directly under his eye was legible. The rest was lost in the fiery interplay of squirming script and had the peculiar property of seeming to give a different meaning at every reading. Considered as a legal document, thought Mr. Feathersmith out of the depths of his experience, it was a honey. It seemed to mean what it purported to mean, yet —

At any rate, there was a clause there that plainly stated, even after repeated readings, that The Party of the Second Part would be duly set down at the required destination, furnished with necessary expense money and a modest stake, and thereafter left on his own.

"The compensation?" queried Mr. Feathersmith, having failed to see mention of it. "You'll want my soul, I presume."

"Dear me, no," responded Satan cheerily, with a friendly pat on the knee. "We've owned that outright for many, many years. Money's all we need. You see, if anything happened to you as you are, the government would get about three quarters of it and the lawyers the rest. We hate to see that three quarters squandered in subversive work — such as improved housing and all that rot. So, if you'll kindly give us your check —"

"How much?" Mr. Feathersmith wanted to know, reaching for his checkbook.

"Thirty-three million," said Satan calmly.

"That's outrageous!" shouted the client. "I haven't that much —"

"There was to be one percent off for cash, Your Vileness," reminded the witch sweetly.

Mr. Feathersmith glared at both of them. He had been neatly trimmed — right down to chicken feed. His first impulse was to terminate the interview then and there. But he remembered that, given youth and opportunity, he could make any number of fortunes. He also had in mind the dismal future forecast for him by the doctor. No. The transaction had to be gone through with. He meekly signed checks for his full balance, and an order on his brokers for the delivery of all other valuables.

There was one more thing to do — sign the pact.

"Roll up your left sleeve," said the witch. He noticed she held a needle-tipped syringe in one hand and a pad dampened with alcohol in the other. She rubbed him with the cotton, then jabbed him with the needle. When she had withdrawn a few cubic

23

centimeters of blood, she yanked the needle out, unscrewed it and replaced it by a fountain-pen point.

"Our practitioners did awfully sloppy work in the old days," she laughed, as she handed him the gruesomely charged pen and the pact. "You have no idea how many were lost prematurely through infection."

"Uh-huh," said Mr. Feathersmith, rolling down his sleeve and getting ready to sign. He might as well go through with it — the sooner the better.

"Your transportation," she added, handing him a folding railroad ticket with a weird assortment of long-defunct or merged railroads on it, queer dates and destinations. But he saw that it ended where and when he wanted to go.

"Grand Central Station, Track 48, 10:34 tonight."

"Better give him some cash," suggested Satan, hauling out a roll of bills and handing them to her. Mr. Feather smith looked at them with fast-rising anxiety; the sight of them shook him to the foundations. For they were large, blanket-like sheets of paper, none smaller than a fifty, and many with yellow backs. Satan also handed over a coin purse, in which were some gold pieces and six or eight big silver dollars. Mr. Feathersmith had completely forgotten that they used such money in the old days — pennies and dollar bills were unknown in the West, and fives and tens in paper so rare as to be refused by shopkeepers. How much else had he forgotten? It rattled him so that he did not notice when Satan disappeared, and he allowed himself to be ushered out in a mumbling daze by the little witch.

By train time, though, he had cheered up. There was just the little journey halfway across the continent to be negotiated: and the matter of the forty years. No doubt that would occur during the night as a miracle of sorts. He let the redcap carry his luggage aboard the streamlined flier and snugged himself down in his compartment. He had not had to bother with having clothes of 'the period' made 'to' order; for the witch had intimated that those details would be taken care of automatically.

His next job was to compose the story he was going to tell to explain his return to Cliffordsville. Besides other excellent reasons,

24

he had chosen the particular time for his rejuvenation so as to not run foul of himself in his earlier personality or any of his family. It had been just at the close of the Spanish War that both parents had died of yellow fever, leaving him an orphan and in possession of the old homestead and the parental bank account. He had lost little time in selling the former and withdrawing the latter. After that he had shaken the dust of Cliffordsville from his feet for what he thought was to be all time. By 1902 there was no member of the Feathersmith family residing in the county. His return, therefore, would be regarded merely as an ordinary return. He would give some acceptable explanations, then take up where he had left off. Sooner or later he would pull out again — probably to Detroit to get in on the ground floor with Henry Ford, and he thought it would be a good idea, too, to grab himself some U. S. Steel, General Motors and other comers-to-be. He licked his lips in anticipation of the killing he would make in the subsequent World War I years when he could ride Bethlehem all the way to the top, pyramiding as he went, without a tremor of fear. He also thought with some elation of how much fun it would be to get reacquainted with Daisy Norton, the girl he might have married if he had but stayed in Cliffordsville. She was cold to him then, but that was because her father was a rich aristocrat and looked down upon the struggling. Feathersmiths. But this time he would marry her and the Norman acres under which the oil field lay. After that —

He had undressed automatically and climbed into his berth. He let his feverish anticipations run on, getting dozier all the time. He suddenly recalled that he really should have seen the doctor before leaving, but dismissed it with a happy smile. By the time he had hit his upper twenties he was done with whooping cough, measles and mumps. It had been all these years since, before he required the services of a doctor again. He made a mental note that when he next reached sixty he would take a few precautions. And with that happy thought he dropped off into sound sleep.

The Limited slid on through the night, silently and jarless. Thanks to its air conditioning, good springs, well-turned wheels, smooth traction, rock ballasted roadbed and heavy rails, it went like the wind. For hundreds of miles the green lights of block signals flickered by, but now and again another train would thunder by on an eastbound track. Mr. Feathersmith gave no thought to those things as he pillowed deeper into the soft blankets, or worried about the howling blizzard raging outside. The Limited would get there on time and with the minimum of fuss. That particular Limited went fast and far that night — mysteriously it must have covered in excess of a thousand miles and got well off its usual route. For when Mr. Feathersmith did wake; along toward dawn, things were uncannily different.

To begin with, the train was lurching and rocking violently from side to side, and there was a persistent slapping of a flat wheel underneath. The blizzard had abated somewhat, but the car was cold. He lifted the curtain a bit and looked out on a snow-streaked, hilly landscape that strongly suggested Arkansas. Then the train stopped suddenly in the middle of a field and men came running alongside with lanterns. A hotbox, he heard one call, which struck him as odd, for he had not heard of hotboxes for a long time.

After about an hour, and after prolonged whistling, the train slowly gathered way again. By that time Mr. Feathersmith noticed that his berth had changed during the night. It was an old-fashioned fore-and-aft berth with an upper pressing down upon it. He discovered he was wearing a flannel nightgown, too — another item of his past he had failed to remember, it had been so long since he had changed to silk pajamas. But by then the porter was going through the car rousing all the passengers.

"Gooch Junction in half a' hour, folks," he was saying. "Gotta get up now — dey drop the sleeper dere."

Mr. Feathersmith groaned and got up. Yes, yes, of course. Through sleepers were the exception, not the rule, forty years ago. He found his underwear — red flannel union suit it was — and his shirt, a stiff-bosomed affair with detachable cuffs and a complicated arrangement of cuff holders. His shoes were Congress gaiters with elastic in the sides, and his suit of black broadcloth beginning to turn green. He got on the lower half of it and bethought himself of his morning shave. He fished under the berth for his bag and found it — a rusty old Gladstone, duly converted as promised. But there was no razor in it of any type he dared use. There was a set of straight razors

26

and strops and a mug for soap, but he would not trust himself to operate with them. The train was much too rough for that.

But he had to wash, so he climbed out of the berth, bumping others, and found the lavatory. It was packed with half-dressed men in the process of shaving. The basins were miserable affairs of marble and supplied by creaky pumps that delivered a tablespoon of water at a time. The car was finished in garish quartered oak, mahogany, mother-of-pearl and other bright woods fitted into the most atrocious inlays Mr. Feathersmith could have imagined. The taste in decoration, he realized, had made long steps since 1902.

His companions were "drummers" — heavy, well-fed men, all. One was in dry goods; one in coffee, tea and spices; another in whiskey; and two of the rest in patent medicines. Their conversation touched on Bryan and Free Silver, and one denounced Theodore Roosevelt's Imperialism — said it was all wrong for us to annex distant properties like the Sandwich Islands and the Philippines. One man thought Aguinaldo was a hero, another that Funston was the greatest general of all time. But what worried them most was whether they would get to Gooch Junction at all, and if so, how much late.

"We're only an hour behind now," said the whiskey drummer, "but the brakeman told me there's a bad wreck up ahead and it may take 'em all day to clear it —"

"Many killed?"

"Naw. Just a freight-engine crew and brakeman and about a dozen tramps. That's all."

"Shucks. They won't hold us up for that. They'll just pile the stuff up and burn it."

It was ten when they reached the Junction, which consisted of only a signal tower; a crossing, and several sidings. There was no diner on, but the butcher had a supply of candy, paper thin ham sandwiches on stale bread, and soda pop. If one did not care for those or peanuts, he didn't eat. Dropping the sleeper took a long time and much backing and filling, during which the locomotive ran off the rails and had to be jockeyed back on. Mr. Feathersmith was getting pretty disgusted by the time he reached the day coach and found he had to share a seat with a raw farm boy in overalls and a sloppy old felt hat. The boy had an aroma that Mr. Feathersmith had not smelled for a long, long time. And then he noticed that the aroma prevailed in other quarters, and it came to him all of a sudden that the day was Thursday and considerably removed from last Saturday and presumptive baths.

It was about that time that Mr. Feathersmith became aware that he himself had been unchanged except for wardrobe and accessories. He had expected to wake up youthful. But he did not let it worry him unduly, as he imagined the Devil would come through when he had gone all the way back. He tried to get a paper from the butcher, but all there were were day-old St. Louis papers and the news was chiefly local. He looked for the financial section and only found a quarter of a column where a dozen railroad bonds were listed. The editor seemed to ignore the Orient and Europe altogether, and there was very little about Congress. After that he settled down and tried to get used to the temperature. At one end of the car there was a potbellied cast-iron stove, kept roaring by volunteer stokers, but despite its ruddy color and the tropic heat in the two seats adjacent, the rest of the car was bitter cold.

The train dragged on all day, stopping often on bleak sidings and waiting for oncoming trains to pass. He noticed on the blackboards of the stations they passed that they were now five hours late and getting later. But no one seemed to worry. It was the expected. Mr. Feathersmith discovered he had a great turnip of a gold watch in the pocket of his waistcoat — a gorgeously flowered satin affair, incidentally — and the watch was anchored across his front by a chain heavy enough to grace the bows of a young battleship. He consulted it often, but it was no help. They arrived at Florence, where they should have been before noon, just as the sun was setting. Everybody piled out of the train to take advantage of the twenty-minute stop to eat at the Dining House there.

The food was abundant — fried ham, fried steaks, cold turkey, roast venison and fried chicken and slabs of fried salt pork. But it was all heavy and greasy for his worn stomach. The fact that the vegetables consisted of four kinds of boiled beans plus cabbage reminded him that he did not have his vitamin tablets with him. He asked for asparagus, but people only looked amused. That was stuff for the rich and it came in little cans. No, no asparagus. Fish? At

28

breakfast they might have salt mackerel. They *could* open a can of salmon. Would that do? He looked at the enormous, floury biscuits, the heavy pitchers of honey and sorghum molasses and a bowl of grits, and decided he would have just a glass of milk. The butter he never even considered, as it was a pale, anaemic salvy substance. They brought him an immense tumbler of buttermilk and he had to make the best of that.

By the time they were were back in the cars, the brakeman was going down the aisle, lighting the Pintach lamps overhead with a lamplighter. The gas had a frightful odor, but no one seemed to mind. It was "up-to-date," not the smelly kerosene they used on some lines.

The night wore on, and in due time the familiar landscape of old Cliffordsville showed up outside the window. Another item he discovered he had forgotten was that Cliffordsville had been there before the railroad was run through. On account of curves and grades, the company had by-passed the town by a couple of miles, so that the station — or depot — stood that distance away. It would have been as good a way as any to approach the town of his childhood, except that on this day the snow had turned to drizzling rain. The delightful clay roads were all right in dry weather, but a mass of bottomless sticky, rutted mud on a day like this. Mr. Feathersmith walked out onto the open platform of the car and down its steps. He viewed the sodden station and its waterlogged open platform with misgiving. There was but one rig that had come to meet the train. It was the Planter's Hotel bus — a rickety affair with facing fore-and-aft seats approached from the rear by three steps and grab-irons, a la Black Maria. The driver had his storm curtains up, but they were only fastened by little brass gimmicks at the corners and flapped abominably. There were four stout horses drawing the vehicle, but they were spattered with mud up to the belly and the wheels were encrusted with foot-thick adhesions of clay.

"Stranger here?" asked the driver, as he gathered up his reins and urged the animals to break the bus out of the quagmire it had sunk down in.

"I've been here before," said Mr. Feathersmith, wondering savagely why — back in those good old days — somebody had not

29

had enough gumption to grade and gravel-surface this road. "Does Mr. Toler still run the hotel?"

"Yep. Swell hotel he's got, too. They put in a elevator last year."

That was a help, thought Mr. Feathersmith. As he remembered the place it had twenty-foot ceilings and was three stories high. With his heart, at least for the first day here; he was just as happy at not having to climb those weary, steep stairs. And, now that he thought of it, the Planter's Hotel *was* a darn good hotel for its day and time. People said there was nothing like it closer than Dallas.

The drive in took the best part of two hours. The wind tore at the curtains and gusts of rain blew in. Three times they bogged down completely and the driver had to get out and put his shoulder to a wheel as the four horses lay belly-flat against the oozy mud and strained as if their hearts and backs would break. But eventually they drew up before the hotel, passing through streets that were but slightly more passable than the road. Mr. Feathersmith was shocked at the utter absence of concrete or stone sidewalks. Many blocks boasted no sidewalks at all; the others were plank affairs.

A couple of Negro boys lounged before the hotel and upon the arrival of the bus got into a tussle as to which should carry the Gladstone bag. The tussle was a draw, with the result .that they both carried it inside, hanging it between them.

The hotel was a shattering disappointment from the outset. Mr. Feathersmith's youthful memories proved very false indeed. The lobby's ceiling was thirty feet high, not twenty, and supported by two rows of cast-iron fluted columns topped with crudely done Corinthian caps. The bases and caps had been gilded once; but they were tarnished now, and the fly-specked marble painting of the shafts was anything but convincing. The floor was alternate diamond squares of marble — black with blue, and spotted with white enameled cast-iron cuspidors of great capacity, whose vicinity attested the poor marksmanship of Cliffordsville's chewers of the filthy weed. The marble-topped desk was decorated by a monstrous ledger, an inkpot and pens, and presided over by a supercilious young man with slicked-down hair neatly parted in the middle and a curly, thick brown mustache.

"A three-dollar room, of course, sir?" queried the clerk, giving the register a twirl and offering the pen.

"Of course," snapped Mr. Feathesmith, "the best. And with bath."

"With bath, sir?" deprecated the young man, as if taking it as a joke. "Why, there is a bath on every floor. Just arrange with the bellboy."

The old financier grunted. He was forgetting things again. He glanced over his shoulder toward the rear of the lobby where a red-hot stove was closely surrounded by a crowd of drummers. It seemed to be the only spot of warmth in the place, but he was intent on his bath. So he accepted the huge key and tag and followed the boy to the elevator. That proved to be a loosely woven, open-cage affair in an open shaft and operated by a cable that ran vertically through it. The boy slammed the outer door — there was no inner — and grasped the cable with both hands and pulled. There was a throaty rumble down below and the car began gradually to ascend. Inch by inch it rose, quivering, at about half the speed of a modern New York escalator. Mr. Feathersmith fumed and fidgeted; but there was no help for it. The elevators of forty years ago were like that. It was just too bad his room was 303.

It was big enough, twenty by twenty by twenty. A perfect cube, containing two gigantic windows which only a Sandow could manage. The huge double bed with heavy mahogany head and foot pieces was lost in it. Several rocking chairs stood about, and a rag rug was on the floor. But the *piece de resistance* of the room was the marble-topped washstand. On it rested a porcelain bowl and pitcher and beside it a slop jar. Mr. Feathersmith knew without looking what the cabinet beneath it contained. He walked over to it and looked into the pitcher. The water had a crust of ice on top of it. The room had not a particle of heat!

"I want a bath. Right away," he said to the bellboy. "Hot."

"Yassir," said the boy, scratching his head, "but I ain't know of the chambermaids got around to cleaning hit yit. They ain't many as wants bath till tomorrow. I kin go look and see, though."

"I've got some laundry, too. I want it back tomorrow."

"Oh, mister — you-all must be from New Yawk. They ain't no such thing here. They's a steam laundry, but they only take up Mondays and gita it back on Sat'day. My ma kin do it fer you, but that'll have to be Monday, too. She irons awful nice. They's mighty little she ever burns — and steal! — why, white folks, you could trust her with anything you got. Now'n then she loses a hand'chuf er some little thing like that, but steal — nossir."

"Skip it," snorted Mr. Feathersmith, "and see about that bath." He was relearning his lost youth fast. There had been times when metropolitan flunkyism had annoyed him, but he would give something for some of it now. He pulled out a dime and gave it to the boy, who promptly shuffled out for a conference with the maid over the unheard-of demand of a bath on Friday afternoon.

One look at the, bathroom was enough. It was twenty feet-high, too, but only eight feet long by three wide, so that it looked like the bottom of a dark well. A single carbon filament lamp dangled from a pair of black insulated wires, led across the ceiling, and gave a dim orange light — as did the similar one in the bedroom. The bathtub was a tin affair, round-bottomed and standing on four cast-iron legs. It was dirty, and fed by a half-inch pipe that dribbled a pencil-thin stream of water. In about two hours, Mr. Feathersmith estimated, his bath would be drawn and ready, provided of course, that the maid should remove in the meantime the mass of buckets, pans, brooms, mops and scrub rags that she stored in the place. One glance at the speckled, choked other piece of plumbing in the place made him resolve he would use the gadget underneath his own washstand.

"I kin bring hot water — a pitcher ur so," suggested the colored boy, "ef you want it."

"Never mind," said Mr. Feathersmith. He remembered now that a barber shop was just around the corner and they had bathtubs as well. It would be easier to go there, since he needed a shave, anyway, and pay an extra quarter and get it over with.

He slept in his new bed that night and found it warm despite the frigidness of the room, for the blankets of the time were honest wool and thick. But it was the only crumb of comfort he could draw from his new surroundings.

The next morning Mr. Feathersmith's troubles truly began. He got up, broke the crust of ice in his pitcher; and gaspingly washed his face and hands. He waited tediously for the slow-motion elevator to come up and take him down to breakfast. That meal was inedible, too; owing to its heaviness. He marveled that people could eat so much so early in the morning. He managed some oatmeal and buttered toast, but passed up all the rest. He was afraid that grapefruit was unheard of; as to the other fruits, there were apples. Transportation and storage had evidently not solved the out-of-season fruit and vegetable problem.

It also worried him that Satan had done nothing so far about his rejuvenation. He got up with the same gnarled, veiny hands, florid face, and bald head. He wished he had insisted on a legible copy of the contract at the time, instead of waiting for the promised confirmation copy. But all that was water over the dam. He was here, so, pending other developments, he must see about establishing his daily comforts and laying the foundation for his fortune.

There were several things he wanted: to acquire the old Feathersmith homestead; to marry Daisy Norton; to bring in the Cliffordsville oil field — wasn't there already Spindletop, Batson and Sour Lake making millions? — then go back to New York, where, after all, there was a civilization of a sort, however primitive.

He took them in order. Representing himself as a granduncle of his original self, he inquired at the local real-estate man's office. Yes, the Feathersmith place was for sale — cheap. The former cook, Anna was living near it and available for hire. It did not take Mr. Feathersmith long to get to the local livery stable and hire a two-horse rig to take him out there.

The sight of the place was a shock to him. The road out was muddy in stretches, and rocky add bumpy in others. At last they came to a sagging plank gate in a barbed-wire fence and the driver dragged it open. The great trees Mr. Feathersmith had looked back on with fond memory proved to be post oaks and cedars. There was not a majestic elm or pecan tree in the lot. The house was even more of a disappointment. Instead of the vast mansion he remembered, it was a rambling, run-down building whose porches sagged and where the brown remnants of last summer's honeysuckle still clung to a tangle of cotton strings used for climbers. They should have a neat pergola built for them, he thought, and entered.

The interior was worse. One room downstairs had a fireplace. Upstairs there was a single sheet-iron wood stove. What furniture that was left was incredibly tawdry; there was no telephone and no lights except kerosene wick lamps. The house lacked closets or a bath, and the back yard was adorned with a crazy Chic Sale of the most uninviting pattern. A deserted hog-pen and a dilapidated stable completed the assets. Mr, Feathersmith decided he wouldn't live there again on any terms.

.But a wave of sentimentality drove him to visit Anna, the former cook. She, at least, would not have depreciated like the house had done in a paltry two years. He learned she lived in a shack close by, so he went. He introduced himself as an elder of the Feathersmith family, and wanted to know if she would cook and wash for him.

"I doan want no truck with any kind of Feathersmith," she asserted. "They're po' white trash — all of 'em. The ole man and the missus wan't so bad, but that young skunk of a Jack sold out before they was hardly cold and snuck outs town twixt sundown and daylight an' we ain't never seed ur heard tell of him since. Jus' let me alone — that's all I ask."

With that she slammed the cabin door in his face.

So! thought Mr. Feathersmith. Well, he guessed he didn't want her, either. He went back to town and straight to the bank. Having discovered he had three thousand dollars in big bills and gold, a sizable fortune for Cliffordsville of the period, since the First National Bank was capitalized for only ten, he went boldly in to see Mr. Norton. He meant to suggest that they jointly exploit the Norton plantations for the oil that was under it. But on the very moment he was entering the portals of the bank he suddenly remembered that the Cliffordsville field was a very recent once, circa 1937, and therefore deep. Whereas Spindletop had been discovered by boring shallow wells — a thousand feet and mostly less — later-day wells had depths of something over a mile. In 1902 the suggestion of drilling to six thousand feet and more would have been simply fantastic. There was neither the equipment nor the men to undertake it. Mr. Feathersmith gulped the idea down and decided instead to make a deposit and content himself with polite inquiries about the family.

Mr. Norton was much impressed with the other's get-up and the cash deposit of three thousand dollars. That much currency was not to be blinked at in the days before the Federal Reserve Board Act. When money stringencies came — and they did often — it was actual cash that counted, not that ephemeral thing known as credit. He listened to Mr. Feathersmith's polite remarks and observed that he would consider it an honor to permit his wife and daughter to receive the new depositor at their home. Personally fingering the beloved bank notes, Mr. Norton ushered out his new customer with utmost suavity.

The call was arranged, and Mr. Feathersmith put in his appearance at exactly 4:30 p.m. of the second day following. Ransacking his mind for memories of customs of the times, he bethought himself to take along a piece of sheet music, a pound of mixed candies, and a bouquet of flowers.

The visit was a flop. Befitting his new status as an important depositor, he took a rubber-tired city hack to the door, and then, to avoid the charge of sinful extravagance, he dismissed the fellow, telling him to come back at five. After that, bearing his gifts, he maneuvered the slippery pathway of pop bottles planted neck down, bordered by bricks and desiccated rosebushes. He mounted the steps and punched the doorbell. After that there was a long silence, but he knew that there was tittering inside and that several persons pulled the curtains softly and surveyed him surreptitiously. At length the door opened cautiously and an old black mammy dressed in silk to match let him in and led him into the parlor.

It was a macabre room, smelling of mold. She seated him in a horsehair-covered straight chair, then went about the business of opening the inside folding blinds. After that she flitted from the room. After a long wait Mrs. Norton came in, stately and dignified, and introduced herself. Whereupon she plumped herself down on another chair and stared at him. A few minutes later the giggling Daisy came in and was duly introduced. She also bowed stiffly, without offering a hand, and sat down. Then came the grandmother. After that they just sat — the man at one end of the room and the

35

three sedate women in a row at the other, their knees and ankles tightly compressed together and their hands folded in their laps. Mr. Feathersmith got up and tried to manage a courtly bow while he made his presentations, thinking they were awfully stuffy.

He thought so particularly, because he had formerly had Daisy out on a buggy ride and knew what an expert kisser she could be when the moon was right. But things were different. He introduced various possible topics of conversation, such as the weather, the latest French styles, and so forth. But they promptly — and with the utmost finality — disposed of each with a polite, agreeing "Yes, sir." It was maddening. And then he saw that Daisy Norton was an empty-headed little doll who could only giggle, kiss, as required, and say, "Yes, sir." She had no conception of economics, politics, world affairs —

"*Aw-r-rk!*" thought Mr. Feathersmith. The thought took him back to those hellcats of modern women — like Miss Tomlinson, in charge of his Wall Street office force — the very type he wanted to get away from, but who was alert and alive.

He listened dully while Daisy played a "Valse Brilliants" on the black square piano, and saw the embroideries her fond mother displayed. After that he ate the little cakes and coffee they brought. Then left. That was Daisy Norton. Another balloon pricked.

On the trip back to the hotel he was upset by seeing a number of yellow flags hung out on houses. It puzzled him at first, until he remembered that that was the signal for smallpox within. It was another thing he had forgotten about the good old days. They had smallpox, yellow fever, diphtheria, scarlet fever, and other assorted diseases that raged without check except constitutional immunity. There was the matter of typhoid, too, which depended on water and milk supply surveillance. And it came to him that so long as Satan chose to keep him aged, he must live chiefly on milk. Cliffordsville, he well remembered, annually had its wave of typhoid, what with its using unfiltered creek water and the barbarian habit of digging wells in the vicinity of cesspools. Mr. Feathersmith was troubled. Didn't he have enough physical complaints as it was?

36

He was reminded even more forcibly of that shortly afterward when he came to, sitting up on the floor of a barroom with someone forcing whiskey into his mouth.

"You fainted, mister, but you'll be all right now."

"Get me a doctor," roared Mr. Feathersmith. "It's ephedrine I want, not whiskey!"

The doctor didn't come. There was only the one, and he was out miles in the country administering to a case of "cramp colic" — a mysterious disease later to achieve the more fashionable notoriety of "acute appendicitis." The patient died, unhappily, but that did not bring the doctor back to town any quicker.

The next morning Mr. Feathersmith made a last desperate effort to come back. There was a bicycle mechanic in town who had recently established a garage in order to take care of Mr. Norton's lumbering Ford and Dr. Simpson's buggy-like Holtzmann. Those crude automobiles thought it a triumph to make ten miles without a tow, had to be cranked by hand, and were lighted at night by kerosene carriage lamps or acetylene bicycle lamps.

"Why not devise a self-starter," suggested Mr. Feathersmith, recalling that millions had been made out of them, "a gadget you press with the foot, you know, that will crank the engine with an electric motor?'

"Why not wings?" asked the surly mechanic. He did not realize that both were practical, or that Mr. Feathersmith had seen better days. The trouble with Mr. Feathersmith was that he had always been a promoter and a financier, with little or no knowledge of the mechanical end of the game.

"It works," he insisted solemnly, "a storage battery, a motor, and a gilhookey to crank the motor. Think it over. It would make us rich."

"So would perpetual motion," answered the garage man.

And that was that.

Dr. Simpson, when contact was made, was even a poorer consolation.

"Ephedrine? Digitalis? Vitamins? Thyroxin? You're talking gibberish — I don't know what you mean. Naturally, a man of your age is likely to get short of breath at times — even faint. But shucks, Mr. Feathersmith, don't let that bother you. I've known men to live

37

to a hundred that didn't stack up as well as you. Take it easy, rest plenty with a nap every afternoon, and you'll be all right. We're only young once, you know."

When Mr. Feathersmith found that the good doctor had nothing to offer better than a patented "tonic" and poultices for his rheumatism, he thereafter let him strictly alone. The situation as to vitamins and glandular extracts was worse than hopeless — the dieticians had not got around yet to finding out about calories, let alone those. Mr. Feathersmith worried more and more over Satan's inexplicable delay in bestowing youth befitting the age, for Forfin had insisted the Old Boy would fulfill his promise if the price was paid. But until that was done, the old financier could only wait and' employ his time as profitably as he could.

He kept ransacking his brains for things he could invent, but every avenue proved to be a blind alley. He mentioned the possibility of flying to the circle that sat about the, lobby stove, but they scornfully laughed it down. It was an obvious impossibility, except for the dirigible gas bags Santos-Dumont was playing with in France. He tried to organize a company to manufacture aluminum, but unfortunately no one had heard of the stuff except one fellow who had been off to school and seen a lump of it in the chemical laboratory: It was almost as expensive as gold, and what good was it?

Mr. Feathersmith realized then that if he was in possession of a 1942 automobile no one could duplicate it, for the many alloys were unknown and the foundry and machine-shop practice necessary were undeveloped. There was nothing to paint it with but carriage paint — slow-drying and sticky. There were no fuels or lubricants to serve it, or any roads fit to run it on.

He played with other ideas, but they all came croppers. He dared not even mention radio — it smacked too much of magic — or lunacy. And he most certainly did not want to be locked up as a madman in an insane asylum of the era. If standard medicine was just beginning to crawl, psychiatry was simply nonexistent. So he kept quiet about his speculations.

Since life had become so hard and he was cut off from any normal intercourse with his fellow townsmen, he yearned for good music. But alas, that likewise was not to be had outside one or two metropolitan orchestras. He went once to church and heard a home-grown, self-taught soprano caterwaul in a quavering voice. After that he stayed away. He caught himself wishing for a good radio program — and he had altered considerably his standards of what was good.

A week rolled by. During it he had another stroke that was almost his last. The New York doctor had warned him that if he did not obey all the rules as to diet and other palliatives, he might expect to be taken off at any time. Mr. Feathersmith knew that his days were numbered — and the number was far fewer than it would have been if he had remained in the modern age he thought was so unbearable. But still there was the hope that the Devil would yet do the right thing by him.

That hope was finally and utterly blasted the next day. Mr. Feathersmith was in the grip in the grip of another devastating fit of weakness and knew that shortly he would be unable to breathe and would therefore fall into a faint and die. But just before his last bit of strength and speck of consciousness faded, there was a faint plop overhead and an envelope fluttered down and into his lap. He looked at it, and though the stamp and cancellation were blurred and illegible, he saw the return address in the corner was "Bureau of Complaints and Adjustments, Gehenna." His trembling fingers tore the missive open. A copy of his contract fell out into his lap.

He scanned it hurriedly. As before, it seemed flawless. Then he discovered a tiny memorandum clipped to its last page. He read it and knew his heart would stand no more. It was from the cute little witch of Fifth' Avenue.

Dearest Snooky-Wooky:
His Nibs complains you keep on bellyaching. That's not fair. You said you wanted to be where you are, and there you are. You wanted your memory unimpaired. Can we help it if your memory is lousy? And not once, old dear, did you cheep about also having your youth restored. So that lets us out. Be seeing you in Hell, old thing.
Cheerio!

He stared at it with fast-dimming eyes.

39

"The little witch . . . the bad, badgering little —" and then an all-engulfing blackness saved him from his mumbling alliteration.

Fighters Never Quit

*The dead can't die — so far as we know, but there may well be yet
other realms, and battles to be fought. And if the invisible dead can
see the living —*

Chief Bos'n Jockens was exceedingly annoyed. And as the
moments slipped into the seconds, and the seconds into minutes, he
became more annoyed. Chagrin was what he felt chiefly, polluted
with dismay and disgust. For he was rapidly becoming convinced
that he was up to his neck in a situation that simply couldn't happen
— not to *anybody*, and least of all him! The bitter pill that the good
chief bos'n had to swallow was this: he had become a ghost! And
Jockens was one of those feet-on-the-ground people who absolutely
did not believe in ghosts. His orations on the subject were well
remembered in every W. O. mess in the fleet. Hence his extreme
mortification.

It all came about when that big Jap battleship came barging
out of the mist and let go with all she had at the already hard-pressed
El Paso. Five sixteen shells at close range can do plenty to a light
cruiser, even if the light cruiser had not already been amply riddled.
The *El Paso*'s reaction was the simple and obvious one she
shuddered as the lethal lumps of steel tore through her sides, then
blew up with a terrific bang. What five tons of hurtling H. E. might
not have completed, her own magazines did. Within five seconds, all
that was left of the gallant cruiser and her crew was a towering
mushroom of smoke and a drizzle of splinters and fragments.

Jockens remembered that explosion vaguely, but the force of
it had been too vast and so instantly applied as to give no time for

41

sensation. He only knew that he had been hurled upward and that, without his feeling it in the least, his limbs had been ripped off him to disappear in a blast of flame. After that came a brief period when all that remained of him was a sort of disembodied consciousness hovering over a patch of flotsam in the water. Then things began to change subtly.

A couple of feet below him floated the splintered loom of an oar. Sloshing about in the water a yard away was a gruesome object which the late chief bos'n studied with a deep and morbid interest. It was horrible, that thing, being only a torn and blackened portion of a human torso to which the neck and head were still attached. But, although it floated face down, he knew from a vivid scar on the back of the neck and a conspicuous mole on the shoulder that what he was viewing was a bit of his own mortal remains. It was that discovery that had convinced him he was dead — certainly a discovery in no way shocking, since few on the *El Paso* had expected any other outcome since their harried flight from the battle of the Banda Sea began. Jockens, in common with many of his kind, was necessarily a fatalist. What was to be would be, and he accepted the present fact with a mental shrug. But dying properly while doing his job was one thing, and the disconcerting tranformation that followed it was another. Jockens most emphatically did not yearn to be a ghost and forevermore haunt the empty ocean over the spot where his ship had sunk.

Yet that was unmistakably what was about to happen. He was becoming aware of taking visible, if not tangible, shape. He now perceived that he was sitting astride that broken oar, clad in immaculate whites and wearing the ribbons of all his many badges, and medals. It was a tenuous and nebulous body he was acquiring, to be sure, but yet a faithful copy of his old one. What disturbed him most was the fact that though he steadily became more and more solid to the eye, he could still see the pale shaft of the oar beneath him even though he had to stare down through his phantom abdomen to see the whole of it. And worse, the oar rose and fell as easily as if it bore no burden. On the heels of that discovery he observed a parallel phenomenon. As he himself grew in apparent solidity, the things he knew to be real grew fainter. The water which bathed his legs took on a misty, iridescent quality and he saw that it did not wet

42

him at all. The fragment of real body paled to a blob of cloudy stuff and eventually disappeared as does a blown-out candle flame, and with it the slender apparition of the oar. In ghostland, it was beginning to be evident, things of the spirit wore the aspect of reality, while the concrete became illusions.

There was almost instant verification of that observation from all about. On every hand his shipmates were popping into visibility, swimming along in the faint and ethereal ocean. They seemed to have a common goal. He turned his eyes that way and saw what it was. The *El Paso*, too, had been reconstituted in the spirit, and was even then steaming slowly along, picking up its men. Jockens rolled over on his side and began swimming for it with steady, even strokes. He was a little disappointed to find that the art of levitation — which the silly ghost believers had always attributed to ghosts — was not his, but perhaps that would come later. Yet swimming in the fictitious ocean served quite well, and he shortly found himself grasping at the lower rung of a Jacob's ladder someone had lowered over the side.

Harkey, the radio gunner, gave him a hand as he crawled over the bead molding and onto the quarterdeck.

"Hi, spook," he greeted, grinning from ear to ear. "How do you like it?"

"Don't rub it in," growled Jockens. It was only last night in that former world that Jockens had completely demolished every argument his superstitious messmate had advanced in favor of a sort of in-between state of afterlife. But under the present circumstances nothing occurred to him to say.

Jockens looked about the decks in astonishment. Things were as trim and shipshape as the day they had been commissioned, except that the spud locker, empty for a week, now bulged with spuds, and more spud crates were stacked on the deck beside it. So all the spuds they had eaten had come back as well! And in a moment similar discoveries were being made elsewhere in the ship. The gunner said his magazines were stuffed to capacity with powder and shell. The engineer reported full bunkers and replenished lubricating oil drums.

"Muster the crew," ordered the skipper, who had been taking the situation in without comment.

43

There were only five absentees — sea-lawyers all and chronic gripers, men whose heart had never been in the war.

"The first rule of ghosthood, it appears," remarked the commander ironically, "is that consciously or subconsciously, you who want very badly to carry on, do. I commend all present for that."

Just then there was a surprising diversion. A youthful seaman — the ship's inveterate cut-up — had stolen out of ranks and was clambering up the ladder to the maintop. He stopped a yard short of the pinnacle and shouted to those below.

"Hey, we're immortal now. Watch what we can get away with!"

With that he let go both hands and dived straight for the deck below. There was the gasp conditioned by long habit. Then the hurtling body struck the steel carapace of a gun housing with a sickening thud, only to slide off onto the deck where it lay motionless, a broken thing. It was all too clear that the neck and arms were broken and that the body was a corpse. Men ran up, but at once were forced to stand back in an awed semicircle. For a flicker of green flame played over the crumpled figure a moment; there was a quick blaze and then the body was no more. There was simply nothing there!

"Hrn-m-m," murmured the surgeon, who had been the first to arrive. "Add Rule 2. A ghost can be killed, if ghostly means are employed. You men had better watch your step."

A hundred pairs of eyes were turned speculatively on the chaplain, but that officer did not see fit to speak. Perhaps the gnawing thought in his own mind as well as that of his silent questioners was, "After the first stage of ghosthood, what? And how many stages? And —"

The general alarm was ringing, and the men broke from their spell and dashed for their battle stations. Very, very faint, but plainly recognizable, the Jap battlewagon and two of its attendant cruisers were approaching. No doubt they wanted to cruise through the floating wreckage in expectation of picking up a prisoner or so, or other information. On the *El Paso* ranges were being taken and ammunition brought up. Battle orders rang out — the big fellow was to be the target."Commence firing!"

The cruiser heeled to the recoil of her broadside, and the control officers watched eagerly for the behavior of their salvo. What they saw was disappointing. The shells must have gone squarely through the oncoming ship, for mountains of white water sprang up just beyond. But it was as if the projectiles had merely passed through a wall of mist. The battleship did not notice. It came steadily on, and the phantoms on board the *El Paso* saw that its turrets had been secured. As far as it was concerned, the battle was over. There was only empty sea on which bits of debris floated.

The battleship came on, slowed, then passed squarely through the flimsy illusion that stood for the sunken cruiser. It was evident that neither could feel the other or have any material effect, and it was equally evident that while the ghosts could see the living Japs faintly, the Japs could not see them at all.

Chief Bos'n Jockens watched the show from his station on the fo'c's'le, and the more he saw the greater did his disgust with his new status grow. It was all very well to be reconstituted in what seemed to be flesh and on a convincing phantom of a ship that was well-fueled, well-armed and well-provisioned. But where did it get them?

There had been a discouraging silence from the bridge ever since that one futile salvo had fallen. The commander had checked fire and waited. Now he was watching the passing victors. Suddenly he sighted something, and a fresh clamor of orders rang out.

"On the machine guns, there! Look aft on that second Jap cruiser — see those solid-looking figures. Let 'em have it!"

The second cruiser was one they had exchanged a few shots with and scored a hit or so before the arrival of the heavy stuff. On the after deck a broadside gun had been dismounted, but not destroyed, as its filmy haziness attested. Alongside it, however, were ranged a score of very material-appearing Japs. The conclusion was inevitable — they must be the ghosts of the dead gun crew.

The machine guns chattered, the smoky tracers leading fairly to their mark, The Japs, still bewildered at the new state of existence which they did not understand, began disappearing by twos and threes in little puffs of dazzling green fire. A wild cheer went up

45

from the decks of the erstwhile *El Paso*. Not a single watcher but comprehended the-significance of what was being revealed. .They could not kill living Japs, but they could send dead ones another leg on the road to Hell!

The same thought had swept the bridge, for as the last of the enemy gun crew flickered out into the unknown second stage of the hereafter, the rudder had been put hard over and the engine telegraphs moved to "Flank Speed." The sailors of the *El Paso* knew without waiting for the orders that would follow what to do. They broke out torpedoes and loaded their tubes. Fresh charges rang home to their seats in the guns. Twenty miles away — over the horizon — there must be the shades of the four Jap destroyers they had just sunk when the battleship came up and made them run for it.

It was less than an hour before they picked them up. The destroyers were heading dismally for their homeland, indicating that the Japanese psychology did not comprehend the possibilities or responsibilities of ghosthood.

"Ha!" snorted Jockens, seeing their state of unreadiness. "Now it's our turn to do a sneak attack."

The attack went home. The second version of the morning's battle was short, and to the attackers doubly sweet. They watched with satisfaction as the phantom foes blew up and sank in quick succession. Five miles farther on they came upon a windfall — a bomber they must have shot down and not known about. It still rested on the waves and its crew was trying to make a take-off. A few bursts of ack-ack disposed of it, leaving once more an empty ocean.

"Now what?" asked the navigator.

"Back to the Macassar Straits and Bali," snapped the captain. "I am not exactly sure what we gain by this, but it's fun — and it smells like progress."

The ship straightened out on a southerly course, but not for long. Late in the day came the lookout's cry, "Sail-ho!" Three pairs of binoculars and a long glass came to bear on the object. It was plainly visible, though miles away; and therefore clearly another phantom. But it was no gray-hulled warship of any modern navy. Beautiful in the low slanting rays of the setting sun, she flaunted many square yards of snowy canvas, complete with studding sails, top royals and skysails. The commander rang down for more blowers on. He wanted to reach the distant clipper before the coming night blotted her out.

The cruiser made it, just at the edge of dusk, and as her screws churned the water astern to rid her of her way, it could also be seen that the clipper flew the Stars and Stripes, though of a design strange to modern eyes. It bore only half the number of stars displayed on the ensign at the *El Paso*'s gaff. The friendly phantom ship was obviously a Yankee of the old China trade, fully a century old, and the smart seamanship with which she backed her sails and got the quarter-boat away was further evidence of it. A few seconds later the boat was being rowed with swift, sure strokes toward the cruiser. A tall, gaunt man whose face was framed by whiskers, but whose chin and upper lip were clean shaven, sat in the stern sheets, tending the tiller.

"Boat ahoy!" hailed the cruiser.

"The *Bethesda*, one hundred and two years and five months out of Boston," came the response, clear but husky, from a voice that must have had far more than that number of years of experience in bellowing orders through a speaking trumpet into the teeth of a gale. "'Ezra Sitwell, master. We want gunpowder, rum and vittles, if we can git 'em."

"Come alongside," replied the voice from the cruiser, and a moment later was giving orders for rigging cargo lights and dropping a ladder over the side. It was Jockens who attended personally to the last item and who was present when the grizzled skipper of a century ago climbed aboard.

Captain Sitwell solemnly saluted; then shook hands all around.

"Howdy, cappen," he said. "Glad to fall in with you. Newcomer to these parts, eh? We heard tell there was a new war on, and that soon we'd be having plenty of company. It gits mighty dull hereabouts some years, what with nothing but typhoons to depend on for recruits and provisions. 'Twas a hundred years ago come September that we wuz caught the same way — typhoon took our sticks out and threw us up on the shore of Shikoku. Fight we tried to, but we were half drowned, and the murdering heathen beachcombers

47

came at us with their wicked knives. I've haunted their coast ever since, picking up fishing boats mostly. But black powder and honest round shot are hard to come by these days, and lately we've had to depend on our cutlasses and sheath knives."

"We'll try to help," said the commander of the *El Paso*. Yet he made no move to order up the supplies asked for, partly because he had little of either and partly because he wanted to know more of this ghostly existence that had fallen to their lot. "Tell me," he asked, "don't ghosts ever die?"

"Nope. Only by violence, and that from ghosts or ghostly stuff."

Captain Sitwell chuckled; "The sea can't hurt us, because it ain't real. Neither are the rocks and shoals —"

"But old age, disease —"

Sitwell shook his head. "Ghosts stay the same age. 'Bout disease — four-five years ago I fell in with a foundered yacht — had a modern doctor on board — had plenty of whiskey on board — we talked all night. He told me about microbes and why they don't bother us. Ornery critters they were, he said, too little and ornery to have souls. So they don't bother us."

. The commander noted the inquiring look that followed the simple explanation, and knew he must do something about the request at hand. "What's your armament?"

"Carronades, muskets and pistols."

The commander shook his head. He had a few hundred pounds of black powder for his saluting battery, but no other ammunition suitable for ancient ordnance. Nor did he have any rum on board. He offered a dozen modern rifles and four one-pounder boat guns with ammunition to match, but the skipper of the sailing ship looked dubious.

"Nope," he said, "I've tried those newfangled things before. We'd best stick to cutlasses and knives, I reckon!"

"I believe we can fix him up, commander," volunteered Jockens:

A moment later men were scouring the storerooms of the ship. Presently they were coming up, bringing the results of their search. All the black powder there was, two kegs of rivets and two more of assorted nuts — which would be useful for grape shot for Sitwell's carronades. There was some other miscellaneous scrap iron, a few sheets of gasket lead, and eight bags of sugar. The *Bethesda*, being manned by the old-fashioned, self-sufficient breed of sailors, could undoubtedly cast her own bullets and make her own rum. To that store of necessities, the cruiser added onions, spuds and eggs, things not easily come by among the, salvage of the Eastern Seas.

"Many thanks, cappen," said Sitwell, beaming. "I'll do all right now. By the way, a couple of weeks ago I spoke a brother clipper down by Tai Wan. He says a lot of you fellows have shown up in the South China Sea and around Java. Says they made a big killing and have cleaned out everything. Last he saw of them; they were going on to India for fresh pickings there. Says they even hunted down a cruiser that's been plaguing us old fellows for twenty years or more — a German ship called the *Emden*. I sure hated that fellow, but all I could ever do was run from him. He wasn't so fast lately, 'cause he was a coal-burner and coal's getting almost as scarce as black powder."

Captain Sitwell said no more. Nor did the frowning captain of the *El Paso*. That last news was not too encouraging. If the sunken Asiatic Fleet had gotten on the job as quickly as. they seemed to have, there was nothing left for his own ship to do. The months ahead looked dreary.

"In your experience, Captain Sitwell," he asked, "is it possible to communicate with the living?"

The *Bethesda*'s' skipper walked to the lee rail and relieved his cheek of an immense load of tobacco juice.

"Wa-al," he drawled, "yes. And no. There's mediums, but mighty few of 'em are any good. You can only send a word or two and they mostly get those mixed up. What they send back don't hardly ever make sense. Anyhow, living folks can't help us much."

"Maybe not, admitted the commander, but he cast a thoughtful eye toward Jockens, just the same. The last of the supplies had been sent down into the *Bethesda*'s boat and Jockens was back, watchful and drinking in what was said.

Captain Sitwell repeated his thanks and made his formal farewells, adding as an afterthought: "They do tell me this newfangled thing you call radio will do it. The messages you send, the living folks call static; but if you could find an operator that was a medium, too, you might get somewhere."

Jockens cocked his head to one side and delivered himself of a solemn wink. Then he disappeared below. Presently he emerged with Harkey, and the pair hurried away to the radio shack. In the meantime the boat had shoved off, the *El Paso* was picking up speed along her resumed course, and the faint running lights of the clipper were dropping fast astern. High up between the masts, an antennae set began crackling out static. Half an hour later Jockens stole softly out of the room and mounted to the bridge.

"Sir," he said, addressing his skipper, "Harkey and me's found the answer. He was always telling me about a niece of his he claims is psychic. I always thought that was so much hogwash, but lately I've been thinking maybe it's not. Anyway, she's in Communications at Honolulu. Harkey just got a message through and she managed to dope it out. We told her we're sunk, and where and how, and what a hole we're in for something to do next. She came back in plain English and said, 'I hear you perfectly and understand. The admiral's here and is interested. He wants to know what can we do for you?' "

The commander sighed. What, indeed, could the living do for the dead?

"Nice try, Jockens," said the skipper, "but I can't think of what to say to him. Can you?"

"Sure, sir." Nobody could see Jockens' wide grin ,in the dark, but it was as big and persistent as a Cheshire cat's. He was about to do some plagiarizing, but under certain conditions and with certain famous phrases, plagiarism becomes a virtue.

"Well?" snapped the commander, his nerves on edge.

"Why, sir, we could turn around and go scouting for live ones. They can't see us, but we can see them. Then we could send word to the admiral where they are, how many, and how they're heading —"

"Swell," answered the skipper, suddenly cheered. The *El Paso* sunk could still partly do her job in the world they had left, though her own guns and tubes would be useless. "Swell," he

50

repeated, "but it doesn't answer the admiral's question. He wants to know what he can do for *us*."

Jockens chuckled.

"Send us more Japs!"

The Giftie Gien

How do others see you — what queer distortions would a bootblack, to whom a man is a pair of dusty shoes, or a barber, to whom he is a head, mostly bald, with a fringe that needs cutting, see of a man —

It was five o'clock. The girls were getting ready to go home and the city salesmen were beginning to come trooping in. Mr. J. C. Chisholm, sales manager of the Pinnacle Office & Household Appliance Corp., folded his pudgy hands across his ample middle and sat back in his chair to watch the daily ritual going on beyond the clear-glass partition that separated his office from the salesmen's room. A bland smile was on his pink face and a stranger might have said that he appeared to be beaming with satisfaction and good will. At any rate, the smile was there, and, as a matter of fact, Mr. Chisholm was quite satisfied with himself. There was not the slightest doubt in his mind — and the incoming orders up to that hour were added proof of it — that he was the best little old sales manager POHAC had ever had. Consequently, he viewed the activities beyond the partition with the utmost amiability.

Miss Maizie Delmar, his secretary, sat beside him, her notebook on her knee and her pencil poised in anticipation of any weighty utterance he might see fit to make. Not that she expected to take any notes for the next ten minutes, for she knew her boss quite as well as he thought he knew everybody else. This was the "psychic hour," as she caustically referred to it when outside the smothering confines of POHAC's. It amused Mr. Chisholm to display his keen powers of observation and his uncanny judgment of people. So she waited with a hard, set face for his first prediction. She knew that he would look at her from time to time to get her reaction, but she was ready for that, She had a little frozen smile and a gleam to put into her tired eyes that she could flash on and off like a light, but she reserved those until they were demanded.

"Har-rum," he observed, "Miss Carrick has now finished dabbing her nose. In exactly forty-three seconds she will fold her typewriter under and slam the lid. Then she will go to the window and look at the sky. It is cloudy, so she will put on her galoshes and take an umbrella."

He started his stop watch. Miss Delmar sighed inaudibly and waited. Of course he was right. Miss Carrick was an elderly and sour spinster and decidedly "set in her ways." She was as predictable as sunset and the tides.

"Forty-four seconds," he announced, triumphantly, snapping off the watch at the bang of the desk top. "Don't tell me. I know these people like a book. Nobody can slip anything over old J. C."

Miss Trevelyan was the next subject for prophecy. She had a well-established routine that was almost as rigid as that of Miss Carrick, though she was of a different type. Miss Trevelyan was a baby-doll beauty of the Betty Boop variety and with the voice to match. At the moment she was regarding herself anxiously in a ridiculously small compact mirror, tilting her head this way and that with quick birdlike jerks so as to better scrutinize nose, cheeks, eyes and ears. After that, as J. C. gleefully foretold, would come the powdering, the lip-sticking, the eyebrow-brushing — in the order named — and eventually an elaborate tucking-in of imaginary wisps of vagrant hair. J. C. didn't miss a bet.

Then three salesmen came in. Jake Sarrat, the big, jovial ace of the wholesale district, slapped the other two on the back, hurled his brief case and kit into a desk drawer, made a brief phone call, and then went out. Old Mr. Firrel wore his usual somber, tired look, and walked slowly to the bare table they had let him use. He unbent his lanky and stooped six feet of skin and bones and began dragging copious sheafs of notes from his brief case. Those he glanced at briefly and began tearing up, one by one. The third, a saturnine little fellow who appeared to be perpetually angry, marched straight to his desk and began scribbling furiously on a pad of report blanks. He was Ellis Hardy, Chisholm's pet.

"Jake," said Mr. Chisholm, confidently, "is working up a big case and wants to surprise me with it. Watch his smoke before the week is over. Ellis has just brought in a big one — stick around, we may pour a drink before we call it a day. As for Old Dismal, he's quitting. The poor dope!"

He twirled his chair around to face a mahogany cabinet. He opened the door of it, took out a bottle and glass, and poured himself a stiff slug of rye. He tossed it off with a grunt and swiveled back.

"That guy is not a salesman and never will be," he snorted contemptuously. "Look at him! He looks like a tramp and as mournful as a pallbearer. When I talk to him about dolling himself up he says he hasn't the dough; when I tell him to cheer up and wear a smile, he croaks about his stomach ulcers. What do I care how hard he works if he never brings the bacon in? Why, if that poor drip ever took a look at himself in the mirror, he'd go hang himself."

Maizie gripped her pencil harder and quoted softly:

"Ah, wad some power the giftie gie us
To see oursels as ithers see us —"

"That's right," exclaimed Mr. Chisholm. "You get it. Take me. I'm always on the lookout for that. If I didn't watch myself, I might turn stout. But no, I'm wise. I don't wait for people to tell me — I go to the gym three times a week and have a good workout. The rubber says there's not a, spare ounce on me. There's no crime in being big — people respect a big man, don't you think?"

"They do get out of their way," admitted Maizie, flashing her stock smile, and batting here eyelids appreciatively. After all, he paid her forty a week and she had a paralyzed mother to support.

"Exactly," he continued, gratified, "and that's only appearance I'm talking about. The big thing is personal relations. Look how often somebody takes me for an easy-mark and tries to slip something over. I fool 'em, don't I? That's because I keep studying myself. I say to myself, say I, 'Look here, J. C., this bird thinks he's smart; now show him you're smarter.' Good system, eh? That's what comes of taking an objective view of yourself. That's why I keep all those psychology books around. You have no idea —
"

"It must be grand to be so masterful, to be able to hold down such a big position . . . and . . . and all that," she said, hoping the blush it cost her wouldn't be noticed.

But there was a diversion at hand. Ellis Hardy was approaching and she knew without being told what was about to happen. In line of duty she listened in — with the connivance of Miss Perkins, the PBX operator — on salesmen's telephone conversations. In fact, she was the modest source of much of Mr. Chisholm's omniscience.

Hardy came in without the ceremony of knocking, and promptly sat down on top of Chisholm's desk. He threw down a sheaf of filled-out orders. A certified check running to five figures was clipped to the top.

"Got 'em," announced Hardy with a self-satisfied smirk. "Eight SXV units, motor-driven, complete with accessories and a year's supply. That's for the head office. I sold 'em four more for the branches."

"Attaboy!" responded Chisholm, doing another rightabout-face. This time he set out three glasses with the bottle. "Moore & Fentress, eh? I told you they would be pushovers. Don't ever say I don't give you the breaks — that was like getting money from home."

"Uh-huh," admitted Hardy, with a reluctant grin. "'Of course that sap Firrel —'

"Never mind Firrel,'" snapped Chisholm, "I'll handle him. The money's the thing."

"Oh, sure," said Hardy, "as soon as my check comes through —"

"Drink up," said Chisholm, waving a deprecating hand. There was no need of Maizie knowing *too* much — she was discreet and loyal and all that, but still —

Firrel was at the door, standing hesitantly as if unwilling to interrupt the conference going on, but fidgeting as if anxious to be on his way.

"Scram, Ellis," said Chisholm, seeing the gaunt old man. "Let me hear what this egg's wail is."

Hardy grinned his sour grin and stepped out, giving Mr. Firrel but the curtest nod in passing. Firrel came in, and not being invited to sit, stood awkwardly before the desk. Maizie felt sorry for the man. He was so earnest, so sincere, such a hard worker — yet he had been with them more than a month and the few commissions he had received could hardly have done more than pay his carfare. It was pathetic.

"Well?" asked Chisholm, hard and cross, as if annoyed at the intrusion.

"I'm quitting," said Firrel. "That's all."

"Suit yourself," said Chisholm, indifferently. "I never begged a man to work for me and I can't see myself starting now. Check out with Miss Delmar. Give her your kit and turn over the list of prospects you have been working on — not that I think they are any good. It's the rule, you know."

"You can go to hell," said Mr. Firrel, very quietly. Maizie noticed that his knuckles were white and his hands tense. "I called in to see Mr. Fentress this afternoon. He told me to. That was a week ago. He said that they had to await the authorization of their Board of Directors before signing an order. I found out what had happened."

"So what?" roared Chisholm savagely. "Do you think we could keep open if we ran on a sometime, if and when basis? Alibis are all you ever have . . . at the end of the quarter . . . when they take the inventory . . . when Mr. Goofus gets back from the West Coast. We want business *now*. That's why I sent Hardy when they called up this morning and wanted to know why our man hadn't been around. *He* doesn't stall and make alibis for himself. He gets 'em on the dotted line. I couldn't let you muff a big order like this one."

Chisholm waved the order under his nose, then laid it face down so the amount on the check would not show.

"Of course," the sales manager went on, in that I-lean-over-backward-being-a-good-fellow manner he assumed at times, "if you really feel that you have anything coming to you for what preliminary work you did, I'm sure I can make Hardy see it that way. He'll cut you in. That's a promise. Would a twenty, say, help out?"

He pulled out his wallet and opened it. Maizie took one glance at the smoldering hatred and contempt in the weary eyes of the man before the desk and then hastily dropped her own to the notebook on her knee. If only someone would sock the porcine jowl of her detested employer!

"You heard me," said Firrel with a cold distinctness that cut. "You can go to hell."

He turned abruptly and walked out. A moment later the outer door slammed.

"Never mind trying to piece out his torn prospect cards, Maizie," said POHAC's eminently successful sales manager. "We have a file of his daily reports. Hardy can work just as well from those."

"Yes, sir," said Maizie. Her rent was overdue, and the doctor had said —

She swept out of the office and down the hall to the washroom. Her nails were biting into her palms and her eyes were brimming. "Oh, the louse," she moaned over and over again, "the louse, the dirty, dirty louse! If I were only a man —"

Then those lines of Burns came to mind again:

"O, wad some power the giftie gie us —"

"That would do,"'she cried fervently. "Hang himself! If he only saw himself as I see him, he'd be lucky if he *could* hang himself."

Seven o'clock came. Mr. Chisholm took one final snort before putting on his hat and turning out the lights. He must be in fine form when he met Mr. Lonigan. Lonigan was an important buyer and he was coming in on the *Rocket* at seven thirty. The evening was already planned. He was to meet the buyer, take him to dinner, then meet the McKittricks in the lobby of the Palace Theater. Mr. McKittrick was the president of POHAC and had six box seats for the show. With him would be Mrs. McKittrick, Mrs. Chisholm, and a certain very personable young woman whom the company employed from time to time to fill in on just such occasions. It promised to be a gay evening, and as soon as he had a chance to

57

whisper to the big boss about the order he had topped the day off with, even McKittrick would concede that he had the best sales manager ever.

Chisholm jabbed the elevator button, whistling merrily as he stood back to watch the oscillations of the telltale above the door.

"Nice night, Jerry," he said cheerily to the elevator man.

"A very nice night, sir," agreed Jerry. But he never took his eyes off the column of blinking ruby lights before his nose. Mr. Chisholm was to be the most mistrusted when he was in a benign mood. It was usually the come-on for some probing and tricky questions. Like, "I saw Mr. Naylor get in your car awhile ago. What a card! He's higher'n a kite tonight. *Ha, ha*." *Any* response to a remark of that sort was sure to mean trouble for somebody.

Chisholm was in an expansive mood and strode along as if he owned the earth. He felt fine. It did not matter that ten of his men had quit that week, and not all of them had been as restrained as old man Firrel in their good-bys. What did he care for the weak sisters? An ad in tomorrow's papers would fill up the anteroom with forty more. If they clicked — weeks from now — so much the better; if not, how could he lose? POHAC's sales department was strictly a straight commission outfit.

He turned through, the park. It was not only a short cut but pleasanter walking, except for the beggars. One met him and whined for a cup of coffee, but Chisholm growled at him and stalked on by. Farther on he came to a place where the path passed through some heavy shrubbery. There were deep shadows there and he hesitated a moment. He would have felt better if a policeman were in sight. Then he reminded himself of what puny creatures most of the panhandlers were and of his own brawn. He walked on.

A man was coming toward him. Just as he supposed, the man was another beggar. He asked for a dime. Chisholm realized it was dark where he was and thought perhaps a dime was cheap insurance against an argument. He stopped and groped in his change pocket for the coin. At that moment something happened. The beggar suddenly grasped his right arm, while another man stepped out of the bushes and grabbed his left. At the same instant someone from the rear locked an arm about his throat and lifted. He was off his feet and choking — skilled hands were exploring his pockets — he kicked and squirmed only to feel the viselike grip on his neck tighten maddeningly. There was an inward plop and something cracked just under his skull with a sharp detonation and a blinding flare of light. Mr. Chisholm had been brutally mugged. Mr. Chisholm was quite dead.

Two hours and a quarter later a group of four were still waiting impatiently in the foyer of the Palace. An angry man from St. Louis sat in the back of a cafeteria eating his supper. He had not been met at the station as promised; neither the office phone, nor McKittrick's or Chisholm's home phones had answered. Not that he minded missing Chisholm particularly — he had always thought him a phony — but he did like the McKittricks. The party at the theater were equally angry, though they showed it less.

"Well," remarked Mrs. McKittrick acidly to her husband in a moment when the others were occupied, "how much longer are you going to wait for that stuffed-shirt of a head salesman of yours?"

"One minute — no more," said McKittrick, glaring at his watch. "If it's any comfort to you, he's being canned as of coming Monday. The office turnover since he's been in charge is something scandalous."

In the other corner of the foyer the smartly gowned creature brought along for the delectation of Mr. Lonigan was growing restive also. She turned to Mrs. Chisholm.

"Whatever could have happened to your husband?" she asked sweetly.

"Drunk, I suppose," answered Mrs. Chisholm calmly. "I hope so. I hear this is a good show and I want to enjoy it, even if we have missed half the first act. My husband, you know, fancies himself as a dramatic critic. He is quite unbearable, I assure you."

"Oh, really?" said the fair young thing. It was best to be noncommittal, she thought, though she had been secretly wondering for some time how long Mrs. Chisholm No. 3 was going to stick it out. No other Mrs. Chisholm had ever finished out the first year, despite the Chisholm legend of what a "way" he had with the gals.

"Let's go on in," said Mr. McKittrick, pocketing his watch.

It was about then that the park police stumbled across the defunct sales manager's broken form. It was already a long time

59

after Mr. Chisholm had temporarily forgotten all about Hardy and Firrel and Maizie and Lonigan and the theater party. For in some places a matter of a couple of hours or so seems longer. It was that way where Mr. Chisholm was.

First, there was all that tiresome marching. Chisholm found himself on a vast gray plain under a dull leaden sky, marching, matching, marching. It was odd .that it tired him so, for it was effortless and .timeless and the distances, though interminable, seemed meaningless. It must have been the monotony of it. And, then, also, he found those marching with him strangely disturbing. Some were healthy-looking men like himself, except that most of them.were gashed or mangled in some way, as if hurled through plate glass or smashed by bombs. Others were haggard and pallid, as if coming from sickbeds. But it was the soldiers that got him most. He had forgotten about the war. It had touched him but slightly, though his impressions of it had been irritating, but not in a flesh and blood way The silly business of priorities, price controls and sales taxes had annoyed him exceedingly, and the outrageous income-tax boosts had infuriated him. Now he was getting another slant on the conflict, for hordes — armies — of soldiers were marching along with him. They were of every kind — Russians, Japs, Tommies, Nazis, even American bluejackets and soldiers — and mingled with them were miserable-looking civilians of every race. A pair of wretched-looking Polish Jews walking near him had obviously been hanged but a short time before. Chisholm edged away from them in horrified disgust.

He was beginning to tumble to the fact that he was dead, and was getting restive with the monotonous tramping across the plain. He had never been a devout man, or even a philosophical one, so he had little idea of what to expect, except that certain childhood memories or notions kept intruding themselves upon his consciousness. Wasn't there some sort of trial coming to him? Not that the prospect worried him much. At least, not very much. For he had always dealt justly with people according to his lights, he insisted to himself. He couldn't help it if there were venal people, or weaklings, or would-be tough eggs that had to be pushed around. Nobody could be expected to get through life without handling such

60

types in the most appropriate way. But where, or where, was the judge that would pass judgment?

After a time the crowd grew thinner. At length the shade of Chisholm noted that he was virtually alone and treading a narrow path that led upward over a shadowy hill. There was no one ahead of him or alongside, but following him at a distance was a considerable multitude of other shades of his own kind. He supposed that shortly after his own unfortunate encounter with the thugs a catastrophe of some sort had developed locally. He could not resist the malicious half hope that it might have been a theater fire. Somehow it irked him that his latest wife should still be alive and fattening on his property while he was tramping these gray wilds. Nor would it have upset him to know that McKittrick had been caught in the same disaster. McKittrick, in his estimation, was a pompous ass whom he would have shown up if he could have lived just a little longer. As far as that went, he could also have viewed with equanimity the decease of the girl that was brought along for Lonigan. He hadn't forgotten the smart of her recent rebuff of him, the little cat!

With such thoughts in mind, he topped the rise and saw a wall with a gate in it before him. The gate was open, so he went on in. He halfway expected to be stopped, or at least greeted by an angel, but things were just the same inside the gate as out — except that there was a voice. The voice cried out in the manner of a train announcer, deep and booming.

"The prototype of Jerome Chester Chisholm!"

Just that. That was all.

Then a demon materialized directly in front of the shade of Chisholm.

"This way, Jerome," he said very politely. He was not bad-looking — for a demon — though he was unmistakably one, having the expected stock properties: a reddish, glistening skin, stubby horns, and shiny jet-black eyes.

" 'J. C.' is what people call me," corrected Chisholm. He had never dealt with a demon before, but since the demon appeared to be friendly he thought he might as well respond with a gesture of his own.

"Better stick to Jerome," advised the demon. "I'll admit it's not pretty, but it's safe. When you start being known by what people *call* you — well!"

Mr. Chisholm sniffed. The demon's words had the faint odor of a dirty crack. He was beginning not to like the demon. Also the import of the unseen aerial announcement was puzzling him. What did it mean by calling him the "prototype" of himself? It didn't make sense.

The demon was skittering along ahead, paying very little attention to Chisholm, who was following along meekly enough. Presently a large building loomed ahead. As they approached Chisholm could see that it was an auditorium of some kind. He could also see that the mob of shades were close behind and that they had no guiding demon with them. Evidently they were following blindly in his own tracks.

The demon turned into the door of the building and led the way up to its stage. It was an auditorium. By the time they had reached the platform, the crowd of ghosts behind were crowding into the place. They soon filled it from wall to wall.

"You must have been a pretty popular fellow," remarked the demon, looking them over, "or the reverse. Notorious, you know."

Chisholm didn't know. He had a reputation, he knew, as a go-getter and a good fellow, but it was a modest one — restricted to his customers, his salesmen, and people he met casually. He hardly expected this turn-out. Moreover, he couldn't recognize anybody in the hall. As he looked them over he was struck with one singularity of the crowd. Many of them bore a family resemblance to him, some rather close, others fantastically distorted. The majority looked like three-dimensional, animated caricatures of him. One especially obnoxious one kept trying to climb up onto the stage. He was far fatter than Chisholm himself had ever been or could ever have been even if he had skipped the gym workouts.

The demon observed the look of profound distaste on Chisholm's face, but only grinned a little and picked up a gavel. He rapped sharply on the table.

"Come to order, please," he said. "The convention is assembled."

There was a momentary hush, and then pandemonium broke out. It was a very disorderly crowd and an opinionated one, from the jeers that were hurled up at the stage. It was hard to pick out what they were saying, but the trend of it seemed to be that practically everyone there wanted to preside or was full of hot ideas that demanded immediate and full expression. The demon was unperturbed. He was an old hand. At intervals he would bang with the gavel. At last he got a tiny bit of silence.

"Fellow heels," he commenced, unblushingly, then paused to see what uproar would follow. There was none. His insult had quieted the tumult like oil on ruffled waters. He cleared his throat and went on.

"We are gathered here to form the ghost of Jerome Chester Chisholm, deceased, erstwhile sales manager of the Pinnacle Office & Household Appliance Corp. We have all eternity, to be sure, but why waste it? Coalesce, please, as rapidly as possible. For purposes of comparison, your prototype is standing here beside me. Take it or leave it. That's your affair."

There were howls of "Chuck him out," "chiseler," "heel," "stuffed shirt," and many, many less elegant epithets. Then an ominous silence descended. The demon quietly pointed to a spot on the stage and the procession started. One by one the specters mounted the stage, marched to the spot and stood on it. Succeeding ones came on, each melting imperceptibly into the one that had been there before. Gradually the resultant figure took on more definite shape and looked far more solid than any single shade in the hall. For many of them were so tenuous as to be hardly visible.

"Would you mind, sir," asked Mr. Chisholm, not knowing any better way to address a demon, "telling me what this is all about? And after this monkey business is over, when do I get my trial?"

"Trial?" The demon laughed. "In one sense you have had your trial. This is the result.. In another sense, this is your trial. In either case, the verdict is already found and the sentence fixed."

"I don't get you," said Mr. Chisholm. "Who are all these . . . er . . . spooks? And what have they got to do with me? They look like a flock of comic Valentines."

"They have plenty to do with you. They *are* you."

"Me! You're crazy. I'm me." He struck himself on the chest.

"No. You are only one aspect of you," corrected the demon. "You are a ghost now, and nothing more. Ghosts are intangible, immaterial things — made of dream stuff, as your poets say. What you call you is your own estimate of you. These creatures flocking up onto the stage are other people's estimates of you. *You* — the you that we recognize — is the composite of them all. Stick around. You are going to learn something." -

Chisholm turned his gaze back at the oncoming file of shades. They were ghastly cartoons of himself, and malicious ones at that. Many of them were unintelligible.

"Hey," he said, "what's that thing coming up — that slender wisp of smoke with the lumpy feet? If that is a conception of me, the guy that thought it up has gone surrealistic."

The demon looked.

"Oh, that. Yes, it's weak. It is offered by a fellow named Percy Hilyer. He roomed with you at school and has almost forgotten you. He does remember that you were lean and lanky then and used to swipe his socks and wear holes in them."

"That's a hell of a thing to hold against a guy," complained Chisholm.

The demon shrugged.

"That is the way reputations are made. How do you like this one?"

"This one" was the rambunctious shade who had tried to take charge of the meeting at the outset. He was egregiously repulsive.

"That," announced the demon blandly, "is the contribution of one Maizie Delmar. Judging from its robustness and solidity, she knew you recently and well."

Chisholm's jaw had dropped and his eyes bulged. The thing was incredible. Not Maizie's. Maizie was regular; dumb, maybe, but they got along.

"I take it Maizie was the tactful sort," remarked the demon with a sly drawl, noting the amazement on Chisholm's loose face. Then, "Here comes one that might suit you better."

It was a fat, squally baby, drooling and flapping its pudgy arms.

"One of your mother's contributions. Her favorite of many. You might admire some, but they are all on the helpless side — not at all in keeping with your hardboiled idea of the way to do things."

Chisholm stood aghast and watched the endless procession. On they came, one vile caricature after another. Nobody seemed to have forgotten him. He expected the Specter furnished by Firrel to be bad. It was. Malice was not its creator, but sheer contempt. Chisholm had to turn his face when it clambered up onto the stage. The office girls' offering differed little from Maizie's except in intensity. The one held by Hardy was a cruel surprise. He had done so much for Hardy. But be had forgotten how he had made Hardy pay through the nose for favors.

The greatest shocks were to follow. He steeled himself for whatever opinions those first two wives held, but the current one had done a devastating job of analysis. Even the demon whistled. Interspersed between the major blows were minor ones, and not always shadowy. Bootblacks, waiters, taxi drivers — on almost every casual contact he had left a mark. Out of the lot there was only one that was glowingly heroic. He could not refrain from asking the demon about it. The demon bent his insight onto the wraith and pronounced:

"A girl you met once — a pick-up. You kissed her on the Drive that night, and then lost her phone number, you lucky dog."

"Lucky?"

"Yes. She never had a chance to know you better."

Mr. Chisholm was glum. It wasn't right to be pilloried that way. They simply couldn't do that to him. To hell with what all those people thought. Who were they, anyhow? A lot of nitwit salesmen and office help, gold-diggers and climbers! He knew he was all right. He had got along. They were jealous and envious, that's what. He nudged the demon.

"Hey," he called, "this is a democracy, ain't it? If these soreheads have a vote, so do I. Don't *I* come in?"

"Sure, sure. It ought to help a lot, too. All these figures are weighted, you have noticed, by degree of intimacy and one thing or another. Since you have probably thought more about yourself than anybody else has, even if you've been wrong most of the time, your opinion counts."

65

Chisholm looked down at himself confidently, and then his confidence began to ooze. His own personality, it appeared, even when viewed from his own standpoint, was more nebulous than he thought. He had never taken himself apart with the critical fury employed by such persons as Maizie, his wives and some others. It looked as if the almost-finished monstrosity standing in the center of the stage was going to be the image handed down to posterity.

"It's not fair," he wailed. "What do all those yapping people really know about me — motives, and all that? I never did anything I didn't think was right, I never —"

"Neither did Nero," said the demon calmly, "nor Torquemada, nor your estimable contemporary, Hitler. Nevertheless, we cannot take an Ego at its own valuation. Not where others are involved."

Chisholm took a shuddering look at the hideous thing that was the summation of all his world thought of him. It was intolerable. That, then, was the verdict the demon had spoken of.

"Your sentence," said the demon, as if he knew the thought, "is to contemplate it from now on. It is all yours — your life's work. At least it's definite, if that is any consolation."

"I can't, I can't," moaned Mr. Chisholm.

"Don't make things worse," warned the demon.

The composite spook had just turned a bright, lemon yellow.

Chariots of San Fernando

Indian legend swore we were headed for a hell peopled with unspeakable devils.

FOREWORD

It may be to the credit of the skeptical scientific attitude that no single important group or individual has accepted the sensational account by Dr. Stephen Taussig of the discovery of new, amazing fauna in the San Fernando country at the Amazon's head-waters. Taussig, sole survivor of the Museum of Living Science Expedition, was plainly deranged when he reached the outposts of civilization. Bits of alleged evidence — a glassy object some ten inches long by-- six wide, of a pointed oval-shape and convex like a cupped hand; a length of coiled, transparent tubing, perhaps thirty feet long and tapering from the diameter of an inch to half as much; and a huge bone, unfortunately shattered in transit to America — have invited curiosity, but not diagnosis.

I came into the mystery by pure chance. I was secretary-companion three years ago to John J. Beazle, a wealthy dabbler in exploration and adventure, with some pretension to botanical and zoological education, and sailed far up the Amazon in his yacht, the *Tethys*. News came of a white man, sick and delirious, at a settlement on one of the uncharted side-streams. We sought the place and found it to be the outpost Cruxite mission of Youmbinque.

Father Hundig, who was caring for the sick man, welcomed our appearance and loans of bedding, ice and medicines. The patient, though wasted, screamed and struggled so that we could not move him from the missionary's cot. Beazle, not much interested, spent most of the days that followed among liquor bottles on the *Tethys*, it was I who heard Stephen Taussig's story, which I have tried to set down in his own words from my short-hand notes.

The specimens mentioned above lay near Taussig's cot. When whole, the bone was as massive as the femur of a dinosaur, some six feet long, with its very center a roughly cubical bulge a foot thick. Tapering both ways from this central lump, the ends of the bone terminated in spherical knobs, ivory-hard and perhaps eight inches in diameter. As it spindled toward these ends, the bone showed round and smooth but for v-shaped grooves running lengthwise from small holes toward the middle.

It was plainly fresh, to judge from the oily moisture and clinging fragments of tough flesh. I was surprised to find no sign of terminal cartilage on the knobs. About this and the two crystal pieces clung an odor of rot, strangely and chemically pungent.

Father Hundig told how Taussig and others had stayed at the mission on their outbound trip some weeks before, and how Taussig had returned in a native canoe, alone but for sullen Indian paddlers, whom he kept in hand at pistol point. Though seriously ill, Taussig begged the priest to take charge of the specimens the boat carried, then collapsed. The Indians paddled away in patent relief.

The recent death of Father Hundig leaves my account almost unsupported, but his diary might prove interesting to scholars with open minds. Meanwhile, here is Taussig's story, to be read either as scientific data or mere curiousa. I am not expert enough to suggest which.

I

Our up-river trip was mostly uneventful. All had been well planned and Dooling, who had previously visited this basin, acted as interpreter and go-between with the Indians. We had no difficulty until we reached the confluence of the Caquini.

You must have heard the Indian legends about the San Fernando as a hell peopled with unspeakable devils. We did not fall into the error of disregarding these entirely; savage tabus are often founded on a practical basis. We guessed that in the region were real dangers, perhaps unknown predatory animals, and we hoped to find them and prove how exaggerated folklore can be.

But neither threats nor promises could induce a single native to accompany us beyond the great falls of the Caquini. We were faced with the unsatisfactory job of going ahead without guides or bearers. The solution of the problem was somewhat disquieting.

Two days journey below the falls, we stopped, at man's uttermost habitation, the village of the Chicupes. The natives appeared more apprehensive about the country just beyond than any of the downriver peoples.

Their fear had created a bizarre custom — each year they selected two prime warriors to go as sacrifices into the unknown land. If one of these should survive, they said, for the space of a single moon, his safe return would show that the devils had been propitiated. Such a survivor would be rewarded with the chieftainship. But none had ever returned.

By a fortunate coincidence, the selection had been made only a few days before we arrived. The two young warriors were undergoing some interesting rites of purification before leaving. After tedious negotiations and the paying of substantial bribes, we arranged to go along with the party that escorted them.

We had bearers at least, but with them came disquiet. If two warriors, and of the best, went into the San Fernando yearly and did not return, what became of them? We could not guess. Neither, I am sure, can you. But we found out.

A short distance from the falls we established a base camp. Beyond here our Indians would not go. The next three weeks were uneventful. We set up our field laboratories and explored the heavy forest, in widening circles. There was little of interest and less of danger in our findings. Hedrick identified some poisonous plants, there were a few snakes and insects, and I shot one wildcat. It was like many another district in the jungle.

Our Indians huddled timorously at our base camp, but we overcame our own sense of vague apprehension. How false were these senses of security we were soon to learn.

As we prepared to move on, only the sacrificial braves, Itai and Tubutu, could be persuaded to help carry our tinned foods, cameras and other supplies. This pair, really splendid youngsters, had slept and eaten apart from their friends, and were seemingly regarded as already dead. Camber remained in charge of the base; with instructions to bring every day as much food and other necessaries as he could carry to a certain advance base we chose as point of departure into the unknown. Hedrick, Dooling and I, with the two Chicupes, pressed on.

Nine miles on our journey, among thinning trees that hinted open savannas ahead, I almost tripped over a neat ball of crushed and splintered bones. Just beyond lay the neatly severed head of a Capuchin monkey. As we gathered to look, there seemed to hang about us a heavy odor more suggestive of the chemical laboratory than the jungle. Hedrick, stooping, identified the smashed bones as belonging to the monkey whose head lay beyond. They were jammed into a rough sphere the size of a melon, broken and pressed as if by some ramming device, and covered with chemical-smelling slime.

"Looks as if it had been chewed up and then spat out" commented Hedrick. "But what jaws could crumple a pelvis like that?"

As to the head, it had been sliced off as smoothly as by a machete, and its hair was dry and clean. None of us could think of an animal large enough to take such a bite with, at the same time, such sharp, guillotine-like incisors. We rejected both lions and anacondas. Whatever had killed the monkey would be in a class by itself, a class unknown to us, a class that might prove decidedly unpleasant to study.

The Indians showed fright, but only for a moment. Steeped in tradition, they seemed to recognize their brotherhood with the monkey's remains. Dooling sniffed the air.

"Silico-ethane," he said. "Where does it come from?" He lifted some slime on a twig. "Here it is. Silicic acid, or I'm an impostor among chemists." He scraped some into a specimen can. "I'll analyze it later."

Hedrick took pictures and we went on.

At the spot agreed upon, where Camber was to come daily, we made a temporary advanced base. It was about noon, so we ate a snack, then Hedrick and I struck out for a quick look around at what was beyond. We took Itai with us to carry cameras and boxes, but Hedrick and I were burdened only with rifles and machetes. Dooling said he would go to work with his chemicals and hoped to have a report for us when we returned.

Before us was flat country covered with a short grass. A mile in front and away to the left rose a low range of hills, fairly steep, but round-topped and covered with grass. In the far distance we could make out the hazy blue profile of a mountain range. To the right was a high cliff, about a mile distant at its closest, and running straight away from us for as far as we could see. This escarpment marked a great fault that elevated the country beyond and made possible the magnificent falls of the Caquini, ten miles behind. There was a little watercourse that followed the cliff down to the Caquini.

We were soon out of the grass and into a thicket of bushes shoulder high. Hedrick stopped in amazement and examined several of the bushes, pulling long pods from them. He shredded the pod, first smelling and then tasting its contents.

"*Ricimus*, of some sort," he said in response to my questioning look. "Must be a variety of castor bean, but I never expected to see it growing wild in South America. I think I can chalk this up as my great discovery of the day. Yours will be the monkey-killer, if you can track it down."

"It didn't leave tracks," I said. "I looked for them."

Hedrick was quite bucked up over his castor beans. I knew what he was thinking, of how nice it would be to see in print *Ricinus Americanus Hedriquensis*. We all have those little vanities.

The area covered by them was fairly extensive. We reached a little knoll, a foot or so higher than the general level, and we could see that they extended all the way to the cliff, and from the forest on our right to several miles to the left of us. We kept on through them as it was by far the shortest way.

A few hundred yards farther on we both were brought up in surprise to find ourselves in a comparatively clear space. The bushes were all down — some uprooted, all of them broken and torn apart and most of the foliage gone. Lanes led in a dozen directions, like the spokes of a wheel. In these spaces the wreckage of the bushes was appalling. The sight suggested a small scale replica of the damage done by elephants. Here was a new situation to ponder. No one had ever heard of an elephant in this country, and anyway, these would have to be midget elephants.

It was not until we had carefully and minutely examined the ground that we got our first clue. We found wagon tracks!

We checked each of the lanes that led in. Each showed the marks of broad tires with a gauge of nearly six feet! Our previous mystification was nothing to what we felt now. How could there be wagons in an uninhabited country lying hundreds of miles beyond populated country where even a cart was unknown? And such wide wagons, and so many, and in such a place?

When we had seen all there was to see, we went on, following the wagon trail that led straightest toward the water and the cliff.

Under foot all the way were the broken and stripped castor plants. Twice before we reached the far boundary of this extraordinary bean patch we came across much wider places where other wagons had converged and had destroyed a half acre or so of the plants.

Our trail led more or less straight to the foot of the cliff and we finally emerged onto a wide sand-bed that edged the clear creek which ran along the foot of the bluff. Our wagon wheel marks continued straight on into the water, and there they ended! We could see there for a few feet under water, but beyond the running stream erased them. The creek was hardly fifty feet wide, the other bank of it was a towering cliff, rising sheer three hundred feet.

"What a country!" said Hedrick, wiping his brow, after we had had a good drink of the clear water, and refilled our canteens. "I'm beginning to think those Indians have something."

After a brief rest, we turned upstream, walking along close to the water where the sand was damp and firm. Presently we came to more wheel-marks. That cleared the mystery for a moment. Apparently the driver had chosen to come upstream part of the way in the river. Then we came to an intricate criss-cross of tracks, indicating dozens of wagons, in and out of the river, in and out of the beans, up and down the sand-bed, like a circus lot the day after. We traversed a mile of this, conversing from time to time, chiefly to explode each other's theories as fast as one would develop some hypothesis to work from.

Even if there had been a reasonable source of wagons, the maze of markings on the sand would still have been of dubious meaning. For one thing, there were no tracks of horses, oxen or other draft animals.

Again, many of the trails were partially obliterated, as if by a drag. We also decided that the carts were two-wheeled, and of various gauges, from six feet to as little as two. As we stooped to measure a trail through the thicket, I saw something round and whitish, half buried in the sand near the bean stalks. I picked it up.

It was a human skull.

Around the brow was a leather strap, stiff and moldy, stitched with copper wire — just such a symbol of sacrifice as Itai wore that moment. Beyond lay bones, human but crushed and compacted, like those of the monkey.

I turned to him, with a sign of inquiry. Brave enough, he drew himself up as if at attention.

"Garzus," he muttered, and passed his left hand thrice across his face — the Chicupe counterpart of the sign of the cross to avert evil. There were tears on his brown cheeks, and he was afraid — mortally afraid — for all that he was a picked fighting man of his people.

III

There was nothing to be gained by lingering over the relics of the dead Indian; if we were to penetrate the veil of mystery that shrouded these strange deaths we must learn more.

An uneasiness, vague at first, but steadily mounting to a sense of profound apprehension, settled upon us. We had not forgotten those hideous legends. Heretofore we had regarded them as the mad inventions of fanatical witch-doctors or the insane imaginings of superstitious heathens. But now we could not help remembering that no matter in what other respects the myths might

73

differ, they had invariably spoken of the horror of this land of fiends as the "rolling death," and always coupled with that expression had been the dread word "Garzus" — a word signifying "dragon" or "hippogriff."

The wonder grew on us as we speculated whether there could be in this accursed country a ferocious race of aboriginees who drove chariots after the fashion of the early Britons. Perhaps in this weird and malignant land there *was* a fearsome creature of a type unguessed; could it be that such a monster drew the war-chariots of the barbarous people of this place? We shrank from that solution. We told ourselves thatwe must not permit ourselves to be swept away by the psychic vagaries of these credulous savages; that we must retain our grip on our common sense; that we must search, and find more clues until we had found the simple, practical explanation that our reason told us must lie somewhere behind these grotesqueries.

Ahead of us the creek bent outward from the cliff to round a vast hemi-cone of detritus, where long ago a section of the cliff had been undercut and fallen down. The widened stream's ripply surface told us that here were shoals that we could cross without serious wetting. Since at this point also there was a convergence of cart tracks leading into the river and evidence of their emergence on the other side, we waded across.

The chariot tracks led around to the downstream face and here we were further astonished to find ourselves in what had every appearance of being a rough quarry. Dozens of half-begun shafts showed where someone had dug into the walls. An inspection of the roughly level floor of the quarry revealed that away from the walls there were a number of mounds of broken limestone and a little slate. Whoever was working here was only interested in the quartz and silicates. On the ground in front of the newest working we found a pile of large quartz crystals mixed with fragments of agate.

I went to pick up a particularly beautiful piece of stone when to my startled disgust I found it covered with slime. As it slithered from my fingers I recognized the revolting odor and texture of the stuff that was smeared on the dead monkey's bones. Half nauseated, I hardly heard Hedrick's cry of astonishment as he pointed to the gobs of jelly lying on the ground on the far side of this collection of rocks. But there they were enough to fill a gallon bucket, scattered about as if dispersed by the nuzzling snout of some feeding beast. As I wiped my hands, Hedrick collected several pounds of it to take back to Dooling. There was no smell in the air here of silico-ethane; this was chlorine, faint but unmistakable!

"I think we have enough material for one night's insomnia," Hedrick said, "and it's getting late. Let's go back to Dooling."

Back in the trees we found Dooling had made an improvised camp and had food cooking, and on a box we could see a beaker and some test-tubes.

"That jelly *is* a silicic acid," Dooling announced, as soon as we joined him, "but just which I don't know. It appears to be an organic variety and there's no telling what the formula for it is."

"Take a look at this, then," said Hedrick, handing him the jar with the stuff from the quarry.

It proved to be the same, or closely similar. The last sample was somewhat stiffer than the slimy stuff from the skeleton.

We talked until late that night, but got nowhere with the baffling data we had collected that day. Being together around a cheery fire, and having warm food tended to allay the qualms of misgiving. Tomorrow might bring a solution to part of these riddles.

IV

Early the next day, we had left two miles of flat plain behind us and were halfway up the side of the first of the foot-hills. We had already passed three sets of long-dried bones, of antelope, this time. The layout was always the same; a compact pile of crushed bones, and within three or four yards, a complete skull, these with antlers. Then we found a fresh set, a kill of not later than the day before.

"That monster not only has a big mouth, but it must be fast," was Hedrick's comment. "It is no cinch to catch an antelope in an open place like this."

We examined the grass; there were two-distinct trails, one down from the top of the hill, the other up. The up-trail, oddly enough showed the signs of the drag behind it, the other not. There could be no mistake, the direction of the bent grass was conclusive. Outside the lines left by the wheels, we noticed many blades of grass, tipped with droplets of a clear yellow liquid. As this golden dew appeared nowhere else, it must have dropped from the hubs of the chariot. Hedrick lifted a drop with a finger, held it under his nose, then gingerly tasted it.

"Crude castor oil," he grunted.

We followed the trails to the summit of the hill, where we found a long, nearly level ridge, marked occasionally by clumps of trees resembling mesquite. Up here there were many marks in the grass, as if a number of the vehicles had paraded up and down, and we observed half a dozen places where trails led straight downward.

Following the trails along the summit, we had just passed a clump of bushy trees, when we wheeled at the sound of a stifled scream from Itai.

Ten yards away a face was looking at us.

It was no human face — only grotesquely humanoid — and gigantic. Maybe it was four feet across, with large, dark, lustrous eyes gazing placidly at us. Between them a long nose, flexible as a trunk, twitched, and below grinned a yard-wide mouth, as full of teeth as a shark's. At each temple clustered what appeared to be curls, and two more clumps showed on top of the head. I was stupid with amazement and horror. I remember thinking that I used to know a barber who looked something like that.

But more ghastly still was the body. It was mounted on wheels that attached to either side of a plumpness like a sort of owl. There were no arms or legs, only a dragonlike tail that swept behind to steady the bulk. The wheels were pale and solid, like the wooden ones on a Cuban ox-cart.

All that we saw in a flash of time. For at once the curl-pads on the monster's head unwound and flicked at us — four darting cables in the air. Itai was closest, and those devil's antennae whipped around his neck, arms and legs, yanking him through the air like a toy on a string. He screamed — once — and then the mouth received him, feet-first, and closed. His head dropped off, neatly severed, and' bounced suddenly away.

Hedrick and I still stared. These large brown eyes closed as if in ecstasy. The thing began to chew, like a ruminant cow. Hedrick fired first, then I — bullet after bullet from our rifles, at point-blank range.

76

There was no effect. It chewed calmly. Lead bullets were like peas tossed at a sofa pillow — I saw momentary dimples as the missiles struck and glanced off. That hide was tougher than armor. Its covering of glassy scales rang musically when hit.

We fired, perhaps two or three clips each, when the monster was satisfied with its snack. Opening its eyes and mouth, it spat onto the ground Itai's crumpled skeleton — then looked at us.

I had some saving instinctive impulse. Dropping my rifle, I swipped out my machete. Hedrick did likewise. The tentacles stretched toward us, more slowly — the thing wasn't quite so hungry now.

We whacked and slashed. My first stroke encountered a strand almost as tough as wire cable. A second blow, more strong and desperate, cut away an eight-foot length, and bright blood flowed. Hedrick was tangled in two of the antennae, lifting him, from the ground as he hacked and hewed.

I rushed, swinging with all my strength, and he fell free. The monster gave a soul-shattering howl, and its eyes crinkled shut in pain, huge tears rolling, into sight. Three of its four tentacles had been wounded, and fell back into coils that spurted blood. Still screaming, the creature threshed itself about with a sweep of its tail and pushed away. I saw prismatic lights on the scales of the back armor.

We pursued the Garzus — we knew that this must be one — and, scientists even in this hour of peril and fear, we saw that it moved by shoving stubby shoulders against spoke-like ribs on the inner faces of the horny wheels. When we came close, we encountered another weapon. The back scales lifted, like hair on an angry cat, and from beneath white smoke gushed upon us. At the same moment the thing hoisted its tail, balancing on its wheels, and coasted away down a swift slope, losing itself behind the clouds of vapor.

It had laid a smoke-screen of silicon tetrachloride.

V

It was with decidedly mixed feelings that we turned back to the spot where we had commenced our fight. But for the accident of

77

position, either one of us might have played the role of Itai, and had the animal been less sluggish after its meal, it would have taken a second victim. The Thing was immune to gunfire, and with its four tough tentacles one man could not withstand it, even if fore-warned. He could only hope to wound it on his way into that hopper of a mouth.

Knowing now the secret of its locomotion, we perceived that the safest place to encounter one would be on level ground. It could hardly move faster than a brisk trot unless rolling free. We shuddered to think what our fate would have been if our party had been charged by a group of them while still on the hillside, for we now understood the technique of the beast's hunting. Yet even on flat ground, the ability suddenly to flick those forty-foot. tentacles made them formidable foes. Yet, the Things must have some weakness; we knew we must study them and find a way to conquer.

The pieces of the antennae stank of silico-ethane and we observed that they were really thick-walled gelatinous tubes. Just what was the function of the wire-thin inner duct that terminated in a sort of nozzle at the tip of the tentacle we could not fathom.

We had a brief discussion, and decided to go on to the quarry and begin our observation. Later we would come back and bury the remains of the unfortunate Itai. We scoured the ridge to make sure there was not another lurking Garzus to swoop down on us after we had begun the descent. Off to the west, the smoke-screen had almost dissipated. Our recent adversary had turned away to the south, several miles upstream from the ford and the quarry.

We found the quarry exactly as we had left it. Sixty feet or so overhead was a hard stratum of sandstone forming a ledge above which we could see the dark mouths of several caves. By grasping at the roots of shrubs growing out from the face of the cliff and taking advantages of the many minor projections we climbed without difficulty to the ledge. Directly under us was the quarry; to the left, beyond the creek, was the sand-bank where the Garzi paraded. We flattened down on our faces, and unslinging binoculars, began our vigil.

Nothing happened for several hours. Once we made out through our glasses another little tragedy on the hillside we had quit earlier. From the crest of the hill came a flash of light, something like a runaway cannon slid swiftly down to where an antelope was grazing, there was a quick gleaming of silvery lariats flailing the air — and there was no more antelope. In a little bit, the rolling thing turned and slowly climbed up the hill and disappeared into a clump of trees.

Intent on this drama, we had not noticed the first approach of a herd of Garzi. But soon there were dozens, slowly rolling up and down the sands, while some browsed in the patch of *Euphorbiaceae*, tearing at the branches of the bean bushes. Among them were many little ones, Garzilli we called them.

The larger Garzi seemed to be engaged in prodding the little ones into promenading, following them closely. Whenever one of the baby monsters would show a tendency to stop or even to slow down, the parent would whack it forward with a resounding side slap of the tail. Now and then an elder Garzus would appear to attack one of the little ones from the side, gripping it firmly with all four tentacles while nuzzling at the near wheel. The Garzillus would make the air hideous with its trumpeting and squealing for a moment, and, then released, it rolled wobblingly away, its soft young wheels bending and caving under the infant's weight.

"Must be teaching 'em to roll!" whispered Hedrick.

In the meantime, several full-grown Garzi had forded the creek and were up in the quarry. We watched their operations with the most intense interest, for of all the clues we had previously found, those in this spot were the least intelligible.

From our excellent observation post we learned to distinguish between male and female. The latter were smaller, but the salient difference was in the snout. The female proboscis was much shorter and thicker, and terminated in a cup-shaped tip of bone or ivory. This tip appeared to be quite thin, even sharp, like a tin biscuit cutter.

We could not see exactly what they were doing among the piles of silicates because usually their scaly backs and tails were to us, but we could see fumes rising and detect the odor of chlorine in the air. Just what acid or in what manner, they secreted it, we shall probably never know, but having poured it out, they waited patiently. From our previous find, we were able; to anticipate the result, they were preparing silicic acid: In a while we were to see them eat it, and others follow and repeat the performance.

Virtually prisoners until the hour should come when this herd would move on, Hedrick and I had ample opportunity to digest what we had seen. Finally, we withdrew a distance into the cool inner part of the cave and compared notes.

We were too realistic not to accept the natural explanation of it. After all, the human being consumes and converts in his lifetime a vast quantity of carbon, salt and other solids. There is small difference between a diet of diamonds and coal and a diet of opals and quartz. It is all a matter of glands and digestive processes.

The Garzus, from its observed diet and excretions, had an affinity for silicon. Its skin and the scales of its armor were siliciculous; it exhaled a silico-ethane, it could produce silicon tetrachloride for protection, and used a silicic acid in digestion. In order to ingest the required amount of the element, it had special glands that enabled it to reduce onyx and quartz to an edible jelly. It was all very reasonable. And it made us anxious to kill and dissect one of the things. Doubtless the more normal diet of animal-flesh was to provide the necessary heat for movement and the operation of its internal laboratories.

Hedrick and I were in fair agreement as to these theories, but we still had the novel method of locomotion to consider. Nature is a great experimentalist, but this example verged on the incredible. I must have been a little dazed by the rapid events of the last two days, for I must admit that I owe the explanation of it to Hedrick's keen mind.

But I was to wait a while before receiving it. When we had finished our discussion of the silicic aspects of the Garzus, we went out onto the ledge to take a look. The herd had gone. They had- gone through the castor plants, a few were still there browsing on the far edge, the others were slowly rolling toward the forest — toward where Dooling and Tuputu were awaiting us!

VI

We scrambled down straight through the ravaged bean growth, crashing through the brittle bushes and acquiring many scratches. As we neared the far edge, we slowed down, and gripping our machetes and keeping a sharp lookout for the Garzi, but it was not until we had emerged on the other side that we saw any.

The sun was behind us, a circumstance that rendered the Garzi ahead of us exceptionally visible, for the rays reflected from their prismatic backs were brilliant and of every hue. There were three of the glittering creatures, their tails to us, at the foot of a tree by our camp site. We could see the flashes from the snaky feelers that were stripping the lower branches from the tree. We advanced boldly, knowing their clumsiness, but stopped about twenty yards behind them. There was no danger as long as we could stay out of reach of the tentacles, we felt that outside of their radius we could outrun the cumbersome creatures should they turn and threaten us. But they were too intent on what was before them to notice our approach.

A shout from above informed us that Dooling was high up in the tree. He was trying to warn us of the monsters; and said there were several more back in the woods. As he spoke, we saw two rolling toward us, one from directly behind the tree, the other from somewhat to the right of it. We ran to the highest of the nearby trees and scrambled up not a moment too soon, for before we were high enough to be out of reach; we each had to straddle a limb and slash frantically at sinuous glassine tentacles.

I did not succeed in doing more than nick the ones grasping for me, but Hedrick managed to cut away a yard or so of the tip of one, and we heard the yelp and howls of its injured owner with grim pleasure. We resumed our ascent until we came to a roomy fork about. fifty feet from the ground. An excited chatter overhead reminded us that we had company. A group of the Capuchin monkeys was huddled there, squeaking and twittering in fright.

Firmly settled, we craned our necks hallooing, until we spotted a khaki patch through the lacery of leaves. That was Dooling perched in his tree, a couple of hundred feet away. After we had cut away some intervening branches so that we could see better, we observed that his tree was not so high as ours, and although he was at about our level, he could go no higher. He, too, had partners in misery, a pair of monkeys like ours. Shouting back and forth, we gave each other the high spots of the day's happenings.

Dooling said that Camber had been there about noon with a good load of provisions. They had visited for a while, and Camber had gone back, saying he would return again tomorrow. Dooling went to work on our notebooks. His first intimation of danger was the warning given him about an hour before by the excited Tuputu.

They watched two Garzi approach, and he fell into the pardonable error of trying to shoot them. Ignorant of the uncanny peril in the innocuous looking curls on the heads of the monsters, he continued shooting until the first one got too close. Tuputu charged it with a machete, and Dooling saw him snatched and devoured in one horrible instant. Under the circumstances, he could think of nothing better than to climb the nearest tree.

We told him he done the only possible thing, but that he was safe now. And when we, said it, we thought he was. We did not know that the Garzus had still another deadly weapon.

We watched the Garzi below us grope the lower branches of our tree with their tentacles, reaching, feeling for us, as if they did not trust their eyes. When we next glanced Dooling's way, we were startled to see that a ring of Garzi about the tree had extended their antennae to the fullest, all pointing at Dooling. They looked in the almost level rays of the setting sun like glistening glass rods. They failed to reach him by about ten feet, but the fumes we now saw jetting from their tips did not. Dooling shouted hoarsely something about deadly gas — chloroform — and frenziedly tried to climb. We saw him cling a moment to a little fork just above his head, then slip away and fall crashing. Like echoes, we heard the thuds of the monkeys as, they plopped to the ground beside him. Helpless to do anything, we had to see the inert forms wrapped in tentacles that fell as quickly as cut ropes and witness the greedy tug of war between two rival Garzi who had simultaneously clutched the body of our friend. We turned our eyes away, unable to endure more. When we had heard the third of the shocking *clops* of decapitating mouths snapped shut, we knew that Dooling was now in the maw of the "rolling death" of San Fernando.

Sick with horror, and despondent over our own futility, we hauled ourselves mechanically higher up the tree. Another twenty feet and we were among the shuddering monkeys.

Soon we had our gas attack. We caught the odor, but our height and a freshening breeze that had just sprung up made it ineffective. Seeing that we did not drop, the Garzi abandoned their posts below us and wheeled off into the forest.

In another hour, the bright beams of the rising full moon illuminated the savanna clearly. Hedrick placed a hand on my arm.

"Let's go down," he whispered, "there is at least one more thing we can try."

He led the way to the other tree, where the scattered remains of our advanced camp lay, rooted and tumbled around by the dragons. He picked up an armful of notebooks and asked me to do the same. Watching our tread carefully, for somewhere about here lay the heads of two of our fellows, we stalked out onto the moonlit plain.

"Damn, the notebooks," Hedrick muttered, "if this hunch works, we can write a book whose dullest page will be worth a ton of this rubbish."

He led on. The breeze was quite strong now at our backs, as if blowing out of the moon behind us. Nowhere was the loom of a bulky Garzus. All about us was grass, and just ahead the shoulder high bushes of the castor bean area.

VII

"Thank God for the wind," said Hedrick, fervently. He tore branches from a bean plant and threw them to the ground. Ripping out a handful of leaves from the notebook he wadded them up. I struck a match and held it to the paper in cupped hands. Five minutes later, a roaring fire was sweeping away from us toward the cliffs. We ran each way along the edge of the plantation, lighting new fires every few dozen feet. In an hour's time we rejoined, and stood for a moment watching the wall of flame as it swept toward the. river. The crackling of bursting pods and stalks and the roar of the receding flame made a tremendous noise, but we did think once we heard the howling of a roasting Garzus.

We returned at once to our scattered camp. It was fairly light in here now, the moon beams coming through from one side and the ruddy glare of the burning bushes from the other. We rummaged about and found a ball of fish-line, and I mounted to our nest in the tree.

Once there, I let the line down, and successively drew up piece after piece of our outfit that Hedrick tied on below. As each item reached me, I would cut off a short length of the line and lash it to a convenient limb. It must have been midnight when Hedrick joined me.

We had boxes of food, six canteens of water, and some of Dooling's chemical gear and. the first aid kit. We took our belts and rifle slings and rigged safety belts. We were all set for a siege We could last in comfort for a week. But that night we could not sleep, there had been too many gruesome things happen before our eyes, and too much of interest. And the coming day was to have its responsibilities. We must warn Camber, for he would come walking along, innocent of the dangers that surrounded him.

Hedrick elaborated his theory of silicon absorption and recombination, and gave me his ideas on the rolling system of locomotion.

"Until we saw these things," he said, "we would have staked our professional reputations that a free joint, like between wheel and axle, would be an impossibility in a living thing. The limb cannot have a connection with the body, and therefore would wither from lack of nourishment. But here, all around us, are examples of this impossibility in actual being. Luckily, there is also the evidence which enables us to see *how*.

"The diet of castor beans serves a double purpose. It provides raw material for the glands of the Garzus which manufacture an organic oil that is both a lubricant and a carrier of living substance to replenish the wheels as they first grow, then wear away. As human body absorbs mercury or lead if rubbed on the skin, so do these horn wheels absorb food from the oil surrounding the axles.

"The females have a bony gadget at the tip of their noses. I am confident if we could find a nest of fresh born Garzilli we would find them with soft, flexible wheels of gristle, and without intervening joint. As they get older, the gristle turns to horn, becomes stiff enough to bear its weight, but the little thing cannot yet move about, it must remain motionless in the lair. This is when the mother brings her peculiar nose into play. She cuts a joint. By

84

this time, the castor oil glands have begun functioning. The oil flows into the incision, soothing it, and thereafter acts as lubricant and carrier of building elements to the severed horn.

"Normally, the horn would again adhere to the axle, just as human bones tend to grow together after a serious joint injury. We can understand now the purpose of the relentless driving up and down of the little ones by the parents. You even saw on several occasions where a mother recut a joint that might have been beginning to freeze. By the time the Garzillus approaches full growth, it has worn definite bearing surfaces on both axle and wheel, its oil glands have taken over their duties, and the rolling joint ceases to require any more attention than our own elbows.

"But suppose we cut off that part of the food supply which provides the oil, like our burning the bean patch. If, as I hope, that is the only considerable supply near here, it is bound to have profound affects. I anticipate adhesions, perhaps complete immobilizations of the wheels. Stalled in their tracks, they cannot replenish their silicon supply, and the chemical exudations of which they are capable will probably diminish in strength. And, unless some other animal is so stupid as to stray within reach of the antennae, they will also lack the blood food they have been getting."

This logic seemed to me to be perfect. The one great question was, how long will it take? Snakes can endure months without food. Would we see this herd, its wheels locked, die all about us? Would it take a week, a month, how long?

Our discussions had used up the night. In the fuller light of the breaking day we began to see the monsters rolling toward us, dosing in on our tree trunk. They were coming back to finish their work of yesterday. Whatever the ultimate effect of the destruction of the castor plants, in the meantime we must find quicker acting weapons.

VIII

As hastily as possible Hedrick prepared a neutralizer for the Garzus chloroform. We tore off our shirts, and were ready to wet them with the solution and bind them to our noses if attacked again.

85

"Camber is coming here about noon," Hedrick said, "and they will surely get him. We've got to get down and head him off."

I had been thinking of that, too. I felt I would as soon die myself as witness another friend gulped down. But there was so little we could do. Now that we knew about the gas, it would be suicidal to descend and try an attack with machetes.

Hedrick produced another beaker from Dooling's box.

"It doesn't cost anything to experiment," he remarked drily. "I am going to mix up a belly-ache for our little playmates. You be thinking of a way to feed it to them."

He went to work with his bottles, weighing stuff by guess. The bubbling, fizzy concoction looked potent. I wondered if the Garzi would snap up a bottle. Their craving for silica might lead them to. Then I remembered that they did not eat crystals raw, they first dissolved them into jelly. Our medicine must be fed to them some other way. That is when I thought of the poor monkeys. I dug in Dooling's box and found a big hypodermic syringe, and a can of chloroform.

Busy with compounding our prescription, we were not watching the Garzi, but at the first whiff of the threatening odor, we bound up our faces with the saturated shirts. The stupefying fumes rose steadily to us. A monkey passed out and fell, straight down. Another, from just above, crumpled and started to slide by us but I grabbed the limp form and half jammed, half hung it in the crotch of a branch. The other monkeys were hanging desperately to the limbs, groggy, barely conscious. Pouring some chloroform onto a piece of shim, I clambered around, putting first one monkey and then another completely out, securing them so that they could not fall. I got a grim comfort out of the condition in which I found them. They were doomed anyway, I could not be blamed too much for using them in the way I had planned. At least there was a promise of vengeance.

As fast as Hedrick could fill the syringe, I brought and held the limp animals until he shot the injection home. I piled the sagging forms around us as best I could on the limbs and branches about us. It took a long time to prepare eight, but eight we needed; one for each of our besiegers.

The gas had stopped before we were ready, but the Garzi were still there, staring up at us with those astonishing eyes.

"Let's go," I said, and began heaving the bodies down.

It was a full ten minutes after the horrid churning before we knew that the gastric juices of the dragons had mingled with our doses. Unprepared for what followed, we almost fell from our perch. Before, we had heard the howls of injured Garzi, when we had hackled at their antennae, but those were as nothing compared to the hideous cacophony that arose now from below. The medley of shrieks, trumpeting, howls and bellowing nearly broke our eardrums, while the threshing about of the agonized monsters made our tree tremble from its uttermost leaf to the very trunk. Slashing about below, the crystal encrusted tails beat wildly against their mates, against the tree, anything solid. In their frenzy and agony, the creatures glands let go with every offensive and defensive device known to them. Gasses squirted from the drooping antennae and from beneath the hard, glittering scales of the back and tail came smoke, the cavernous mouth belched other gasses and vomited gobs of bloody jelly.

It was with grim, sardonic joy that we viewed this spectacle. If the extraordinary structure of the Things had allowed it, they would have wallowed and squirmed, but bound as they were by those colossal wheels, they could do nothing but yowl and thresh about, whipped here and there by the dragonish tails. The exudation of the smokescreen, an instinctive reflex, quickly blotted them from our vision. What followed we could only guess at, it was much too thick below.

"I figured they had acid stomachs," was Hedrick's bland comment.

After a bit, when the smoke had cleared somewhat, all we could see were a few smoky trails, leading away. If Hedrick's prescription had proved fatal, they had gone away to their hidden lairs to die. We left the remnants of our field laboratory and the food supplies that were in the upper branches. We climbed down, and machete in hand, took the back trail to the base camp.

We were halfway there when we met Camber. We turned him back and walked along beside him. He was inexpressibly shocked at what we told him, but we could see the gleam of disbelief in his eyes. He heard us out, but as we neared the base camp his revealing comment was:

"It's a tough country — a good night's sleep will do you both good."

We fell onto our cots like men struck by an axe.

When we woke Camber felt that he ought to make the usual trip to the advance base. He still believed that Dooling and the two Indians were camped there. We reiterated our story in vain. He persisted in treating us as sick mien, spoke of tropical fever and the like. Futilely, as it later transpired, we tried to impress him with the reality of the tragedy we had survived.

A couple of mornings afterward, when we got up for our breakfast, we found Camber gone. We selected the sharpest machetes in the camp and hastened after him. I need not tell you the rest, Six miles away we found the head and the thoroughly masticated bones. The incredulous, as well as the credulous, are sometimes led to fearful dooms.

The Garzi, then, still moved about their domain. We got our notes in order, and started to mix more of Hedrick's prescription, but had used up several ingredients. Because we must, we retreated into the thick forest through which we had first come, knowing that no wheels could follow us there.

Our natives were as nervous as when last we saw them. Perhaps they wondered what had become of our companions, but none deserted. At the end of a week, Hedrick and I scouted back into Garzus territory.

From the tree that once gave us refuge we surveyed the country beyond. Fire had swept away most of the castor beans. About two clumps that had survived thronged numerous Garzi, apparently fighting over the inadequate supply. We camped that, night at the edge of the thick forest.

Next morning we saw none of the Garzi and no castor beans at all. Venturing into the open, we spotted a grotesque shape standing motionless on the charred plain, and further on another. Approaching the nearest one, we found that it whipped its tail savagely and reached with its tentacles, but did not move on its wheels. We closed in, gingerly chopped off its tentacle-tips and pressed in to prune them as close as we could.

He could not turn those wheels — they were frozen. After experimental slashes, we sliced away some of his lifted scales. Finally, with repeated stabs in the exposed softness, we killed it amid weird and mournful howls.

An axe from the camp enabled us to strip away the tough bulk, until we had freed the axle-bone and wheels. While I finished the stripping of the axle, Hedrick, examining some of the exposed viscera, screamed.

I whirled to help him, but I staggered back, choking and momentarily blinded, from a cloud of vile yellow-green gas.

His machete had thrust into an organ, from which the venomous juice had squirted into his face. He was unrecognizably disfigured by its deadly acid!

I lashed his body to the axle-bone and from our belts and gun-slings rigged myself a harness. Then, dragging the chassis of the Garzus, I struck along the creek margin toward the falls. I passed stilled Garzi — singly, in groups, once a mother with three young — and with gloomy satisfaction knew that they must linger where they were, to starve for want of castor beans, quartz and blood food. One still rolled, very slowly, after me, but easily I distanced him and came to our base camp.

There stood perhaps a dozen Garzi, the last of their great race. Necessity had driven them on creaking wheels into this country where for ages they had existed only in legend. About them lay the strewn wreckage of our camp — boxes, our valuable notes, instruments. Our canoes were crushed by the blind thrashings of the starved beasts. Up several trees hung some of our Indians, but scattered on the ground were many brown heads of crushed victims.

By now, none of the raiding Garzi could move freely. Casting off my harness, I approached, machete in hand. One after another I cut away the groping tentacles — twice I was nearly snared and eaten — and it was an afternoon's dreadful, exhausting work.

The surviving Indians watched me, and this conquest of demons before their eyes gave me the prestige with which I carried out the last phase of the adventure; I bullied them down from their perches, made them load a single unsmashed canoe with a few salvaged supplies and the specimens I had saved. The chassis of the Garzus could not go whole, and so I hewed away the wheels, saving only the axle-bone.

The trip down-river to the mission lasted a week. When the Indians, still horrified, tried to desert me and my relics of their dreaded demon-enemies, I kept them at the paddles with a leveled pistol. And I reached here, and then the cumulation of horror, fatigue and perhaps sickness brought on by that whiff of acid-gas, blacked out everything.

That is the end of Taussig's narrative. He came home with us aboard the *Tethys*. How that heavy axle-bone came to be broken is one of the mysteries — both Taussig and I think that the Indians who handled it deliberately chopped it up as a magical rite. Anyway, his story did not suit those who heard it at home. The Garzus remains unrecorded among the fauna of the upper Amazon, but it may be that in the future some man of daring and faith will go into the Caquini country and find those telltale remains.

But before he goes, let him come to me. I know where Taussig lives today — he runs a taxidermist's shop on Ninth Avenue, and refuses even to discuss the affair save with me, to whom be thinks he owes much. Perhaps I can persuade him to show the model of a Garzus which stands hidden on a closet shelf in the back of his shop. Even though small and stationary, it is frightful enough to be convincing.

Vengeance In Her Bones

The messenger from the Navy recruiting office found old Captain Tolliver in his backyard. The   crabby, sour-visaged housekeeper took him as far as the hedge back of the house and pointed the retired mariner out to him. Captain Tolliver was reclining in a ragged canvas deckchair taking the sun. He had on faded dungarees, soft and pliant as linen from hundreds of scrubbings, and the stump of his handless left arm rested carelessly on his lap. The peg-leg that matched it lay in alignment with the one good leg. The captain had his eyes closed, comfortably drinking in the sun's good heat, when he heard the crunch of the messenger's step on the gravel walk that separated the vegetable from the flower beds. The old skipper's hearing was still alert, though, and at the sound he raised his lids and looked inquiringly at the newcomer.

"Commander Jason's compliments, sir," said the bluejacket, "and would you please step down to the office. He has a ship for you."

Captain Tolliver smiled feebly, then he closed his eyes against the glare. His eyes were not overstrong these days — the doctors had said something about incipient cataracts.

"Commander Jason is confusing me with my son. He already has a ship, working out of West Coast ports. My sea-going days are over. Forever."

To emphasize his point he waved the stump of his left arm, and lifted the peg-leg slightly.

"No, sir. It's you he wants. He was very clear about that. He has a ship that only you can command. She's a rogue. They say she will obey no other skipper. He says they have waived your physical defects and will give you all the help you need. But they've got to have you."

The captain shook his head.

"He's wrong, I say. There is no such a ship. There was one once, but she rotted her life away in the back channel. They sold her finally to a wrecking company and broke her up for scrap. All I have to say to that is whoever bought that scrap had better have a care as to how they use it. For she was a vindictive wench. The *Sadie Saxon* bore grudges and would have her way no matter what you did. . . ."

"Yes, sir," said the messenger, eagerly, "that's the ship — the *Sadie Saxon* — a cargo type vessel! They've put her back in commission but she won't leave port. They need ships now that America is at war. Every ship. That's why they need you. The commander says please come. If you want, he'll send an ambulance."

"The *Sadie Saxon*," whispered the old captain, suddenly rapt with nostalgia for World War days when he and she were in their prime.

Then aloud, "He needn't bother about the ambulance. I can get there under my own power, son. Give me a hand so I can get up and go dress. The old uniform still fits, thank God."

Captain Tolliver's senility seemed to drop from him as a cloak the moment the well-worn blue garments were back on his lean frame. He looked a little ruefully at the tarnished gold lace on the sleeves and at the cap device the years had tinted with green mold, but nevertheless he brushed the uniform carefully, squared his shoulders, and marched down the steps without availing himself of the sailor's proffered arm.

"So they didn't break her up after all?" said the captain, as they waited at the curb in the hope a cruising taxi would come by. "How come? I know she was sold."

"Too expensive. She was part of a contract for scrap to be sent to the Japs some months ago, but they only worked three days on her. She killed nine men the first day they brought their cutting torches aboard, all of them in different ways. One of her booms crashed down the second day and smashed five others. On the third day seven suffocated in a hold, and two slipped and fell overboard.

92

The men said she was jinxed and threatened to call a strike. So they put a tug alongside and hauled her back to her old berth."

Captain Tolliver chuckled.

"For the Japs, huh? She knew it even before they attacked Pearl Harbor, but I might have told 'em. But what's this about her *refusing* to leave port. Doesn't that sound a little silly to you?"

His faded old eyes twinkled when he asked the question. It was one that did sound silly, when a person came to think about it. Yet he knew it was not silly and one an experienced sailorman would answer as seriously as he could.

"There's no other word for it, sir," replied the bluejacket, soberly. "She was refitted at Newport News, given a crew and loaded with cargo. They took her out to make a voyage to Spanish Morocco, loaded with grain and automobile tires. But she wouldn't pass the Thimble. Her rudder jammed and she piled up hard, and at high tide, too. It took four days to pull her off. They took her back to the yard and looked her steering gear over. It was okay. So they started her out again. That time she sheered out to the other side and grounded near Willoughby Split. The third time they tried to take her out, she piled up in the dredged channel and blocked all shipping for hours. The yard still insisted there was nothing wrong with her steering gear and suspected sabotage —"

"I know," said the captain, "They didn't find any evidence of it."

"That's right. They gave her crew a clean bill of health and ordered to sea once more. She won't budge. She had steam up and stood a good dock trial, but once she was out in the stream her propellers quit turning over —"

"With full throttle, of course," remarked Captain Tolliver calmly.

"Yes, sir. With full pressure in the boilers and throttle wide open. All she would do was drift until she banged into a dock.

"The tugs got hold of her and tied her up again. The engineers swear her engines are all right and there is no reason why she won't run. She just won't — that's all."

A taxi rounded the corner and caught the sailor's hail. As it slid to a stop before them the captain made one final remark.

"I see. They looked up her record and found she was always that way. Except when I had command of her. Well, I know what is on that little tub's mind and what to do about it. It won't be orthodox, but if they want her in service it is the only way."

"What's that, sir."

"Give her her head," said the old man cryptically, then stiffly climbed into the cab.

It was a week later that Captain Tolliver arrived at Norfolk Navy Yard. An aide of the admiral in charge of transport took him to the dock where she lay. She looked spick and span and new and a painter's stage swung under her near bow, and was to play her part in keeping supplies going Eastward in spite of havoc to the West. Tolliver climbed up onto it with some difficulty and patted one of the shiny plates of her nose.

"Up to your old tricks, eh, Sadie?" the astonished aide heard him say. "Well, everything's going to be all right now. We'll go hunting together."

Was it the wash of a passing tug that caused her to bob suddenly up and down that way? The aide shrugged his shoulders and was glad he was in the regular outfit. He would hate to have to go to sea through the war zone on a rogue ship under the command of a decrepit and senile madman of a skipper.

"I am ready to take over," announced Tolliver when he was back on the dock, "whenever those three men whose names I gave you have been replaced by others more acceptable."

"Acceptable to whom, sir? I repeat that they are loyal American citizens despite their German ancestry. They have been investigated fully."

"Acceptable to me as representative of the ship," answered the captain with all his old dignity. "When they are off we sail. Not before. Perhaps it is prejudice — Sadie's funny that way — perhaps your investigation was not as comprehensive as you think. That's your problem."

The aide laughed. The old lunatic, he thought, but I'm stuck I guess. They said give him anything he asked for.

"Very well, sir," was what he said out loud.

94

Captain Tolliver waited patiently beside the bow until the last of the three scowling men had come down it laden with their bags and dunnage. Then he mounted to the deck and went straightway to the bridge. His hand reached for the whistle pull. A long, triumphant scream of a blast split the air.

"Stand by your lines," bellowed the old man through a megaphone, "and tell the tug never mind. We won't need her."

Two hours later the *Sadie Saxon* swept through the dredged channel, picked up and passed the entrance buoy to the bay. Throbbing with the vibration of her churning screws and rising and falling to the heavy swell outside, she shook herself joyfully at the smell and feel of the open sea. Cape Henry and Cape Charles Lights soon faded behind. The captain set a course for Bermuda, for the ship's orders had been changed. After the long delay in setting out the situation was different. She was to rendezvous with a Gibraltar bound convoy at the island.

Mate Parker came up to take the watch. It was a cloudy, dark night and the ship was running without lights.

"Keep a sharp lookout," warned the captain, "and handle things yourself. I don't want to be called unless something extraordinary occurs."

"Aye, sir," acknowledged the mate surlily. By rights he should be the skipper of this cranky tub — not this doddering old fool.

The captain got down the ladder the best way he could and groped along the darkened decks until he came to the door of his room. He did not undress at all but lay down in his bunk as he was. The *Sadie Saxon* could be counted on to do the unexpected at any time. He closed his eyes wearily, for the excitement of the day had taxed his strength to the utmost. In a moment he was fast asleep.

It must have been well after midnight when he was roused from his deep slumber. Mr. Parker was standing over him with a look of concern on his face.

"She's gone crazy again, sir," he reported, "and we can't do a thing with her —"

"Don't try," directed the captain. "What she doing?"

"Turned sharp to the left about fifteen minutes ago and is turning up about twelve revolutions more than her proper speed. The helmsman can't do anything about it.

Neither can the engineer. She won't obey her wheel or throttle. What do we do — fold up and call it a day?"

Captain Tolliver sat up in his bunk.

"Oh, no. By no means. You'll be awfully busy shortly. Turn out all hands at once. Man your lifeboats and have them ready for lowering. Shut all water-tight doors below and see that there is plenty of shoring handy in case the peak gets stove in. Have the collision mat ready. That's all."

"But the steering?"

"Just let the wheel go. She'll steer herself. She knows where she wants to go. I don't."

The mate left and the old man dragged himself to his mismated feet and began the laborious journey to the bridge. Once he was up there he made sure that the searchlight was ready to turn on in case he needed it. After that he could only wait.

The wait was not long. Fifteen minutes later there was a shock, a grinding, bumping of something under the fore-foot and along the keel. The ship's engines stopped abruptly, then began backing. Captain Tolliver reached for the engine room telegraph and rang it to "Stop."

The ship stopped.

"Collision forward!" shouted the lookout in the bow. "We just ran down a small ship of some sort."

Tolliver could hear the boatswain and his gang dropping into the fore hold to see whether the damage was serious. Then he spoke quietly to the mate who was on the bridge beside him.

"You may put your boats in the water now, Mister. I have a hunch we just ran down a Nazi sub. I'll put on the light as soon as you are lowered."

The mate left on the run, more mystified than ever. A man came up from forward and reported the peak was full up to the waterline but the bulkhead abaft it was holding and the ship seemed to be in no danger.

"Turn on that searchlight," ordered Captain Tolliver, "and sweep aft."

There was a chorus of gasps as the light stabbed out into the murk and almost instantly lit on a large black object rearing up above the waves. It was the bow of a submarine, and even as they sighted it it slid backwards into the deep. But in that brief glimpse they saw several men plunge overboard, and as the light swept to right and left the bobbing heads of a dozen or more men could be seen in the water.

"Pick up those men and be smart about it," yelled Tolliver through his megaphones to the boats. Then he watched as they dragged the survivors into the boats and rowed back to the ship, He watched as they hoisted the boats in and housed them at their davits.

"Put those men under guard," he directed, "and get back on your course. Things will be all right now." And with that he went below to pick up his night's sleep where he had left off.

The arrival of the *Sadie Saxon* at Bermuda caused quite a stir. Many were the congratulations upon the ship's luck in blundering across a U-boat and ramming it in the dark. The two officers and eleven men rescued from the crash were most welcome to the British Intelligence officers. Hasty arrangements were made for quick repairs to the ship's damaged bow. She had missed the convoy for which she was intended, but there would be other convoys and the little delay was well paid for by the bag of the undersea wolf. Captain Tolliver took his praise modestly.

"It's not all luck," he said. "It is a habit of the *Sadie Saxon*. If you will look up her record in the last war you will see she has done that sort of thing before."

By the time the ship was ready for sea again the hubbub had died down. Captain

Tolliver took the position assigned him with entire calm and confidence. It was a big convoy and made up of three columns of ships. The *Sadie Saxon* was given the post of danger and honor as the lead ship of the right-hand column. But destroyers frolicked about ahead and on the flanks. It would be costly for any submarine to tackle that well-guarded flotilla.

For three nights they went eastward, steaming without lights and in formation. There was no alarm other than the appearance overhead one day of a trio of scout bombers marked with the black and white crosses of Germany. The anti-aircraft guns of the escorting warships kept them at too great a height to do any damage, and so drove them away. But after their appearance old Captain Tolliver knew anything might happen. The *Sadie Saxon* had behaved most peculiarly all the while they were in sight, vibrating almost as if she had dropped a screw.

"Steady, old girl," whispered the skipper into the binnacle, "you'll have to get used to those. They're an innovation."

It was the night after that that the big attack occurred. The long triple column of ships was plowing along through a dark and misty night and thirty officers on as many bridges were staring anxiously into the murk striving not to lose sight of the tiny blue stern light of the ship ahead. Under the circumstances mutual collision was much more likely than a hostile attack. The orders were strict — maintain radio silence at all costs, never show a light under any circumstances, and above all, keep station.

But the *Sadie Saxon* cared next to nothing about commodore's orders. At ten minutes past four in the morning she balked, her engines churning violently at full speed astern, to the consternation of the black gang who had had no bells to that effect and were caught off guard. Captain Tolliver was on the bridge when it happened and called sharply to the forward lookouts:

"Look sharply close aboard! What do you see?"

The ship was turning rapidly to starboard, her rudder jammed hard over, while the helmsman strove wildly to bring the wheel back the other way.

"The wakes of two torpedoes, sir — no, four — five — nine! Coming from starboard, sir."

The streaks of phosphorescent light were visible now from the bridge. The *Sadie Saxon* was turning straight into them; she would pass safely between a pair of them.

The aged skipper acted with an alacrity that surprised even him. He yelled for the searchlight and with his own hand pulled the whistle into a strident blast of warning. The searchlight came on and threw its beam straight ahead. There, in a line, were three gray conning towers — three submarines on the surface and in fairly close formation. The nearest destroyer saw them too and at once plunged toward them with its guns blazing. Geysers of white water shot up about the nearest one. A couple of seconds later a bright flash told of a six-inch hit squarely at the base of a conning tower. The other two subs were diving hard, but the one that was hit did not dive. Or did not dive the regular way. It rolled slowly over toward the Sadie Saxon, spilling frantic men from its torn superstructure, then settled to its grave.

The leading freighter of the middle column suddenly blew up with a bang, lighting up the sea like day. A moment later the second ship of the left-hand column burst into flames. At least two of the nine torpedoes fired had found a mark. But the subs that fired them had no opportunity to fire more. They had been ambushed in their own ambush, and already three destroyers were racing back and forth over the spots where they had last been seen and dropping depth-charges by the score.

Similar activities were going on on the other side. Apparently there had been other subs waiting there as well.

The *Sadie Saxon* lay still where she was until the survivors of the two ships destroyed had been brought on board. Then she unaccountably turned due South and ran for an hour at full speed. There she stopped and refused to budge another yard. It was well past the dawn then and a destroyer could be seen on the horizon behind still searching for vestiges of their attackers.

"Signal that destroyer," the captain said, and tell him to come over here. We've got one spotted."

The destroyer came up within hail, and its captain delivered a blistering message through what must have been an asbestos-lined megaphone.

"Will the second on that ship kindly relieve that blithering idiot in command and put him under arrest? The —"

"The sub's right under me," Tolliver yelled back, "playing possum a hundred feet or so down." The ship started moving ahead. "Come in and drop your eggs. Then lock me up if you want."

He turned to Parker who was in a quandary as to what to do. The performances of the ship had shaken his nerve. He had begun to wonder whether *he* was the crazy man. Tolliver ignored him. Instead he walked out to the wing of the bridge and watched the destroyer do its work.

Huge seething hummocks of water rose as the ash-cans exploded under the surface. Four of them had gone off and the destroyer was coming back for a second run across the same spot. But there was no need. A half mile away a black nose, appeared for a moment on the surface, stuck its beak up into the air, then with a loud hissing of escaping air fell back weakly into the water. Where it had been were three bobbing heads. There *had* been a sub under there!

"Thanks," flashed the destroyer, "well done. Rejoin convoy."

They went past Gib without stopping and made the hazardous trip to Alexandria without incident other than a few sporadic and ineffectual raids by enemy aircraft. At Alexandria Captain Tolliver found this message waiting for him; it was from ONI.

"You are a better guesser than some of our experts. The three men you tipped us off to are in jail. They planned to seize the ship and divert it to a Norwegian port. Congratulations."

The skipper gave a brief snort and then crammed the message into a pocket with his one good hand. Then he learned that on the voyage home he was to carry the convoy's commodore. The "commodore," a retired Navy captain, came aboard and looked around.

He did not say much until they were out of the Mediterranean and well to the west of Portugal. By then they had been joined by many other ships and were steaming in a formation much like the one before, with the difference that this time, being flagship, they were more nearly in the middle of the flotilla.

"You seem to have a remarkable ability to spot submarines, Captain," he remarked. "What is your secret?"

"Me?" said the skipper indignantly. "Hell, I can't see a submarine in the dark or under water any farther than the next man. All the credit is due to Sadie. She *smells* 'em. She hates 'em, too."

"Yes. I know. She rammed several in the last war, didn't she? And didn't they make her into a Q-ship?"

100

"She did. She was. If you'll look down there on the pedestal of the binnacle stand you'll see some file marks. There are fourteen of 'em now. Each one stand for a U-boat. Or raider. I tell you, she don't like Germans. She was a German herself, you know, but they didn't treat her right. She has a grievance."

"Now, Captain," laughed the commodore, "don't you think you are carrying your little joke too far? After all . . ."

"Do you know the story of this ship?" asked Tolliver fiercely, "well, listen."

It was close to midnight then and a bright moon was shining. The silhouettes of the ships about were distinct as black masses against the glittering white-kissed sea. The two officers went on talking, but their eyes were steadfastly kept ahead. This was a night when anything might happen.

"In 1914 this ship was spanking new. She was the *Koenigen von Sachsen* or something of the sort, freshly turned out of the Vulcan Works at Stettin. The outbreak of the war caught her at Hoboken and they tied her up for the duration. But when we joined the war in '17 and took her over, her innards were something pitiful to see. Her crew had dry-fired her boilers and they were a mass of sagging tubes. The vandals cracked her cylinders with sledges, threw the valve gear and cylinder heads overboard, and messed up all the auxiliaries. They fixed the wiring so it would short the moment juice was put on it, and they took down steam leads and inserted steel blanks between the flanged joints. In other places they drove out rivets and replaced them with ones of putty. I tell you she was dynamite, even after they fixed up the boilers and main machinery.

"Naturally, having a thing like that done to you would make you sore — especially if you were young and proud and the toast of the Imperial German merchant marine. But that was not all. On her first trip across — I was mate then — a sub slammed a torp into her off the north of Ireland and it took her stern away. Luckily she didn't sink and another ship put a hawser on us and worried us into Grennock where they fixed her up. That would have been bad enough, but on the trip home she smacks into a submarine-laid mine off the Delaware Capes and blows in her bow. We had to beach her near Cape May.

"They rebuilt her again and we set out. But her hard-luck — or mistreatment rather — wasn't at an end. In those days our Secret Service wasn't as good as it is now and a saboteur got aboard. He gummed up things pretty bad. So bad that we caught afire and almost sank in mid-ocean. It took some doggoned hard work to save that ship, but help came and we stayed afloat. Well, that was the end of her patience. She went hog-wild. After that, no matter whether she was in convoy or not, whenever anything that was German was around — sub, torpedo, raider or what not — she went after it, and never mind engine room bells or rudder. Her whimsies cost me a hand and a leg before we were through, but I didn't mind. I figured I could take it if she could.

"She broke the hearts of three captains. A lot of captains, you ought to know, object to having the ship take charge. They said she was unmanageable and chucked their jobs. That left me in command, though at the time I didn't rate the job. Knowing something of her history, I knew better than to interfere. Her hunches are the best thing I know. No matter what she does . . ."

"Hey!" yelled the commodore, thoroughly alarmed, "watch what you're doing."

The *Sadie Saxon* had sheered sharply from her course and was heading directly across the bows of a ship in the column to one side of them. It was too late then, even if the *Sadie* had been tractable, to do anything about it. A collision was inevitable. The commodore reached for the whistle pull, but Tolliver grabbed his arm and held it.

"Wait," he urged, "this means something. I know her."

An angry, guttural shout came from the bridge of the ship whose path they were about to cross. Then came the rending crash as steel bit into steel — thousands of tons of it at twelve knots speed. The other ship had rammed the *Sadie Saxon* just abreast the mainmast and she heeled over sharply, spilling deck gear over the off rail. At once pandemonium reigned in the convoy as ships behind sheered out to avoid compounding the already serious collision.

At once fresh confusion succeeded. The ship that was the victim of the *Sadie*'s caprice suddenly dropped her false bulwarks and the moonlight glinted off the barrels of big guns both fore and aft. Harsh orders sounded in German and the guns began spitting

102

fire. Shells began bursting against ships on all side as the raider that had insinuated itself into the midst of the convoy began its work. Escort ships began dashing toward the scene, worming their way through the scattering freighters so as to get to a spot where they could open fire.

"I told you," said Captain Tolliver, serenely. "You can always trust her."

But she was sinking, and the crew were lowering what boats they could. The commodore was one of the first to leave, since he was in charge of the entire expedition and must transfer his flag to a surviving ship. Tolliver stayed behind. There was not room enough in the boats for one thing, and his faith in the durability of the *Sadie Saxon* was unlimited. He had seen her in worse plight many times before.

The raider had succeeded in backing away, but it, too was in a perilous condition. Her bows were torn wide open and she was fast going down by the head. She continued to fire viciously at everything within reach, paying especial attention to the crippled *Sadie Saxon*. A shell struck her funnel and threw fragments and splinters onto the bridge. One fragment struck Captain Tolliver in the right thigh and he went down with a brief curse. Another pair of projectiles burst aft among the rest of the crew who were engaged in freeing a life raft from the mainmast shrouds. It must have killed them all, for when shortly afterward a destroyer ranged alongside and hailed, there was no answering cry.

Tolliver hauled himself to the wing of the bridge and managed to cut an opening in the weather screen. He looked out just in time to see the flaming remnants of the raider sink under the moon-tipped waves. The freighters had all gone and the destroyers were charging off in a new direction. Apparently submarines, working in conjunction with the camouflaged raider, had made their appearance. Tolliver watched a moment, then was aware of a growing faintness. His leg must be bleeding more than he thought. In a moment everything turned black.

It was broad daylight when he came to again. Another peep showed him an empty ocean. The convoy must have gone on, as it was proper and correct it should. And then he heard the burr and roar of airplanes overhead. They swooped low, machine-gunning the decks systematically on the assumption men were still aboard. One, more daring than the rest, swopped in between the masts. *Sadie Saxon* was trembling in every plate and rivet.

"Steady, girl," murmured the now delirious captain, laying his check against the bridge deck and patting it gently with his one hand, "you can't handle those, I know. But we've done enough, you and I. We can't keep afloat forever."

Her answer was typical. He had no way of knowing how deep she was in the water, or what her trim, but she heeled violently to port — hung there a moment, then turned quietly over on her side. The instant she chose to do it was just as the daring raider plane was diving beneath her radio antennae, ready to drop its final bomb. Captain Tolliver heard its wings snap off and its body crash as the whipping, heeling mast struck it. There was a final burst of flame, and the rest was cool, green water. The old sea-dog felt the waves close over him, but he was smiling and content.

"Bless her old heart," was his last thought, "she even got one of *those*."

Heaven Is What You Make It

She was a very determined woman. She was determined to fight in battle and did, and died. And thereafter — she was determined to make the heaven she was misdirected to suit her —

I.

Commodore Sir Reginald Wythe-Twombley, R. N., D. S. O., et cetera, sighed deeply and twisted unhappily at his gray mustaches. Damn these strong-minded women — especially the American variety. Why do they persist in pushing their noses in where only men belong?

"Well?" she demanded. She did not tap her foot, or plant her hands on her hips. It was unnecessary. That "well" contained both. And a lot else.

The harried commodore sighed again. As if he didn't have trouble enough already. He could only suppose she had done it that way in London, too. How else could she have obtained that absurd letter from the minister? Yet he had to dispose of her.

"But, my deah," he protested, "after all! As a nurse, now, or a lorry driver that would be practicable. But to go into a Commando unit as just . . . just . . . why —"

"The letter is clear," she reminded him, icily.

She stood there, imperturbable and determined. She was big for a woman — a darkish blonde with cool gray eyes and a chin that might have been chiseled out of granite. Her passport gave her age as thirty-three. It may really have been that, but she was of the type that did not suggest queries as to age. Her most salient characteristic was competence. She fairly oozed efficiency at every pore.

The commodore coughed.

"It happens" — he tried to hedge —"that . . . uh . . . there are none of our units in the Orkneys just now. Of course, if you are very insistent about it, you could wait here at Kirkwall, but I assure you you would be more comfortable in . . . well, Edinburgh, let us say."

"What about the *Tordenskjold?*" she asked, with a firmness that reminded him painfully of a former governess. "I understand it is about to raid the Yigten Islands and Namsos Fjord."

"Quite so," he admitted, grudgingly. At least she seemed to be well informed. "But it is officered and manned entirely by Norwegians, Danes and Frisians. You would not —"

"I speak all the Scandinavian languages fluently," she said, coolly. "Moreover, to save you your next remark, I might remind you that I have been principal of a school in the Gowanus Canal section of Brooklyn for the past ten years. I've handled roughnecks and hoodlums beside which even your dreaded Nazis are gentle. As for these fine men who will be my comrades — Well!"

The commodore surrendered. He hated to do it, for the *Tordenskjold* was going on something very much like a suicide mission, but he reached for a pad of blank chits. He scribbled a few lines on it, and then his initials. He felt himself a weakling, for the first time in many years, in taking the easy way out with this woman. But she still stood there, unmoved, looking at him and waiting. Then he called his orderly.

"Have the cart out," he told the marine, "and take Miss . . . Miss —"

"Miss Ida Simpkins," she supplied, without a quiver of an eyelid or a trace of thanks.

"Er, Miss Simpkins," continued the commodore, "to the dock at the North Anchorage in the Flow. Put her in the Norwegians' boat and then return."

The marine saluted, and picked up Miss Simpkins' bag.

She sat stonily beside the driver all the way, looking neither right nor left. Once or twice the driver attempted conversation, but he spoke a strange archaic language that was neither Scandinavian, Scotch nor yet Gaelic. The marine sat moodily in the back of the cart with the bag for company. Like his superior, he sighed, too, from time to time, for he was a veteran of the last war and knew that such things as this had never happened on earth or in heaven before.

The kommandor-kaptein of the quaint old cruiser received her with more equanimity than any other military man she had encountered since her strange quest began — the Saturday after Pearl Harbor. He merely read her papers through, asked three crisp questions, and assigned her to duty. She was to be the bridge messenger on the starboard watch. She was told where she could sleep and eat, and that was all there was about it. Dusk was already at hand, and shortly the old ship and the destroyer *Garm* would be stealing out through Hoxa Gate. Tomorrow promised to be foggy, so that under its cover they might possibly reach their destination after all. It was on those things the captain was thinking, not on the unorthodox addition to his crew.

It was early in the evening of the next day that they began to close with the rugged land. The mists had held and the sea had been calm. Except for a heavy ground swell that made the vessel wallow constantly, the voyage had had no outstanding feature. The men, grim-faced and ready, and bundled up in heavy clothes, stood always by their guns, which were loaded and trained outboard for anything that might loom suddenly on their beam.

It was just at seven bells it happened. The fog had been thicker for the past half-hour, when suddenly it lifted. A scant three miles away .a large ship was charging along, throwing spray over her bridge at every swell she met. Its silhouette was unmistakable. She was a Nazi cruiser. In another instant the guns of all three ships were blazing.

The little *Garm* looked as if she would capsize, as she heeled under hard-over rudder and full speed to make her torpedo attack, but her larger consort clung doggedly to the old course. After that first moment, nothing was very clear. Geyserlike splashes bloomed suddenly close aboard, with deafening noise as the sensitive shells exploded on contact with the water. Spray showered the ship, and in it were deadly shell fragments. The *loitnant* of the watch received one such in his left eye and another in the knee. He fell to the deck with a brief groan.

"Get Fenrik Janssen," he muttered. "Quickly."

Miss Simpkins ran aft to where she knew he would be, by the 5.9" battery control station. But just as she was well clear of the bridge, another salvo struck. That one was a fair straddle, and many things happened, fore and aft. The bridge went up in a fountain of flame, smoke and splinters, and with it the captain and the wounded lieutenant of the watch. The after turret spouted fire heavenward, which meant it had been penetrated and whatever powder was exposed ignited. It was clear that the minutes left to the faithful old warship were numbered.

Miss Simpkins sprang to the nearest broadside gun, where she saw the trainer — a mere boy — sagging in his saddle. She embraced him with capable arms and lifted him out; then laid him gently on the deck. Half his head was gone. After that she climbed quietly into the place she had thus vacated, and grabbed the handles of the training gear. She flattened her face against the buffer of the sight and found the Nazi cruiser. She tried the handles, and found that by turning them this way and that, she could bring the vertical crosswise she saw inside the telescope so that it would be in alignment with the German's principal mast. She supposed that that was the idea, so she held it there, though every few seconds the gun beside her would go off with a snapping bark that nearly caved in her eardrums. Moreover, it jolted her to her very skeleton as it lashed backward in its recoil, and the muzzle blast smote her from head to foot.

But she clung on, doing her bit as she saw it — saw bright blossom after bright blossom flower on the hated enemy's side, and saw the orange ripple of flame that marked his return of the compliment. She knew from the acrid smoke that drifted past her own nostrils that her own ship was afire, but she noted with grim delight that so was that of the Nazis. For an instant she got a glimpse of the sinking destroyer, itself blazing from stem to stern. And then she saw the vast explosion that rent the German. She saw that instantaneous blot against the sky, shot through with flame, and knew it was the *Garm*'s last torpedo that must have done it, for suddenly she realized that her own gun had been silent for fully a minute now.

Indeed, there was no sound whatever about her, except the wild hiss of escaping steam and the crackling of flame. There was an almost inaudible moaning somewhere in the murk, but not the boom of cannon. She slid off her seat and looked about her. All she could see through blistering smoke were the legs of a dead man lying directly behind the gun. That would be one of the loaders. Then something struck the ship a blow that shook it as if it had hit a rock at full speed. Almost in the same instant there was a concussion of such stupendous violence that Miss Simpkins had only the vaguest impression of it. She only knew she was being hurled upward and outward. The dying Nazi must have delivered its own torpedo as its swan song — that was her only thought.

She was very numb about the whole thing. It had all happened so quickly, and she had been utterly unprepared. She did know, though, that she had done her best, and hoped it had helped. She was starting to fall then, and wondered how it would feel to drown. Or did it matter?

It was then that what she thought was her delirium started. There was a jumble of wildly mounting music, queer triolets that reminded her somehow of Wagner and grand opera — though it must have been from a record she had heard somewhere, since she thought opera both sinful and a waste of time and money. There was a distant, but approaching chorus of yoo-hooing —" *Yohohoto, yohohoto*, aia*ho!*" it went. Last of all she saw the horses! A cavalry charge from the skies! Dozens of galloping horses were bearing down on her, and on each was mounted a fierce Amazon, armored and helmeted and waving a spear and yelling at the top of her lungs.

"So death is like this," thought Miss Ida Simpkins, bitterly, "and I always supposed it would be angels who would come, not heathen apparitions."

She was not far from the water by then. The dark waves were rushing up to meet her. It was at that moment that a great white charger swooped beneath her and a strong left arm swept her into its embrace. It was a woman's arm, and snowy white, and in the next instant Miss Simpkins felt herself pressed against two breasts incased in golden chain mail. They were zooming upward next, and the Amazon rider of the horse, a powerful woman with honey-colored hair, was bending forward to kiss her.

"No, NO!" screamed Miss Simpkins, fighting fiercely at her.

But it was of no use. The warrior blonde's full red lips were against hers, full of tender kiss. Miss Simpkins tried one final struggle, but to no avail. She was in cool darkness now. There was no woman, no horse, no ocean — nothing. And Miss Simpkins knew exactly what that meant. Ida Simpkins was *dead.*

In blackness there is no sense of time. Who knows? Perhaps there really is no time. Nor was there time in the gray stage that followed. It was a formless sort of gray, like the inside of a cloud, where there is nothing overhead or beneath or to any side. But Ida Simpkins had a kind of awakening. She was aware of herself again. She was capable of memory, and thought, and even reasoning. It puzzled her, was she dead, or wasn't she, Maybe she had been picked up and was merely sick. Or could it be that all her ideas of the hereafter were not exactly correct after all. Perhaps this was a transition stage of some sort.

For her ideas of the hereafter had always been most definite. It was a thing that had interested her profoundly, and she had been wicked enough — though a devout and unyielding Methodist — to read the outrageous beliefs of all the pagans, and even the mistaken views of some of the other sects of her own general faith. There was nothing in any of it that resembled this endless grayness. It was tedious, maddeningly monotonous.

She tried thinking about her past; of her strict upbringing, and how steadfastly she had always hewed to the line. She remembered well those days of schoolteaching in blighted districts, of physical instruction, and of having to learn not only boxing and wrestling, but jujitsu, so as to be able to handle the tough boys she taught. All that seemed so long ago now, though in reality it could have been but a few months. For her martial career had been a short one. One brief day, to be precise, leaving out of account the two months' battle she had had to get the opportunity to die the way she did.

Ida Simpkins had always been a profound pacifist. It was one of her many strict ideals. Smoking, drinking and gambling were wrong to her because they were injurious and wasteful, as well as sinful. Fighting and war were wrong for the same reasons, except

110

that war embraced all the vices on such a grand scale as to be the most hateful of them all. The rape of Europe and China had offended her sense of propriety, but she had entertained the feeling that those crimes were foreign affairs. That in a sense it was due punishment for their own foul crimes. Were not the Chinese pagans? Were not the French and Viennese notoriously loose-lived? All right-thinking persons knew those things.

It was war for America that she was against. The draft was wrong, any preparation was wrong, since it implied the recognition of that which should be firmly denied. It was Pearl Harbor that jolted her out of that beautiful but impractical belief. It was late that Sunday when she first heard of it, and all that night she lay in harrowing combat with herself. Must one fight, or should one turn the other check? Ida Simpkins was in a dreadful dilemma. For she was a good Christian, as she understood the term, but when it came to the cheek-turning business she was notoriously stiff-necked. Her struggle with herself went on through that night and the next and next. It was nearly dawn on Wednesday when she arrived at her decision. At that moment she threw pacifism overboard and went all out for belligerency. Thereafter, she practiced it with all the fanatical fervor she applied to her other ideals.

It was not until Saturday of the same week that she penetrated the last barrier and came face to face with one of the Powers That Be. Sorry, no, they told her in Washington, but we have no battalion of death — not yet. Maybe there will be a Woman's Auxiliary Service later, something on the order of what the British have, but that is a long way off. That was enough for her. She wangled a passport and managed to get to England. There she pestered an already overburdened War Ministry until she got the coveted letter she sprang on the bewildered commodore at Kirkwall. She battered down his defenses. She got to the front. And now — now the war was over, as far as she was concerned.

She quickly tired of memories, being no introvert. The perpetual grayness began to pall on her. Was it going to be like this all Eternity? She had a wholesome respect for Eternity. Eternity was a long time, and one should arrange his life so that it would be spent in reasonable comfort. She remembered all that from a very long way back, and had faithfully followed the rules taught her.

Was this interminable grayness to be the reward?

But she was in the beginnings of awareness of other things than mere featureless grayness. There was a sense of physical contact, of lying jackknifed face down on a moving something. As her senses became acuter, her impressions became clearer. She was lying across something short-haired and warm, and it had a detestable horsy smell. She could feel muscles and bones working beneath her, and then she knew that she was nearly naked. All that she had on were her panties, and a firm hand held them by the seat in a tight grip.

This is madness, she thought at first, until her dying dream began slowly to piece itself together again in her consciousness. But what troubled her most just then was the sense of being undressed. In her dazed and buffeted condition while at the trainer's seat at the gun, she had not noticed that the blast of every shot or every nearby bursting shell had blown some garment to shreds and entirely off her. All that was left, apparently, were the panties. But those, thank goodness, were durable — being, as they were, heavy knitted bloomers. But what was she doing face down on the shoulders of a galloping horse, and who was it holding her on? Then the dream stood forth in perfect clarity. That woman — *ugh!*

Ida Simpkins opened her eyes and squirmed. All she could see was the plunging shoulder of the horse and a white human leg from the knee down. It was a naked leg — like her own, only plumper, or perhaps beefier would be the word. Ida clawed at the charging horse and tried to get upright, to slide off behind — anything. It was disgraceful for her to be in this grotesque pose — her, Ida Simpkins, formerly mistress of Gowanus Settlement House! Who did this so-and-so who had kidnapped her think she was, anyhow?

But the so-and-so's grip was unbreakable. However, she quickly shifted it to an embrace, and before Miss Simpkins knew what was happening, she had been picked up, upended, whirled about, and set astride the horse facing her captor.

"Hail, hero! Yo-*ho!*" shouted the beefy blonde. "I'm Brynhild —"

Her mouth dropped open and Ida thought for a moment she was going to fall off the horse. The horse seemed to sense something, for it slowed its mad gallop to an easier pace.

"Y-y-you're a woman!" gasped the Valkyrie, as if the utmost in sacrilege had been done. "How did I get hold of —"

"Of course I'm a woman," snapped Miss Simpkins.

"But it was a ship full of Norse heroes," protested the Valkyrie, "fighting against odds. Me and my girls —"

"My girls and *I*," corrected Miss Simpkins, firmly.

"My girls and I were watching from afar," continued Brynhild, still so taken aback by the scandalous error she seemed to have committed that she accepted the reproof meekly. "You were the last survivor, serving nobly at a gun and surrounded by raging flames. The ship blew up and you went up with it. I gathered you up in fragments as you rained down. It might have been better if I had had a bucket. I must have mixed things up — somehow."

She finished lamely, and shook her head dazedly. War in the good old days was not like this. All you had to do then was gather up a spare arm or ear or so, and maybe a head, and you had *all* your hero — and nothing else. The way things were going now, a poor battle maiden never knew what she was getting.

"So what?" Miss Simpkins wanted to know, entirely unmoved by Brynhild's discomfiture: "What am I being taken for a ride for? Why did you horn in on my affairs, anyway

"Because," explained the badly rattled daughter of Wotan, "I thought you were a Norse hero, and should be taken to Valhalla along with the others. See them — over there? And Bifrost ahead? The bridge that only gods and heroes may cross?"

Miss Simpkins looked, blinked and looked again. Sure enough, a whole squadron of cavalry was charging along their flanks, each steed with a Valkyrie and a sailor astride. She had to twist her head to see the bridge, but there it was, unmistakably — a great, glorious rainbow that had thickness as well as breadth, rearing itself above the clouds they rode upon.

Brynhild did not look happy.

"Were you really a warrior," she asked, finally, "or did I make a terrible mistake? According to the Law, no woman has, or ever will, set foot within Asgard."

"I was aiming a gun," replied Miss Simpkins sharply, "if that's what you mean by being a warrior. By the way, how long have I been dead?"

"A long, long time," answered Brynhild, cryptically, "and in the other direction."

Ida Simpkins thought that over. Dead a long time, huh, and headed for Valhalla! She knew her mythology, having studied it and taught it to the tough brats of Red Hook. Up to this moment everything was regular — providing only she were ancient Norse. There was the business of death in battle, the death kiss of the Valkyrie, and the translation to Valhalla. That, she knew, lay just over the bridge that was close ahead. It was a rowdy place, as she recalled it, but —

"If you hadn't been so darned hasty," reproached Miss Simpkins, with considerable acidity, "my own people would have got me. As it is, I don't know how to get back. I guess we'll have to go on now, even if it breaks your old law. It's a fool law anyway. I'm not going back to the gray place, I can tell you that, sister."

"We'll see what Heimdall says," said the Valkyrie, in some dejection. "He's the guardian of the bridge."

Ida Simpkins said nothing, but squirmed around so as to face the way the charger was going. The whole situation was bitterly clear now. It was a tough break to die and get taken to the wrong heaven through someone's clumsy interference, but if that was the way it was to be, so it was to be. At least, before she made any hasty decisions, she meant to look the place over and see what possibilities it had. It might be a sinful thing to spend Eternity in a heathen heaven, but who knew? There might be a purpose behind it.

That was the sweet, consoling thought that sustained her. Didn't missionaries spend their lifetime among the benighted heathen? She could not but be thrilled.

Come to think of it, had *any* missionary *ever* penetrated so deeply into the territory of the misguided and the nonbeliever? She saw a great mission ahead, and the light of battle came into her cold gray eyes and the granite mouth set itself on the old familiar lines. On to Valhalla! Ida Simpkins' work bad just begun !

II.

The passage of Bifrost was a truly nerve-shaking experience. The frail but beautiful bridge quivered, swayed and bucked under the thunderous hoofs of the cavalcade bearing the honored dead. Ida looked down once only and gasped. The bridge was built of nothingness — a curious web of interwoven strands of fire and air and water. Its dazzling iridescence was almost more than human eye could bear.

Then they were at the summit of the great bow. Brynhild's steed, and the others following, slowed and came to a halt at what appeared to be a tollgate barring the road. At the right was a gold-plated shack, set upon a bracket extending out over an abyss so deep that Miss Simpkins dared not think about it. By the side of the door hung a huge trumpet. In the door stood a tall, fair young man in silvery armor. That must be Heimdall, keeper of the bridge and chief greeter of the fallen heroes.

He stepped out and unlatched the gate.

"You did well, Brynhild," he remarked, making a sign for the rest of the cavalcade to pass. "This will prove the greatest hero of them all. I have sharp eyes and ears, you know, and can see and hear for thousands of miles and thousands of years. This is a day that will never be forgotten in Valhalla."

Miss Simpkins compressed her lips still more firmly. That was just what she was thinking. But as she looked down at herself, it annoyed her to be in her present state of dishabille. She yearned for more adequate covering than the gray panties, useful though they were. Heimdall must have read the thought, for he entered his golden shack and at once reappeared with an armful of cloth and glittering hardware.

"With the compliments of Alberich, King of the Dwarfs," he said, bowing. "Magic has been worked into these garments. While they are intact, no man can harm you."

"Intact or not intact," snapped Miss Simpkins, "just let one try!"

But she snatched at them and, although it irked her to dress herself by the side of a public road with a flock of leering dead

seamen galloping by, she managed to get the outfit on, though
Brynhild had to help her with some of the straps and buckles. By the
time the job was finished, she was rigged out in a style similar to that
affected by the Valkyries, except that she was given a short sword
instead of a spear.

"But what will papa say?" asked the worried Brynhild.

"Ah," smiled the ever-agreeable Heimdall. "I wonder."

Brynhild helped Ida mount, much to the latter's annoyance,
but she found she could not manage herself very well in the
cumbersome gold armor. Then they thundered on in the wake of the
other heroes, hearing a gentle farewell toot of Heimdall's horn as
they left.

They galloped down the other half of the bridge and into the
shimmering, gold-leaved grove called Glasir. Even the ultra-
practical Miss Simpkins was impressed by it, for it was all it was
cracked up to be, not like the fabulous "palace" Heimdall was
reputed to have atop the bridge. After a little they came out onto an
extensive flat place. Ida Simpkins' reaction was that she had entered
a vast airdrome, for the field was large enough to accommodate the
armies of the world, and beyond stood an immense building that
could easily have housed a score of Zeppelins. But she knew from its
silvery, fluted walls, and the roof of overlapping golden shields that
it must be the great hall of Valhalla. Distant as they still were from
it, she could hear the resounding cheers of the old-timers as they
hailed the newcomers. Ida Simpkins tightened herself for the coming
fray, for she intended to take no nonsense from any of them, not
even Wotan himself.

"Don't forget," cautioned Brynhild, icily, for she was heartily
sick of her find, "that when papa presides over the veterans, he styles
himself Valfather."

"It's all one to me," said Miss Simpkins, indifferently. She
firmly resolved never to board another horse again without at least
thick stockings on. This one shed horribly and she knew the insides
of her bare legs were plastered with white felt.

They rode in through a portal that would have admitted a
battleship, and straight up through an aisle made through a mob of
howling, armored men — huge, beefy, red-faced men, all of them,

116

many with red or yellow beards and drooping walrus mustaches. On a dais far ahead, stood a spare man in armor, wearing a winged helmet. As they drew nearer, Ida could make out the missing eye. Yes, that was the Valfather.

Just before the throne, the horse stopped abruptly, and Ida slid off — over its neck and head. She got up crimson, furious with Brynhild, the horse, and herself. But neither Wotan nor Brynhild were looking at her.

"Another Valkyrie?" Wotan was asking, looking a little baffled. "My memory seems to have slipped. Really. I must see Mimir soon. Who was her mother, and in what country did she live? Perhaps I may recall the incident."

Miss Simpkins was not to be put upon. Before Brynhild could answer she spoke up for herself.

"I'm *not* a Valkyrie. Catch me traipsing all over the country picking up strange men, and dead ones at that! And you can't make me wait on tables here, either. It may be a technicality, but I'm a hero, and as such I want my rights."

"A hero?" asked the Valfather, dumfounded, rolling his one good eye solemnly from first one of them to the other.

"That's what *I* thought," said Brynhild, defiantly, "and that's what Heimdall says. He let her across the bridge. That's something."

"Oh, dear," said the Valfather, anxiously. "Those Norns are holding out on me again. Why didn't I know about this before?"

Miss Simpkins could think of nothing appropriately tart to say to that. Nor did she care to. For she was beginning to relax a little and there was something about the bewildered old man that appealed to her. He seemed so good, yet so utterly impractical. She regarded him for a moment with speculative eyes. A man like that had possibilities — salvage possibilities, that is. Under firm management, he might eventually amount to something. At the moment, he seemed completely lost in the face of the inexplicable situation that had suddenly confronted him. And not unnaturally, for it must be embarrassing to a self-styled god who supposedly knows the past, present and future to its utmost detail, to have something laid in his lap that wasn't in the book. Something had to be done.

"Well, I'm here," snapped Miss Simpkins. "When do we eat?"

"Yes, yes, of course," said the Valfather, hurriedly, and clapped his hands. A tall old geezer with a shiny bald head and flowing white beard stepped forth, plucking a few tentative notes on a bejeweled harp he carried.

"Sound mess call, Bragi," said the god of all the heroes, and sank limply onto his throne.

"Just take any vacant seat, dearie," said Brynhild in Ida's ear. "You're on your own now."

Miss Simpkins gave her a dirty look, but it was wasted on dimpled shoulder blades. Brynhild was making for the kitchen. A Valkyrie's work is never done.

In the meantime the milling crowd of heroes were beginning to sort themselves out and line up along the many long troughs that covered the floor of the vast hall. There were benches on one side of the troughs, and the warriors were shucking their outer armor and stacking it beside the place they meant to sit. Ida had a look about. Wotan seemed to have gone to sleep. There seemed to be no course open except to follow the catty advice she had just received. So she walked over to the nearest table where men were beginning to seat themselves. They were spread out pretty well, but there would easily be room for another if they would move over a little. She came up between two big huskies and pushed them gently but firmly apart. Then she unbuckled her sword belt and laid it down on the bench. She was reaching for the corselet buckles when the storm broke.

"Hey," said the big bruiser on the right, "what's the big idea? Get in the kitchen where you belong and hurry up with the chow."

Her answer was to unsnap the holdings of the corselet and fling it on the bench. Then she calmly sat down beside it. A roar went up that filled that entire side of the hall. A hairy paw snatched at the back of her neck and a blustering voice began to say something. Whatever it was, it never got said, for it turned into a howl of pain and rage. A small but strong thumb was digging into a vital nerve of the gripping paw, and another small but strong hand had seized the elbow farther up. There was a mysterious twist, a heave and another twist, and the hero went flying headfirst across the trough and lit face down a dozen feet beyond. He skidded on, plowing up the sawdust for another yard or so, then sat up with a groan.

"That," announced Miss Simpkins, calmly, standing now and facing the circle of amazed heroes that had come up, "is known as the Kata Otoshi, or Shoulder Overthrow. A very tricky race of warriors called Japs invented it. Do any of you want to make something of it?"

There was a gleam in her eyes that had not been there since the day of the big riot back there on the back water front of Brooklyn. It seemed that nobody cared to make anything of it. Moreover, fighting in the hall was a breach of etiquette. They would have all afternoon for that out on the field.

"To set you straight," she added, "I'm a certified hero, like it or not."

Suddenly there was a great gust of laughter throughout the hall. Her victim was getting dazedly to his feet, rubbing his skinned nose with one hand.

"Ha, Gunnar," yelled one tall Viking, "how does it feel to be tossed on your ear by a woman?"

Gunnar growled and turned away amidst the guffaws of the crowd. He went over to another table and sat down, leaving his arms and armor where he had left it on the seat beside Ida Simpkins. She swept them off onto the floor to make more room beside her. Everywhere the men were sitting down now, though there was much conversation going on behind the backs of hands into ears. Heimdall's prophecy had matured faster than most. It was indeed a day to be remembered in Valhalla. For few of the heroes had a greater reputation for toughness in a rough-and-tumble than Gunnar, brother and slayer of Sigurd, the lover of Brynhild. The reverberations in Asgard would not die down for ages:

But a distraction was at hand in the form of food. Columns of Valkyries were deploying into the hall, each Valkyrie either bearing a huge tray of smoking meat or a horn of mead. They had shed their armor and were now in long white gowns with their yellow hair hanging free about their shoulders. Still other Valkyries were coming along the bench side of the troughs, handing out drinking vessels. One stopped sulkily beside Ida and handed her a silver-mounted white stein. It was a ghastly-looking thing, being fashioned out of a freshly scraped human skull. The mouth, nose and eyeholes had been deftly plugged with chased silver.

"What's this thing?" demanded Miss Simpkins.

"Your drinking mug," answered the handmaiden. "It is made from the head of one of your enemies. You got fourteen, according to our count, but the other thirteen are not made up yet. They'll be up later."

"Take it away," said Miss Simpkins, firmly, "and bring me a glass of water. I don't drink mead, and I won't drink out of that thing."

"Water?" echoed Skaugul, for that was her name. "What is this 'water'?"

"Water," reiterated Ida, "the stuff they fill lakes with — what they poison to make liquor of."

"But here everyone drinks the lovely mead —"

"Up till now," snapped the ex-schoolteacher. "Now, listen, don't start any arguments with me. I've passed all the tests and here I am — a hero. As such I rate anything I want. If these dumbbells are content to guzzle the slop they do, that's their affair. I want water. Get me?"

Skaugul took on the same unhappy look that Ida had noticed several times on Brynhild's broad face. She went away. Presently she came back — and with water. In the meantime the line of Valkyries had passed by on the far side of the trough,, filling skulls as they came, and dumping enormous quantities of what looked and smelled like barbecued pig into the troughs.

"*Skol!*" rang out tens of thousands of booming voices in unison, as all lifted their drinking mugs and emptied them. Miss Simpkins took a sip of her precious water. She had already noticed a lot of things about the service that were going to be bettered before she lived much longer; but, after all, Rome wasn't built in a day. Her companions up and down the line were grabbing up joints of the roast pig with both hands and cramming them into their mouths. The entire Valkyrie force was now concentrating on the almost impossible task of keeping the mugs filled. Miss Simpkins ignored them all. Instead, she fumbled amongst her cast-off armor and found her little sword and drew it. With it and the one hand she could not

120

help getting greasy, she sliced off a small sliver of the part of the carcass in her section of the trough.

It was not bad, though a little gamy, and she ate another slice. Her fellow heroes had already gone through their first joints and, after some intermediate burping on a truly colossal scale, had tackled their seconds. A few hearty eaters were even yelling for thirds, which were promptly brought on the run by the obedient Valkyries. After a little they began giving up, one by one, and sat back on their benches in sated contentment, taking only a gallon or so of the abundant mead as the ultimate chaser. Miss Simpkins beckoned Skaugul, who had been hanging around somewhat frightenedly in the immediate background.

"No vegetables? No greens? No dessert?" demanded Ida, coldly, knowing perfectly well there were not.

But Skaugul merely looked blank and a little scared. She bobbed her head in what might have been an attempt at a curtsy of a sort, then scurried away. It was a long time before she returned, but return she did, and with a bowl of dark-green leaves. Her guest glowered at them.

"From the tree Yggdrasil," said the poor little Valkyrie, trembling. Ida did not know it, but Skaugul had always thought a lot of Gunnar. Next to Thor, she always told the other girls —

Ida was glaring at her.

"Greens, you said," Skaugul explained, timidly. "Heidrun eats them. Maybe you could."

"Who's Heidrun?"

"She's the goat — the one that gives the mead." By that time Skaugul was on the verge of collapse. Greens this strange female hero had asked for, and greens she had brought — the only green thing on Asgard. It was all very weird, but there was at least the precedent of the goat. So Skaugul saw no harm in mentioning it.

"Skip it," snorted Miss Simpkins. She was going to have to tackle this problem nearer its source. There was no use in punishing the child more. She tried to close her ears to the mouth-smacking and belching that filled the hall about her. She thought grimly for a moment on this subject also. What beasts uncontrolled men can be, she thought. And when Ida thought about control — well, there was only one proper kind of control in Ida's mind. That was the Ida-

121

directed variety. She, might have begun to do a little planning then and there, but at once a great shout filled the hall.

"Let's fight!" it boomed, and on the instant the men were heaving their stuffed bulks off the benches and clambering into their harness. A number were already dressed and on their way out. Ida looked at her own little pile of gilt junk and decided to leave it where it lay. It might do for ceremonial occasions, but in a fight it would be a distinct handicap to her. For she firmly intended to attend the fight. It was the custom, and she was resolved to follow the customs. Oh, she would modify them, bit by bit, but still she would not buck them.

"I'm Sigmund," bellowed a towering blond giant beside her. "How's for a little scrap? Berserk, you know, with no holds barred." She noted that he had left off his hardware as she had done. "I want to get the hang of that stunt you worked on Gunnar. Ha, ha, ho, ho, haw, haw!"

"Lead the way," she said, crisply.

They were late getting onto the field. By the time they arrived practically everybody had teamed off and were going at it hammer and tongs. There were many styles of fighting in progress. Some combats were duels, others between groups. Some men fought in full armor with buckler and long sword, others dispensed with the shield and flailed about them with eight-foot two-handed swords that were about as light as crowbars of the same length. Still others used war clubs and maces, and some hammered away with mailed fists. There were wrestling matches as well.

Some of the fights had already terminated, for the ground was beginning to be strewn with stray heads, severed arms and legs, and not a few of the heroes lay on their backs, split from shoulder to navel by some lucky swipe of a battle-ax. Miss Simpkins picked her way through the carnage with considerable disgust, though she knew that they would all come alive when mess call sounded again. Oh, what a wacky place, and how lucky for them that she had at last got there!

They eventually reached a comparatively clear spot, about a mile from the hall. Until then they had had to duck and dodge repeatedly to avoid losing their own heads through the backsweep of the sword of some fighter too intent to note what was going on

122

behind or beside him. Ida stopped, and Sigmund walked on beyond about twenty paces. Then he turned, vented a tremendous roar, and charged.

She stood stock-still until he was almost upon her. At that, she gave but a little bit — just enough not to be bowled over by the impact. She did not go into action until his arms were already about her, ready to begin a bearlike squeeze. Then a lot of things happened fast. Something gouged him in the small of the back, and a sharp elbow was sticking in his throat. Sigmund hit the ground, bit out a hunk of turf, and came up yelling.

He closed again, but that time she did not throw him. She grabbed one hand and crossed his arm with hers. Then she snuggled up to him and twisted. He howled with pain and refused to go down on his knees as any mortal would have. So she increased the pressure by a hairbreadth and was slightly sickened by feeling and hearing the bones pop. Not that it mattered. They would be whole in time for dinner.

He staggered back, looking incredulously at his dangling arm, folding it up and down across its break to make sure there was no mistake about it.

"W-wh-what . . . how?" he stammered.

"The first maneuver," she replied primly, "is known as the Sora Towoshi, or Sudden Fall. The second treatment is called Ude Ori, or the Arm Break. You should have dropped to the ground. Then I would not have had to spoil your arm."

He could only gaze and fiddle with his arm in blank amazement. Yet he towered a good foot above her and probably tipped the scales at three hundred flat. It wasn't reasonable!

Ida Simpkins was aware of a sudden hush on the battlefield. Hundreds of whole and manned heroes had knocked off their encounters and were hurrying up to see the fun. In a moment there was a deep ring about them, listening open-mouthed to the stories being told by the score or so that had witnessed Sigmund's trimming. There were deep curses, or heavy sighs, depending upon the temperament of the auditor.

"It's magic," whispered one, but in the voice of the gale.

"Stuff and nonsense," whipped out Miss Simpkins. "Who said that?"

A burly man clad in red-gold armor, complete with shield and broadsword, stepped sheepishly forward.

"Me. Hogni. I say it's magic. But it will not avail against an armed man. Not a man of courage and skill."

"Yeah? Well, come on and do your stuff. I'll show you the Taka Tooi. It's not magic, but it'll stop *you*."

Hogni seemed to regret his outspokenness, for he showed no anxiety to put his words into action, but the hoots and jeers of his messmates soon stimulated him into action. He twirled his sword and charged in the same reckless bull-fashion that Sigmund had. A gasp that must have made every leaf on Yggdrasil quiver rose from the watching crowd. For the woman stood quietly waiting, the only tense thing about her her eyes. Then he was upon her, with his sword upraised for the smashing cut that would have split her to the pelvis. But it never fell. Like lightning, a hand shot up and grasped his wrist, yanking the charging hero forward, and twisting at the same time. In the same split second she interposed her heel behind his and gave a sidewise shove. Hogni spilled quite neatly a couple of yards away.

Ida gave him an appraising look as he scrambled, muttering, to his feet. He was really enraged now, as the whole of Valhalla made the welkin ring with their ribald comment. He forgot his shield and sword and was coming at her full tilt, grasping and ungrasping his huge paws. She calmly turned her back on him and started to walk away.

She felt the wind on the back of her neck as he reached out for her. No eye among the bystanders was quick enough to see what followed. Some said she merely stooped and that he dived over her. Others said she tossed him. Whatever she did, Hogni was through for the afternoon. When they turned him over and took stock of his condition, his head lolled indifferently in any direction. That hero broke his neck.

Ida Simpkins had had enough, too, but she did not want to admit it. She was grateful now for Tim Hannigan, the big cop on the beat back home. He used to come into her gym and work out with her, and taught her tricks for some she taught him. But at that, throwing heavy men around is work, and Ida was hard put not to give vent to panting. She tried to walk past the crowd and back to the hall, but they would not have it. They clustered about her, all thoughts of fighting any more that afternoon gone by the board. They wanted to know what the new hero was called, and how she could defeat three of Valhalla's best champions with such seeming ease.

"The name," she said, very precisely, "is Miss Ida."

"Misaeda," they told the ones in the back ranks who might not have heard. "The champion calls herself Misaeda."

To answer the rest called for a speech, and to make a speech she needed wind. For that she needed time. So she asked the nearest huskies to kindly make a pile of handy corpses so she would have a rostrum to address them from. Then she stood back, breathing heavily, while they dragged the bodies up and heaped them, topping them off with a layer of shields that served very well as a floor. She climbed up onto it and motioned them to assemble in front of her. When everything was right, she began.

"You call yourselves heroes. Perhaps you were. You call yourselves champions. That you are not, and I'll tell you why. You don't live right. You gorge yourselves with rich, unbalanced foods, and dim your wits by guzzling liquor. You're fat and flabby and you don't care, because no matter what happens to you, you'll be revived enough to continue with your hoggish stuffing at the next meal. You lack skill, too. Fighters, bah! You're a lot of butchers. You have strength, bad as your present condition is, but you don't know how to use it. I guess that covers it."

She stopped abruptly and started to descend from her macabre rostrum. But they would not let her — just as she had planned. They wanted to know more — how to get in trim, how to fling giants about the way she did. She heard them in grim silence. Yes, she would teach them a lot of things — all but the last. That would be her secret, or at least until her control was established beyond possible challenge.

"All right," she flashed back at them, "if you mean it, get to work! Strip off that armor. Then line up out there in as many ranks as you please, but with room around every man enough to swing his arms and body about without interfering with his neighbor."

She waited while they stripped down to their underwear and got in gym formation, issuing the appropriate orders to correct the formation. When all was set. she started. The Swedish movements she gave them, from A to Z, demonstrating each from her high, perch, then calling off the numbers. In half an hour they were sweating profusely. At the end of the hour, nine shamefaced champs lay quietly down and quit, winded and aching in every muscle. But she went relentlessly on, until she caught sight of the Valfather walking across the field accompanied by the faithful Bragi. She allowed them to stop for a rest, and awaited the coming of the all-highest.

"What manner of fighting is this we have today?" he asked mildly, as he came up. "I have seen strange ways of fighting in the world, but never a thing like this."

"Oh, we're not fighting now," she explained, "but getting ready to fight. You see I've got to get the b —" — she bit off the "bums" that came so readily to her lips and substituted "heroes" — "to get the heroes in shape to fight. It may take months. They're in awful condition now, what with lack of exercise, inadequate diet and all."

The Valfather's single eye bulged a bit. What this female hero was saying had the ring of madness. It was astounding. Lack of exercise? Why, his heroes had fought to extinction twice daily for aeons. Inadequate diet? Why, his boys could outeat, and did, any men of comparable weight and occupation in the world. Only giants could exceed them. What was this thing Brynhild had brought up from earth and Heimdall had passed over the bridge?

"I'll talk to you more about it later," she promised him. "Right now I want to let these men go, and look over the commissary arrangements."

Paying no further heed to the Valfather, she stood up straight again and yelled for attention. The weary warriors struggled to their feet, many, cramped from their momentary rest.

"Dismiss!" she said, and started to get down. But they stood staring at her. She turned back. "Dismiss, I said. It's all over for today. Scatter. Rest. Do anything. We'll take the next lesson right after breakfast tomorrow."

Down on the ground, she addressed herself to the Valfather once more.

"I'd like to see the back of the house now, please. Who is the chief cook and bottle washer?"   •

"Back of the house? Bottle washer? The chief cook is Andhrimnir, but we haven't any of those other things."

"You show me, pop," she said, taking Bragi by the arm. "We ought to be able to give it the once-over before supper, don't you think?"

The venerable Bragi looked startled, but he nodded. So they started back across the field. It was a winding course, for the spent warriors lay everywhere — whole for a change, but more miserable than if they had been hacked in pieces. There was only a second's pain when an ax cleaved an arm away, but reaching for the sky for minutes at a time left aftereffects. But there was not a hero there but was resolved to go on doing it. They were beginning, in a formless sort of way, to hate this Misaeda, but at the outset she had aroused their admiration. Now every man of them wanted to fit himself so he could do the things she had done. And each, as he groveled and panted, looked forward to the day when he could fling people around — beginning with Misaeda.

III.

As in many palaces and the "grand hotels" of earth, the back of the house at Valhalla was as dismal as the recesses of an outmoded penitentiary, in sharp contrast with the gilded exterior. The kitchen was dark, gloomy, and dirty, with a bloodstained earthen floor. Innumerable cobwebs hung from the undressed rafters. A huge caldron stood in the middle of the room, and in the far corner a tank of heroic dimensions. The walls were lined with racks to hold the mead-carrying horns, and the stench was terrible. The most obnoxious features of the place, however, were the pigsty and the cook himself.

Andhrimnir was a giant — and an ultra-fat one. He sat dozing on a stool six feet high, but his bulk was so great that his posture was a squat. He had nine chins and five bellies, lying fold upon fold, and his face was coarse and stupid. He was snoring stertorously as Misaeda entered.

In the pigpen — which lacked only grandstands to qualify as a bull ring, so immense was it — stood a colossal boar, surrounded by thralls. One thrall, far larger than the rest, was maneuvering before the pig with a heavy poleax. The pig was watching him anxiously with an expression of utter woe, and all the while great tears rolled out of his tiny red eyes and dripped from his snout. Misaeda thought she had never seen so miserable a creature.

"That is Saehrimnir," explained Bragi, proudly. "It is him we eat thrice daily. He has just been magically reassembled from the remains of the dinner. When the thrall kills him, Andhrimnir will awake and thrust him into the pot. It is a very neat and economical arrangement."

"It's outrageous," pronounced Misaeda, looking at the poor animal with rare compassion. "Wait until the S. P. C. A. hears about this. Why, to slaughter the same beast three times a day, day after day, for years and years . . . Oooooh!"

She shuddered. There was that angle, of course. But she was also thinking of such collateral issues as monotony of diet — which the drunken heroes never seemed to notice — trichinosis, a constant threat, and vitamin deficiency.

The ax fell, the pig squealed, and Misaeda plugged her ears with her fingers. All slaughtered pigs squeal, but few pigs are of elephantine proportions. Saehrimnir's squeal might well have served as the signal for an air alert for the entire Atlantic coast of America. The cook, Andhrimmr, heard it, even through his deep slumber, and stirred. Misaeda hurried out a side door, dragging Bragi behind her.

There Misacda saw something that froze her into her customary stance of cool self-possession. Hundreds of weary Valkyries sat on benches that ran along the outer back wall of the palace, waiting for the next mess call. But what caught Misaeda's eye was Brynhild and one other person. They were standing apart, Brynhild and a sly, sneaky-looking, undersized man, whispering together. At Misaeda's sudden and unexpected appearance amongst them, they both looked up, started guiltily, then exchanged knowing glances. The little man smiled a quick, crooked smile, nodded, then disappeared abruptly — much as a light goes out. Brynhild stalked to the nearest bench and sat down, trying to appear indifferent. Misaeda knew, without being told, that the little man was Loki, the Norse god of mischief. There was trouble brewing, and it was being brewed for her. Her immediate disposition of it was a disdainful sniff.

"Now," she said to the fatuous Bragi, "what about this mead stuff? Where does it come from, and how do they handle it?"

"Ah, yes," said he, "the lovely mead. Follow!"

He led her past the seated rows of fagged Valkyries to the place where an open trough entered the kitchen wall. The trough was quite similar to an irrigation or mining flume, and conveyed a gurgling, sticky amber liquid that smelled to high heaven. Valhallic mead, consisting as it does of thirty percent honey, thirty percent pale ale, and forty percent alcohol, *would* be smelly. The legions of flies blackening the planked sides of the flume did nothing to detract from the general nauseousness of the scene. Now Misaeda understood the big tank that stood in the corner of the kitchen, and why it was relatively easy for the harassed waitresses to satisfy the Gargantuan thirst of the Valhalla warriors. Or Einheriar, as Misaeda had just learned they were collectively called.

She insisted on tracing the flume to its source, so the unwilling Bragi had to trail along. In a couple of minutes they came upon the obvious source of the myriads of flies. Just abaft the kitchen was the golden-wired corral within which the horses of the Valkyrie squadrons were kept. They may have been celestial horses, but they conformed closely in their habits to the earthly and mortal kind.

The trail led on through the golden grove, then upward. At length the gold-leaved trees gave way to green, and she knew that they were in the famous upper bow of the great tree Yggdrasil. It was a forest in itself, with many levels and ramps leading from one to another. She saw many kinds of darting and flying animals, or others placidly browsing — squirrels, eagles, ravens, owls, and stags. But the flume led on, wide open all the way.

At last she found the source. High in the uppermost branches was a filthy platform on which stood a goat, no doubt the goat Heidrun that Skaugul had mentioned. It was a noble animal, if size is any criterion of nobility, for it matched the pig Saehrimnir in dimensions, standing some forty feet from ground to spine. It ate steadily from the leaves of the overhanging bough and its udder continually streamed the fresh-made mead into the trough that it bestrode.

"Why couldn't that animal give milk just as well?" asked Misaeda, with pointed scorn.

"She could. She did," said Bragi. "But who wants milk? We worked magic on her to change it. Neat, eh?"

Misaeda's sniff, to his poetic mind, did not constitute a satisfactory answer. She was unaware of it, and if she had been aware would not have cared a farthing, but at that moment she added one more name to the list of her nonfriends. Miss Simpkins had a way of getting people to do what she wanted them to do, but she lacked the art of making them like it.

"I've seen enough," she announced, having finished a thoroughly disapproving survey of the placid Heidrun.

"Asgard was a dreary place," remarked the innocent Bragi, as they left, "until we had mead. Heavens, you know, are always dull. One has to do something about it after the novelty has worn off. Think of it, I've been here centuries and centuries with nothing to do but sound mess call three times a day and render a ballad now and then on request!"

Misaeda's reply was a super-sniff. Might we say a snort?

Supper that night was a repetition of dinner. Tons and tons of the unfortunate Saehrimnir's flesh and thousands of gallons of the potent mead vanished. It was accompanied, as before, by millions of cubic feet of belly gases erupted by the contented Einheriar. Altogether, according to Misaeda's lights, it was a most disgusting performance. To her further disapproval, the meal was accompanied by some very flagrant flirtations between the heroes and the willing Valkyries. It appeared that the evening meal, unlike breakfast and dinner, was to be followed by exhibitions of prowess in the field of love rather than in fighting.

"You see, my arm is all right now," said Sigmund, who had seated himself beside her. He demonstrated.

"If it's still there a second from now," she told him, "I'll tie it into a knot with the other one."

He removed the offending arm with a hurt and baffled look. He had certainly tried his best to make this female hero feel at home — offering her a challenge and all that — but everything he did seemed to be wrong. He furrowed his handsome blond brow a moment, then thought of the obvious *mot juste*.

"Silly of me, wasn't it?" asked the warrior. "One hero trying to make another. Sorry. Naturally, now that we have female heroes, we'll have to have some masculine Valkyries to match."

"Sir!"

And that was the extent of Misaeda's supper conversation. Sigmund hung around for a while, but found it discouraging. When Bragi appeared on the stage for the evening's ballad, he seized the occasion to vanish quietly in the crowd.

Misaeda got through that awful evening somehow. Then some magic was performed. The long troughs and benches disappeared as in a dream. In their places were lines of golden couches. Apparently taps was close at hand.

She picked a couch in the very center of the hall, since, being a hero, she had to sleep there with the others. But for the edification of her neighbors, she most pointedly drew a circle about it with her sandaled toe before she retired. To people steeped in the traditions of potential magic it was sufficient. She did not enlighten them as to what the purpose of the circle was, or what would happen to anyone rash enough to cross it, but the exhibition of the day had been enough for them all.

Morning brought breakfast, and after breakfast came the forenoon of combat time. But that morning the throngs of warriors waited. Their routine had been upset. They simply didn't know what to do. It was Misaeda who told them. Calisthenics again. And she also hinted that those who went easiest on the mead would have the best chance of sticking it out until noon. Because she meant to work them to a frazzle, and did.

All the while, the Valfather sat dejectedly on his throne, contemplating the gloomy future and the puzzling and unprecedented and unpredicted present. He was a sad and disillusioned man, godling, or what you will. , He had traded an eye for all-knowledge and wisdom, and had undergone other harrowing experiences in order to make himself more fit as the leader of his people. He knew, or thought he knew, the ultimate culmination of all his efforts. And that culmination was defeat, extinction, and obliteration. Pure tragedy. Nor was there any way out. So the Norns had foretold it; so it would come to pass. It was they who had all knowledge of what had been, what was, and what was to be. Yet at no time had there been mention made of a female hero coming to Valhalla. It was that that troubled him most. Had he given his eye in vain? Were the Norns completely dependable?

Only last evening Loki had come to him. He did not like or trust Loki, but what the fellow had said seemed sound advice. Loki had insinuated that perhaps this female hero who had unaccountably appeared within the walls of sacred Valhalla might be a giant in disguise. How else could one so frail fling heroes about, breaking arms and necks?

So he himself, Wotan, the All-Highest, master of runes and prophecies, had cut runes and studied them. The answer was blank. The woman was no giant, no sorceress — a simple Norse hero cut down while resisting the hated Cimbri. There was no choice left him. He had to follow the advice of the tricky Loki and seek the aid of the reluctant Norns. It was a thing they should have told him, and had not. It was his right and duty to demand an answer. So he sent Loki as the messenger. Loki was due back at any moment.

It was in this manner that things stood when Bragi tinkled his harp and sounded mess call that momentous day. It was in this manner that things stood when the strange hero, Misaeda, and her heaving and flabbergasted disciples staggered off the fighting fields into the grand mess hall of Valhalla. Not one of them, not excepting Misaeda — though she knew dirty work of some stripe was afoot — had any inkling of what was coming.

Before they could sit down, Bragi tinkled his harp and sang out the call to "attention." The panting heroes stiffened where they stood. The tableau on the thronal dais told them something big was about to happen. Loki was there, trying to look self-effacing and unimportant, as was his wont — and Loki's presence always meant trouble. Also the chief Valkyrie was there, Brynhild, looking extremely satisfied with herself and glowing with virtuous triumph. The Valfather was slumped in his throne chair fingering a carved bit of a stick.

After a moment he handed it to Bragi, and commanded, "Read!" Bragi took it, cleared his throat, and began.

"Hark! A message from the wise sisters:

In Hlidskialf sits Odin,
His rule is empty.
Misaeda, amongst the Einheriar,
Usurps him.
Wroth are the Dises,
Their sooth unheeded.

Signed:
URDAR, VERDANDI, SKULD. THE NORNS.

There was a hush that was painful.

"What say the Einheriar?" asked the bard.

The Einheriar exchanged a lot of sidelong glances, but not one of them saw fit to say anything. They all had visions of fair hands pushing at their throats, twisting their wrists and arms, or other unorthodox contortions that would make them subject to the ridicule of their fellows. No hero cared to stick his neck out. Not one of them opened his trap. Let the gods handle it.

The Valfather stirred himself. He snapped out of his defeatist lethargy long enough to get to his feet and declare.:

"The self-styled hero, Misaeda, having wormed herself into our midst and violated our hospitality, is hereby expelled from Valhalla. The masters-at-arms will take appropriate measures."

Gunnar and Sigmund, who were the masters-at-arms, exchanged significant looks. It took no clairvoyant to read their meaning. It was simply, "How?"

Misaeda accepted the challenge. From where she stood in the center of the hall she called out in a high, clear voice:

"Fiddlesticks! I've got something to say about this."

Then she started forward, the armored men clankingly making way for her. They were keenly interested. Scarcely one of them but whose cheeks still burned and ears tingled with some sharp rebuke of the morning. They respected Misaeda, but they would gladly have seen her turned wrong side out. They loathed Loki, the trickster, but they credited him with being smart. They loved their Valfather, but knew he could be thunderous and pompous as all get-out on occasion; and they also knew that Brynhild was nobody to be trifled with. They looked forward with considerable relish to what would happen when Misaeda tangled with that trio.

They had not long to wait. Misaeda was at the foot of the throne. She was mounting the dais! She was up with the big shots, where only gods and demigods dared stand!

"Listen, everybody," she began. "I didn't want to come to this lousy heaven of yours. I'm stuck with it. And it's that dumb woman's fault." Here she flung an accusing finger at the astonished Brynhild.

"She can't distinguish between right-thinking people and your kind. But I'm here, and I mean to make the best of it. Let the old Norns be wroth! What are we here for? To waste our lives in debauchery and stupid dueling, or to prepare for Ragnarok —"

A gasp from tens of thousands of throats in union almost sucked in the walls. Ragnarok, the unmentionable, shouted from the platform! It was hideous; it was blasphemous; it was unthinkable. All the world knew about Ragnarok and dreaded it, but never spoke of it. The ultimate fate of the world was the most hush-hush thing imaginable. Nobody was supposed to know it but the Valfather, Mimir, and the Norns. And all mankind, and godkind, and giantkind, and dwarf and fairykind joined in the conspiracy. If the good and kindly old man who was their chief god chose to kid himself that only he knew the future, they would not disillusion him.

The Valfather's lone eye bugged.

"Did you say Ragnarok, my, child?" he asked anxiously. "Are you, perchance, a fourth Norn, that you know the unknowable?"

"Do I look like one of those crack-brained old women?" she countered. "Why do you have to be a Norn to know what everybody knows and has always known? This cockeyed set-up you have here is headed straight for a fall, and it's no secret, but you sit here day after day mooning about it and grieving over what you think can't be helped. Well, I'm not usurping anything. I'm trying to help you, that's all. If you expect to make any showing at all at Ragnarok, we'll have to get this bunch of bums in better condition. They are fat and flabby, and their kidneys are all shot from swilling mead . . . oh, my, they're *terrible!*"

The Valfather's single eye was roaming the sea of upturned, eager faces. He did not like in the least the turn the conversation had taken. Cats were being let out of the bag by droves. And, to his amazement, the assembled throng of heroes took the nasty reference to them with meek silence. If this woman kept on talking, it was hard to say what would come out next.

"Suppose we adjourn this hearing to my chambers, my dear," suggested he, solicitously. "It must be trying to talk before so many."

"Very well," Misaeda snapped back, "but that rat" — indicating the fawning Loki by a contemptuous jerk of the thumb — "and that cat" — meaning the indignant Head Valkyrie —"don't sit in. I've got things to tell you for your own good."

The Valfather winced. Sometimes Frigga talked like that, too. He knew from a wealth of experience that whatever was for his own good was going to be hard to take. He sighed audibly. Women were like that, though, and you had to make the best of them.

"This way, my dear," he said resignedly. Then, turning to Bragi, "Tell 'em to sit down and eat. We'll put out a release later."

In the interview in the chambers — which were the usual barnlike rooms Misaeda had observed elsewhere in Valhalla, palatial only because of the vast areas of gilding — the ex-headmistress of the Gowanus Settlement School did not pull her punches.

"Are you going to be a sap all your life?" she began, with her customary disregard for tact. "You're all tied up in knots in the silliest, most impractical mythology ever invented by drunken poets. And all you do about it is sit and suffer. Or else you go off the reservation entirely and squander months down in Midgard breaking up families and impairing the morals of minors. Do you think it's *right?*"

She spoke with a bitter fierceness that drove him straightway into the corner. He was on the defensive from the first onset.

"Wh-wh —"

"No. Of course you don't. You're a decent guy — at heart. But you're too darn gullible. You believe you've got to do these things because they're in the book. Nuts! If you set yourself up as

135

chief god in this wacky world, why don't you work at it? *Do something.*"

She paused for breath, glaring at him with open disapproval. He floundered for a moment and managed a weak, "But what can I do?" when she was back at him.

"What can you do? Plenty! You swapped an eye for knowledge that everybody has. Go back and get your eye and tell old Mimir to go and jump in his own ocean. You keep fooling around on the advice of three crazy old women who are doing their best to make a monkey out of you — and succeeding. Bosh! I know as much about the future or anything else as they do. You are worrying about the giants, and the dog Garm and the wolf Fenris. Well, I ask you. What has Garm and Fenris got that is so terrible? Bad breath — halitosis, they called it in my age. Get yourself a gas mask, that's all there is to that. And you're worried about the dragon Nidhug that is gnawing at the roots of Yggdrasil. Why don't you kill it now, while the killing is good? Why wait until they all gang up on you? Snap these heroes out of their chronic jag, and swat the frost giants. Swat the fire giants. Send expeditions everywhere, one at a time. Then you'll have no Ragnarok."

"But, my dear," protested the harassed Valfather, "you don't understand. Ragnarok is far in the future. There is nothing we can do about it now. We have peace. Don't you understand? If we do the things you urge, we upset the status quo. That is always bad."

"Nuts. Excuse my frankness, but I -seem to remember a gentleman bight Chamberlain. He talked like you did — of 'Peace in our time.' There was another, somewhat before him, who said, 'After me the deluge.' That's you, on both counts. I ask you again, are you going to be a dope all your life?"

The Valfather was much distressed. *Nobody* had ever talked to him like that — not even Frigga, in her most uninhibited moments. One of the tremendous advantages of the godhead was the immunity to unmasked opinion. His satellites had always been Yes-men, and there was no denying it — he liked it. He must get rid of this troublesome female hero, with her sharp tongue and utter lack of respect of authority. He had the fleeting idea of summoning Brynhild and having her take this Misaeda back to where she had found her and dump her in the ocean. He stammeringly mentioned it.

"Not a chance," was Misaeda's tart reply. "Your stupid, bungling system wished me on you, and I stick. You've hauled me back a couple of millennia and there is no place for me to go. But if I can't have the Christian Heaven I'm entitled to, I'll do what I can with this one — on a give-and-take basis. I'll help you, you help me. Between us, we can make Valhalla a decent place to live. As for Ragnarok — that's in the bag."

Wotan tried to digest that. For he had never had much use for women except in a limited sense, and all she had said was rank heresy. Try as they might, the Aesir could not hope to survive Ragnarok. It was so written in the sacred runes. It had been foretold by the Norns. Mimir bad confirmed it. Wotan himself knew it from the prescience he had so dearly bought. This Misaeda talked sheer sophistry. Yet she talked it with such an air of determined confidence that his own self-confidence was shaken. Perhaps in a case like this compromise was in order.

"My dear," he said, after a lengthy communing with his own thoughts, "I have reconsidered my expulsion order. I believe you are truly a hero from Midgard. As such, I shall let you remain in Valhalla. More than that, since you appear to have practical ideas, I shall make you chief of the Einheriar. Handle them as you will — with Ragnarok in mind. But not a word of that to them, do you hear?"

"I hear," she acknowledged grimly. The fable of the Camel in the Tent was not far from her mind. First a foothold, then control. What more could a sincere, ambitious girl ask? Well, a few things. And she asked for them.

"Very well," she added. "I'll do it. But I need a little help."

"Ask it."

"I want," she began, "first of all, that when we eat this hog Saehrimnir next, that he'll stay eaten. Get me? After that, I want herds of cattle, flocks of chickens, and some sheep. Get Mimir to furnish fish twice a week — he has plenty, and the Einheriar need variety."

The Valfather nodded approval. But he hadn't heard the half of it.

"I want," she continued, "ten thousand thralls with oxen and plows to turn up the south recreation pasture. I need only the north one for my exercises and drills. After that I want it planted in vegetables. I want cabbages, spinach and potatoes. I want asparagus, lettuce, radishes and artichokes. I want onions. Garlic. Corn and wheat."

"It's a big order," murmured the All-Highest. "Moreover, the heroes won't eat that stuff. I know 'em."

"They'll eat it," she assured him, with a stabbing glance of those steely gray eyes, "and like it. I'll guarantee it."

"All right," sighed the Valfather. "Go on."

"I want that fat cook fired . . . the kitchen thoroughly cleaned and painted white inside — not gold . . . and that mead-producing goat turned back into a normal goat —"

"But, my dear, the heroes will not drink milk —"

"They will drink milk," affirmed Misaeda, determinedly. "But not in such quantities as they have been drinking mead. That calls for cheesemakers. Which brings up another item. Send a squadron of Valkyries down to Midgard and have them pick out a few score deserving housewives, instead of swashbuckling killers, for a change. What we need up here is homemakers — not these floozies you hire as body snatchers."

"Floozies?" queried the Valfather, wrinkling his noble brow.

"Hussies, if you like the word better. That's all half these Valkyries are. What goes on here after dinner at nights is simply scandalous, no less. I won't have it."

By then Wotan was in such a state of confusion that he could only nod acceptance. Inwardly he was cursing the Norns for not having let him in on this thing in advance and told him what to do. He was a simple, primitive war god, and not versed in the technicalities that now confronted him.

"What else?" he asked meekly.

"I guess that's all for now," said Misaeda, relenting. She knew just how far to push a thing on a single interview. She had learned that with countless contacts with high-school board officials. Up here in Asgard she had all Eternity in which to work. What could not be done today could be done tomorrow. The Valfather bowed her out. She marched by him primly, out onto the platform, and down the steps to the floor of the hall. The meal was over, as she well knew from the chorus of burps and the clicking of toothpicking. But she stalked to her seat, nevertheless, and sat down as if nothing out of the way had happened.

"I saved some chow for you," whispered Sigmund, leaning over and opening his tunic. Underneath his sweaty shirt was a side of ribs, greasy and underdone, but still warm.

"Thanks," said Misaeda, laconically, taking it and pretending to nibble. She was fed up with pork, but in her own peculiar way she was gratified. At least one of the heroic dead was showing symptoms of incipient good manners.

That night Misaeda lay on her golden couch — within the magic ring — and thought and thought. So far, so good. In a day or so she would introduce a balanced diet; her system of calisthenics was already doing marvels. Next would come the business of teaching the defunct heroes table manners; the matter of appointing corporals and sergeants and the teaching of squads right and similar basic maneuvers. After that the Blitzkrieg tactics.

Then an errant breeze wafted to her the odor of ten thousand spent warriors lying on the weather side of her. Oh, yes. There must be showers, too, and some arrangement about laundry.

Misaeda sighed. A woman's work is never done, she told herself for the nth time. These poor, poor men — so helpless, so goofy. It was lucky for them she had come amongst them! Tomorrow there would be much to do. She was so ecstatic in her previsions that she did not note or even hear the somnolent mutterings of the hero on the next couch.

"Ah, god," he moaned, "Misaeda! What next?"

The Old Ones Hear

Yesterday our forces occupied the island of Aea.
Axis War Communiqué

The promontory loomed ahead, vague and shadowy. Behind it, dark against the starry western sky, lay the remainder of the small island. The commander who sat in the stern sheets leaned forward and spoke quietly to the men on the after-most thwart.

"Land ahead," he said. "Pass the word forward to make no noise."

Under the dim starlight the men sent the whispered message on its way. The scantily dressed lieutenant and midshipman who sat on either side of the boat officer shivered and pulled their blankets tighter about their shoulders. Their blouses had been ripped apart and blown off by the terrific blasts of the bombs that had sunk their ship.

The boat went on. All was silent except for the faint ripple under its bows and the swish of quickwater along the sides. Even the wounded were quiet, though the faithful mast groaned once or twice as the hastily rigged sail slightly shifted its position.

It was a strangely assorted boat load, those men huddled together on the thwarts and in the spaces between. Thirty-odd of them were various ratings of his majesty's ship *Peeblesshire*; nine were Anzacs, all wounded; four were what was left of the crew of a cargo ship sunk four days before. The oddest was a queer old Greek, clad in his quaint skirted uniform. He had been the Anzacs mountain guide and had fought with them from Mount Olympus, down

140

through the desperate stand at Thermopylae, across the flanks of lofty Parnassus, past Delphi to the water's edge. A little touched, they thought him, for when they had rigged the mast he produced a leather bag as if from nowhere and hung it on the mast by the nock of the sail. "For good luck," he had grunted, by way of explanation. Ever since, he had sat doggedly on the third thwart and never taken his eyes off it.

The commander peered anxiously ahead. It had been a hard trip, even though luck had been with them, just as the old Greek had foretold. They had driven more than sixty miles through the winding waterways of the Gulf of Corinth and that of Patras, and always with a miraculously favorable breeze. Not once had a roving Stuka found them, nor the prowling coastal motorboats. But they had had to leave their ship in a hurry and there was room only for men, not for spare stores of provisions and water. The wounded were very miserable, and some were near death. The commander wondered what the island was, and whether it held capture for them, or haven.

There was not a glimmer of a light to be seen. Nor could his keen, night-piercing eye detect that there had ever been a light on the end of the jagged cape which he passed close aboard. He gave the tiller a touch and headed up into the cove that lay inside. Suddenly he started. For dead ahead, square across his bows, he could distinctly see the masts and upperworks of a cruiser. It was an enemy cruiser. He knew that at a glance from its fat, single stack with a deal of rake to it. He had laid his sights on a sister of it, not two weeks before, and watched her disappear in a gush of flame, smoke and splinters.

"Douse the sail," he ordered huskily, and put his tiller up.

The sail came down with a rush and with remarkably little noise, but the nails of the commander's disengaged hand were biting hard into the palm. He expected momentarily to hear a staccato challenge or be fixed in the prying beam of a searchlight. There were such things as picket boats, too, which might be lurking anywhere. But there was no challenge. The ship was as dead, apparently, as a hulk left to rot in some back channel.

The boat had way enough upon it to neatly round the stern of the alien warship. He eased it off a little and studied his unexpected adversary more closely. There was not a man on deck, so far as he could see, and, astonishingly enough — for it lacked only an hour or so to the dawn — her, colors flapped at both bow and stern, for all the world like noontime on a gala day.

"Out oars," he whispered, and waited patiently while the extra men slid off the thwarts and lay down out of the way in the soggy bilges. Of a sudden a daring idea had come to him. Perhaps the bulk of that cruiser's complement were on shore, and the remainder, certain of their safety, had been celebrating an easy victory over an undefended island. It might be that they were all drunk. He had heard that discipline on some of those ships was not of the best.

"Give way together," he ordered, and pointed the nose of his overladen craft toward the unguarded gangway.

For several minutes there was only the rhythmic stroke of the oars and the sound of water dripping from their uplifted blades as they swept forward for the next impulse. The commander steered her deftly, and after a few more low-spoken orders, felt the bow graze the platform of the accommodation ladder. Ready hands grasped at stanchions, and the rowers boated their oars without a sound. The moment they were along-side, the commander leaped like a panther to the landing stage and swiftly mounted the ladder.

There was no one at the top of it. A quick turn around the deck revealed nobody. He listened at a hatchway and at a ventilator. The ship was silent as the tomb, except for the faint throbbing of machinery far-below decks. He went back to the gangway and beckoned his men to come up.

They swarmed up the ladder, all of them that could walk, gripping what pistols and rifles they had contrived to keep with them in their hurried evacuation. There was a low conference and the group split up into several smaller squads. They parted, some going forward, some aft, the remainder below. Fifteen minutes later they reassembled, as had been agreed upon.

"A rum thing, sir," said a petty officer. "Not a living soul in the ruddy ship. But there's lights below and some auxiliaries running. They left a few burners going, so there's some steam in the boilers, though their water's low."

"How long will it take to get steam enough up to move her?" asked the commander sharply.

"Two hours, sir. Maybe less."

"Get at it. Mr. Torkingham!"

The lieutenant acknowledged.

"Have the wounded men brought up out of the boat and put 'em to bed. When you have found yourself some warm clothes, go up on the bridge and get acquainted with all the gadgets there. When there is steam enough to work the anchor engine, heave short. We're getting under way in two hours."

"Aye, aye, sir."

"I notice there's not a boat on the ship. Every set of skids and davits and all the booms are empty. I'm curious about that. While you are making ready, I am going to take a pull ashore and find out what has happened. I'll be back shortly."

The commander waited stolidly at the top of the gangway while the injured men were being carried up. He was concealing his impatience as best he could, for he felt he could not leave this unknown island without some explanation of his bizarre landfall. Never in all the histories of the navies of the world had there been a precedent for it. To leave a modern warship all standing with not even an anchor watch or a water tender on board! It was incredible. Not even during the darkest, undisciplined days of the Menshevik revolution at Kronstadt had it a counterpart.

He thought back over the escape and the marvels of the previous day and night. When he had left the shattered *Peeblesshire* she was an inferno of raging flames. There had been no opportunity to salvage a chart. Yet the boat had found her way through the winding channels to this place he did not recognize, and always with a good, stiff following breeze that veered and hauled as if to order. He wondered quizzically about the queer old Greek and his "windbag" and his talk of good luck. Well, they had had f air winds. And as for good luck! Just now he stood on the quarterdeck of a ship quite as good in some respects as the one he had had blown from beneath him. And he had taken it without a vestige of a struggle. He was short-handed, of course, but he could manage.

It occurred to him to ask the men about the Greek. He wanted to question him as to what island this was, how it lay as regards Cephalonia, and how far from Cape Matapan. But none of the men knew where he had gone. No one had seen him since they made the gangway. He had not come on board. He was not now in the boat. Maybe, feeling himself safe among his own people and his duty done, he had swum ashore.

The commander shrugged. It did not matter greatly. He had never been able to get anything out of the old fellow, anyway, but scarcely intelligible mumbles. He picked out a few men for a boat's crew, then slid down the ladder and into the boat. By that time it was full light, though still gray, and he could see that the pull would not be a long one.

He stood up in the boat on the way in, examining the shore. Ahead of him was a quay of antique masonry, hung over with green moss. Alongside it lay the abandoned cruiser's boats — power boats, pulling boats, even life rafts ripped from the bases of the masts — but in none of them was a boatkeeper. The desertion of his prize's crew had been absolute and complete.

To the right and left stretched sandy beaches, studded with the protruding ribs of vessels left to go to wrack many years before. They marred the beach as the straggly, yellow teeth in the gums of a hag mar her smile, transforming it into something sinister and ominous. As he drew close; he saw one peculiar relic and he knew it from its unique shape. It was covered with green patina of many centuries, but it could have been but one thing — the bronze ram of an ancient trireme.

He mounted the worn treads of the ancient steps of the quay with misgivings that grew with every foot of progress he made. This unknown islet — and he thought he knew them all, for he had cruised this coast many times since his midshipman days — appeared to be the graveyard of ships. Was it subject to a strange and swift pestilence? If so, why had it not been mentioned in the "Sailing Directions"? A sense of disquiet, unease, descended upon him, far more disturbing than had been the roar of the plunging Stukas or the screaming of their deadly bombs. He wondered whether he should go on or turn tail and fly. But curiosity drove him forward.

"Wait here," he said tersely to the boat crew, and strode off up the gentle slope, doing his best to quell the thrills of expectancy, amounting almost to fear, of imminent disaster.

There was no town to be seen, nor houses of any sort. Nor were there tilled fields. The place was more of a park, lovely in its grassy stretches, and spotted with clumps of trees and hedges. He found a path which ran between two winding rows of bushes and followed it for some distance. At a turn farther on he caught a glimpse through the copses of an establishment of some sort on the top of the hill.

"Ah," he thought, "the villa of a rich playboy, perhaps a retired munitions millionaire, or an exiled grand duke."

He stopped to survey it, though he could see little except the red tiles of its roof and the olive grove surrounding it. But his viewing of the place was cut short in an unexpected way. Before he knew what was happening, a horde of snapping wolves descended upon him. There, were hundreds in the pack and they swarmed about him, leaping and snarling.

He drew his pistol, but hesitated to use it. He did not want to advertise his presence on the islet. He pivoted on one leg and kept himself in an incessant swinging, kicking at the fangs of those animals that threatened him most. Once or twice he succeeded in landing a vicious kick squarely in the jaws of the plunging brutes, and after that the others kept at a more respectful distance. He noticed then that they were not truly wolves, but near-wolves — a noisy pack of blustering jackals, willing and eager to pull down a lamb, but not overbold when it carne to man. Yet they surrounded him, and their ceaseless yapping and snapping annoyed him. He could defend himself, but hardly progress.

Again a miracle happened. In his turning and twisting he had put his back to the villa on the hill, but now he heard a vibrant, contralto voice berating the creatures in tones of withering scorn. He did not recognize the odd dialect she used, but he did know the biting end of a black-snake whip when he saw one. The end of a long lash flashed by him, nicked a patch of yellow hair from the rump of one of the howling doglike creatures, which promptly slunk away, yelping and whining miserably. He heard the whistle and snap of the lash again and the distressed cries of another victim. He wheeled to see who his rescuer might be.

145

His senses reeled, and he could only gasp. The wielder of the lash was a woman; he had already surmised that from the voice. But nothing in his previous life had prepared him for what he saw. He was gazing at a woman, but such a woman as exists ordinarily only in visions and dreams. She was the incarnation of ideal voluptuous beauty, but at the same moment she was also the incarnation of cold, vindictive fury as she laid mercilessly about her with her whip. Her hair, under the touch of the first ray of the morning sun, was, as a mass of flame, and there was an uncanny, quality to her flashing green eyes which had the curious property of seeming to repel yet attract irresistibly at the same moment. There was hardly a detail of her exquisite figure he did not take in at that first startled glance, for she wore only a filmy veil of a garment that revealed more than it hid.

She seemed suddenly to become aware of him, as if she had not observed him before. Raging scorn melted from her face and she took on an expression of utter tenderness and longing that was more than he could bear. In that instant she cast her whip away from her and stretched out her arms to him in passionate welcome. He staggered forward blindly, all thought of ship or duty vanishing from his mind. He only knew that unless he reached her and embraced her, the drum-like roll of his throbbing pulses would drive him mad.

Yet he had taken not more than one or two strides before her manner altered again, and he froze where he stood under the compulsion of her, calm, imperious gaze. She was cold and haughty now, and queenlike, and regarded him with a cool, appraising look that was almost as terrifying as had been her fury and her ardor.

"You are a Briton, our ally?" she asked, a trifle hesitantly. "The man Hermes brought?"

"Hermes?"

"Oh, you wouldn't know, of course. He assumes many forms." She relaxed her forbidding attitude and permitted herself a little smile. "But you were not to come upon my island. You were brought to take that hideous, smoking iron galley away —

"But its crew — what became of -them?"

She stooped and picked up her whip, flicking it tentatively as she did. The wolfish animals which had been cowering and whimpering about. her feet slunk a little farther away.

"Have no fear of them. They will not return to interfere with you. Later, when I have disciplined them properly, I shall take them to the other side of the island and turn them into the pasture with my swine. Those are they who came to me from the sky." She seemed to be laughing inwardly, as if at a pleasant reminiscence.

The softening of her mood brought back his earlier yearning with all its imperativeness. He sprang forward to snatch her into his arms, but she recoiled and looked at him with something like horror.

"No, no!" she cried. "Not you! You are our friend, our ally. It cannot be. Take what the: gods have provided and go. It is a privilege few have had who have stepped upon this island and dealt with me, but it is so ordered. Go!"

The kaleidoscope of emotions to which he had been subjected in this last strange hour showed a new phase. A chilling sense of awe began to grow upon him as the monstrous truth of what he had seen and heard began to dawn upon him. He looked at her now with something akin to fear, yet there was a degree of grudging respect in it, too. That these long dormant ones should stir themselves now to help, if only a little, was something to be honored. He felt impelled to bow.

"I will go," he said quietly, "at once. But tell me — I must know, for my sanity's sake — who are you?"

Her eyes widened, as if she were deeply hurt.

"I? In the old days I had a name, but that does not matter now. I am everywhere, anywhere, and my work is always the same — I turn men into beasts."

She shuddered, and her look changed. It was a horrible mixture of passion and power — and agony. "Go!" she said.

Not According to Dante

*Hell wasn't what it used to be — but he found, waiting for him, a
very special, private hell all his own —*

For a long time he continued to lie face down on the hard
pavement in the cold, gray light of that curious land where there was
neither night nor day.

He had no way of knowing how long he had slept, nor did he
care. His sense of time had long since left him. How long, he could
not guess. It could have been a matter of hours, it might easily have
been an eon or so. He only knew that after seemingly interminable
wanderings through dark glades, and after the passage of many
rivers, he had eventually come to a place where a path struck off
from the broad, downward highway and led straight up the steep
mountainside. He had looked dully upon the two signs, then chosen
the easier road. And then, faced with yawning portal in a great,
gloomy wall that barred his way, he had lain down to rest.

Before arousing himself he thought for a while on his
previous journey, but it was all very vague and nebulous. In the
beginning there had been another gate, and chained to it was the
carcass of a dog — a three-headed dog, as he remembered it, badly
emaciated. He had gone through it and walked along a river — the
Acheron. He knew the-name, for some historical society had
evidently been along before him and marked the old historic spots
with neatly embossed metal signs on iron stakes stuck into the
ground. He had- crossed another river lined with gaunt trees whose
charred limbs still overhung the now dark river. It must have been a

148

great sight once, that flaming Plegethon, but no longer. Cakes of hardened asphalt was all that there was left of it now.

And he remembered vaguely crossing the Styx at least fourteen times and wondering at its spiral course. He had done that by means of a modern causeway that cut straight across it, but he had not failed to note the aboriginal .ferry landing at the place he first encountered it. He wondered whether the crude skiff lying there with wide open seams had been the ferry, a peeling sign announced the fare to be one obolus. Another sign pointed toward a low, rambling building covering many acres. It said "Waiting room for shades." Somehow it suggested that the ferryman was inefficient — or temperamental, which comes to the same thing.

At another river, prompted by the sign, he had washed the blood off his forehead and face and off his bloody knuckles. Somehow he could not recall the other details that went before. That river had been named Lethe. Miles beyond — thousands, for all he knew, and a long way past the dead town of Tartarus — he had come to that steep hill and the path leading up it.

He chuckled as he remembered the signs. The one a little way up the cliff said: "To the Pearly Gates." The one by the road said: "To —" The rest was blotted out and scrawled below were the words "the other place." That was the work, no doubt, of a prig bound up the mountain.

Pete Galvan stirred uneasily and began to think of getting up. The stone flags he was lying on had already made deep dents in him and he had rested long enough. The impulse to go on was strong within him. He dragged himself to a half-sitting position and began to regard the dreary landscape about him.

It, like the rest, was gray and formless. Only the wall farther down the road had shape. He dropped his gaze to the stones underneath him and cast about to see whether any of his belongings had dribbled from his pockets to the-pavement. His eye caught the inscription on the stone immediately below. It said, curiously enough, "Take this, it will make you feel better." Just that, and nothing more.

He looked at the next one. It said, "I'm sure she will like it." How odd, he thought. The adjacent four or five had simply this:

149

"Never again!" He let it go. He couldn't hope to understand everything he saw. He got up and strolled on down toward the gates.

They were big ebony gates, each leaf a hundred feet wide and three times as high. At the bottom of one a small door, had been cut, and in it a sliding panel, for all the world like the door of a pre-repeal speakeasy. Above the keystone of the granite arch were cut these words:

"Abandon all hope, ye who enter."

"Huh!" commented Pete Galvan. Then he knocked.

No one answered, so he stepped back a few paces and began tearing up the pavement. It was after about the third or fourth of the paving blocks had bounced off the black doors that the cover to –the peephole slid back and a beady black eye glared out.

"Knock that off!" came a snarling, screeching voice. But on the instant its tone changed to jubilation. Galvan saw the eye disappear and at the same time heard:

"Hey, fellows, what do you think? A customer! Whee!"

There was a rattle of chains, and the small door stood open. Galvan at once pushed on in.

He was considerably startled by his reception. It was hearty, but brief.

He was hardly inside the place than hundreds of little red imps-rushed him, abandoning their card and crap games. The hellions were none of them over four feet high, and all wore stubby little horns like those of a bull yearling. The tiny, ruddy devils were also equipped with venomous, barbed tails which they lashed furiously all the time. Galvan would have been completely bowled over by them, despite their small, size, if it had not been that they rushed him from all sides at once.

"He's mine, I saw him first!" was what they were yelling.

But just then a superior demon of some sort made his appearance. - He, unlike the imps, was quite tall and had a set of really fearsome horns. He carried a long blacksnake whip, with which, in conjunction with his tail, he promptly began lashing the howling little fiends.

"Scat!" he hissed. "Back — all of you — or I'll take you off the bench and put you back on Cave –Relief." He planted a sharp, cloven hoof squarely in the stern sheets of one and drew an ear-splitting yowl. Then he jerked a nod toward Galvan. "Come into the office. Let's see what you rate

Galvan followed stolidly into a room let into the right-hand tower flanking the gates. The demon sat down on a handy potbellied cast-iron stove that was gleaming ruddily, and began inspecting the grime under his hideous talons. Behind a desk sat a sour-looking and very bedraggled angel.

"Name and denomination?"she asked, acidly, poising a quill pen.

"Galvan, Pete. None," he answered categorically. Then, "Say, what's going on? Where in Hell am I?"

"At the gate, dumbbell," spoke up the demon, shifting his seat slightly. The hair on his goat's-thighs was beginning to smoke. It smelled abominably. "Where else in Hell did you think?"

"But I don't believe in Hell," protested Galvan.

"Oh, yeah?" said the demon, resuming his manicure.

"Silence!" snorted the angel, crossly. She was jabbing a buzzer. In a moment an imp came, capering about and making absurd faces.

"Get me file Number KF-2,008- 335," she snapped. "And ask Mortality whether they have anything on a P. Galvan, and if so, why they didn't notify me. We could have had the quarantine furnace lit off."

"Yessum," said the imp, and turned a back -handspring out the door.

"Not for us," she announced, disgustedly, after a cursory study of the asbestos-bound dossier the little hellion brought back with him. "He's not a Methodist, or a Baptist, or anything. He's not even dead! Belongs in Psychopathic, I guess."

"Nuts," remarked the demon. He spat viciously at a rat that had just nosed into the room. The rat scampered back into its hole with smoking fur, and there was a faint aroma of vitriol in the office. "Not a damned customer in months," he bemoaned.

151

"You are being redundant again, Meroz," she rebuked him, primly. "What other kind of customer could you get?"

"All right, *all* right," replied Meroz, testily. "Well, what do I do with the gink? He can't go back, and if we send him on by himself as likely as not that W.P.A. gang in mid-Gehenna would grab him and go to work on him. Then there would be Hell to pay —"

"Oh, those unemployed wraith producers," she admitted reluctantly and with obvious annoyance, "you're right, Meroz —"

"Ha!" snorted he, ejecting two slim clouds of smoke from his shiny vermilion nostrils. "So after eighty-seven millennia of nagging, Eli Meroz is right once, huh? Think of that!"

The Deputy Recording Angel bit her lip. It was a regrettable slip.

"I mean," she hastened to say, still flustered, "that we can't afford to have any more jurisdictional disputes. After that last case the Council of Interallied Hells —"

"Yeah, I know," yawned Meroz, "but I'm asking you — what am *I* supposed to do? This bozo shows up here and some nitwit lets him in. Now *I'm* stuck."

"I know!" she cried. "You can escort him across. I'll make out a passport for him and you can get a receipt from the psychos." She reached for a sheet of blank asbestos.

"You could scratch it on a sheet of ice just as well," observed the demon with heavy sarcasm. He sighed wearily. Hell was not what it used to be.

"Galvan, Pete — U.S.A. — Earth — Solar System," she wrote, "Galorbian Galaxy — Subcluster 456 — Major cluster 1,009 — Universe 8,876,901 — Oh, bother the rest of it. *They'll* know."

She wrote some more. Then she affixed the Great Seal of Hell and under the stamped name of Satan, Imperator, she scribbled her initials.

"And here's the receipt," she added. "Delivered in good condition the soul —"

"I haven't got a soul," said Galvan, sullenly.

" — the soul of one Pete Galvan," she went on serenely, "a Class D sinner."

"Class D?" demanded Galvan, angry now. "Is that the best I get? After all the booze I've drunk and —"

"Come along," said Meroz, taking a couple of turns around his gesticulating arm with his tail. "You rate the D for vanity — otherwise you'd cop no more'n a G or H. You gotta be really tough to get up in the pictures in this place. Some day you might read 'Tomlinson'."

The road inside was just as dreary as that outside the big black gate. On every side was the same monotonous gray landscape, broken only by the profile of ugly black dikes. Overhead was a lifeless pall, more like the roof of a vast, unlit cavern than a sky. The only hellish touch was the whiff of sulfur dioxide that Galvan scented once in a while. On the horizon, far off to the left, was a single spot of light. That was the ruddy glow on the underside of some low-hanging smoke that seemed to indicate a minor conflagration beneath.

Meroz, who had walked this far in silence, gestured toward the glow with his remarkably flexible tail.

"That," he said, moodily, "is the only job we've had this year. A train hit a bus in the Ozarks, and there were a lot of people in it — coming back from a revival meeting."

"Hillbillies," said Galvan, scornfully.

"Yeah," grinned the demon, "but they look good to us. They believe in us. It helped a lot with the unemployment situation. We're practically shut down now, you know."

"I don't get it," said Galvan, ducking and striking at something that had just pinged down and hit him in the back of the neck. He fished out a bit of brown string and threw it away. "I thought you did your stuff for all eternity. What's the line about the 'fire that is never quenched' or something like that? How about the ten billion dead sinners that did believe in you? Awk!"

Something stung him on the cheek, then fell to his lapel, where it stuck. He flicked it off, it was another string — a black one this time.

"Oh, those? They're still going strong. It's this Billy Sunday Wing that's so hard hit. It's the same old story — overexpansion. You see, during that wonderful war you put on to end war there was a great revival of the, old-school hell-fire and damnation brand of religion. The Stokes trial may have helped, too, though some of us think the other way. Anyhow, we built this wing. Now look at it. Thousands of square miles of brimstone lakes and not a pound of sulfur has been burned in more than one or two percent of 'em."

"It don't add up," objected Galvan, doing a little mental arithmetic. "You made a crack back there about a lot of millennia. How do you fit that into a quarter of a century?"

"Oh, me ?" the demon said. "That's easy. You see, His Majesty knew I was a very earnest tormentor and was already at the top of the imp classes. He promoted me to Demon, Second Class and transferred me here to handle the gate detail. I jumped at it. How was I to know the place was going to be a flop?"

He paused in his stride and produced a flask from somewhere — probably a kangaroo pouch, for the fellow wore no clothes.

"Have a slug?" he offered, hospitably. "It's Nitric, C.P. — a lot better than issue vitriol."

"Thanks, no," said Galvan, sniffing. The demon took a long pull and vented a grateful hiss.

Galvan winced again as a shiny object bounced off his forehead. He stooped and picked it up. It was a gilt collar button, and had evidently been stepped on. He tossed it away, wondering where it had come from, but Meroz, bucked up by his liquor, was talking again.

"Well, to make a long story short, Old Nick had to establish Relief —"

"In 1920 or so?"

"Yes — way back there. He's very proud of it. It's his own invention, you see, and quite appropriate to the locality. It appears he'd been keeping books on us all along, and everybody knows we are not exactly saints. So first there was Cave Relief, then came the W.P.A. —"

"That sounds familiar."

"Really? Wraith Prodders Aid is the full of it. Nine tenths of our work is sticking the sinners with pitchforks, as you probably know. Nowadays the old boy keeps 'em busy — well, *reasonably* busy — cleaning up the grounds —"

Blam! A complete 1918 model tin lizzy struck the road not ten yards in front of them and disintegrated into flying fragments of cast iron. It must have fallen from a great height.

" — just such stuff as that," went on the demon serenely, "only it's mostly little things — half strings with knots in 'em and such trash."

"Where," Galvan wanted to know, "does the stuff come from?"

"I'll bite," said the demon, "where does it come from? You know the habits of the living better'n I do. All we know is that it just shows up. It's mostly junk, but why do they send it here?"

Galvan enlightened him.

"I'm damned," was all Meroz could say.

Miles farther on they could hear ribald singing ahead. As they came closer they could see a string of trucks going by on a crossroad. By then the dull-red reflection on the horizon was abreast of them.

The truck's were piled high with lemon-colored sulfur, and on the top of each truck there sat a group of wild imps, waving tridents and singing lustily. Upon sighting Galvan they broke into a string of invective that would have delighted and astonished an old bos'n. But after a sharp snarl from Meroz they cut that out and returned to their singing.

"The next shift going over to No. 16 — that's where the Arkansas hillbillies are. That job took quite a lot of 'em off relief, what with the loaders and the brimstone haulers and three shifts of prodders. Besides those you've got to figure two blacksmiths on the job all the time —"

"Blacksmiths?"

"Yeah. Those prongs melt down. They have to weld new ones on every hour or so. Of course, they could throw the shafts away and simply use new ones — Satan knows there are stacks enough of them around, rusting — only" — wistfully —"business *might* pick up."

Eventually they came to the other side. There was another wall, but not so high. In it was set a moderately small gate, with ornamental bronze doors. The demon led the way on up to it and stopped.

"End of the line," he said. "Here's where you get off."

Pete Galvan had-passed through two gates of Hell already with the minimum of emotion, but as he stared at this one something flopped inside his viscera and turned clean over. It was with a definite catch of the breath that he read the inscription over the door. It was:

Welcome, Petie!

A bronze plate beside it carried further interesting news. The first two lines read:

Marantha Middlebrook,
Architect and Donor
Anna Middlebrook Galvin,
Assistant and Co-donor

Below was this information :

Messrs. Freud, Jung and Adler, Consultant Soul Engineers, have inspected and mapped this place.

"Well, well," said Meroz, cheerfully, reading over Galvan's shoulder. "Look who I've been with all this time. A guy with a private, personal Hell, no less. Unholy Beelzebub! It must be something to work in a joint like that."

He suddenly sprouted a pair of flapping bat's wings ending five feet above his head in curving clawed finials.

"But then," he added, "this new fangled stuff is out of my line. S'long, kid, and take it easy. It's the first million years that are the hardest."

With that Meroz polished off another swig of his bonded Nitric and swirled upward and off with a heavy flapping of wings. Pete Galvan watched him go with considerable regret. Then he turned and walked slowly toward the door. Those inscriptions had worried him a lot. For Marantha Middlebrook was his maternal grandmother, and she had died before he was born. Why should she have designed a Hell for him And yet more mysteriously, why should the other one — Anna, his Mother? And then be saw that the door was ornamented with bas-relief.

The left leaf carried a representation of a beetling, overhanging cliff with a narrow path winding along the face of it supported by jutting ledges. In the canyon below twisty things were intertwined — snakes or giant worms, they might be either. The right-hand panel was covered with diminutive figures, some running about frenziedly with hands clapped to the ears. Other. agonized ones were clawing at the smooth inner sides of eggs that seemed to surround them. And as Galvan looked wonderingly at the designs, the doors opened smoothly and quietly of their own accord. On the other side was — blackness, velvety utter blackness. There was no one, either human or diabolical, in sight. The doors, apparently, had opened of their own accord.

Like a somnambulist, Pete Galvan marched straight ahead into the, darkness, and did not notice that the doors folded shut behind him as he did.

It was not until he came up against a wall of cold, hard granite that he looked backward and realized that the dark was all about him. He put out a hand to one side. There was another dripping granite wall; on the other side the same thing, beaded with cold moisture. Galvan experienced a momentary fright — he had walked into a blind alley. He took three hasty steps back — he wanted to get out badly; he had suddenly remembered that Meroz was to get a receipt signed by somebody and had gone off without it. He must call him back. The he came up against a fourth wall, squarely trapping him.

Cold sweat trickled down his taut face. Something brushed his hair and an upflung hand scraped its knuckles against more damp granite, close overhead this time. Galvan lost all control and screamed.   Shrieking, he beat wildly against the hard barriers that shut him in. He felt as if he was suffocating and that his life depended upon his being let out on the instant.

For a long-time he kept that up, until he fell panting and sobbing to the stony floor, weak and exhausted.

157

He must have slept, or fainted. For when he returned to consciousness his environment was so different he knew that the change could not have taken place without his being aware of it. A smooth surface bore down on him from above, barely touching the point of his hose, his chest and the tips• of his toes. He tried to rise, but could not. He tried to raise his hands, but could not. They were at his sides, and the pressure against his knuckles told him there were also boards penning him in laterally. Then the awful truth burst upon him. It was a coffin he was in. He was buried alive!

Again he struggled for breath — the last one, it seemed to be. Yet in his frenzy of despair he screamed without restraint until he could scream no more but lay quivering with helpless panic. In time he lapsed into a state of dull apathy, too weak and hopeless to struggle more. And that was when he noticed the cold draft of air blowing down upon his shoulders.

He pulled himself together and tried to think the thing through. It must be that if he was in a coffin, it was one wit open ends. Inch by inch he wriggled upward. And inch by inch he made progress. There was nothing to stop him. He continued, and after he had gone a long foot or so, he was aware there was a little more room around him. A few yards more and there was some gray light, enough to let him see he was in a narrow tunnel. At the end of what could have been an hour he sighted the full light of day — a circular blob of bright sunshine shining into his rabbit warren. He could roll over then and make the rest of the way on hands and knees.

Once he was outside in the blessed space and light, he drew a deep breath and rested, reproaching himself for his mad panic. If he had not let the shutting of the door upset him, he would no doubt have found the tight tunnel and escaped through it long before. In fainting he had doubtless fallen directly before it, and later, in his restless coma, he must have wriggled well into it. So in that manner, strengthened by the glorious sunlit and unlimited space, he laughed the incident off. Now he could get about his business of exploring this Hell his forbears had so kindly bequeathed him. What had he to fear? Had he not already passed the Hells devised by twenty-five centuries of ancestors and been none the worse for it? He began to take stock of this sunlit place where he was.

He appeared to be on a broad stone platform at the base of a high cliff. He got up and walked out a little way from the cliff so he could look up at it better. But to his surprise the flat rock was not so wide as he though, nor so flat. A few paces away it began to slope down, until it took such a sharp angle that he doubted his footing. Then to his horror he observed that it came to an end anther yard below him. And beyond that was nothing — nothing but empty air. Through the violet haze of great distance he could just make out another mountain range on the other side of the incredibly deep valley that lay between the one he was on and it. He stood precariously on the brink of a precipice of unguessable height. And at that moment of horrid realization, his foot slipped!

Galvan fell flat on his face and clung for a while with outstretched hand to the slippery rock. This time he resolutely fought off panic, but he did not dare move until he was quite sure of the grip on himself. When that time came he crawled cautiously upward until he was once more on level stone.

It was clear that he was on the shoulder of a mountain and the ledge he was on curved both ways out of sight. Which led up and which down he could only guess and he told himself it did not matter, though, all things considered, he preferred to go down. But the nature of the ledge soon settled that problem for him. To the left, after about forty steps, he found that I narrowed to nothing. He retraced his steps and took the other trail. For a well-defined path he noticed now, led from the mouth of the cavern he had come out of.

The ledge narrowed in that direction, too, but not unbearably. At the end of some minutes he found himself walking along the ledge that was still all of four feet wide, and he took the precaution to keep his eyes glued to the path immediately in advance of his feet. He dared not so much as glance over the edge, for the earlier glimpse of that sheer drop of many thousands of feet had frozen him to the marrow and covered him with goose pimples. Nor did he neglect to keep his left hand trailing against the cliff wall, caressing it with his fingertips as he went along. He was hideously uncomfortable, nevertheless, and it was only the occasional sight of old footprints in sandy patches that reassured him sufficiently to keep him going. If others had come this way, he could make it too, he told himself frantically.

It was when the ledge and cliff turned from stone to clay that cold fear again beset him. His first warning was when his trailing fingers struck an embedded stone and clung to it a moment while he debated exactly where he was going to place his foremost foot next. As he relinquished his hold upon the stone, it became dislodged and thundered down the face of the precipice in the vanguard of an avalanche of loose earth that tumbled down in the wake of it. Galvan gasped and flattened himself against the vertical clay bank as the torrent of dirt and gravel roared past him. When the dust had dissipated, he stared with bulging eyes at the path he had just come over. It was not there! Behind him there was only a crumbly, vertical wall down which a few belated pebbles were bounding. Faint sounds from below told him that the avalanche was still crashing earthward, despite its already long fall.

Pete Galvan's skin was white as snow and cold as he stood there against the treacherous wall of clay. He was afraid to make a movement, yet he knew he dared not stay. For the path beneath him, disturbed by the recent dirt fall, was sloughing away by inches and sliding into the depths.

With a heart thumping like a pounded tympanum, he forced himself to edge along. A little further he discovered to his horror that the path was not only narrower — something less than a yard — and softer, but blocked here and there by obstacles. He could step over most of them, but eventually he came to one that was too big. It was a boulder that stood waist high, and he wondered how it got there, for the cliff above hung out over him like a sidewalk awning.

He paused and studied that boulder for a long time. He must pass it, but how? It touched the bank on the one hand and protruded over the precipice's edge on the other. It was too high to step over, and the path beyond was too unstable to sustain a body landing from a jump. There was but one course left. He must climb up onto it, then down again.

Pete Galvan bent over and placed both hands atop the boulder, then brought up a wobbly knee. The rock trembled a little and Pete froze in his awkward position. But the rock did not roll, so he transferred a few more pounds of his weight to the pressure of his hands and the advanced knee. Again the rock, trembled, but did not roll. With the courage of despair Galvan put his full weight upon it and drew up the idle leg. The boulder teetered wildly, dust rose from the canyon as the rotten soil below the boulder began shedding itself away. The boulder turned sluggishly, then like a startled hare it bounded downward, tons of dry clay tumbling after it.

Galvan leaped wildly forward as he felt the rock turn beneath him. His heels struck the path beyond, and it in turn crumpled beneath him and fell rumbling down the cliffside. He never knew how his hand managed to connect with that root but it did. An instant later he was dangling over the chasm, clinging to a gnarled tree root that stuck out of the face of the cliff.

To his tortured mind it was all of a century that he hung there expecting every moment to have to let go and drop. Though his ,eyes were firmly shut, the bare thought of the bottomless abyss under him was vastly more painful than his cramped hand and the 'agonized arm muscles. He knew that the end was at hand, yet he clung on, to the last eternal moment. And then, just as sheer horror was about to turn to black and irrevocable despair, he made that last superhuman effort. Summoning up his last ounce of reserve, he twisted and grabbed with the other hand. It, too, caught a root. He had a respite!

That trip up the face of the crumbling cliff was as arduous a one as man ever made, but he made it. Though he was winded and weak as a baby, he did not cease his exertions until he had placed a long distance between himself and the maddening brink. He found a spot among some trees on top of that tableland and threw himself down in the grass. He tried to sleep.

A tree nearby creaked. Yes, *creaked*. He thought at first it was a rocking chair with a loose rail, then it seemed that it was a door with unoiled hinges. He listened to its rhythm with growing disgust, but hardly ,had he adapted his ears to it than the damnable thing changed its rhythm. It not only dropped one creak from the series, but the next three were irregularly spaced. Then it took up another rhythm.

More sounds were added — the zooming buzz of some wheeling insect, now blatant, now requiring straining ears to keep up with it. Then came a pattering as of naked feet on concrete, a noise that meant nothing to him, but annoyed him intensely; last of all, the raucous "caws" of a race of cynically derisive birds. Galvan stood it as long as he could, then rose and fled the place. A flock of carrion birds he had not noticed earlier rose as he did and sailed in ever-widening circles above him, swooping now and then as if to bite at him.

Galvan ran on, until he could run no more. Then he stopped, panting. His feet were sore and cut and he wondered how he had become unshod. He had quite forgotten that he had thrown his shoes away while on the slippery ledge. But he wished now he had not, for his feet felt indescribably uncomfortable. They were not only hurt from the running, but some nasty, oozy stuff had stuck to them and was squeezing up between his toes. He looked down at them, wishing for water with which to wash them.

Despite the other horrors of this inherited Hell, he knew when he looked at those feet that he had attained the ultimate. He was standing barefooted in two inches of blended caterpillars and groveling, blind worms, and as far as the eye could reach the ground was covered with them. The vile creatures slithered and crawled, working over and under each other, and both varieties trailed a repulsive slime. But the most sickening detail was that fully half the caterpillars were covered with ulcerated knobs that grew and grew until they burst with a faint plop, throwing gouts of dirty orange liquid in every direction. And wherever those drops of infection struck, fresh ulcers grew. Galvan's own legs were speckled halfway to the knees with dirty orange droplets, and those spots itched unbearably. He watched wild-eyed as the ulcers formed.

He paused in his wild race away just once. That was in a sand spot not quite covered by the odious caterpillars. The violent rubbing with sand that he gave his rotting flesh was only an added pain. Then he knew that sand, or even water, if he had it, would not be enough. He must get somewhere where more drastic treatment — amputation, perhaps — was available, for he could not bear the thought of having those ulcers climb higher than they were already — at midthigh.

He charged on, trampling the squirming, hateful pests underfoot, not caring any longer where he went, so long as it was away from those diseased foul worms. He did not see the edge of the cliff until he was at it. Nothing could check the momentum of his plunge.

Down, down he went, turning slowly over and over as he fell, now glimpsing blue sky and bright sun, now the gaunt face of the unstable cliff, now the canyon bottom rushing up to smite him. He set his teeth and waited — waited for that terrible final impact that would blot out all the other horrors of this Hell.

When it did come it was a blessed relief. He struck headfirst and there was one sharp crack — hardly worse than an ordinary knockout. There was a brief explosion of light, and he slipped into cool darkness.

"He'll do now," Pete heard a feminine voice say, and he felt cool fingers relinquish his wrist after placing it back on the bed. He opened his eyes to see a girl in nurse's uniform and two white-smocked men standing looking at him.

"A-are you demons, too?" Galvan stammered, looking at them with one eye. The bandage over his head covered one. The question seemed to him to be a perfectly logical one. If, as the inscription on the gate suggested, this was his own private and personal Hell, doctors would do as well as anything for tormentors. He couldn't forget a curtain dentist.

One of the doctors laughed. "That is a matter of opinion, sonny. But you'd better knock off going around breaking up religious services or you'll have some real demons after you. The way those Holy Sons and Daughters of the Pentecost went after you when you tried to bust up their service should have taught you that. Do you remember? You started a free-for-all and they crowned you and tossed you out on your ear."

"I don't remember nothing since I washed my face in that River Lethe," mumbled Pete Galvan, sullenly.

The first doctor looked at the second one quizzically. The other nodded.

"It's all in here," he said, tapping a roll of shorthand-covered sheets of paper. "He was delirious most of the night. The nurse on duty recorded the high spots. Most of it is commonplace enough, but what interests me in the case is that it was his own unprompted mind that designed that last gate — especially . . . uh . . . the inscription

163

over it. It is little mysteries like that that make my job fascinating at tines."

"Oh. You mean the stuff about his mother and grandmother?"

"Exactly. Of course, we already had a history of dipsomania, and in these ravings we get a glimpse of demonomania, claustrophobia, acrophobia and mysophobia, but those, as you know, are run-of-the-mine symptoms. But he also rather clearly indicates that his grandmother was one of the old orthodox with an active New England conscience. I suspect his mother tried to do without any. He inherited the inevitable conflicts and no doubt added a few embellishments of his own —"

"Say, doc," interrupted Pete Galvan, bored with talk that had nothing to do with him that he could see, "did you know I've been to Hell and back? And what's more, it's a private, special Hell built just for me? Gee, ain't that something!"

But the doctor was looking at him disapprovingly.

"Oh, you don't believe it, huh?"

"Yes, son, I do. You were in Hell the live-long night."

Train for Flushing

What if the Flying Dutchman were in command of a subway train instead of a ship?

They ought never to have hired that man. Even the most stupid of personnel managers should have seen at a glance that he was mad. Perhaps it is too much to expect such efficiency these days — in *my* time a thing like this could not have happened. They would have known the fellow was under a curse! It only shows what the world has come to. But I can tell you that if we ever get off this crazy runaway car, I intend to turn the Interboro wrong-side out. They needn't think because I am an old man and retired that I am a nobody they can push around. My son Henry, the lawyer one, will build a fire under them — he knows people in this town.

"And I am not the only victim of the maniac. There is a pleasant, elderly woman here in the car with me. She was much frightened at first, but she had recognized me for a solid man, and now she stays close to me all the time. She is a Mrs. Herrick, and a quite nice woman. It was her idea that I write this down — it will help us refresh our memories when we come to testify.

"Just at the moment, we are speeding atrociously *downtown* along the Seventh Avenue line of the subway — but we are on the *uptown* express track! The first few times we tore through those other trains it was terrible — I thought we were sure to be killed — and even if we were not, I have to think of my heart. Dr. Steinback told me only last week how careful I should be. Mrs. Herrick has been very brave about it, but it is a scandalous thing to subject anyone to, above all such a kindly little person.

165

"The madman who seems to be directing us (if charging wildly up and down these tracks implies *direction*), is now looking out the front door, staring horribly at the gloom rushing at us. He is a big man and heavy-set, very weathered and tough-looking. I am nearing eighty and slight.

"There is nothing I can do but wait for the final crash; for crash we must, sooner or later, unless some Interboro official has brains enough to shut off the current to stop us. If *he* escapes the crash, the police will know him by his heavy red beard and tattooing on the backs of his hands. The beard is square-cut and there cannot be another one like it in all New York.

"But I notice I have failed to put down how this insane ride began. My granddaughter, Mrs. Charles L. Terneck, wanted me to see the World's Fair, and was to come in from Great Neck and meet me at the subway station. I will say that she insisted someone come with me, but I can take care of myself — I always have — even if my eyes and ears are not what they used to be.

The train was crowded, but somebody gave me a seat in a corner. Just before we reached the stop, the woman next to me, this Mrs. Herrick, had asked if I knew how to get to Whitestone from Flushing. It was while I was telling her what I knew about the busses, that the train stopped and let everybody off the car but us. I was somewhat irritated at missing the station, but knew that all I had to do was stay on the car, go to Flushing and return. It was then that the maniac guard came in and behaved so queerly.

"This car was the last one in the train, and the guard had been standing where he belongs, on the platform. But he came into the car, walking with a curious rolling walk (but I do not mean to imply he was drunk, for I do not think so) and his manner was what you might call masterful, almost overbearing. He stopped at the middle door and looked very intensely out to the north, at the sound.

"'*That* is not the Scheldt!' he called out, angrily, with a thick, foreign accent, and then he said 'Bah!' loudly, in a tone of disgusted disillusionment.

"He seemed of a sudden to fly into a great fury. The train was just making its stop at the end of the line, in Flushing. He rushed to the forward platform and somehow broke the coupling. At the same moment, the car began running backward along the track by which we had come. There was no chance for us to get off, even if we had been young and active. The doors were not opened, it happened so quickly.

"Then he came into the car, muttering to himself. His eye caught the sign of painted tin they put in the windows to show the destination of the trains. He snatched the plate lettered 'Flushing' and tore it to bits with his rough hands, as if it had been cardboard, throwing the pieces down and stamping on them.

"'That is not Flushing. Not *my* Flushing — not *Vlissingen!* But I will find it. I will go there, and not all the devils in Hell nor all the angels in Heaven shall stop me!'

"He glowered at us, beating his breast with his clenched fists, as if angry and resentful at us for having deceived him in some manner. It was then that Mrs. Herrick stooped over and took my hand. We had gotten up close to the door to step out at the World's Fair station, but the car did not stop. It continued its wild career straight on, at dizzy speed.

"'*Rugwaartsch!*' he shouted, or something equally unintelligible. '*Back* I must go, like always, but yet will find my Vlissingen!'

"Then followed the horror of pitching headlong into those trains! The first one we saw coming, Mrs. Herrick screamed. I put my arm around her and braced myself as best I could with my cane. But there was no crash, just a blinding succession of lights and colors, in quick winks. We seemed to go straight through that train, from end to end, at lightning speed, but there was not even a jar. I do not understand that, for I saw it coming, clearly. Since, there have been many others. I have lost count now, we meet so many, and swing from one track to another so giddily at the end of runs.

"But we have learned, Mrs. Herrick and I, not to dread the collisions — or say, passage — so much. We are more afraid of what the bearded ruffian who dominates this car will do next — surely we cannot go on this way much longer, it has already been many, many hours. I cannot comprehend why the stupid people who run the Interboro do not do something to stop us, so that the police could subdue this maniac and I can have Henry take me to the District Attorney."

* * *

So read the first few pages of the notebook turned over to me by the Missing Persons Bureau. Neither Mrs. Herrick, nor Mr. Dennison, whose handwriting it is, has been found yet, nor the guard he mentions. In contradiction, the Interboro insists no guard employed by them is unaccounted for, and further, that they never had had a man of the above description on their payrolls.

On the other hand, they have as yet produced no satisfactory explanation of how the car broke loose from the train at Flushing.

I agree with the police that this notebook contains matter that may have some bearing on the disappearances of these two unfortunate citizens; yet here in the Psychiatric Clinic we are by no means agreed as to the interpretation of this provocative and baffling diary.

The portion I have just quoted was written with a fountain pen in a crabbed, tremulous hand, quite exactly corresponding to the latest examples of old Mr. Dennison's writing. Then we find a score or more of pages torn out, and a resumption of the record in indelible pencil. The handwriting here is considerably stronger and more assured, yet unmistakably that of the same person. Farther on, there are other places where pages have been torn from the book, and evidence that the journal was but intermittently kept. I quote now all that is legible of the remainder of it.

Judging by the alternations of the cold and hot seasons, we have now been on this weird and pointless journey for more than ten years. Oddly enough, we do not suffer physically, although the interminable rushing up and down these caverns under the streets becomes boring. The ordinary wants of the body are strangely absent, or dulled. We sense heat and cold, for example, but do not find their extremes particularly uncomfortable, while food has become an item of far distant memory. I imagine, though, we must sleep a good deal.

"The guard has very little to do with us, ignoring us most of the time as if we did not exist. He spends his days sitting brooding at the far end of the car, staring at the floor, mumbling in his wild, red beard. On other days he will get up and peer fixedly ahead, as if seeking something. Again, he will pace the aisle in obvious anguish, flinging his outlandish curses over his shoulder as he goes. '*Verdoemd*' and '*verwenscht*' are the commonest ones — we have learned to recognize them — and he tears his hair in frenzy whenever he pronounces them. His name, he says, is Van Der Dechen, and we find it politic to call him 'Captain.'

"I have destroyed what I wrote during the early years (all but the account of the very first day); it seems rather querulous and hysterical now. I was not in good health then, I think, but I have improved noticeably here, and that without medical care. Much of my stiffness, due to a recent arthritis, has left me, and I seem to hear better.

"Mrs. Herrick and I have long since become accustomed to our forced companionship, and we have learned much about each other. At first, we both worried a good deal over our families' concern about our absence. But when this odd and purposeless kidnapping occurred, we were already so nearly to the end of life (being of about the same age) that we finally concluded our children and grand-children must have been prepared for our going soon, in any event. It left us only with the problem of enduring the tedium of the interminable rolling through the tubes of the Interboro.

"In the pages I have deleted, I made much of the annoyance we experienced during the early weeks due to flickering through oncoming trains. That soon came to be so commonplace, occurring as it did every few minutes, that it became as unnoticeable as our breathing. As we lost the fear of imminent disaster, our riding became more and more burdensome through the deadly monotony of the tunnels.

"Mrs. Herrick and I diverted ourselves by talking (and to think in my earlier entries in this journal I complained of her garrulousness!) or by trying to guess at what was going on in the city above us by watching the crowds on the station platforms. That is a difficult game, because we are running so swiftly, and there are frequent intervening trains. A thing that has caused us much speculation and discussion is the changing type of advertising on the bill-posters. Nowadays they are featuring the old favorites — many of the newer toothpastes and medicines seem to have been withdrawn. Did they fail, or has a wave of conservative reaction overwhelmed the country?

"Another marvel in the weird life we lead is the juvenescence of our home, the runaway car we are confined to. In spite of its unremitting use, always at top speed, it has become steadily brighter, more new-looking. Today it has the appearance of having been recently delivered from the builders' shops.

I learned half a century ago that having nothing to do, and all the time in the world to do it in, is the surest way to get nothing done. In looking in this book, I find it has been ten years since I made an entry! It is a fair indication of the idle, routine life in this wandering car. The very invariableness of our existence has discouraged keeping notes. But recent developments are beginning to force me to face a situation that has been growing ever more obvious. The cumulative evidence is by now almost overwhelming that this state of ours has a meaning — has an explanation. Yet I dread to think the thing through — to call its name! Because there will be two ways to interpret it. Either it is as I am driven to conclude, or else I...

"I must talk it over frankly with Nellie Herrick. She is remarkably poised and level-headed, and understanding. She and I have matured a delightful friendship.

"What disturbs me more than anything is the trend in advertising. They are selling products again that were popular so long ago that I had actually forgotten them. And the appeals are made in the idiom of years ago. Lately it has been hard to see the posters, the station platforms are so full. In the crowds are many uniforms, soldiers and sailors. We infer from that there is another war — but the awful question is, 'What war?'

"Those are some of the things we can observe in the world over there. In our own little fleeting world, things have developed even more inexplicably. My health and appearance, notably. My hair is no longer white! It is turning dark again in the back, and on top. And the same is true of Nellie's. There are other similar changes for the better. I see much more clearly and my hearing is practically perfect.

"The culmination of these disturbing signals of retrogression has come with the newest posters. It is their appearance that forces me to face the facts. Behind the crowds we glimpse new appeals, many and insistent-'BUY VICTORY LOAN BONDS!' From the number of them to be seen, one would think we were back in the happy days of 1919, when the soldiers were coming home from the World War.

My talk with Nellie has been most comforting and reassuring. It is hardly likely that we should both be insane and have identical symptoms. The inescapable conclusion that I dreaded to put into words is *so* — it must be so. In some unaccountable manner, we are *unliving* life! Time is going backward! '*Rugwaartsch,*' the mad Dutchman said that first day when he turned back from Flushing; 'we will go backward' — to *his* Flushing, the one he knew. Who knows what Flushing he knew? It must be the Flushing of another age, or else why should the deranged wizard (if it is he who has thus reversed time) choose a path through time itself? Helpless, we can only wait and see how far he will take us.

"We are not wholly satisfied with our new theory. Everything does not go backward; otherwise how could it be possible for me to write these lines? I think we are like flies crawling up the walls of an elevator cab while it is in full descent. Their own proper movements, relative to their environment, are upward, but all the while they are being carried relentlessly downward. It is a sobering thought. Yet we are both relieved that we should have been able to speak it. Nellie admits that she has been troubled for some time, hesitating to voice the thought. She called my attention to the subtle way in which our clothing has been changing, an almost imperceptible de-evolution in style.

We are now on the lookout for ways in which to date ourselves in this headlong plunging into the past. Shortly after writing the above, we were favored with one opportunity not to be mistaken. It was the night of the Armistice. What a night in the subway! Then followed, in inverse order, the various issues of the Liberty Bonds. Over forty years ago-counting time both ways, forward, then again backward — *I* was up there, a dollar-a-year man,

171

selling them on the streets. Now we suffer a new anguish, imprisoned down here in this racing subway car. The evidence all around us brings a nostalgia that is almost intolerable. None of us knows how perfect his memory is until it is thus prompted. But we cannot go up there, we can only guess at what is going on above us.

"The realization of what is really happening to us has caused us to be less antagonistic to our conductor. His sullen brooding makes us wonder whether he is not a fellow victim, rather than our abductor, he seems so unaware of us usually. At other times, we regard him as the principal in this drama of the gods and are bewildered at the curious twist of Fate that has entangled us with the destiny of the unhappy Van Der Dechen, for unhappy he certainly is. Our anger at his arrogant behavior has long since died away. We can see that some secret sorrow gnaws continually at his heart.

"'There is *een vloek* over me,' he said gravely, one day, halting unexpectedly before us in the midst of one of his agitated pacings of the aisle. He seemed to be trying to explain — apologize for, if you will — our situation. 'Accursed I am, damned!' He drew a great breath, looking at us appealingly. Then his black mood came back on him with a rush, and he strode away growling mighty Dutch oaths. 'But I will best them — God Himself shall not prevent me — not if it takes all eternity!'

Our orbit is growing more restricted. It is a long time now since we went to Brooklyn, and only the other day we swerved suddenly at Times Square and cut through to Grand Central. Considering this circumstance, the type of car we are in now, and our costumes, we must be in 1905 or thereabouts. That is a year I remember with great vividness. It was the year I first came to New York. I keep speculating on what will become of us. In another year we will have plummeted the full history of the subway. What then? Will that be the end?

"Nellie is the soul of patience. It is a piece of great fortune, a blessing, that since we were doomed to this wild ride, we happened in it together. Our friendship has ripened into a warm affection that lightens the gloom of this tedious wandering.

It must have been last night that we emerged from the caves of Manhattan. Thirty-four years of darkness is ended. We are now out in the country, going west. Our vehicle is not the same, it is an old-fashioned day coach, and ahead is a small locomotive. We cannot see engineer or fireman, but Van Der Dechen frequently ventures across the swaying, open platform and mounts the tender, where he stands firmly with wide-spread legs, scanning the country ahead through an old brass long-glass. His uniform is more nautical than railroadish — it took the sunlight to show that to us. There was always the hint of salt air about him. We should have known who he was from his insistence on being addressed as Captain.

"The outside world is moving backward! When we look closely at the wagons and buggies in the muddy trails alongside the right of way fence, we can see that the horses or mules are walking or running backward. But we pass them so quickly, as a rule, that their real motion is inconspicuous. We are too grateful for the sunshine and the trees after so many years of gloom, to quibble about this topsy-turvy condition.

Five years in the open has taught us much about Nature in reverse. There is not so much difference as one would suppose. It took us a long time to notice that the sun rose in the west and sank in the east. Summer follows winter, as it always has. It was our first spring, or rather, the season that we have come to regard as spring, that we were really disconcerted. The trees were bare, the skies cloudy, and the weather cool. We could not know, at first sight, whether we had emerged into spring or fall.

"The ground was wet, and gradually white patches of snow were forming. Soon, the snow covered everything. The sky darkened and the snow began to flurry, drifting and swirling upward, out of sight. Later we saw the ground covered with dead leaves, so we thought it must be fall. Then a few of the trees were seen to have leaves, then all. Soon the forests were in the full glory of red and brown autumn leaves, but in a few weeks those colors turned gradually through oranges and yellows to dark greens, and we were in full summer. Our 'fall,' which succeeded the summer, was almost normal, except toward the end, when the leaves brightened into paler greens, dwindled little by little to mere buds and then disappeared within the trees.

"The passage of a troop train, its windows crowded with campaign-hatted heads and waving arms tells us another war has begun (or more properly, ended). The soldiers are returning from Cuba. *Our* wars, in this backward way by which we approach and end in anxiety! More nostalgia — I finished that war as a major. I keep looking eagerly at the throngs on the platforms of the railroad stations as we sweep by them, hoping to sight a familiar face among the yellow-legged cavalry. More than eighty years ago it was, as I reckon it, forty years of it spent on the road to senility and another forty back to the prime of life.

"Somewhere among those blue-uniformed veterans am I, in my original phase, I cannot know just where, because my memory is vague as to the dates. I have caught myself entertaining the idea of stopping this giddy flight into the past, of getting out and finding my way to my former home. Only, if I could, I would be creating tremendous problems — there would have to be some sort of mutual accommodation between my *alter ego* and me. It looks impossible, and there are no precedents to guide us.

"Then, all my affairs have become complicated by the existence of Nell. She and I have had many talks about this strange state of affairs, but they are rarely conclusive. I think I must have over-estimated her judgment a little in the beginning. But it really doesn't matter. She has developed into a stunning woman and her quick, ready sympathy makes up for her lack in that direction. I glory particularly in her hair, which she lets down some days. It is thick and long and beautifully wavy, as hair should be. We often sit on the back platform and she allows it to blow free in the breeze, all the time laughing at me because I adore it so.

"Captain Van Der Dechen notices us not at all, unless in scorn. His mind, his whole being, is centered on getting back to Flushing — *his* Flushing, that he calls Vlissingen — wherever that may be in time or space. Well, it appears that he is taking us back, too, but it is backward in time for us. As for him, time seems meaningless. He is unchangeable. Not a single hair of that piratical beard has altered since that far-future day of long ago when he broke our car away from the Interboro train in Queens. Perhaps he suffers

174

from the same sort of unpleasant immortality the mythical Wandering Jew is said to be afflicted with — otherwise why should he complain so bitterly of the curse he says is upon him?

"Nowadays he talks to himself much of the time, mainly about his ship. It is that which he hopes to find since the Flushing beyond New York proved not to be the one he strove for. He says he left it cruising along a rocky coast. He has either forgotten where he left it or it is no longer there, for we have gone to all the coastal points touched by the railroads. Each failure brings fresh storms of rage and blasphemy; not even perpetual frustration seems to abate the man's determination or capacity for fury.

That Dutchman has switched trains on us again! This one hasn't even Pintsch gas, nothing but coal oil. It is smoky and it stinks. The engine is a woodburner with a balloon stack. The sparks are very bad and we cough a lot.

"I went last night when the Dutchman wasn't looking and took a look into the cab of the engine. There is no crew and I found the throttle closed. A few years back that would have struck me as odd, but now I have to accept it. I did mean to stop the train so I could take Nell off, but there is no way to stop it. It just goes along, I don't know how.

"On the way back I met the Dutchman, shouting and swearing the way he does, on the forward platform. I tried to throw him off the train. I am as big and strong as he is and I don't see why I should put up with his overbearing ways. But when I went to grab him, my hands closed right through. The man is not real! It is strange I never noticed that before. Maybe that is why there is no way to stop the train, and why nobody ever seems to notice us. Maybe the train is not real, either. I must look tomorrow and see whether it casts a shadow. Perhaps even *we* are not...

"But Nell is real. I *know* that.

The other night we passed a depot platform where there was a political rally — a torchlight parade. They were carrying banners. 'Garfield for President.' If we are ever to get off this train, we must do it soon.

175

"Nell says no, it would be embarrassing. I try to talk seriously to her about us, but she just laughs and kisses me and says let well enough alone. I wouldn't mind starting life over again, even if these towns do look pretty rough. But Nell says that she was brought up on a Kansas farm by a step-mother and she would rather go on to the end and vanish, if need be, than go back to it.

"That thing about the end troubles me a lot, and I wish she wouldn't keep mentioning it. It was only lately that I thought about it much, and it worries me more than death ever did in the old days. *We know when it will be*! 1860 for me — on the third day of August. The last ten years will be terrible — getting smaller, weaker, more helpless all the time, and winding up as a messy, squally baby. Why, that means I have only about ten more years that are fit to live; when I was this young before, I had a lifetime ahead. It's not right! And now *she* has made a silly little vow — 'Until birth do us part!' — and made me say it with her!

It is too crowded in here, and it jolts awfully. Nell and I are cooped up in the front seats and the Captain stays in the back part — the quarterdeck, he calls it. Sometimes he opens the door and climbs up into the driver's seat. There is no driver, but we have a four-horse team and they gallop all the time, day and night. The Captain says we must use a stagecoach, because he has tried all the railroad tracks and none of them is right. He wants to get back to the sea he came from and to his ship. He is not afraid that it has been stolen, for he says most men are afraid of it — it is a haunted ship, it appears, and brings bad luck.

"We passed two men on horses this morning. One was going our way and met the other coming. The other fellow stopped him and I heard him holler, 'They killed Custer and all his men!' and the man that was going the same way we were said, 'The bloodthirsty heathens! I'm a-going to jine!'

Nellie cries a lot. She's afraid of Indians. I'm not afraid of Indians. I would like to see one.

"I wish it was a boy with me, instead of this little girl. Then we could do something. All she wants to do is play with that fool dolly. We could make some bows and arrows and shoot at the buffaloes, but she says that is wicked.

"I tried to get the Captain to talk to me, but he won't. He just laughed and laughed, and said,

"'*Een tijd kiezan voor — op schip*!'

"That made me mad, talking crazy talk like that, and I told him so.

"'Time!' he bellows, laughing like everything.' 'Twill all be right in time!' And he looks hard at me, showing his big teeth in his beard. 'Four — five — six hundred years — more — it is nothing. I have all eternity! But one more on my ship, I will get there. I have sworn it! You come with me and I will show you the sea — the great Indian Sea behind the Cape of Good Hope. Then some day, if those accursed head winds abate, I will take you home with me to Flushing. That I will, though the Devil himself, or all the — ' And then he went off to cursing and swearing the way he always does in his crazy Dutchman's talk.

Nellie is mean to me. She is too bossy. She says she will not play unless I write in the book. She says I am supposed to write something in the book every day. There is not anything to put in the book. Same old stagecoach. Same old Captain. Same old everything. I do not like the Captain. He is crazy. In the night-time he points at the stars shining through the roof of the coach and laughs and laughs. Then he gets mad, and swears and curses something awful. When I get big again, I am going to kill him — I wish we could get away — I am afraid — it would be nice if we could find mamma —"

This terminates the legible part of the notebook. All of the writing purporting to have been done in the stagecoach is shaky, and the letters are much larger than earlier in the script. The rest of the contents is infantile scribblings, or grotesque childish drawings. Some of them show feathered Indians drawing bows and shooting arrows. The very last one seems to represent a straight up and down cliff with wiggly lines at the bottom to suggest waves, and off a little way is a crude drawing of a galleon or other antique ship.

This notebook, together with Mr. Dennison's hat and cane and Mrs. Herrick's handbag, were found in the derailed car that broke away from the Flushing train and plunged off the track into the Meadows. The police are still maintaining a perfunctory hunt for the two missing persons, but I think the fact they brought this journal to us clearly indicates they consider the search hopeless. Personally, I really do not see of what help these notes can be. I fear that by now Mr. Dennison and Mrs. Herrick are quite inaccessible.

The Goddess' Legacy

When man bites dog, they say, that's news. It's news, too, when a waiter tips his customer. I saw that done not long ago — quite surreptitiously to be sure — in the dining room of the Hotel Angleterre, in Athens. To say that I was amazed would be to put it mildly, for I knew both men and the thing was impossible. It was not that Herr Scheer took the gold — for gold it was, strangely enough — but that Mike Pappadopoulos should have offered it. I would have thought that Mike would let himself be torn apart by wild horses before trafficking with the enemy. But there it was; I couldn't blink it. The fierce old patriot must have broken under the strain of sustained tyranny. No other explanation of the bribe was tenable. For bribe I took it to be, and wondered what extremity had driven the old Greek to the necessity of giving it.

The part played by Herr Scheer in the furtive transaction was no mystery at all. He was simply a murderous, blood-sucking leech of the type all too frequent in Europe these days. I had known him for some time as the traveling representative of an optical house in Berlin and as such had often had business dealings with him. But with the coming of the troops of the occupation forces he promptly dropped the mask and showed himself in his true colors. Anton Scheer had been the advance man of the dreaded Gestapo. It was from his long-prepared secret lists that hundreds of victims for arrest and spoilation were selected, and from those same lists that the few Hellenic Quislings were appointed to puppet administrative posts. Now that he was the resident chief of Hitler's secret operatives, his cruelty and rapacity knew no bounds. It was also common knowledge that his zeal for his beloved Fuehrer and Fatherland was

179

not untinged by keen self-interest. In other words, Herr Scheer could be "had." Enough money, discreetly conveyed, would unlock the tightest prison gates.

No, the sight of Scheer's curt nod and the clutching hand below the table top was no surprise to me. It was in character. My astonishment arose from the fact that old Mike had paid.

The first time I ever saw Mike was on the Acropolis one bright moonlight night about four years ago — shortly after my company had made me their Near Eastern manager with headquarters at Athens. As any American would have done, I visited the ancient rock at the first opportunity and promptly fell under the spell of the magnificent ruins atop it. Thereafter I became a frequent visitor, and soon learned that the best condition under which to view the old temples was when the moon was up. On such nights the shattered colonnades of the Parthenon stand forth in all their noble grandeur, the chips and scars mercifully softened by the silvery light. And it was on such a night that Mike first spoke to me.

I was prowling about in the ruined temple of Athena when I came upon him. He was standing rigid, as if in a trance, gazing fixedly upward into nothingness. It was in the naos, or inner sanctum, and where he stood was before the spot where tradition had it Phidias' superb ivory and gold figure of the goddess once sat enthroned. By the mild light of the moon I could see that there were several baskets on the pavement at his feet and they seemed to be filled with olives. There was a tray, too, in which were folded cloths of what I took to be embroideries. I paused and looked at him a moment, but in his rapt state he did not notice me. I was but a few feet from him, but not wishing to disturb him, I passed on.

After a brief stroll through the remainder of the interior, I went outside and climbed onto a segment of a fallen column. There I sat for a while, drinking in the splendor of the night and marveling at the perfection of the lines of everything about me. I must have fallen into a deep reverie which lasted longer than I was aware, for when I was aroused again the entire aspect of the ruins had changed, owing to the shifting shadows of the moonlight. I started, then observed that the man I had seen inside the temple was standing beside me and his baskets sitting on the ground nearby.

"You are not one of us," he was saying, and I suddenly knew that it was his voice that had awakened me from my vivid waking dream, "yet you seem to see — the power, the sublimity and the glory of it all —"

"Who could fail?" I asked, looking back at the noble facade, broken though it was.

The simplicity and purity of its lines should have moved the crudest savage. And yet I was startled to realize that I had not been thinking in terms of aesthetic values at all, but dreaming of quite other things. I had been dreaming of a long past time when the rocky summit was dazzlingly crowned with snowy white new marble structures and thronged with gayly dressed people and armored warriors. It is true that in the picture I saw the delicately carved and unbroken cornices and the rich friezes and pediments studded with perfect statuary set off by backgrounds of magnificent reds, deep blues and gold.. But it was on the people that I was intent. I saw wealthy aristocrats march by with slaves bearing heaped-up platters in their train. Those fruits of the field I knew were being brought as offerings to their divine patroness and protector. Eager young men in bright armor were there, too, swarming into the temple for blessings and inspiration to victory in the campaign they were about to begin. Then, so real was my illusion, I was about to follow them into the sacred edifice to see what ritual the priests of Athena followed, when the words of the enigmatic Greek broke the train of my reverie.

"She, Pallas," he said, with his strange dark eyes fastened upon me as if he read my every thought, "is the kindest and wisest of them all. Under her strong aegis none can hurt us. It was against that shield that Xerxes and his Persian hordes beat in vain. She is, and always will be, the guardian of this city and all the cities of Hellas."

"Is?" I said, cynically. The thought that just flitted through my mind that, whatever Athena's power may have been once, it had long since gone. Since the repulse of the Persians, Greece had been overrun many times — first by the Romans, then the plundering Goths, and finally the Turks. It was centuries before the last of them was dislodged.

"Yes, *is*," he said fiercely. "She sleeps, it is true, but her power is not gone. You yourself shall see it. I promise you."

181

"You are a pagan?" I asked. An hour earlier I would have thought that too fantastic a question to put to anyone in these modern times, but it did not ruffle him.

"I am," he said simply.

I looked away from him and at the ruined temple standing in the mellow light of the moon. A queer duck, I thought, perhaps a little cracked. Then I turned to ask another question. Were the baskets he had with him filled with his own offerings? His delusion might be that complete. But when I looked at where he had been he was not there. Nor were his baskets. He was gone. And the hour being late. I slid from the stone and made my way to the grand stairway that led to the sleeping city below.

The next day a cable sent me to Smyrna and thence to Stamboul. I was gone for weeks and when I came back to Athens a full moon again rode in the sky. That night I revisited the Parthenon and again saw the mysterious man with his baskets of olives and fruits, but he ignored my presence. Again he took them into the naos and, as before, brought them out again. That, I argued, was an unusual procedure if the contents of the baskets were meant as offerings.

A day or so later I had a partial answer to that. While strolling through a crowded market street, I came upon a booth presided over by the man of the Parthenon. On its counters various products .of the country were offered for sale. The embroidery and lace displayed were exceptionally fine and I bought several pieces of it. He took the money without a word or flicker of recognition.

For a few minutes I stood hesitant, then walked away with a peculiar crawly feeling of the skin. There was something distinctly uncanny about the market stall and the queer man who tended it. Though the choicest fruits and the finest needlework of the street were for sale there, few perions stopped to look and fewer still to buy. I watched them pass with expressionless faces and unseeing eyes, as if they did not see the place. Two priests came striding down the street, and, when they approached the stall, they plucked up the edges of their habits and walked softly by with averted faces as if fearful of contamination.

The peddler himself — the man of the Parthenon — had something about him that was singularly disturbing to the peace of mind. I cannot say what that was unless it was the impression he gave of utter and infinite age. Or, perhaps, agelessness. Absurd as the statement may seem, I would not venture to guess his age within a century or so — , or a millennium or so for that matter. That was odd, too, for in most of the details of his appearance he might have been a well-knit, hale man of about forty. It was the profound wisdom that one saw in his weary eyes that bespoke great age. He had the look of one who had lived for eons and had long ago tired of it.

Bewildered, I left, carrying my parcel hugged to me tightly. Down the street a little way I encountered a local man I knew, and asked him about the proprietor of the market stall, but he shook his head. He did not know whom I meant. Nor did any others of the several I asked. It was not until I got to the hotel and asked the ancient concierge about him that I found one who knew the man I meant. Even he looked uneasily about before he spoke, as if it was a matter to be whispered, not to be blurted out.

"You are favored," he said, cryptically. "Not many know Mike of the Parthenon. I do not, except that he is not what he seems to be. My grandfather knew him well, but then my grandfather was a silent man. I do not know what Mike's real name is or what his story."

That was all I could draw from him. Needless to say, that little whetted my curiosity to the utmost and there were few moonlit nights after that that I failed to spend part of the night on the Acropolis. The enigmatic Mike was always to be found there, and gradually he became used to my presence and occasionally spoke. I was careful not to say or think anything that might offend him, and little by little his discourse grew less guarded and more fluent. In the end there were times when words would burst forth from him in a fervid torrent.

The talk was never about himself, but of Pallas Athena and her lovely temple, or of her subjects and their vicissitudes. Night after night I listened eagerly, inexplicably aware that I was hearing things only partially guessed by archaeologists, and that often wrongly. He told me of the earlier temple on whose site the present

Parthenon had been constructed; of the labors of the multitudes of slaves in quarries and in transportation to make the later building possible. From him I learned which of the groups had been designed by Phidias and which by others, and of the perfect craftsmanship of the sculptors Agoracritus and Alcomenes. He described also the long missing sculptures pilfered or destroyed by vandals.

Whenever he touched on that theme his tone took on a vindictive bitterness of the most intense sort. The man he hated most heartily was the Venetian, Morosini, who had bombarded the Parthenon with artillery in the year 1687. That act alone would have incurred Mike's undying hatred, but Morosini compounded it with what he viewed as sacrilege. In an attempt to rob the building of one of its pediment statuary groups, he had his soldiers rig for the job of lowering the marbles. But in their clumsiness they dropped the goddess' own chariot and shattered it to bits on the pavement below. Mike hinted darkly that for that impiety Morosini had died horribly some time after.

He also spoke rancorously of the many misuses made of the building by temporary conquerors of Greece. One of the emperors, Constantine, had converted the pagan shrine into a church dedicated to St. Sophia. Later the Turks transformed it into a mosque. As a self-appointed apostle of Athena, Mike detested Christian and Moslem alike, but it was Turkish embellishment to the Parthenon that angered him most. They had defiled its classic lines by erecting a tawdry minaret — an offense even more grave than their later use of the building as a powder magazine. He assured me that its architect, even as Morosini was to do later, had faced frightful retribution for the deed. I was left to infer that Athena, or her agent, had performed the executions.

All that and more he told me. I took it for the most part in silence. I marveled at the extent of his historical knowledge, but wondered that he should be so wholesouledly devoted to a goddess long enough dead to have degenerated to the status of a mere myth, useful only to poets and their ilk. At times I came near to twitting him on Athena's many failures to protect her people — her vaunted protection seemed to me to have failed lamentably during the last twenty centuries. But I forbore. I had come to like the man and did not want to wound him. It was not until the blackening war clouds over the Balkans actually broke and the neo-Roman legions began hammering at the north-west border that I ventured to murmur something about the time having come for Athena to rouse herself and show her power.

"Bah!" he snorted. "For those yelping jackals? They attack only because they think the prey is sick. They do not matter. It is those who will come later that are terrible. It is with those she will deal."

The situation worsened fast and soon my business troubles prevented me from spending much time outside my office. Roumania was betrayed, and Bulgaria. The Nazis were overrunning Serbia. Then came the day when the panzer armies rolled into Greece. They were not stopped on the slopes of Mike's revered Olympus, nor yet at the historic pass of Thermopylae. I thought of the queer pagan and wondered whether even the thunderbolts of mighty Zeus himself could prevail, even if faith could reanimate him. No, Zeus, Athena — all the old gods — they might still live in a few solitary hearts, but they had lost their potency.

Athens fell. The Nazi juggernaut crushed it, then rolled on to other conquests. They left behind them regiments of black-shirted scavengers to pick the bones. They left, too, their own minions — such as Herr Scheer and his storm troopers — to do their own peculiarly discreditable work. All of that was bad, but the crowning insult came when the invaders flaunted their arrogant banner of the hooked cross above Mike's beloved Parthenon. The Acropolis was closed to all civilians; Moreover, the hungry harpies denuded the market of all its edibles and any other thing of value. Mike's shop was looted and wrecked. His temple was defiled. Mike's occupation was gone.

It must have been a month after that before I saw him again. That was when he appeared as a waiter in the dining room at the hotel, and I learned that he went by the name of Pappadopoulos. He chose to ignore me, but I watched him with interest, since I knew the implacable hatred in his heart toward all the fat and greedy exploiters he served. Yet he went about his work with all the unctuous suavity of his adopted calling, and the serene composure of his bearing was almost incredible. I could not help but admire the man. There are few who can bear themselves well when their most precious bubble bursts — when their dearest vision proves to be but a barren mirage. That, I knew, had happened to Mike. Greece groaned miserably under the heel of a new oppressor, yet the long-ago- gods lay inert in their graves. It was, pathetic.

And then that monstrous thing happened. One night he leaned over Herr Scheer's shoulder and whispered something. Then the rest, as I have related — S cheer's cold acknowledgment, the passage of the bribe. It was astounding.

I pretended not to see. I turned away and busied myself with the food on my plate. But before I did I saw that at least one other than me had also seen. That one was a Major Ciccotto, an officer of the local garrison whose power far exceeded the nominal rank he held. It was Ciccotto who had earned eternal infamy by his ruthless seizures of food. His raiding of the people's granaries had turned Greece into a land of gaunt, fear-ridden, starving people. At that moment it is hard to say which I loathed most — the cruel Scheer, or the rapacious Italian. But he had seen. The-greedy glitter in his piggish eyes was the confirmation of that. I arose and left the room, overwhelmed with disgust.

A few hours after that I encountered Mike in an upper corridor of the hotel. He was carrying a tray of empty dishes and I stopped him.

"You had better be more careful," I warned. "I saw gold pass tonight. Others may have seen, too. With all these harpies about, you know —"

"I hope so," he said, with a queer, grim smile. If he had been a man less intense, I am sure it would have been a grin. And with that astonishing reply he pushed past me and went on down the hall.

I fairly gasped, for to openly display real money in the Angleterre's dining room was comparable to exposing a crippled lamb to the sight of a pack of hungry wolves. Except for me, every man present was a predatory agent of one or the other of the Axis powers. I shuddered for Mike's personal safety.

My misgivings were amply justified the very next day. Mike was absent from his usual station in the dining room. So was Scheer. But the next day Mike showed up, looking considerably the worse for wear. His lips were badly swollen and cut, one eye blackened, and there were other signs of having been severely manhandled. But he waited on his customers with his usual outward serenity. It was beyond my understanding. I took a furtive look at the nearby table where Ciccotto sat. He was watching Mike eagerly, and presently I saw him beckon him to his table.

Mike went as meekly, I thought, as a lamb to the slaughter. In obedience to the major's imperative gesture, Mike stooped to listen. There was a moment of urgent whispering, then Mike nodded and went away. He came back in a few minutes, made a pretense of brushing crumbs from the table, and I saw his hand slip into his pocket and out again. Again a few gleaming gold coins changed hands! It was utterly baffling. I tried not to think of it any more.

Business took me away from Athens for several days and when I came back I had to go consult with my firm's banker. Jimmy Duquesne was his name; he was an old friend and one who could be counted on for an unlimited amount of off-the-record gossip. When we had finished our commercial transactions he led me to a back room where we sat down over cups of coffee.

"These totalitarians," he sighed, wagging his head, "what a nose for loot they have! It's incredible. You know how scarce gold is — has been for years — in Europe. Well, I'm swamped with it."

I lifted my eyebrows. What he had just said was strangely interesting. But I made no comment.

"Three days ago," he went on, "that unspeakable butcher Scheer came in. He had two bagfuls of it, all he could carry. He cleaned me out of paper marks and drachmae. Naturally, I had to give him literally bales of the worthless stuff in exchange. Then yesterday in walks that skunk Ciccotto with another lot of it. I could not possibly pay him off with what I had in the vaults, but, luckily, he was content with a draft on our Milan branch for the required number of lira. Now where do you suppose they found the stuff?"

"I wouldn't know," I answered, quite truthfully, though I could guess where a *little* of it came from. "Was it in bullion or coin?"

"Coin," he exclaimed, "and what coinl Much of it must be museum pieces worth I don't know how much. There was everything from a Roman *aureus* to modern. Turkish pounds —

187

medieval ducats, crowns, guilder — I don't know the name of half of them. I bought solely on the basis of weight."

He broke off and flicked the ash from his cigar with a worried look.

"Well?" I knew there was bound to be a sequel. No bank under the fiscal control of Nazidom could have a hundred-weight of metallic gold in its vaults without repercussions.

"All day today," he said dismally, "I have been overrun by secret agents — Gestapo and Ovra men. They want to know all about the gold. Where it came from, who brought it, what they said, what I paid — everything. The inner circles, it appears, are running wild."

"They would," I said grimly. "They want their share."

"Perhaps," he said, thoughtfully. "But there is more to it than that. You see, both Scheer and Ciccotto have disappeared. Without a trace!"

Things happened fast after that. Big planes dropped down daily, bearing fresh inquisitors from Belgrade, Bucharest, Vienna, even from Berlin. New contingents of Gestapo men, high-ranking army officers, and other mysterious persons swarmed out of them and descended upon the bank demanding information. Others of their stamp kept corning from Italy, also bent on the combined purpose of plunder and finding their missing predecessors. For each batch of operatives who had come before had disappeared shortly after their arrival. It was eerie. All Athens held its breath.

There were no clues, no bodies found, nothing. Men came simply to disappear. Others trailed them to find out why, only to disappear themselves. Savage reprisals were taken. Greeks were rounded up by the thousands and herded into prisons and camps, charged with being Communists, Jews or traitors. A tight curfew was imposed and severer food restrictions made on an already starved people. Yet the disappearances went on. Hundreds of Himmler's men vanished like so many extinguished candle flames. The Italian garrisons were denuded of their officers. Athens was an unhealthy place for invaders, apparently. The Germans wanted to know why, but no one broke. The conquerors were up against a blank wall.

"I wonder how long Adolf and Benito can stand the strain?" remarked Duquesne one day. "According to my computations half a thousand of their smartest and most unscrupulous gumshoe men have faded from the picture. It is a deep well that has no bottom."

Evidently the Powers That Be came to the same conclusion. An abrupt change of policy toward Greece took place. The curfew and food restrictions were lifted and the jails emptied. A benevolent old Italian general was sent to be governor and the severity of the occupation was relaxed in many ways. Gestapo men and Ovra agents were still to be seen, but the grapevine had it that those few had strict orders to forget about their missing predecessors, and also to forget all about gold, whether for personal account or for the coffers of "the party."

Oddly, the wave of disappearances promptly ceased.

Mike of the Parthenon coughed discreetly and I looked up. He was standing by my side in his usual obsequious way and with a napkin folded across his arm.

"They have hauled the swastika down and opened the Acropolis again," he said, and there was a gleam of exultation in his eyes, "did you know? You see, the shield of Athena still protects."

"So it appears," I said. Then I recalled that there was to be a moon that night. "Shall I meet you in the Parthenon later?"

"No," he said. "At another place. You almost came to believe. Then you scoffed. I want to show you with your own eyes. Meet me at the end of the street in an hour."

I found him at the place appointed. He was half-hidden behind a low stone wall. Nearby was tethered a pair of donkeys. We mounted those and rode off. In a little while we were following a twisty hill trail skirting the shoulders of Mount Lycabettus. The country grew more rugged as we progressed, until at last we came to a low cliff that blocked our way. There we dismounted and he led me through the brush and along a path I would never have found by myself. We had not gone a great way when we turned abruptly into a clump of shrubbery hugging the cliffside. He drew back an armful of the tangled branches and uncovered a dark and gaping hole.

"Crawl in," he said.

I hesitated. It was a small hole, hardly thirty inches high by about as wide. Many persons had already disappeared — non-Greeks all — and here I was alone with a man who many would have thought demented. But my curiosity overcame my fears. I dropped to all fours and crawled into the black cave. I could hear him scuffling along behind me, and once or twice he warned me to watch out for my head where the ceiling was low or where we were about to make a turn.

After a dozen yards of such progress, the winding passage widened and I could no longer feel the brush of the rocky roof against my back hair.

"You can stand up now," he said, and flashed on a torch.

The place we were in appeared to be a sort of antechamber to the cave. Tortuous passages ran off from it in all directions, each floored with soft white sand. He beckoned me to follow and preceded me down one of them. It ended blind, but just before it ended I came upon a shallow hole dug out of the sand. A few gold coins of antique vintage lay scattered around it.

"That is where Scheer got his first gold. He made me show him where it was."

Then he wheeled and led me past several other wing passages. He flashed a light down one.

"Same story here — Ciccotto's gold find. He threatened to have me shot unless I told him."

He hurried on. In another divergent tunnel he showed me four leather bags neatly packed with gold coins. They were sitting on the sand and a short spade beside them. Footprints led away toward deeper recesses.

"They came back looking for more," he explained. "I think they went farther into the cave to scout out other deposits." He said it with a ghastly chuckle that chilled the soul.

"And got lost?" I asked. Some caves are like that. I pictured rotting corpses and whitening bones deeper within the labyrinth.

"Lost!" he cackled. "Yes. They are lost. Lost forever."

"I am a poor guesser," I said, sitting down on the sand and looking straight at him. "If your purpose in bringing me here was to explain something, explain it."

"I brought you to convince you," he said, with immense dignity, "that the shield of Athena still protects. These baubles" — and he indicated the packed bags of gold with a contemptuous gesture of the hand —"are only bait. The gods have always been wise enough to know that the only kind of men whom they need fear

190

are the greedy ones. And it is by their own greed that the gods slay them. Shortly I will show you what happened to the German Scheer and the Italian and all the others who followed them.

"It was an easy matter to lure them here. I had only to pretend to be in distress — I told them I had an aged aunt in prison charged with harboring a wounded British soldier. I offered money for a favorable consideration of her case. Scheer said it would take much money. I gave him gold. He wanted more. They took me to the police station and submitted me to much abuse. At length I agreed to show him where I got my money. It was from an old temple treasure, I told him, buried in a cave. I showed him the way in and the way back. He left that first night because he had all he could carry. I knew he would go back for more. I knew, too, that he would not be content with merely what I had shown him. He would search the whole cave. The Italian Ciccotto behaved exactly in the same way. It was very simple."

"But of so many," I asked, "why did not some come back?"

"The legacy of Athena, of which I am the earthly executor, has extraordinary properties. There are vast fortunes buried in these caves — things so valuable that once men look upon them they cannot leave. Come!"

Mike led me into a transverse passage for a long way. As we proceeded it was unnecessary for him to use his electric light, for the cavern was bathed in a soft and mysterious luminosity of a faintly rose hue. He turned into a doorway on the right.

"This room is no longer used," he said.

I looked in. It was a huge semicircular room much along the lines of a Grecian theater. Directly opposite the door was an empty raised stage or dais. Between it and the doorway the amphitheater sloped upward. But the room was not empty. It was crammed with statuary.

"Examine them," Mike directed.

You have seen habitat groups in museums? It was something like that, except that the figures here were of mixed nationalities — all ancient.

There were hooded Egyptians, and many Romans — , some togaed, others incased in armor. The figures were of stone, cleverly

191

and perfectly carved, but were dressed in the habiliments of living men of the era. The figures must have stood where they were for many centuries, for many were nude with only the moldy fragments of their former clothing lying at their feet. Much of the armor was encrusted with rust and scale, though here and there a golden casque bespoke an aristocrat. The faces all had one thing in common: the features were frightfully distorted as if in an ecstasy of horror.

"Come," he said. "I will show you another room — more modern."

It was a duplication of the first, except the type of statue had changed. Here stood big-muscled, athletic figures of men, all beautifully executed in white marble. Over their shoulders heavy animal skins were flung, and there were other skins wrapped about their middles. There were many Turks there, too, and soldiers of a type I took to be Janizaries. As before, the stony faces registered utter terror. Many of the figures had their arms thrown halfway up, as if the sculptor had caught them in the act of warding off some fiendish thing that threatened them.

Mike led me through the throng of statuary much as one would tread a sidewalk mob when the persons in it are intent on studying a bulletin pasted on a wall. For it was noteworthy that all the figures had their faces turned the same way and their stony, eyes fixed on a spot in midair some yards above the empty dais. He stopped at one and tapped it on the shoulder.

"This one was Morosini," he said, with cold venom, "the chief ravager of her shrine. But we must go. There is one other room to see."

I was brimming with questions, for nothing shown me yet had shed much light on the mystery of the recent disappearances. Where had the gold come from — especially the modern coins? Who had executed the vast assemblage of life-sized figures, and why were they entombed in this hidden and unknown spot? Were any of the more recently missing Gestapo men still alive?

"The modern gold," he said promptly, as if I had asked the questions out loud, "is the tribute of the faithful. I and those before me have long sold the offerings of the peasants who still have faith — you saw my market booth. Its profits are buried here. The other questions will answer themselves soon."

192

He lapsed into silence and took me back in the direction whence we had come. Presently we came to the passage by which we had entered and he turned deeper into the cave. I saw that loose gold was scattered along the path, a tempting lead to go farther. Suddenly Mike stopped before an open door.

"The other rooms were abandoned long ago," he said. "They became too full. It is in this one that Athena presides during the intervals when she is awake. Her sleeping compartment is in the rear, but that is forbidden to mortal man. Here, put on these."

He handed me a pair of peculiar-looking binoculars, and I noticed he had a similar pair for himself. They were a sort of cross between prismatic binoculars and spectacles, for the lenses were blanked off and there were hangers to hook over the ears. I found when I put them on that I could see perfectly well, but the images came to me through artificially widened eye-spacing, giving me a keener perception of depth. They were quite as satisfactory as straight vision, but I could not help wondering why he insisted on my wearing them.

"Now," he directed, "take my hand and walk backward."

We backed into the remaining hall. We had gone only several strides until I stopped with a gasp. I had passed and was now facing a portrait statue of a German Gestapo man I knew! The marble figure stood rigidly with the contorted expression of stark horror on his chiseled features I had seen elsewhere. His clothing was modern to the minute. I had seen the man and in those very clothes not three weeks before. It was a figure of one of the missing men, dressed in that man's clothes!

We went on. I passed a replica of an Italian major, more Gestapo replicas. At length Mike jerked me to a halt.

"Here Here is Scheer," he said. It was. Except for the fact he was in marble and not in the flesh and that his horrified expression differed from the one of smug arrogance I had been accustomed to, there was no whit of difference.

"Now," said Mike, "turn around."

I turned. The dais before me was not empty as the others had been. Upon it was a colossal throne-chair — at least twenty feet in height. Over the back of it a cloak of cloth-of-gold was thrown and atop it perched a huge, solemnly blinking owl and beside him a snow-white cock. A slender silver lance of some fifty feet in length leaned against the chair, a coiled serpent lay on the step before it. On the right side of the chair an immense golden shield stood. It was adorned with intricate carvings and I started to take off the glasses I wore in order to study its'detail better.

"Don't, youfool!" said Mike, harshly, gripping my wrist with fingers of steel. "Do you want to be like the others? That is the aegis — the shield of Pallas. You cannot bear the naked sight of it — use your mirrors, man!"

I did not quite understand, and then, as I looked again, I did.

In the midst of the shield, where another shield would have a boss, there was a head. My blood chilled at the sight of it and I felt goose flesh pop out all over me. My hair lifted and I knew that my face was as twisted in the same horrified contortions as those of the cold figures all about. For the face of the head on the shield was indescribably hideous — horrid fangs protruded from a misshapen and lipless mouth — wild eyes filled with living hatred and immeasurable fury glared out from beneath frightening eyebrows — and all about the vile face the writhing hair of the head twisted and untwisted. It was not hair, but a mass of hissing snakes.

I wanted to scream, to faint, to die. The sight was intolerable — no man could bear it. A blessed blackness blotted out my vision. I realized I had gone blind, but I was grateful for it. That did not matter, for I had clutched at myself and found reassurance — my flesh was still warm and yielding — *I* had not been turned to stone. For at that moment I knew what it was that I had gazed upon, and how I had been saved. It was by looking through the prismatic mirrors, even as Perseus had when he severed that frightful head from its former body. I had forgotten until then that he had gratefully presented the bloody, writhing trophy to his patroness and that she had set it in her shield.

"Medusa," I murmured, half hysterically, "the Gorgon, Medusa."

"Yes." said Mike of the Parthenon, grabbing me firmly by the arm and leading me way, "it still has power. Her aegis is impregnable —"

194

I heard no more. Even the memory of that hideous sight was unbearable.

Doubled and Redoubled

He was in a rut, doing the same things every day — because every day was one day!

The very first thing that startled Jimmy Childers that extraordinary, repetitive June day was the alarm clock going off. It shouldn't have gone off. He remembered distinctly setting it at "Silent" when he went to bed the night before, and thumbing his nose derisively at it. He was a big shot now; he could get down to the office, along with the Westchesterites, at a quarter of ten, not at nine, as heretofore.

He rose on an elbow and hurled a pillow at the jangling thing, then flopped back onto the pillow for a moment's luxurious retrospect.

Ah, what a day yesterday had been! The perfect day. The kind that happens only in fiction, or the third act of plays, when every problem is solved and every dream comes true all at once. He grinned happily. This time yesterday he had been a poor wage slave, a mere clerk; today he was head of a department. Until last evening the course of true love, as practiced by himself and Genevieve, had run anything but smoothly; this morning she was his bride-to-be. Twenty-four hours ago the name of Jimmy Childers was known only to a few hundred persons; all today's papers would carry his pictures and the commendations of the police and the mayor. Yesterday —

But why go on? Today was another day. Jimmy pulled himself together and got out of bed, making a slightly wry face as he did so. One only reached the utmost pinnacle once in his life; today,

196

after yesterday, could only be anticlimactic. At ten he must hit the grit again. It would be a new kind of a grind, pitched on a higher level with higher and fresher ambitions, but a grind nevertheless. And so thinking, he reached for his clothes.

And that was when Jimmy Childers received jolts number two, three and so on! For the neatly wrapped packages delivered late yesterday afternoon from Livingston & Laird were not on the chair where he had placed them for the night. Nor was the nice, new pigskin wallet and the two hundred-odd dollars he had kept out as spending money from his race-track haul, anywhere to be seen. Even the empty jeweler's box that had contained Genevieve's ring was gone. Burglars!

Jimmy frowned in puzzlement. His door was spring-locked, but it was bolted, too. There was no transom, and the window was inaccessible from any other. It didn't make sense. He thought he would hardly make a row about it yet. Moreover, he was consoled by the thought that before going on his shopping spree yesterday, he had dropped by the bank and deposited a flat thousand. For reassurance, he slipped a hand into the inner pocket of his dangling coat and drew forth the little blue book.

The book was here, but the entry was not! Jimmy's eyes popped in unbelief. The last entry was May 15th, and for the usual ten dollars. Yet he remembered clearly Mr. Kleib's pleasantries as he chalked up the one-grand deposit. Why, it was only yesterday!

He glanced up at the calendar that hung behind the door. Each night he crossed the current day off. Last night he had not crossed it, but encircled it in a triple circle of red — the day of days! He suddenly went a little sick at the stomach as the rectangle of black figures stared back at him. The fourteenth of June was neither crossed off nor encircled. Jimmy Childers sat down and scratched his head, bewildered and dazed. Had he dreamed all that he thought had happened? Could it be that today was the fourteenth, and not the day after? Trembling a little, he finished dressing.

For a time he pondered his strange feelings. He tried to account for the disappearance of the things he had bought, remembering that the boys rooming down the hall had a way of borrowing without always telling. They *might* have come in last evening while he was out. As to the loss of the wallet, a pick-pocket might have lifted that, and he tried to recall occasions when he had been crowded or jostled. He gave it up. There was only the old hag on Riverside Drive, who had held out a scrawny, clutching hand for alms. Surely she couldn't have been the thief! He smiled to recollect her fawning gratitude when in his exuberance he had unexpectedly given her a five-spot, and her mumbling as she tottered on her way.

No. None of it fitted. As a matter of fact, now that he was going into such details, he remembered distinctly getting home *after that*, and putting the wallet and empty ring box on his dresser, winding the clock, and the rest. He sighed deeply. It was all so screwy.

He walked briskly from the house. He had decided to say nothing about his loss to Mrs. Tankersley. Upon second thought he would wait until he got to his office, then he would ring up the police commissioner personally. Hadn't he told him only yesterday that if he ever needed anything just give him a buzz? Jimmy felt very grandiose with his new connections. He had completely conquered his jitters when he stopped at the tobacco stand on the corner.

"Gimme a pack," he said, "and extra matches."

The clerk handed the cigarettes over, and then in a low, confidential voice added, "I gotta hot one for you today — Swiss Rhapsody in the first at Aqueduct. She's sure fire, even if she's a long shot. The dope is straight from Eddie Kelly —"

"Wake up," laughed Jimmy Childers, "that was yesterday!" He started to add, "Don't you remember my dropping by here last night and handing you a 'C' for the tip?" but for some reason choked it. The fellow evidently didn't remember it, or something. The situation was cockeyed again. So Jimmy said that much and stopped.

The clerk shook his head. "Not this nag. She hasn't been running."

"O. K.," said Childers, on a sudden impulse, and digging into his watch pocket he fished out four crumpled dollar bills. That was what he had to live on the rest of the week. "Two bucks — on the nose."

"You ain't making a mistake, pal," said the clerk.

The words startled Jimmy Childers more than anything else that had happened. Syllable for syllable the last exchange of sentences were identical with what had passed between them yesterday this time. Jimmy had the queer feeling, which comes over one at times, he was reliving something that had already happened. Hastily he pocketed his cigarettes and backed out of the place.

Downstairs in the subway station he snatched a paper and just made the crowded train, squeezing in the middle door into a solid mass of humanity. He was anxious to see whether his exploit in foiling the Midtown Bank robbery had made the first page or not, but it was not for several stations that he had the opportunity to open up his paper. Then he muttered savagely in dissatisfaction. The dealer had worked off yesterday's paper on him! He had read it all before — June 14th, PARIS FALLS. Bah!

"The young men of this generation have no manners whatever!" bleated a nagging, querulous voice behind him, and he felt a vicious dig at his ribs.

"I beg your pardon," he exclaimed, automatically nudging away to give what room he could.

"People go around sticking their elbows in other people's eyes, trying .to read sensational trash!"

"I'm very sorry, madam," reiterated Jimmy Childers, making still more room. He was looking down into the snapping eyes of an acid-faced old beldam, and the sight of her made chills run up and down his spine. This very incident had occurred to him in every detail only yesterday. He felt very queer. Should he drop off and see a doctor? No, he decided, it was that damn vivid dream that still hung on to him.

Then, when the flurry caused by the tart old woman's eruption had subsided, he stole a glance over the shoulders of his neighbors. Some were reading one paper and some another, but they all had one thing in common. They were yesterday's papers! And their readers seemed content!

"Hell's bells," ejaculated Childers, "I *am* nuts."

At Thirty-fourth Street he got no shock, for the mad stampede of the office-bound herd is much the same, whatever the date. It was when he stepped into his own company's suite that fate biffed him squarely between the eyes again. Biff number one was that none of the other clerks took any special notice of him as he walked past the desks. The expected shower of congratulations did not materialize, nor for that matter, did the sour look of envy he expected to see on Miss Staunton's face. It was just like any other morning. It was just like yesterday morning, to be even more specific.

But he did not stop at his old desk in the outer office as he always had hitherto. He walked boldly on to the private office of the manager of the foreign department. It was not until he was within a pace of it that he halted in his stride, open-mouthed. The lettering on the door was not new gold-leaf at all, but the black paint that had always been there. It said simply, "Ernest Brown, Mgr."

He stared at it a moment, then turned and slowly made his way back to his old hangout in the clerk's offices. He hung up his hat and coat and sat down at the desk he had worked at for the past five years. Presently the office boy came bearing the trays of mail. Childers watched the deck of envelopes fall onto his blotter with tense anxiety. Somewhere in that batch of mail ought to be a test of his sanity. Or was it the reverse? He couldn't be sure. That damn dream had him so mixed up, he couldn't tell reality front pipe dream any more.

"I'm going to call my shots, from now on," he told himself. With a hand that was close to trembling he pulled a pad toward him and wrote down:

Acceptance and check for two hundred and fifty dollars in this morning's mail for a story I tossed off in my spare time and sent to the *Thursday Weekly*.

He turned the pad upside down and shot a cautious glance about the office. No one was paying him any attention. He ran through the envelopes. Yes, there it was. He almost tore the check as he snatched it out. Yes! The unexpected had happened, an impossible thing — his first effort at writing had been bought! He read the inclosed letter feverishly. Word for word it was the one in his dream. Now he knew that yesterday had not happened. For the *Weekly* wouldn't send out two checks for the same yarn. Would the rest of the day go the same way? It did.

At nine thirty the messenger came and told him the boss wanted him at once. Jimmy Childers went with alacrity. For twenty-five minutes he had been sitting there, alternately chilled with fear and glowing with anticipation.

"Childers," said the Old Man, "we've watched you for some time and we like your style. Beginning tomorrow you'll have Mr. Brown's job in the foreign department. The pay will only be two hundred, but remember that we are jumping you over a lot of other people. You may take the rest of today off."

"Thank you, sir," said Jimmy Childers with every appearance of calm acceptance of his just dues as a capable employee, but all the time queer tremors were playing hob with his inner workings. "But if it's all the same, I'll hang on as I am until noon at least. I would like to clean up my present desk before I leave it."

"A very commendable spirit," said the Old Man, cracking his cold face into the first smile he had ever let Childers see. That, too, had been in the dream. Childers was not sure whether he looked forward to the rest of the day with apprehension or what. It was a little disconcerting to know beforehand just how everything would turn out.

When he got back to his desk a puckish mood seized him.

"Oh, Miss Walters, will you take a letter, please."

"A-hum," he said, in his best executive manner, when she had settled beside him with her notebook. "To Mr. E. E. Frankenstein, Cylindrical Metal Castings — you know where — dear sir. In reply to your offer of this date of the position of stockmaster at your foundry, I beg to inform you that the job does not interest me and the salary you mention is ridiculous. Yours very truly — and so on and so on — the new title, you know."

"Why, Mr. Childers," exclaimed Miss Walters, "I didn't know they were trying to get you —"

Childers cocked an eye at the clock. He had timed it nicely. The messenger was approaching with a telegram in his hand.

"Read that to me," he said to the stenographer, with a lordly wave of the hand.

She tore the yellow envelope open and read the message aloud.

"How did you know?" she asked, wonder in her eyes.

"Hunch," he said laconically, and lit a cigarette.

"By golly," he told himself, "the dream is coming true, item by item." In succession he rang up Genevieve and made a date for that night; and then his bookmaker and doubled his bet on Swiss Rhapsody. Then he fell to thinking about the affair at the Midland Bank and that took some of the glow off. Hell, that fellow with the machine gun didn't miss him by much! Should he go through with it? He decided he would, for there were several details he had missed in the flurry of excitement in the dream. Moreover, he had pleasant memories of the fuss that was made over him afterward, not forgetting the standing reward of one thousand dollars offered by the protective agency. If he were to be married, and now he was sure he would be, any extra cash was very welcome.

He took the *Weekly*'s check and strolled out of the office. First he stopped by the haberdashers and spent a most pleasant hour selecting gay ties, a suit, hat and various other items. Then, leaving the delivery address, he made his way to the bank.

He had a very queer feeling as he went through the portals — that uncomfortable sensation of having done it all before. His upward glance at the clock and the fact that exactly 12:03 registered firmly in his memory was a part of it. But he nerved himself for the ordeal and went straight to his usual teller's window.

He had just shoved the money under the wicket and knew uneasily that goose pimples had risen all over him when the expected happened. A low, husky voice said almost in his ear.

"Stand as you are, bud. Keep your hands on that marble shelf and don't turn around. This is a stick-up."

Then the voice said to Mr. Kleib: "Shell out — everything in the cage but the silver!"

Now!

Childers deliberately and without sense of direction, except that of the voice, kicked backward with all his force. He felt something soft give and then his heel crunched against bone. There was a curse and a moan, and he heard the clatter of the gun on the floor and the soft thud as his man slid to the marble.

In that instant pandemonium reigned. A huge howler over the door began its siren wail, Tommy-guns rattled, men shouted and women screamed.

Like a flash Jimmy Childers dropped to his hands and knees just as a stream of whizzing bullets spattered against the marble cage front. He grabbed up the fallen gun and turned it on the man that was firing at him, a short, stocky thug in a light-gray suit. He saw the man drop, and as he did another rushed past, headed for the door. Jimmy let the gun fall and launched himself in a flying tackle, grabbing at the fleeing gangster's knees.

The next couple of seconds was a maelstrom of sensation and confusion. Then he was aware of looking at the pants legs of some big man in blue, and a heavy Irish voice saying:

"Leggo, son, you've done enough. We've got him now."

Childers unwrapped his arms from the bandit's knees and got up. His heart was pounding wildly and he knew his clothes were a wreck, but it was a glorious moment and he didn't care. A circle of men were around him, men with notebooks and cameras and flashlight bulbs, snapping pictures and asking questions. Next, a big police car screamed its way to the front door, and in a moment he was receiving the unstinted congratulations of a fiery little mayor and his police commissioner.

"Nice work, Childers," said the latter. "Those eggs have been wanted a long, long time. If there is anything I can ever do for you, call on me."

Then the president of the bank came and whirled him away to the club for luncheon. What a day! Had so much ever happened to one man before in so short a space of time? And how odd that he had dreamed it all, even to the date of the vintage on the label of the sauterne the banker ordered with the lunch!

Suddenly he realized it was close to two thirty and the first at Aqueduct was probably already run. He excused himself and hastened over to Kelly's place.

"I'll take it in big bills," he said to Kelly, as he went in.

"Optimistic, ain't you?" was Kelly's rejoinder. "Didja ever hear of nine horses falling down and breaking their legs in the same race? Well, that's what it'd take to let that milk-wagon nag —"

"They're off," announced the fellow with the headphones on.

"I'll still take it in big bills," said Jimmy, serenely.

"I'm damned," was Kelly's only comment, a couple of minutes later.

Jimmy Childers had two free hours that somehow were not covered by the dream. He remembered vaguely that he had deposited most of his winnings and then gone for a walk in the park. That he did, but his thoughts were so in the clouds and his pulse pounding so with the sense of personal well-being and triumph that he hardly remembered jumping impulsively into a cab and going to the most famous jeweler's in the world.

Later he mounted the steps in Genevieve's house, the ring snuggling in his pocket. He knew exactly how he was to be greeted — for once the pout would be off her face and in its place jubilant excitement. For the evening papers were full of his exploits at the bank, and the reporters had brought out the fact that that morning he had been made manager of the foreign department. The auspices for a favorable reception to his umpty-teenth proposal were good, to say the least.

They went to dinner, just as he knew they would, at the most expensive place in town.

Jimmy ordered carelessly, without a glance at the card.

"Yes, sir," said the waiter, with that bow that is bestowed only on those that know their way around.

"Why, Jimmy," she tittered, "you seem to be perfectly at home here."

"Oh, yes," he said carelessly, as he flipped the folds out of his napkin. He did not see fit to tell her that in the dream of yesterday — or was it today? — it had been only after thirty minutes study of the intricate card, to the tune of many acrimonious comments by Genevieve and the obvious disapproval of an impatient waiter, that he had picked that particular combination of food and drink. But it had been eminently satisfactory, so why not repeat?

As the evening wore on he found himself more and more eager to get to the place where that culminating kiss occurred. *That* was something he could repeat *ad infinitum*, whether in the flesh or a dream. And when it came, he was not disappointed. After that they had the little ritual of the ring, and still later his departure. His soul soared as it had never soared before.

Or rather, he reminded himself, a trifle ruefully, as it had never soared before in waking life. For after all, the day's triumphs had had just a little of the edge taken off by his certainty that they would occur.

And as he digested that thought, he concluded he would go straight home and to bed. After all, last night the only thing more he had done was stroll on the Drive, after paying the cigar-store clerk his tip, wrapped in his own glorious thoughts. No other incident had occurred worth reliving, as his pleasure at being able to give such a generous handout as a five-dollar bill was somewhat marred by the repulsiveness of the beggarly old crone who had received it.

So he went straight to his room, locked and bolted the door, and prepared for bed. Just before he turned off the light he surveyed the chair piled high with his purchases with immense satisfaction. Tomorrow he would go forth dressed as his new station in life required. His eye caught the calendar, and instead of striking out the day with his customary black cross, he encircled it twice in red. Then taking good care that the clock was wound, but not the alarm, he went to bed.

The very first thing that startled Jimmy Childers that extraordinary repetitive June day was the alarm clock going off. It shouldn't have gone off, He remembered distinctly setting it at "Silent" when he went to bed the night before, and thumbing his nose derisively at it. He was a big shot now; he could get down to the office with the Westchesterites, at quarter of ten, not at nine, as heretofore.

He rose on an elbow and poised himself to hurl a pillow at the jangling thing. And then, THEN —

"Good Heaven!" he mumbled. "I've done all this before."

Angrily he bounded out of bed and choked off the offending clock. It took only a swift glance around the room to check the items some quick sense told him were missing. There were no packages from the haberdasher's, nor ring box. And the calendar stared at him unsullied by red-penciled marks. It was the morning of June 14th!

205

He dressed in sullen rage, grumbling at his fate. He couldn't stand many double-barreled dreams like that one — they were too exhausting. He'd better see a doctor. And yet — yet it was all so *real*. He could have sworn that all those things had actually happened to him — twice! But then he stopped, more mystified than ever. They had differed somewhat in detail, those two days. He stopped and stared at himself in the mirror and noted he appeared a bit wild-eyed.

"I'll experiment, first," he decided, and hurried out, slamming the door behind.

At the cigar stand he asked the clerk. "How do you go about betting on the ponies?"

"I can take it," said the fellow, unenthusiastically.

"Here's two bucks," said Jimmy, "put it on Swiss Rhapsody — to win. I hope there's such a horse?"

"If you're not particular what you call a horse," said the clerk, with an air of sneering omniscience. "I'm surprised they let her run at all."

"Why?"

"It takes her so long to finish it throws all the other races late."

"Oh," said Jimmy Childers, but he let the bet stand.

He did not waste three cents on a paper that morning. One glance at the headlines was enough. He had practically memorized its contents two days before. But when he got in the subway he was very careful to give the nasty, quarrelsome-looking old woman who blocked his path as wide a berth as possible.

"Whippersnapper!" she exclaimed venomously, noting his scrupulous avoidance of her. There was a little flurry as people glanced up and had a look at him, then they went back to the reading of their stale newspapers. Jimmy Childers groaned. Was he in some squirrel cage of fate? Did everything have to always come out the same way, no matter what his approach? He resolved to make something come out differently, no matter what the cost.

This time he opened his letter containing the literary check without a tremor, and without joy. He knew he would spend the money, and how. He knew, too, that the things he purchased with it would vanish overnight, leaving him to do it all over again tomorrow. When the messenger came to tell him the big boss wanted him at once, Childers said coldly:

"I'm busy. Anyhow, it's no farther from his desk to mine than it is from mine to his."

The messenger gaped with awe, as if wondering whether lightning would strike. Then he stumbled off toward the chief's office.

"I don't think you understand, Childers," the big boss was saying a moment later, as he stood by Jimmy's desk. "Brown has left and we're giving you his job. It pays two hundred, you know."

"Not enough," replied Childers, gruffly.

"It's all we can afford just now," said the boss pleasantly. "But that's our offer. Think it over. It will be open for a week."

Jimmy Childers stared at his retreating back.

"Gosh !" he muttered. "And I got away with that!"

He went through the bank routine with little change, although he did think something of telephoning the police a tip-off and letting it go at that, but for some unknown but compelling reason he had to go through his act personally. But the thrill was gone. His walk in the park was much less joyous, as the more he tried to digest the strangely repetitive nature of his life the last three days, the more unhappy he became.

"It's like that old song about the broken record," he muttered sourly. "All the kick's gone out of things now." He didn't even bother to go to the jeweler's to select the ring. He knew the stock number by heart. So he merely phoned for it.

The kiss that night was up to par, which was some solace, but aside from that, getting engaged was not so much fun. There was no palpitation of the heart as he hung on her words, wondering what the answer would be. He already knew damn well what the answer would be. What kind of a life was that?

That night he threw the alarm clock out the window.

The very first thing that startled Jimmy Childers that —

"Damnation!" he growled, at the first tap of the awakening bell. He threw, not a pillow, but a heavy book, and watched with grim satisfaction as the face crystal smashed to tiny bits.

When he went out he avoided the cigar stand and took a bus, not the subway.

"Insufferable !" snorted the old hellion he sat down beside. He gasped. It was his nemesis of the subway. Apparently she had decided to vary her program a bit, too. He changed seats and listened with reddening cheeks to the titters of the other passengers.

At the office he had an unexpected telephone call. It was from the clerk at his corner cigar stand.

"Oh, Jimmy," he said, "I guess you were late this morning and didn't have time to leave your bet — so I placed one for you. Hope you don't mind?"

"What horse?" asked Childers, glumly.

"Swiss Rhapsody. She's a long shot, but —"

Jimmy hung up and stared at the phone in front of him. He just couldn't get away from this thing.

All day long he tried to ring changes on his routine, and with astonishing minor results. But as to the major outcome there was never any difference. He was promoted, he won money, he saved the bank from robbery, he got engaged.

And the days that followed were no different. In the main, the events of June 14th had to be relived and relived until he found himself wincing at every one of the events that once had impressed him as such tremendous triumphs. Finally one day, during the hours usually devoted to the stroll in the park, he flung himself into a psychiatrist's office.

"Hm-m-m," commented the doctor, after he had smitten Childers' knees with little rubber mallets, and had scratched him on the feet and back with small prongs. "All I see are a few tremors. What's on your mind?"

"Plenty," said Jimmy savagely, and poured out his story.

"Hm-m-m," commented the doctor. "Interesting — most interesting."

He scribbled a prescription.

"Take this before you go to bed. It is simply something to make you sleep better. Then come back tomorrow at this same hour."

"Just one question, doctor."

"Yes?"

208

"What is today's date?"

"The fourteenth." The doctor smiled indulgently.

"And yesterday's?"

"The thirteenth. Come back tomorrow, please."

On the dot Jimmy Childers showed up at the doctor's office the next day — June the fourteenth, according to Childers' calendar. As he barged into the waiting room he was accosted with a chill:

"Name, please?"

He looked at the nurse in astonishment. Why, only the day before he had spent the best part of an hour dictating the answers of a questionnaire to her! He gave her a blank stare.

"The doctor is seen only by appointment," she added, looking at him disapprovingly.

"I . . . I made one yesterday," he stammered. "I was here . . . was examined!"

"You must be wrong," said she, sweetly. "Doctor just returned from Europe this morning."

"Oh, hell!" snarled Childers, and rushed from the place. He saw at once what a jam he was in. He had added another piece of furniture to his merry-go-round. That was all. He could very it within limits, of course, but he would never get anywhere.

Jimmy Childers charged up and down the walks of the park in a frenzy. If only Sunday would come — something to break this vicious circle. But no, there was no way to get to Sunday. With him it was always Friday.

That night he skipped the call on Genevieve. Instead he called her up and made some flimsy, insulting excuse. All she said was:

"You old fibber. You're just shy. The ring came up and I'm *so* thrilled. Of course I'll marry you, you silly, boy."

Weak and trembling he hung up. In his hand was a steamship ticket to Buenos Aires on the *Santa Mosca*, sailing at eleven p. m. He would try that on his jinx.

He got aboard all right, despite some arguments about a passport, and turned in at once, after dogging down the port and carefully locking the door. He took three of the tablets the doctor had prescribed instead of the one mentioned in the directions. If it were a dream, he ought to knock it now — different room, different bed, different environment, different everything. Jimmy closed his eyes. That night, the first for many a June 14th, he went to sleep with a ray of hope.

The very first thing that startled —

"Oh, Heaven!" sighed a haggard Jimmy Childers, as he shut off the clock, "another day of it."

He went through the Red Book almost name by name. He shook his head hopelessly. He had tried almost everything from chiropractors to psychiatrists. Then he found a name that somehow he had skipped. It was under necromancers. At once he grabbed a taxi and flew to the address — a stinking hole under the Williamsburg Bridge.

"Sorry," said the macabre person he contacted, sitting placidly among his black velvet drapes in a "studio" calculated to send a strictly normal person into the heebie-jeebies, "but I only deal with the dead. That is my specialty. Now if you want a corpse raised, or anything like that —"

"No, no," said Jimmy hastily, and paid his fee and left. Outside he shuddered at the memory of the funereal atmosphere of the faker's joint. He hoped fervently that *this* episode wasn't going to get embroidered into the design. His error was in not knowing what a necromancer was. He went back to the Red Book. It just had occurred to him that perhaps under sorcerers or thaumaturgists was what he wanted.

He found a lot of them, mostly in Harlem, and made a list.

The first four were as unsatisfactory as the necromancer, a circumstance that was very trying to Jimmy, for he could visit only one a day, using the blank two hours usually spent in the park. All the rest of the time he had to devote to the tedious business of being promoted, winning money, foiling robberies or making love.

But the fifth man was very much to Jimmy Childers' liking, after he recovered from the shock of the first interview. He found him in a dilapidated office in a shabby neighborhood in Greenpoint, and on the door was crudely lettered the frank but somewhat disconcerting legend, "Master Charlatan." Nevertheless Jimmy went boldly in.

"Ah," said the seer, after gazing for a while in a crystal sphere before him. "I perceive you are the victim of a blessing that misfired."

Jimmy Childers brought his eyes back to the bald-headed, fishy-eyed fat man who had guaranteed to help him. While the master charlatan had been in his semitrance Jimmy had been examining the charts that hung about. Obviously the man he had come to was versatile in the extreme, for there were diagrams of the human palm, knobs of the human cranium, weird charts of the heavens, and all the rest of the props that go with standard charlatanry.

"Now tell me something about this original fourteenth of June," said the sage. "How long ago was it, according to your reckoning?"

"Months and months," moaned Jimmy, thinking back on the intolerable monotony of it all.

"Can you recall the exact details of the first day — I mean the very first one — the prototype?"

"I doubt it," confessed Jimmy. "You see, I've, wriggled around and monkeyed with it so much that I'm all balled up."

"Try," said the wise one, calmly.

Hesitantly Jimmy Childers told his story, as best he could remember it, all the way to his going to bed the night of the genuine fourteenth of June.

"Now you begin to interest me," suddenly said the master, opening his eyes from the apparent slumber into which he had relapsed the moment Jimmy had begun talking. "Tell me more about that beggar woman on the Drive. Was she toothless except for a single yellow fang? Did her knuckles come to about her knees? Was she blind in her left eye?"

"Yes, yes," agreed Jimmy eagerly.

"Aha!" ejaculated the seer. "I thought so. Minnie the Malicious!" He made a note. "I'll report this to the Guild. She was disbarred long ago — for malpractice and incompetence."

Jimmy looked mystified.

"She used to be a practicing witch," explained the great one with a shrug, "now she is just a chiseler. You know . . . cheap curses, pretty enchantments and the like. But just what did she say to you, and *most particularly*, what kind of wishes did you make just after you left her?"

"Well," admitted Jimmy, "she came up whining and asked for a penny. I was feeling pretty high, so I gave her a five-spot."

"That was a mistake," murmured the sorcerer.

"That's all," said Jimmy, suddenly concluding. "She mumbled something, and I walked on."

"But you wished something?"

"Well, I do remember — don't forget what a wonderful day I'd had — that I was wishing every day was like that, or that I could live it over again, or something of the sort."

"Be very exact," insisted his interrogator.

"Sorry," said Jimmy.

"Let's go into the Mesmeric Department," said his consultant, leading the way into a shabby interior room. "Now sit there and keep your eye on the little jeweled light," he ordered.

It seemed only an instant before Jimmy woke up. The master charlatan was sitting in front of him placidly looking at him.

"Your exact wish," he said, "was a triple one, as I suspected. They usually are. Here are your mental words, 'Oh, I wish every day was like this one; I wish I could live it over again; I wish I'd never seen that old hag, she gives me the creeps.' "

"So what?" queried Jimmy, recalling it now.

"When you gave her such a magnificent present, she mumbled out that you would have your next three wishes granted. Oddly enough, if she had been an able practitioner, nothing would have happened —"

"That doesn't make sense," objected Jimmy.

"Oh, yes it does. You see, your last wish would have had the effect of canceling the others, as you would never have met her, see?"

"It is a little involved," frowned Jimmy.

"Yes, these things have a way of getting involved," admitted the wise one. "However, since she was a low-powered witch, so to speak, only the first wish came fully true, that is, every day — for you — was like that one. By the time you had gotten to the second one some of the punch was out of it. You didn't quite live it over

212

again. You had the power of varying it a little, which was a very fortunate circumstance, as otherwise you would have gone on doing it forever and ever."

"You mean I'm cured!" exclaimed Jimmy delightedly.

"Not so fast. When we come to the last wish, her power had petered out almost altogether. It did not do away with the fact that you had met her, but it was strong enough to cause you to avoid meeting her any more."

"I see," said Jimmy, hoping he really did.

"Now what you've got to do is to live that day over once more — the first one, mind you — including meeting Minnie; only the minute she mumbles, reverse your wish. That cancels everything."

"But I can't remember that day well enough —"

"I'll coach you," said the mesmerist. "While you were hypnotized I took it all down, every detail."

An hour later Jimmy Childers rose to go. He paid over to the magician all the money he had just collected on Swiss Rhapsody. The old man dropped it into his pocket with just the-hint of a chuckle.

"By the way," asked Jimmy, on the threshold, "what day is this?"

"That, my friend," replied the master charlatan with an oily smile, "is a mystery I'd advise you not to look into. Good day!"

Catalyst Poison

It was a wonderful idea, the thought solidifier — until the idea went whacky!

Oh yes, I knew Eddie Twitterly and I knew Rags Rooney. Come to think of it, I introduced them. And I knew all about their stunt from the very beginning. It's my job to know people and what's going on. How do you think I could how my job on the *Star* if I didn't?

My paper wouldn't print the lowdown on the Big Day because they thought it was too fishy. That a fellow with literally millions a day income should jump the traces and behave like Eddie did, was just too much for them. It shows you how little some editors understand human nature. There was nothing fishy about it to me, because I knew Eddie so well, knew how temperamental he was.

Eddie was smart as hell. All those degrees he had and the jobs he'd held are proof of that; but he was unreliable. He couldn't stand routine. That's why they kicked him off the university faculty. He didn't fit in the factory atmosphere they have up there, the regular hours and same old grind, month in and month out. Eddie was the kind that gets steamed up over something, goes at it hammer and tongs, day and night, and then all of a sudden drops it like a hot potato. Whenever he reached the fed-up stage, he'd go on a bat; and when I say bat, I *mean* bat. He'd stay blotto for ten days and, likely as not, wind up in a psychopathic ward somewhere.

The psychiatrists said he had an inner conflict. He was part scientist, part artist, and it's a bad combination. His hobby was modeling. Sometimes, right in the middle of a scientific investigation, he'd get the yen to do some sculpting, and off he'd go. It muddled his work in both fields and kept him from being a big success in either. Then he'd get to thinking about *that*, and the next you'd know, he'd be draped across the bar somewhere telling the mahogany polisher all his troubles.

I bumped into him one night, shortly after he lost that physics professorship. It was at the Spicy Club, and from the looks of things, Eddie was celebrating his liberation from academic life. I had Rags Rooney with me. Now Rags is an utterly different type. He's a gambler and promoter; backs fighters and wrestlers, ordinarily, but he'll take a part of a Broadway show, or stake a nut inventor, or lay his money anywhere he sees a sporting chance. Sometimes he cleans up, sometimes he loses his shirt, but generally speaking he picks winners.

That night Eddie kept harping on some wild plan he'd just hatched to tie up his science to his art. When we found him, he was already at the talkative stage, and he proceeded to pour it on us. I was surprised to see how interested Rags got, because the whole proposition sounded screwy to me. But, after all, Rags had played long shots before and come out ahead of them, so I began to pay more attention.

Eddie's hunch, as near as I can remember it, was to build a machine based on these newfangled notions of the atom. You know the idea; that there is no such thing as matter; that everything is simply a lot of electric charges zipping and zooming around and bouncing off each other. According to him, butter and steel are just different combinations of them, revolving at different speeds. All right, he'd say, if it's electrical, you can upset it by electricity; change one to the other, or to something else — a brick, or even a pint of red ink.

From that, he went on to tell us that feelings and thought are electricity, too. Brain cells are little batteries, and when you think, currents run back and forth in your brain. I hadn't heard that one before, but Eddie insisted that it's so; said that the current could even be metered. Well, the payoff was that he thought he could hook the two things together. If he had a machine to amplify his mental powerhouse and focus it on something — anything, even air, is always a flock of swirling electrons — he could make the electrons jump the way he wanted them to. Whatever picture was in his mind would form there.

"Just think," he said, "with my Psycho-Substatiatior I could model without clay or tools. When my thoughts solidify and I see any faults and want to change them, all I have to do is think the revision. And if it comes out all right, then I imagine the material I want — marble or bronze, or even gold — and there it is! No casts to make, no chiseling, no manual work at all — a finished piece."

It must have been the crack about gold that made Rags sit up and take notice. Whatever it was, before I realized what was happening, they'd made a deal and were shaking on it. Rags was to put up the money, Eddie the brains, and split fifty-fifty on what came of it. I thought then — and I haven't changed my mind — that it was a mistake. I couldn't imagine the two of them getting together on what to do with the machine when they got it built. Spoke to Rags in the washroom about it, and warned him how flighty Eddie was.

"Hell," he said, "I've been handling sporting talent all my life and they don't come any more temperamental. This guy'll be a cinch."

I didn't see either of them for a long time — months. One night, I dropped into Rags' apartment to chin a minute with him and his missus, and the minute I got inside, I knew I oughtn't to have come. There was a first-class family row going on. I tried to duck, but she grabbed me and began laying it into me, too.

"You started all this," she said scornfully, "you and your chiseling boy friend! Thirty thousand smackers is what that no-good souse has taken this poor fish for — and look at what we get!" Boy, she was sore.

She dragged me over to the table where there was a little white statuette. It was a comical thing, not bad at all; a potbellied little horse with a big mournful eyes, made out of some white stone, but, of course, not good for much except a gimcrack.

Then she started raving again, and I learned more about Rags' home life in the next fifteen minutes than I ever dreamed of before.

"And him sounding off all the time about how he makes his living outta suckers," she snorted, "but if he hasn't been taken for a ride this time, I never saw it done. He's bought a half interest in what that dope thinks about! Imagine! Why, wine, woman, and song is all that poor louse ever thinks about, and you know what a rotten voice he has."

"What's his voice got to do with it?" Rags growled.

She gave him a dirty look. "That's why he concentrates on the other two."

Rags jammed on his hat and gave me the sign to come along. We went town to Mac's place and Rags threw down a coupla slugs before he said a word.

"Oh, everything's all right," he said in a minute, "only I see where I gotta get tough with the guy. He's not practical. The machine works like he said. What he thinks about comes out. But what the hell good is it if his mind runs to goofy doll horses? I ask you. And it could just as well been a ten-pound diamond. But that's not all. To celebrate, he goes on a four-day binge. I just found him. Two of the boys are sitting with him now in the steam room down at the gym. Soon as they cook it out of him, *I'm* going down and work on him."

I didn't say a word. Eddie's geared for two speeds, full ahead — his own way — and reverse. If Rags was going to put pressure on him, I figured all he'd get would be a backfire.

They must have compromised things after a fashion. Next I heard, Rags was going around town trying to peddle a statue, a gold one this time, for a price like a couple of hundred thousand. I wanted to keep track of things, because I saw a good story coming up when the secrecy was off, so I hunted him up.

Sure enough, the statue was Eddie's second creation. It was gold, but Rags was ready to chew nails.

"The museums won't touch it," he complained, "say it's ugly. But where else will you find so much dough?"

He was right. It was ugly, terrible. A sloppy, bulging, fat, nude woman.

"Rent it to a photographer for the 'before' picture for a reducing ad," I suggested; then, seeing he was in no joking mood, I asked how it happened.

217

"Live and learn," said Rags, sad-like. "Like a dumbbell, I let him have his way. He was dead set to do statuary, so I says, 'O.K., but be sure to make it outta something I can hock in case the art part misses.' So he says, 'I'll do a Venus,' and I says, 'Shoot, only make her gold.; Well, he's got funny ideas about women. At the start, she was skinny enough to be an exhibit in a T.B. clinic, I kept saying, 'Put some meat on her,' thinking all the time about the weight of it when I went to sell it. He was sore at first, then he got to giggling and did what I said, and how!"

"What the hell," I told Rags. "You're sitting pretty. Go down to Wall Street and look up some of those millionaires that are moaning about the gold standard. The law says they can't hoard but they can own golden works of art."

He took my advice and found a buyer all right, but getting that quarter of a million so easy was what ruined him. It made him greedy. Rags had made hits before, like I said, but never anything like that. Now that he had a taste of big money, he was hungry for more and hiked the limit to the sky. He was all for quantity production, and since he had plenty of cash, he began to rig for it.

In planning gold by the ton, common sense told him they couldn't go on working in Eddie's third-floor studio. That plump Venus damn near caved the joists in. rags found a place near the foot of Forty-fourth Street, in the block west of Eleventh Avenue. It was an abandoned ice plant, a big barn of a place with a dirt floor. Eddie had to dismantle his machine and take it down there, then work for two or three months making parts for the new and bigger machine with it.

The day they were ready to ride with the new equipment, Rags asked me to come down and watch it work. The place looked like a cross between an iron foundry and a movie studio. The floor was laid out in grids, four of them, each with moulds for two hundred gold bricks. Pointing down at them was a circle of vacuum tubes mounted on high stands with reflectors back of them. At one side was a sort of throne where Eddie was to sit. Wires, ran all over the place. Rags filled up the molds wit water, and left a hose dribbling into the header so there'd be plenty of additional water to make up the difference in weight.

Eddie put up a last-minute battle about having to do something as tedious as thinking up hundreds on hundreds of little gold bars, all alike. But Rags couldn't see anything but bullion. He had sweat blood trying to get rid of the fat Venus and he wanted no more of it. At five thousand dollars apiece, the gold bricks were in handy, manageable units, and the sum of them was a fortune. Two million a day is good pay, even if you don't like the work, Rags argued. I have to admit that the argument would have sold me. Eddie grumbled some more, but he focused his apparatus on the first bank of molds, put on his metal headpiece, and got on his throne.

As soon as the tubes lit up, the water began to turn pink, then a ruby red. Colloidal gold, Rags whispered. Eddie must have taught him that word. In about two hours, the first quarter of a the job was done. All that time, Eddie had sat there, frowning, concentrating on the idea of twenty-four-carat gold lying in neat rows of pigs. He looked pretty tired and disgusted when he finished, but he only stopped to eat a sandwich. He growled at Rags some more, then tackled the next batch. I struck around. You don't get to see anything like that every day.

In the afternoon, Eddie filled up Grid No. 3. He complained a lot about his head aching, but Rags wasn't listening to him. He was pacing up and down, gloating over the gold, or else sitting in a corner, figuring on the backs of envelopes. Eddie was limp by the time he got to the last set of molds, but Rags kept egging him on, yelling at him like a regular Simon Legree to hurry up, think faster and harder, so it would all be done before night. I felt sorry for Eddie, but all he did was sigh and slip his helmet on and go to work.

It was about an hour later that things began to go sour. I heard Rags yipping, and went over to where he was. He looked scared. The molds under his feet were full of some gosh-awful, fluffy, pinkish mess.

"That's horrible," he said, sniffing the air. Then he ran over and began shaking Eddie.

Eddie had been sitting with his eyes closed, mumbling something to himself, but when Rags pounded him, he snapped out of it, shut off the juice, and came down to see what the excitement was about.

Eddie was puzzled, too, for a minute, then he began laughing.

"Tripe," he said, "that's what it is–tripe!" and then went off into another fit of laughing.

Rags was glaring at him all the time, wondering what was so funny. "Whadya mean, tripe?" he wanted to know, sore as hell.

"Why," said Eddie, as soon as he could get his breath, "I guess I must have gone nuts thinking about nothing but gold. Now I remember. I got to thinking what a lot of tripe this whole thing is; kept saying it over and over, *'This is a lot of tripe.'* Ha-ha-ha! And that's what I got!"

Well, they had it round and round. All Rags could see was a million dollars spoiled by sheer inattention, right when his mouth was watering for big money. But after they'd jawed awhile, Eddie agreed to clean up the tripe, make it into gold, but later on after he'd had some rest. Then I asked Rags what he was going to do with so much gold, when he had it.

"Sell it to the bank," he said, cocky as you please.

When I finished telling him about the gold laws, he was worried.

That night he went down to Washington to find out where he stood. What they said to him, I never knew; but after that , gold was *out*. Rags came back damning the administration like a charter member of the grass-roots conference. But he was already full of new plans. He showed me the schedule — so many tons of platinum, then so much silver, and so on. I warned him he was hunting trouble, driving Eddie like that. I thought it was a miracle that Eddie hadn't torn loose after the tripe episode. He usually did when he was fed up with anything.

"I've taken care of that," said Rags in an offhand way. "I've got to go abroad. I'm going to Amsterdam to find out how many diamonds the market can take without cracking. While I'm gone, to be sure nothing'll slip, I've fixed it with the O'Hara Agency to keep a guard on the place, so nobody can get in or out. Eddied don't know it yet, but he'll be comfortable enough. I had a bedroom fixed up down there, and a kitchenette, and I hired a Filipino boy to stay and cook for him. He'll have to keep busy, and he can't get in trouble.

"Oh, izzat so?" I told him. "Well, you don't know Eddie. That boy could get in trouble in Alcatraz. When he gets a thirst, he can think up ways and means that'd surprise you."

Rags wouldn't listen to me, and now he's sorry. It was bad enough to lay out all that monotonous work thinking up truckloads of platinum, but to lock Eddie in that way, without even telling him about it, was just plain damn foolishness. I knew Eddie'd hit the ceiling as soon as he found it out; and whenever he did, it was going to be just too bad.

And when it happened, it was exactly that way.

I went down there one night, about a week later. It was drizzling, but I felt like a stroll, and I was worried a little about Eddie, locked up I that old plant practically alone. When I got almost to the door of it, one of O'Hara's strong-arm men stepped out from behind a signboard and flagged me down. I showed my card and told him I was a friend of Rags and knew all about the layout, but it didn't get me by. Yet I did want to know how Eddie was taking it, so I slipped the fellow a fin, and he talked.

The second night after Rags had gone, Eddie came out of the plant and started uptown. The watchmen headed him off and turned him back. Eddied didn't understand at first, and cut up quite a bit. They handled him as gently as they could, and finally shoved him through the door without roughing him up too much. It was when he heard what Rag's orders were that he went wild. He went back inside, but a couple of minutes later the door popped open and Eddie kicked the goo-goo out and threw his baggage after him.

"Tell Rooney," he yelled to the dicks, "there's more ways of choking a dog than feeding it hot butter." And with that he slammed the door and barred it.

That sounded bad to me. I wanted to know the rest, and the O'Hara man went on. The next night, they heard sounds of a wild party going on inside. That was strange, because they had kept close watch on the place and knew nobody had gone in. But there it was — singing and laughing, plenty of whoopee. And it had been going on ever since!

I listened, but I couldn't hear a thing. Then we could make out a faint groaning.

221

"Oh, said the operative, "that's all right. Too much party. You know. They were fighting last night. At least, we could hear the guys bawling the girls out, and they were crying."

"Girls?" I asked. "What girls?"

"See that crack over the door?" he said. "We piles some boxes and barrels up and took a squint through there. It was something to see, I can tell you — a perfect harem, like in the movies, only more so. Five or six dames, dolled up like nobody's business, all eating off of big gold platters and passing jugs of drinks around. The only guy in there is this Twitterly, rigged out like a sultan, with a pair of 'em on his lap, handing the stuff to him. What a life! And they pay me to stand here in the rain to keep him in! Where would he want to go? He's got everything. Come on, let's hop down to the coffee pot and get on the outside of some hot chow. This joint don't need watching."

It was raining in earnest by then, so I went back to the Star office to file some copy. It must have been well past midnight when I came out. The rain seemed to be over, so I started for the subway on foot. In Forty-third Street, near Eighth Avenue, I saw a crowd standing around the window of a cafeteria, peeking in, and some of them were staring up at the swinging sign out over the sidewalk. There was a ladder against the building and I could make out a cop near the top of it struggling with something perched on the sign. The cop was wriggling and cussing, and whatever was up there was pecking at him and hissing away at a great rate.

Just then the crown let out yelps. "There's another one!" somebody said, and they all ran out to the edge of the curb, looking upward all the time. On the very end of the sign sat a fuzzy little thing, hardly bigger than your fist, but it had a tail about a yard long that hung down and curled up at the end. Its eyes shone like a cat's. Oh, more than that, they flamed — bright violet, not greenish or orange, the way a cat's do.

"He's already got four of 'em down," a fellow told me, meaning the cop. "They're inside."

I pushed into the cafeteria, and there were some others, sure enough, sitting in a row along the counter. They seemed to be harmless enough, after you got over their looks, but what they were was something else again. They may have started out to be marmosets, but something sure went wrong with them. One was a bright-lemon color, another heliotrope, one emerald green, and the other a little bit of everything. They kept flipping out forked tongues, the way snakes do, and hissing. But those violet eyes were what got you. They gave you the creeps.

The cop outside came in, carrying the latest one he'd caught, a sky-blue one, with purple stripes. Two curbstone naturalists were poking at the little animals and arguing about what they could be. In the midst of that, we heard sirens outside and a police patrol car dashed up. A cop got out of the car and came into the restaurant towing a sleepy, bald-headed man who looked like he hadn't quite finished dressing.

"Do you see what I see?" the cop with the blue monkey asked him, soon as he was inside, throwing me a wink.

"Did you get me out of bed for a gag?" snapped the bald-headed man, huffy as could be. "It's a publicity stunt!" And with that he stalked out.

"A fat lot of help that zoo expert turned out to be," the cop that brought him said. "Stay with it, Clancy; the S.P.C.A. wagon'll be here soon."

I'd seen all I wanted to see, so I blew. Down the street about a hundred feet I began to feel something dragging against my shins at every step. It was dark there and I couldn't see very well, at first, but it felt like I was in high grass. I stopped and looked down. I was up to my waist in hairy, palpitating stuff! I could see a lot of little knobs swaying up and down about the size of baseballs, and each little knob had a pair of pearly lights on it. They were dim, dim as glowworms, but there was something scary about it.

I must have yelled, because people came running up behind me, but they stopped some little distance away. As they did, the bobbing balls and the grassy stuff spread out all over the street like smoke. The way they heaved up and down and slid sideways at the same time made me sick at the stomach. Then I had a better look. They were spiders! Not the hard-boiled, tough kind of spider, with hair on its chest, but the old-fashioned wiry granddaddy longlegs — except that these must have been all of thirty inches high! I must have been pretty jittery, because the next thing I tried to do was climb a brick wall.

I found that was impractical, so I pulled myself together and began to wonder where they came from and what to do about it. They were scattering all over the street then, going away from me, and the other people were backing away from them, yelling.

Presently the emergency truck came and the boys tumbled off and started to work on the spiders. They shot a few, but soon quit that. It would have been an all-night business; there were thousands of them. Some of the cops began whanging them with nightsticks, but all a longlegs would do when it was swatted was sag a little, then come up for more. Finally, one of the cops began gathering 'em up by the legs, tying 'em in bundles with wire. The first thing I knew, the whole crowd had joined in and were having a lot of fun out of it. In a little while they had most of them tied up in shocks, like wheat. I never thought I'd live to see the day when they stacked bales of live spiders on the sidewalks of New York, but that's what they did that night.

A couple of dozen of them got away and went jiggling out into Times Square, with a lot of newsies chasing them. The cops let them corner what were left, because another call had come in. several, in fact. Strange varmints had popped up in two or three nearby places. I didn't know what was happening, any more than anybody else. Some thought a big pet shop had been burglarized and the door left open, and some others thought this and that, but none of it made sense.

I went with the emergency truck next to Forty-fourth, the other side of Eighth Avenue, where a big serpent was reported to be terrorizing the neighborhood. The moment we got there, we saw the serpent, all right. We couldn't miss. It was big, and it was luminous! I should say the thing was a hundred or more feet long and a yard thick. It was made of some transparent, jellylike substance, a deep ruby red, but inside we could see its skeleton very plainly and a couple of dogs it had eaten.

The cops tried to shoot it at first, but that was a waste of time. The bullets would go through — you could see the holes for about a minute afterward. Then the holes would close up. Three or four dozen slugs didn't faze the thing. The tried to lasso it, but that didn't work either. In the first place, it was slick and slimy, and could wiggle right on through. Besides, the slime seemed to be corrosive. When a rope did stick for a few seconds, it dropped apart, charred shreds.

Next they chopped at it with axes. They picked a place about midway of the snake, or eel, or whatever you want to call it, and went to it, two men on a side. It was like chopping rubber, but they did get it in two. Then the fun began. The after piece sprouted a head, then sheered out and took the other side of the street. Both the original serpent and the detached copy stretched out to full length, and in a few minutes the cops had two snakes to worry about, instead of one.

"Forget the axes," said the lieutenant; "we gotta think of a better one than that."

It was all very exciting to me, but the main effect it had on the cops was to make 'em sore. They had nearly everything in the world on that wagon I the way of equipment, and none of it any good in a case like that. Finally somebody brought an acetylene torch into action, and that was the beginning of the end. That is, the end of that particular pair of monsters. When the flame hit 'em, the parts just hissed, shriveled up, and disappeared. In a little while there was nothing left of them except the skeletons of the two dogs and some charred meat that hadn't been digested.

A police inspector drove up in time to see the finish. "I'm glad you boys found the answer," he said, "because there's plenty more. Everything the other side of Tenth Avenue is blocked with 'em. Let's get going."

"Blocked" wasn't the word; he ought've said "buried." When we got over there, we found the fire department and about a thousand other cops already there. The avenue had been cleared, but the first four or five streets above Forty-second were packed with squirming, bellowing, hissing monsters. In some places they filled the street almost to the second-story windows. Everything that crawls, and a lot more, was all mixed up there. After one look, I knew that gelatin eel was hardly worth remembering. In this jam ahead of me were centipedes a half block long, lizards, snakes, animals that didn't look real, storybook animals, dragons, griffins, and the like. The firemen had snared a thing built along the general lines of a crocodile, but it was covered with mirror scales instead of the usual kind. It sparkled beautifully whenever it'd thresh around.

The people in the tenements were awake, and taking it hard. The women and children were on the roofs, or upper levels of the fire escapes. The men stayed lower down, some of them poking at the monsters with curtain poles, bed slats, or anything they had. On the avenue side, firemen had ladders up and were taking the people out as fast as they could. Cars and trucks kept rolling up with more men and equipment. I understood they had sent out a general alarm for all the welding torch equipment in the city. Soon they had lines of flames working into the cross streets.

I watched them burn and slaughter the creatures for a while, but anything gets tiresome. Daylight came and I was getting hungry. I did think of Eddie several times, and wondered how he was making out, cooped up in that old plant. He was entirely cut off from me, probably surrounded by these monsters, but it never occurred to me to worry about him. I knew he had thick brick walls around him, and only one door, and that barred. I broke away and went back to midtown for some breakfast.

While I ate, I looked over the papers. The extras were not out yet, and there was nothing in them except rather facetious, wisecracking accounts of the marmoset and spider episodes. Then I heard somebody say the militia had been called out, and that the police commissioner had set up temporary headquarters in a shack in Bryant Park. I decide that was the place to go to find out what else'd happened besides what I'd seen myself.

They had already built a stockade or corral there, and in it were a number of the monsters that had been taken alive somehow or other. There was a crowd of scientists hanging around, too, and a funny-looking lot they were. I walked through them, admiring the variety of the layout of their whiskers and listening to their shop talk. Some were taking notes and making sketches and were very serious about the whole business. Others were scoffing openly and saying it couldn't be, there were no such animals. The rest simply stood and looked. I guess they were what you'd call the open-minded ones. One bird had brought his typewriter and was sitting on a camp stool, pecking away to beat the band. I asked him what he was doing and he said he was writing a book. The title was "Phenomenal

Metropolitan Fauna." Pretty good, huh? That's what I call being a live wire.

I flashed my card on the guard at the headquarters shack, and went in. A clerk was handing the commissioner a phone.

"What now?" I heard the old boy say, in a weary tone. Then he threw the phone down and tore his hair. "Pink elephants," he said, to nobody in particular, and I thought he was going to break down and cry. "Three of them, coming up Forty-second Street."

"That's going too far," said the A.P. man, tearing up his notes. "I'm through. Some Barnum is putting over the biggest hoax yet. I won't be a party to it."

I started to leave. I wanted to see how they handled the elephants, but something new was coming in over the phone, so I waited. That time it was the report about the sea serpent. Up till then I hadn't given a thought to the marine aspects of the plague, but I hung on, listening to the details.

A sea serpent had slid into the river a little above the Forty-second Street ferry and turned down the river. The battleship *Texas* happened to be coming up the stream at the time and sighted it. They did some fast work and got a couple of motor sailers over and began chasing it. I will have to check back the files to find out what became of that sea serpent. My recollection of it is that it got away; dived and disappeared somewhere in the upper bay. But the *Texas'* boats stayed with it to the end, and I heard they had a grand time, bouncing one-pounder shot off the thing's head. It had awful hard scales and they couldn't dent it. But it must have been timid, because it kept going as hard as it could and never once tried any rough stuff on the launches. One whack of that tail, and it would have been all over for them.

You understand by now, I guess, that those monsters were not really ferocious; they just *looked* bad. They didn't bite, most of them, but they'd jolt you into psychosis if you were the least weak-minded.

I suppose I seem awful dumb, now that we know what it was all about, not to have guessed earlier what was making the plague of monsters. But there was so much happening, and so fast, my brain didn't work like it ought. I might never have tumbled if Rags

Rooney hadn't come rushing in, wild-eyed. He had landed an hour before from a transatlantic airplane and had been trying to get to the plant.

"Where's Eddie?" he fairly panted, grabbing my arm.

"At the plant," I told him, "by your arrangement."

"Can't you see?" moaned Rags, agonized. "He's done it again! The plant is the center of this mess, and Eddie's turning these things out with the Sicco . . . Psy . . . never mind, you know. He's got the horrors, the D.T.'s, like the doctors said he would, if he didn't lay off. We gotta stop him!"

I dragged Rags over to the commissioner and we finally made him understand. He was not what you'd call a quick thinker, but that day he'd try anything. In a minute we had the Edison substation on the line and were telling them to cut the juice off the plant.

"It's already off, a voice said. "The circuit breakers just kicked out, and won't stay in. They must have a bad overload down there, or a short."

That was the worst possible news. "Gosh," I thought, "Eddie's already put out a couple thousand cubic yards of assorted animals since midnight, including three elephants at one crack, without blowing any fuses. What *can* be coming now?"

The commissioner saw something was up, so he went with us, taking us in his car. We tore down Forty-second, blasting the air with our siren. About a block west we met the elephants coming along, docile enough, some national guardsmen leading 'em. I'd heard of pink elephants all my life, but you've got to see one to really know. I think it's the peculiar shade.

We had to park at Eleventh Avenue. There were still plenty of reptiles and minor pests packed around the plant, but flame throwers were slowly cutting their way into them.

The eaves of the plant were still oozing a few small snakes and bats, but the big door was open. The elephants had done that, I suppose. Overhead there were several army and navy planes swooping, machine-gunning the vampires, pterodactyls, and what have you that took to the air. To the side of us, a little way off, were a couple of three-inch field guns that they'd sent down in case something really big and unmanageable should come out.

We heard a big noise down at the plant, and when we looked at it again, we saw the roof begin to rise and the walls to bulge, bricks popping in every direction. Everything fell to pieces, and as soon as the dust cleared away, we were looking at the most gigantic, frightful-appearing thing there ever was, not even barring dinosaurs. It was fat and loathsome and hairy. There was no head, nothing but a gaping red mouth, full of bayonet-like teeth, with a ring of octopus tentacles around it. It began groping around with the tentacles and started picking up the small-fry monsters that were within reach. I saw it tuck away a plaid camel with one feeler while it took a coupla turns around a unicorn with another. Then the artillery let loose.

The curator fellow that was writing the book by the corral had wormed his way through the police lines and had been standing close behind us for some time. He pulled me by the sleeve.

"Beg pardon," he chirped, "but did I understand your friend to say that Twitterly was in there operating a machine by which he could telepathically control chemical changes?"

"Something like that," I admitted, not wanting to say too much.

"He was a good physicist, and a chemist, too. I am surprised he permitted ethyl alcohol to enter the reaction. It's a very unreliable catalyst. Tricky, *quite*."

229

Transients Only

An expert ghost-manager ought to be able to do a lot for a Washington boardinghouse caught between OPA ceilings and a triple-decker mortgage, at that!

"Charles," said the mother, "you annoy me dreadfully."

"Sorry, mom," replied Charles without getting up or turning his head, "what have I done now?" He was lying stomach down on the floor, reading volume two of Lindemyth's celebrated work, "Spectral Character as Deduced From Behavior." The chapter immediately before him dealt with "Motivation."

"It is not what you have done, Charles," said his mother firmly, "but what you haven't done." She sighed. "You have no ambition; you're content with being a mere soda jerker; all you do is moon around the house, reading fool books about spooks. And here, when Granny is about to lose her house, we can't do anything about it except sit back and let the bank take it. You're a man now — or at least you are as big as a man. You ought to be beginning to take on some responsibility. Though Heaven knows how you'll ever get anywhere with your head crammed full of rubbish about ghosts and things."

She sighed another reproachful sigh, pushed the cat out of her lap and rose. Charles rolled over and sat up, slamming the book shut as he did. "Apparitions and manifestations are very interesting phenomena," he said, "and properly manipulated might be very beneficial —"

"There you go with your big words again," she snapped it him, and picked up his book gingerly, holding it at arm's length as if the very contact with it might contaminate her. "I suppose, you are trying to say that spooks are some earthly good. Well, if you'll show me just one instance . . . just one, I say . . . when a ghost is any use at all, I'll take back all I ever said. Fiddlesticks! If there was such a thing as ghosts, the best they'd be would be a pesky nuisance."

"Yes, mom," he said meekly. He knew from long experience that there was no use arguing with his mother when she got off on that track. He got up languidly from where he sat, unfolding all his six feet of gawky lankness.

His mother glared at his mouth, hanging weakly open; noted for the thousandth time his pimple-spangled face and neck, his vacant dull eye and ill-kept hair; and wondered what curse she had been under that this changeling should have been foisted on her. But she knew that nagging did no good; she had tried that long enough. So she sighed once more and said wearily, "I do wish you'd get a better job." Then she went back toward the kitchen.

Charles sat down in the chair she had vacated, picked the cat up and reinstated it. Then he looked thoughtfully into its provocative green eyes as he softly stroked it's fur. He was pondering the complex of problems that somehow in the last five minutes had knitted themselves all into one, come to a crisis, and demanded solution. There was the sordid business of making moneywhich bored him, but which was expected of him. There was the old battle about his fondness for lore of the supernatural and phantasmal. And now there was the present family emergency — Granny and her involved financial affairs.

Granny was incredibly ancient, but somehow she managed. For one thing she had a house, an old brick affair on "O" Street, not far from Dupont Circle. In bygone days when the great foreign embassies were clustered about that circle the house had been thought a mansion. But long since it had been cut up into many small rooms, occupied for the most part by low-paid government clerks. The pittances paid in by the tenants had heretofore been enough to feed and dress the old lady, but there had never been enough over to more than pay the taxes, keep the antiquated   plumbing in working order or the roof from leaking unbearably. There certainly was not enough to do anything about reducing the triple layer of mortgages. Indeed, during the depression years there had not been

231

enough income even to keep abreast of the interest. In those days the banks were generous — being already glutted with fore-closed real estate — but now that was changed. Another great war was on, the city's landlords were in their seventh heaven. One could grant cot space as a gracious favor and still charge a price for it that would have shamed a Capone. That being so, the bank became obdurate. It was time, they said, to fork over a little cash. Or else.

Charles contemplated that ultimatum for a long while. He was fond of his granny in his own peculiar way, and he hated to see the old house go. So he puckered his brow and thought. In all fairness it should be said that Charles was not the goof he looked. It was not that he lacked brains or ability that set him apart from the herd and made him seem inferior. It was that his brain operated in a realm unconsidered by most other people. His thoughts ran in different channels, and though often arriving at the same destination as those of the more orthodox thinkers, proceeded by a route exceedingly devious and bizarre. Now that he faced a dilemma caused by his grandmother's financial crisis and made difficult by his peculiar attitude toward life, he let the queer mechanism of his mentality slip into gear and begin grinding its way out of the mess of conflicting desires that beset him.

In a little bit he came to several conclusions. Out of his analysis emerged one prime villain. That villain was the governmental agency known as the OPA. It was that supposedly beneficent office that had upset the apple cart. They said Washington rents were too high. They froze them where they were. Worse, they walked back the cat and pushed them down to levels near where they used to be. That was what was ruining granny. For the prices of the things. she used were up. It did not help her that every room and cubbyhole in the house was occupied by a paying tenant, or that there was a constant stream of eager would-be tenants forever at the door. Notwithstanding the demand, she could only get so much. Therefore, unless something was done speedily she would surely lose the house.

Charles arrived at another very clear fact. The OPA was too big to be bucked. Also the bank was too big to be bucked. He had neither powerful friends nor money. The problem defied all solution by ordinary means. But then Charles rarely thought of things in ordinary terms. He gazed into the enigmatic green eyes of the purring animal on his lap and knew at once what he must do. The time for reading and theorizing had past. The time for action had come. He must put his books away and apply the special knowledge he had acquired and the curious talents he knew he must possess. He reached his decision. What could not be done by usual means must be done by the unusual. He required assistance from the spectral world. And that indicated most clearly that' he must seek out a ghost and take counsel with him.

Some would have thought that a queer decision. Not Charles. It was so obviously a reasonable one that he would have thought it silly to even challenge it. Writs, warrants and injunctions mean nothing to ghosts. Ghosts could get away with things that no mortal could hope to. Hence the imperative need for making contact with a first-class phantom at once.

"Oh, mom," called Charles. "I'm going out for a while. When I get back I'll fix up things for granny."

He dumped the cat on the rug, spent five minutes in his room, and then was gone. Ten days later his mother anxiously frowned and chalked off another date on the calendar.

"Charles is *so* queer," she muttered unhappily. "It's going on two weeks now, and all he said was that he-was going out for a while. I do wonder what he's up to."

Charles was traveling. When he left home he withdrew what money he had in a savings bank and bought a rickety old flivver. Then for days and days he hunted ghosts. His jalopy browsed through side roads and country lanes, always on the lookout for gaunt and abandoned houses. There were not many, for the war boom was making itself felt all over the country. Few houses were vacant; and of those, fewer still had the reputation of being haunted. Charles made it a rule to spend his nights in such houses, but the experiences were disappointing. Either the spectral population of the region had emigrated or were ineffective practitioners of their art. For though he slept in many gloomy and dilapidated places, not once did he experience anything that could not be explained rationally. Stairs and floor boards did creak, but houses do settle. Loose tin screeches in the breeze, and sudden chilling eddies of night air often give ghostly effects, but not sufficiently so to convince a connoisseur such as Charles. Not that he had ever seen a ghost in the flesh, so to speak, but his reading had been most extensive.

Then one day, when he was about ready to give up in disgust, he saw the place he was after. It was in central Pennsylvania, and it met every specification the most exacting ghost hunter could demand. It was on a hill well off the highway, and there was no gate in the fence or road to it that Charles could see, so he stopped beside the road and gazed up at the somber place in frank admiration. It bore all the stigmata of an accursed spot. It not only looked as a haunted place would look, but seemed to exude a mysterious and ominous something that chilled the-flesh and filled the heart with foreboding. Charles was thrilled to the marrow. At last!

Though it was mid-July and everywhere else the fields were lush and green and the trees in heavy leaf, the hill on which the house stood was as a negative oasis. What trees there were were stark and lifeless, gray or black or a scabrous white, except that to some still clung a few dried brown leaves of some long-past autumn. Where grass should have been there was but brakes of sear brush, thorny and wiry. No living thing was to be seen except a wheeling carrion bird patrolling his beat high above the house itself.

The house was too far away to be clearly distinguishable, but there was an air of brooding tragedy about it that was unmistakable. It must have been very old, and untenanted for many a year. Its roof sagged, one of its chimneys had toppled, and all the windows gaped darkly vacant as do eye sockets in a skull. And as Charles looked he thought he heard the vibrant tones of a great gong struck, followed by a piercing scream. He listened to the uncanny sounds with something akin to glee. Then he drove on, for it was yet early in the afternoon.

Four miles beyond he came to the village. He parked his jenny and approached an elderly bearded man who sat on the steps of a store whittling diligently on a sliver of white pine board.

"Can you tell me, mister," asked Charles, "what is the history of that empty house back down the road?"

The old man looked up at him, studying him with manifest disapproval. Charles did not realize that the jubilant leer he wore added no beauty to his pimply and allegedly moronic face.

"The less you know about that house, bud," croaked the ancient, "the better off you'll be. You shouldn't even have looked at it. It's poison. It's jinxed. There's a ha'nt on it."

"Somebody murdered there once upon a time?"

"Couldn't say. Nobody knows. It's always been ha'nted."

"Anybody ever prove it?"

"Uh-huh. Plenty. Back in the eighties the two Tarbell brothers and another fellow went there on a dare to spend the night. They was found hung the next day — up in the attic of the house. Every ten years or so some other smart-Aleck would get the yen to go and see whether the place was haunted, as if anybody with ears couldn't hear the yells and screaming that go on there without getting closer'n a mile to the place. They all hung themselves or went crazy."

"Did any scientists ever look into it?" persisted Charles.

"Yep. The very last guy that went there. That musts been all of twenty years ago. He was a professor fellow from New York — called hisself a psychic-research worker. He went up there one dark, stormy night. We found him next day wandering in the fields, his hair white as snow and his skin as yellow as a lemon. The stuff he babbled was something awful — what you could understand of it, cause he kept on screaming and goin' into fits whenever he'd try to talk. Si Hall's oldest boy — a kid about like you — went crazy just from hearing him. They took 'em off to the insane asylum, but I don't think the professor lived more'n a week, after that."

"Nobody would care, then, if I went down there and spent the night?" asked Charles.

"You're darn tootin' somebody cares," said the old man dryly. "We got too tarnation many graves in our Potter's Field now to be addin' any more at the county's expense. Take my advice, young spud, and keep on goin' aheadin' the way you are."

"Thanks, pop," said Charles.

The sun was setting when Charles found the place where the old road had gone in. Few vestiges of the road were left, and there was no gate. Someone had replaced it with a barbed-wire panel years before and put up a sign against trespassing. But Charles let neither impediment stop him. He dismounted from his jalopy and clipped

235

the strands of wire with a pair of side-cutting pliers. Then he boldly drove in.

Things started happening at once. The tin lizzie bucked, snorted and backfired, but he fed'her more gas, yanked savagely at the spark; and forced her through the dead grass and brush that covered the old trail. But the confident, cocksure Charles almost screarned when he became acutely aware of something cold and slimy slithering down his neck. It was as if someone had emptied a bowl of ice-cold gelatin inside his shirt front except that this stuff squirmed and crawled. It slid past his belly and came to a wiggly stop just above his lap. It was his first real experience with spectral artistry, and his reflexes won. Before he could stop himself he had ripped his clothes open and was tearing at the substance with clawing hands. But there was nothing there! Then Charles laughed. No, it was not the crazed laugh of a man suddenly demented. It was a low, deprecatory laugh — the kind a person uses when he appreciates the joke is on him. Pretty slick. Good old ghosty. Charles had the consoling feeling that his quest was near, its end.

The car pushed on up the hill, but complainingly. It groaned and vibrated as if it bore tons of load and the grade were ten percent instead of a mild three. Then the going got rough and bumpy. Charles looked out and saw that by some mysterious and silent process all his tires had gone flat. At that moment the engine coughed its last and died. A moment's inspection under the hood showed there was nothing the matter. Lizzie simply did not choose to run.

It was nearly dark by then, and Charles saw to his surprise that he was much nearer to the house than he thought. It was also much farther to the gate than he thought. It would be impossible to return to the highway on foot and reach it before pitch darkness came. Pretty clever, thought Charles. This spook's technique is good!

He left the car and trudged ahead. He observed now that he had been wrong about the lifelessness of the old farm. Great, torpid, repulsive-looking toads were everywhere. They did not move, even to avoid being stepped on, but they, stared at him with malevolent yellow eyes and squished nastily whenever he happened to plant his foot on one.

There were snakes, too, squirming off the weedy path and hissing venomously. Charles strode on, delighted. Things could not possibly be better.

Something white and roundish, like a misshapen bowling ball came bounding out of the brush and rolled to a stop before his feet. There was scarcely any light left then, but enough to let Charles see that the object was a freshly severed human head — that of a fair young woman with honey-colored hair. He tried to step around it, but it perversely managed to be always where he was about to put his foot. So he calmly kicked it out of his path and went on, despite the fact that as he did a soul-chilling wail rent the air.

Though Charles' confidence in his mastery of himself — thanks to his earnest study of the learned Lindemyth and others — was unabated by these little incidents, yet it troubled him that, now that night was falling, the gloom deepened so fast, for he had hoped to reach the doorway of the house before pitch dark arrived. But hurry as he would, unseen things, like wiry creeping vines, caught and dragged at his feet. He stepped out of them time and time again, but by the time he reached the ruined house there was nothing he could distinguish about it but its bulk looming in the inky blackness.

He found the door — by groping — and pushed it open, heedless of the raucous screech of its rusty hinges. Then he was inside in Stygian darkness. The door slammed to with a bang, agencies unimaginable shot bolts home with resounding clunks, and heavy chains were being arranged. Charles knew by those sounds that the door was closed and barred. He knew better than to feel behind him to verify the fact, for he was almost certain that by then there was indeed no door at all! For the first time that evening qualms of unease shuddered through him, and he felt the goose flesh rise and his back hair bristle. But he turned his mind at once back to Lindemyth and repeated to himself the consoling words; " — all such manifestations must be accepted for what they seem to be, and the investigator on no account should attempt to rationalize the irrational."

Charles' train of thought was rudely interrupted. He stumbled and fell face down. A swift exploration with his hands revealed that the obstacle was the torso of a man, recently trimmed of its extremities, judging from the pool of sticky liquid in which it lay. He chose to ignore it, and scrambled to his feet. He went on, but at a slower pace. The floor was tricky, being full of holes of indeterminable depth. He skirted several such and eventually found the stairs. Up above there was a wan light that seemed to emanate from the house itself — incredibly faint and of a phosphorescent green, but almost enough to see by, though one could never be sure.

Near the top of the stairs Charles came upon a fresh impediment. It was the swinging corpse of a hanged man. It oscillated erratically, and all of Charles' efforts to duck past it were in vain. After the fourth try he thought of a way to bypass it. He took off his necktie and tied it firmly about the feet that thrice had kicked him. Then he hauled out the other end, dragged the dead feet to the banisters and lashed them there to the handrail. Somewhere in the ghastly greenish gloom above him a demoniac chuckle broke the silence. Charles went on up the stairs. The pallid light was getting brighter. Soon, perhaps, one might actually *see*.

The upper hall was full of phantasms. They were amorphous creatures, scuttling about the floor or dashing here and there on batlike wings. Some howled, some twittered, others moaned lugubriously. Invisible hands plucked at Charles' clothes, unseen fingers twitched his hair. Prickly things flapped against, leaving his skin slimy and tingling. Once a pair of soft arms stole about his shoulders and he was startled to feel warm, moist lips pressed against his cheek in passionate caress. Then the little mouth bit, and bit hard — right into the jugular.

"Lay off," growled Charles, giving the lady apparition a savage jab in the midriff.

She evaporated like a cloud of drifting smoke. Then Charles saw a truly astonishing thing — the one thing perhaps that he was quite unprepared for. The lights came on suddenly and the hall was in full glare. A man appeared. He was well built and good-looking, in khaki shorts and a polo shirt. He seemed normal in every respect, even when he wheeled and bellowed at the cringing monsters that had drawn away from him and were huddled along the walls.

"Scat, you hellions," roared the man. "Back.to your stinking caverns. Begone!"

They went. The man turned and approached Charles with outstretched hand and a beaming smile on his face.

"Glad to see you, Charles. Welcome to Haggard House." The handclasp he gave Charles was firm and real. "I trust this vermin —"

"Oh, no," said Charles, "not at all. I presume you are Mr. —"

"Throckmorton, sir, and at your service."

Then he vanished amidst peals of mocking laughter. That is, all of him vanished except the hand and forearm that still clung in friendly greeting to Charles' palm. It was disconcerting, especially since it drooped like a bit of rubber hose. Charles stared down at the odd fragment, for a moment stupefied. He turned it over in his hands rather dazedly, after which he made a masterly effort to regain his self-possession. He loosened the grasp of the clutching fingers, and nonchalantly tossed the grisly souvenir of his host down the stairs. There was a dull boom and a flare of crimson flame when it struck. Then the darkness came back.

Charles tried the door to one of the rooms. It gave before his touch and, he looked in. That time, he shrieked without reserve. Prepared though he was by the sage's and Strobius, the inhabitants of that room were more than mortal eyes could endure. What he saw was unutterably horrible, indescribable. He backed away, leaned against the jamb of the door and vomited freely and frankly. After a short spell of violent trembling he took up his quest again.

The next room was filled with scores of pairs of balefully gleaming eyes that glared at him in the darkness. He shut that door, too, and passed on. Every room but the last was stuffed with weird horrors. Even that one; but its horror was relatively moderate, both in conception and execution. In the middle of a large four-poster bed lay a giant skeleton, calmly reading a newspaper by the light of his own luminous bones. He stirred clackingly as Charles entered, bent his eyeless gaze upon him for an instant, and then went back to his reading.

"Sorry," said Charles, walking straight to him, "but you'll have to scram. I'm getting tired of the show and want your bed so I can sleep a while. You can carry on again tomorrow."

"Oh, yeah?" said the skeleton, without looking up.

"Yeah."

Charles reached over and got a good grip with one hand on the vertebrae of the neck and with the other grabbed the pelvis. He straightened up and heaved the collection of bones hard against the wall. It flew apart at the impact and its pieces scattered over the floor. As their illumination faded out, Charles crawled into the bed and pulled the covers up. Then he turned over and went fast asleep.

It must have been near dawn when he woke again, for by then the moon had risen and a great beam of its silvery light flooded in through the window. Charles was slightly discomfitted when he awoke by the realization that he must have been screaming, for his heart was pounding fiercely, his throat was sore, and his neck muscles rigid and tense. He lay back and relaxed; then suddenly remembered what it was that had troubled his sleep. He looked up, and there it was, dangling from a rafter. It was his own body, hung there by his own hands.

"I gotta have a look at that," said Charles, intensely interested and quite calm again.

He crawled out of bed and walked over to it. But it swayed too much and was hung too high for him to see it well. He found a chair and stood up on it, face to face with his dead self.

Yes, the resemblance was astonishing! He tried to bend over to examine it more closely, but found he could not. Something restrained his neck. He looked at his counterfeit double again, but that time what he saw was a different story. He was not looking at himself hanging, but at a mirror! Most damning of all, he noticed now that in addition to the rope around his neck by which he was suspended, his ankles had been caught and tied in a loop of his own necktie and hauled over and lashed to a staircase rail!

The full horror of his situation, burned into Charles' soul, and for one awful moment his sanity almost left him. He tried to cry out, but the strangling cord about his neck would not let him. But just before he slid into the blackness of irrevocable death, his common sense came back to him.

"Shucks, Mr. Throckmorton," he said, without the slightest difficulty, "I'm surprised at you. I thought you were a high-powered spook. And then you go and pull an ancient gag like this on me. You're getting stale, or tired, or something, Mr. Throckmorton. Why don't you go take a little nap?"

240

Blam! Charles, found himself sitting hard on the floor. He got up; a little sheepishly, and found the bed again. Five minutes later he was snoring serenely.

The day dawned bleak and gray, with driving mists. Charles woke up quite normally. He had been wrong about the bed. There was no bed or any other furniture. There wasn't anything. He was lying on the bare floor of a cobweb-festooned room which was in an advanced state of disrepair. The ribs of lathing showed through where patches of plaster had fallen away, water dripped through rents in the roof. Charles got up and examined himself. He was all there except for the necktie. He supposed he would find that on the way downstairs.

It was an uneventful day, spectrally speaking, The only manifestations Mr. Throckmorton chose to make were a series of odors. At times he would afflict the house and vicinity with waves of that unpleasant smell one encounters in morgues. There were other stinks, all offensive, usually of the putrescent order. All of which delighted Charles still further. For it indicated that his host was indeed a competent practitioner, since he could put across his illusions regardless of the hour. Charles rightly — so he learned later — supposed the reason for the paucity of exhibits that day was that Mr. Throckmorton's shade was exhausted from his efforts of the night. The presence of the imperturbable Charles — well, the *almost* imperturbable Charles — must have been a heavy jolt. For Charles knew full well that most normal beings would have fled screaming and babbling from the house at the first onslaught, whereas he had stuck and forced the shade to go through his whole bag of tricks.

However, Charles was wrong on that last assumption. Throckmorton had not exhausted his repertoire by any means. The second night he treated Charles to an entirely different series of newer, bigger, and better horrors. It was very trying, but Charles weathered the grueling test. Then came the day — another day of relative inaction, marked, only by an assortment of apparitions of the type generally associated with the screaming-meemies. On the third night Mr. Throckmorton went all out. In addition to a troop of demons, he brought earthquakes, lightning, and ultimately fire. The illusion of the house burning to the ground and its walls caving in was the best of the lot. But Charles, not to be outdone, chose the hottest region of the blazing structure for his own counter-demonstration. There he quietly lay down in the midst of the phony roaring flames — and went to sleep.

Mr. Throckmorton was the first to break. Charles had just made a trip to his stalled automobile for another package of sandwiches when he found his host had materialized again. This time he wore the habiliments of an ordinary businessman. He was sitting in the doorway of the house, morosely staring at the ground and biting his lips in unconcealed mortification. Charles approached him with all due civility. He did not want to humiliate the specter. His entire aim was to test him, first, and then to bring him to a state of mind where he would be amenable to reason. For Charles had important and pressing business to transact with the ghost.

."Nice place, you've got," said Charles, by way of opening. "You put on a good act, too."

"*Gr-r-r-r*," said Mr. Throckmorton, out of the depths of his disgust. "Don't kid me. The act stinks. It *must* stink. I must be slipping." He was very miserable. His deflation, was complete...

Charles, waited politely, saying nothing.

"Tell me, kid," asked the unhappy phantom, "why did you go out of your way to come here and discredit me who have done you no harm? Why am I persecuted like this?"

"Oh, shucks, Mr. Throckmorton, you've got me wrong," Charles hastened to assure him. "I think you're swell. Really I do. As a matter of fact, you're just the sort of ghost I'm looking for. I've been shopping around for one and you're the first I've bumped into that actually knows his onions."

"But, kid," groaned Mr. Throckmorton, still unappeased, "if I'm so good, why didn't I scare you? I have everybody else. I've driven strong men to madness and wise guys to suicide. What did I do wrong this time?" It was almost-a wail.

"Because I believe in you," said Charles with fullest sincerity. "They didn't. That's why they cracked up."

"Huh?" The ghost wavered and almost vanished at that astonishing statement. "Y-you mean it was the other way around, don't you?"

"Not at all." Charles was very glad of the chance he now had of airing some of the special knowledge he had been at such pains to acquire. "Strobius in his monograph on 'Successful Haunting' treats of that very particularly. He calls it the 'Phasmic Paradox.' He points out that ghosts differ from all other myths in that their power is derived from disbelief in them, not belief."

"I always bogged down when it came to philosophy," complained Mr. Throckmorton.

"It's not so complicated," said Charles. "You didn't scare me because I do believe in you. I know you are an illusion, even if you do look as solid and real as that doorstep you're sitting on. My senses accept what they see and feel, but my judgment is unaffected. I can take it or leave it — either way. Now if I didn't believe, I would also see and feel you, but since my judgment refuses to believe what my senses report, it gets into a panic and goes to pot. It's as simple as that. To a fellow like me who knows what it's all about, the wackier the stuff you pull, the easier it is to believe in it. As an illusion, of course."

"Sounds involved," remarked the specter. "but maybe you're right."

Charles then sketched out the predicament of his grandmother, and made his proposition. "Oh," said Mr. Throckmorton: "I take it you want me to haunt the bank officials so they'll relent. Or is it the OPA guys you want me to go after?"

"Neither. It's Granny's house I want haunted."

"But, kid," remonstrated the ghost, "that doesn't make sense. No ghost ever helped a house by haunting it. Look at this one. Why, if I went there I'd scare all the people out of it in a couple of shakes. After that the house wouldn't be worth a damn to her or you or the bank or anybody else."

"Oh, I don't know," insisted Charles. "It depends on how we handle it."

They argued on for quite a while. At first the apparition that represented the long-departed Throckmorton refused categorically to have anything to do with the project. It was silly. The kickback would be terrible. Better leave well enough alone. Moreover, he liked his present stand. He had haunted the place steadily and with

243

signal success for the better part of a century. He felt-he owed it to the community not to leave.

"I have quite a reputation here, you know," he said very proudly, as if everyone didn't know.

"What does it buy you?" asked Charles sharply. He had not read the wise words of the sages for nothing; he knew more about spectral motivation than many ghosts did themselves. Ghosts, as Strobius several times remarked, were lamentably lacking in the analytical approach to their own problems. Charles promptly pursued his question with a clincher.

"Ghosts lead lonely lives, don't they? And the only fun they can ever hope to get out of it is scaring people, isn't it?"

"Er, yes," admitted the phantom grudgingly.

"O. K. Let's look at the record. You've gotten so good that nobody in his right mind will come near you. You've had just one customer in the past twenty-five years, and you went at him so hard that you drove him nuts in the first fifteen minutes. How long before you expect to hook another sucker? But if you come to Washington with me I can guarantee at least —"

Charles poured on his sales talk. He *had* to have the aid of Mr. Throckmorton. So he kept on hammering. Mr. Throckmorton began to weaken. His resistance become more and more feeble, until finally he surrendered.

"All right. I'll give it a fling. They won't miss me here for a while."

Charles brought the flivver to a halt before, his grandmother's house. The drive had taken longer than he expected, for it was close to midnight when they arrived. He leaned over and spoke to the invisible passenger beside him.

"This is the house. Hop to it. See you tomorrow."

The shade flitted away with a faint sighing sound; Charles drove calmly on.

When he let himself into his own home, his mother heard the key grate in the lock and came running anxiously out of her room. She clutched her errant child to her and patted him feverishly on the back.

"Where, oh where have you been so long, Charles?"

"Ghost hunting, that's all," he said. "Granny'll be all right now."

"You poor, poor. child," the alarmed mother soothed, "you run on to bed. You must be tired. Tomorrow we will go out to St. Elizabeth's and see the doctor."

"Why?" he asked, amazed. He wasn't sick and he wasn't crazy. One explanation suggested itself. "Granny hasn't been here *already*, has she?"

"Why, of course not, Charles. What an odd question. You know she hasn't left that house of hers for years. Why would she come here this time of night?"

"Dunno. Hunch, maybe —"

There was an imperative double ring at the front door. Charles started guiltily. He had either dawdled too long at the garage, or else Mr. Throckmorton —

The opening of the door revealed a cop and a taxi driver standing on the steps. Between them they supported Granny, who was in a complete state of jitters. She was weaving about and making little twittering noises, sobbing spasmodically now and then by way of emphasis.

"A stroke, mum, or a nightmare," said the cop. "I found her wandering in the street. She said she was all right, but she wouldn't go back to her house, no matter what happened —"

"Ooooh!" wailed the old lady.

"Knowing she was kin to you, I brought her here."

They took her in and put her to bed. She was in a bad way at first, but a couple of slugs of chloral quieted her down. She kept muttering about the terrible things that were going on in her house, but Charles comforted her.

"Don't worry, Granny. I'll go over in the morning and straighten things out. Leave everything to me."

With that he went to bed and slept the sleep of the just. All was well within his peculiar private world. Mr. Throckmorton had lived up to his instructions faithfully and promptly.

Charles was true to his word. Bright and early the next morning he walked over to Granny's place. But early as it was, there were many of the neighbors on the sidewalks, standing about in little clusters, whispering among themselves and looking at the old "O"' Street house with something akin to awe. Admittedly the house did look a bit the worse for wear, for a number of its windows were broken, and bits of personal effects strewed the tiny front yard. An ominous sight to Charles was the fire truck parked before the house, not to mention a police car, a service car from the utility company, and a press car. Had Mr. Throckmorton's easy successes gone to his head, and in his excitement had he let go and really gone to town?

As he neared the stoop, Charles passed close to several of the knots of people. He heard snatches of what they were saying. "'Explosion? . . . No, police say no . . . But people were screaming and jumping out the windows . . . Where did they go? . . . Don't know, can't find any . . . Oh, no, couldn't have been murder, there wasn't any blood . . . What was all the screaming for?"

Charles displayed his door key to the cop in charge. The fire truck was pulling away and the other inspectors were going.

"What seems to be the trouble, officer?" Charles asked, squirming miserably inside himself.

"Damfino," said the cop. "When a lot of people take a notion to leave a house all at once and don't bother to open doors or windows when they do — well, they must have been a hurry. That's all I can say. We've gone over the joint with a fine-tooth comb and we can't find anything wrong. You say you are the grandson and business manager of the owner? Swell. You take over then. I'm sick of it."

Charles went on in and looked around. The tenants had left in haste; there could be no doubt of that. Splintered doors hung crazily; and every kind of personal possession could be seen scattered over the doors — stockings, letters, cameras, burst suitcases, all manner, of things. He went over the house from basement to attic. Not one of its thirty-six tenants had stayed. The exodus was complete. Which was exactly what he wanted, though he deplored the abruptness with which it had been conducted. Which in turn reminded him to call in the neighborhood handy man to do something about rehanging the doors and re-glazing the windows.

They worked all morning. By a little after noon Charles had the situation well in hand. He had been entirely unable to raise Mr. Throckmorton, either by calling to him out loud or using a telepathic summons. No doubt the phantom was off somewhere asleep, resting from his exertions of the night. Meantime Charles collected the tremendous quantity of abandoned impedimenta and stored it neatly in one of the basement rooms. He made the beds and swept out. The house had every appearance of being back to normal. Charles also received a piece of gratifying news. The carpenter told him that the neighborhood had settled down, content that they had doped out the explanation of last night's mystery. "The kind of people that are coming to Washington these days!" they said; the rough stuff was the natural result of a drunken party. So he stepped out onto the stoop and hung up the sign, "Vacancy."

The first to ring the doorbell was a tall, well set-up man who exuded vitality and confidence from every pore. Judging from his prosperous, confident air, Charles took him to be a high-pressure salesman come to the city to grab his share of commissions. He carried two heavy, handsome bags.

He, snapped up the first room shown him — the best in the house — and expressed amazement to find so comfortable a room. He shelled out the twenty dollars called for by the posted ceiling price for the room with a haste that was almost pathetic.

"It's only fair to tell you," warned Charles, "that some folks say this house is haunted."

"Ha, ha, ha!" laughed the fellow. "Swell. After sleeping for two weeks on billiard tables and in barber chairs, I'd rent a vault in the cemetery if they'd put a cot in it and put in a shower bath. Bring on your spooks."

"Yes, sir," said Charles, but whether in acknowledgment or agreement he did not make clear. By the time he was back downstairs there were two more prospective tenants. He installed them both at once. One was an arthritic old gentleman who managed the stairs only with the greatest difficulty. The other was a very determined-looking young female who said little, and that tartly. She disapproved of everything shown her, but she took a room and paid for it. She had been commuting from Baltimore for a week and knew a good thing when she saw it.

Charles was gratefully counting the morning receipts when two more applicants came. They were giddy young things from the Midwest, come to Washington in search of secretarial jobs. They

247

asked, not too hopefully, whether there was any chance of getting a room.

"Oh, yes," smiled Charles, employing his newly acquired professional manner. But halfway through the formation of his smile it froze as was, crooked and incomplete. For down the stairs stole that gruesome, awful, morguish smell, and the two noses facing him wrinkled in dismayed disgust. One of the gals gagged feebly. Charles tried frantically to communicate with Mr. Throckmorton, sending out an appealing telepathogram —"Lay off, lay off . . . not now . . . not yet."

But Mr. Throckmorton's ghost was too occupied to notice. From the upper reaches of the house came an angry roar followed immediately by the thudding crash of a heavy piece of furniture overturned. The roar rose swiftly in pitch and intensity like the siren of a departing destroyer, until it reached a wailing howl that was suddenly damped by a choking, startled gasp. At that moment the super-salesman appeared briefly at the top of the staircase, then came down it at one fell leap, touching nothing on the way. Charles, remembering the fate of some of the house's other doors, thoughtfully snatched the front one open just in time to let the plunging tenant pass through. Then he turned to see that the departing guest had bowled over one of the waiting prospects. She had sat down hard against the baseboard, and was regarding him with a pained expression.

"My word!" giggled the other would-be secretary still on her feet. "It must have been a very important appointment he forgot."

Charles had no time to reply. More was going on above. A female voice was scolding in biting words — a nerve-racking scream — wolfish cries — the clink of shattering glass. Then the young woman of the acid manner — no longer acid — came down the stairs. Whatever the alleged weakness of her sex or the presumed handicap of her hampering skirts, she did well. She neatly tied the super-salesman's record of getting down the stairs and out of the house in virtually no time at all.

Charles glanced down at the two still with him in the hall. But they were out of the picture. They had folded limply and lay quietly Where they fell. He was still staring blankly at them when he realized he must make way for still another tenant leaving. It was the crippled gentleman who apparently had elected to try *his* hand at the stairway record. He failed to better it, perhaps because he neglected to bring his cane along; but at least he made a commendable effort. Charles caught no more than a glimpse of him as he flashed by on the way out, but he did see the green about his gills and the wild expression in his eyes.

"Dear me," thought Charles, and he started over to resuscitate the girls. But some, subconscious sense of urgency had already aroused them and they were crawling whimpering toward the door. Their eyes were averted from him, and the moment they crossed the threshold of the house, they jumped to their feet and scurried down the steps.

"Changed their minds, I guess," observed Charles, ruefully, thinking of the twelve cash dollars that each would have given him for Granny's account if they only had not been interrupted and disturbed. "I must speak to Mr. Throckmorton about this. He promised faithfully to pull his punches. We'll never get anywhere this way."

Upstairs he looked around upon a fresh crop of wreckage. He was pleased to note that the salesman had left behind a brand-new portable typewriter. The total of all the abandoned belongings would add up to a tidy sum, for he felt quite certain that not one of the owners would dream of coming back to claim them. Nevertheless, he tuned his mind to its most powerful telepathic wave, and his soul softly vibrated.

"Mr. Throckmorton. Oh, Mr. Throckmorton, please."

"Yes, Charles:"

The whisper came from smack in the middle of his ear, tingling and buzzing as if a bumblebee had lodged there, and there was a clammy, frigid quality about it that was maddening. It startled Charles more violently than any of his hectic experiences in ruined Haggard Hall. He had the wild impulse to soar straight up like a rocket and out through the roof. But he remembered who and where he was, and the sound counsel contained in the monumental work of Hans Friedrich Schutzner von Oberschutzen "On Handling Obstreperous Ghosts." He got a grip on himself and said very quietly but firmly, "This won't do, Mr. Throckmorton. We must have a little talk."

* * *

Out of the conference between carnal and spectral minds came compromise. Subsequently there was a brief transition period during which several desirable changes were made in the routine of the house, and at least one physical addition. After that all was well. Everyone concerned was happy, save perhaps the army of persons who were granted the privilege of spending a few interesting, if not entertaining, hours in Granny's old house.

Granny was happy, though nothing could induce her to go within blocks of her former home again or speak of what befell her the night she so precipitately left it. For her resourceful grandson was doing well by her. He met duly all the notes as they were presented, and one by one he retired the junior mortgages. In addition, he bought her another and smaller place in which to spend her remaining years. She never understood quite why he was succeeding where she had failed, for she herself had been a good manager and her house was never empty. But one gets old, and new brooms sweep clean.

Needless to say, the bank was happy. It got what was due it on the date due, which is all that any bank ever asks. Nor did the OPA have ground for grievance. Its rules were complied with; there were no protests or complaints. The "O" Street house was the least of their worries.

As for Charles — well, Charles was content, too. Granny's house was saved. Every dime of rental he took in went scrupulously into her account. He himself was well heeled, too. Not long after he took charge he found time to open up a small shop dealing in secondhand luggage, clothing, and other personal belongings. It was a very profitable shop, for his main costs were rent and clerk hire. His stock cost him only haulage — from that basement room in the "O"' Street house. But his greatest delight was the augmented library dealing with the occult that his profits had enabled him to buy. The possession of that, coupled with daily association with the indefatigable Throckmorton, soon made him the world's outstanding authority on ghostly affairs.

He was often tempted to join the ranks of the great by writing an authoritative work himself. It would be nice to see his

250

volumes on library shelves. But then, whenever he considered the revelation's he would have to make, and when he looked at the growing bank balances under his control, he would put the doing of it off. Much as he would have relished seeing his name in golden letters on a book cover, he also was aware that the number of persons who shared his limited interest were small. It would not do to ignore the old fable and kill the goose that laid the golden eggs.

For he had composed a lesser piece of writing, which, while not literature nor dignified by the aura of scientific pretension, was paying him daily royalties far and above what he could hope to obtain by exposing his secret to the world. Not that all of this lesser composition was secret. Far from it. Only half. The other half was posted frankly and boldly on the wall beside his desk in the vestibule of the "O" Street house. It hung beside the price schedules for the establishment nailed to the wall by a minion of the OPA. It read:

WARNING!
This house is reputed to be haunted.
THEREFORE:
In self-protection it must insist upon compliance with the following house rules.

1. Each prospective tenant must sign a release to the management against any future claim for loss of property or acute mental distress due to allegedly spectral depredations.

2. All rentals must be paid weekly in advance.

3. No rentals will be refunded for any reason.

4. Rooms abandoned without notice to the management will be at once rerented.

5. Property left unclaimed by departing tenants will be sold for storage charges after thirty days.

Those rules sewed up the tenant. Not that any departed one of them had ever shown up again to claim his property or ask a refund of what he had paid. But, as Charles put it to Mr. Throckmorton's faithful shade, "just in case."

The unpublicized other half of Charles' small but effective brochure was posted elsewhere — pasted face to the wall in the back of a tiny closet in the attic where the phantasmal self of the ex-Mr.

Throckmorton rested during his leisure hours. They were for his personal guidance and the more orderly conduct of the business of the house. They were short and to the point.

HAUNTING REGULATIONS

1. Be moderate always. It would be awkward if a departing guest should develop a major psychosis. Not too much heat!

2. Never put the pressure on until the guest's baggage has been delivered. It is a valuable by-product.

3. No rotten odors when the inspectors of the Health Department are around.

4. Complete fade-out whenever a prowl squad of the Psychic Research Bureau is on the premises.

5. The bathrooms are the preferred spots for staging manifestations. I had that old-fashioned spiral, sliding chute-type fire escape installed for just that reason. The dissatisfied tenant has a quick and easy way out with a ready exit over the back fence. If you stick to that procedure the incoming tenants will not be disturbed by the departing ones.

Yes, everybody was happy. Even the Throckmorton ghost. He grumbled a bit at first, to be sure, but he soon accepted the new regime. He complained that the full scope of his artistry was denied him, but was answered with the pointed reminder that what he lacked in quality he was more than compensated for in quantity. The house had a capacity of three dozen occupants, and while the native Washingtonians quickly learned to shun the place, each new train that rolled into Union Station brought fresh loads of prospects. Boys distributing handbills tipped them off that in Washington there was at least one place where a "few" vacancies might be had — if one hurried. And, as the venerable Throckmorton knew, after his long exile in desolate Haggard House, thirty-six fresh and gullible victims a day is nothing to be sneezed at. That each was compelled to pay the full — controlled — weekly rental was neither here nor there. That part was his partner's payoff. It was give and take.

"Ho-hum," yawned Charles, as he appraised the resale value of the leavings of the night before. "Not bad, not bad." No matter how many came and went, there were always more to come. He skimmed through a packet of letters and glanced at some intriguing photographs. He often stumbled onto such items as those infinitely valuable if offered discreetly to the right market. Only twice did he find anything the F. B. I. was acutely interested in. But he had no use for more personal items. To offer them for sale would have seemed to him dishonorable, smacking of treachery and blackmail. For Charles was a boy of high sense of honor. His business methods, while unique, were strictly on the up-and-up. It was no fault of his that people went on ignoring the marvelous literature on the subject of phantoms and the art of haunting. If they chose to persist in *not* believing in ghosts — well, that was their hard luck.

Children of the Betsy B

The author tells of a little steam launch — that grew up and ran away to sea!

I might never have heard of Sol Abernathy, if it hadn't been that my cousin, George, summered in Dockport, year before last. The moment George told me about him and his trick launch, I had the feeling that it all had something to do with the "Wild Ships" or "B-Boats," as some called them. Like everyone else, I had been speculating over the origin of the mysterious, unmanned vessels that had played such havoc with the Gulf Stream traffic. The suggestion that Abernathy's queer boat might shed some light on their baffling behavior prodded my curiosity to the highest pitch.

We all know, of course, of the thoroughgoing manner in which Commodore Elkins and his cruiser division recently rid the seas of that strange menace. Yet I cannot but feel regret, that he could not have captured at least one of the Wild Ships, if only a little boat, rather than sink them all ruthlessly, as he did. Who knows? Perhaps an examination of one of them might have revealed that Dr. Horatio Dilbiss had wrought a greater miracle than he ever dreamed of.

At any rate, I lost no time in getting up to the Maine coast. At Dockport, finding Sol Abernathy was simplicity itself. The first person asked pointed him out to me. He was sitting carelessly on a bollard near the end of the pier, basking in the sunshine, doing nothing in particular. It was clear at first glance that he was one of the type generally referred to as "local character." He must have been well past sixty, a lean, weathered little man, with a quizzical eye and a droll manner of speech that, under any other circumstances, might have led me to suspect he was spoofing — yet remembering the strange sequel to the Dockport happenings, the elements of his yarn have a tremendous significance. I could not judge from his language where he came from originally, but he was clearly not a Down Easter. The villagers could not remember the time, though, when he had *not* been in Dockport. To them he was no enigma, but simply a local fisherman, boatman, and general utility man about the harbor there.

I introduced myself — told him about my cousin, and my interest in his boat, the *Betsy B*. He was tight-mouthed at first, said he was sick and tired of being kidded about the boat. But my twenty-dollar bill must have convinced him I was no idle josher.

"We-e-e-ll," he drawled, squinting at me appraisingly through a myriad of fine wrinkles, "it's about time that somebody that really wants to know got around to astin' me about the *Betsy B*. She was a darlin' little craft, before she growed up and ran away to sea. I ain't sure, myself, whether I ought to be thankful or sore at that perfesser feller over on Quiquimoc. Anyhow, it was a great experience, even if it did cost a heap. Like Kiplin' says, I learned about shippin' from her."

"Do I understand you to say," I asked, "that you no longer have the launch?"

"Yep! She went — a year it'll be, next Thursday — takin' 'er Susan with W."

This answered my question, but shed little light. Susan? I saw I would do better if I let him ramble along in his own peculiar style.

"Well, tell me," I asked, "what was she like — at first — how big? How powered?"

"The Betsy B was a forty-foot steam launch, and I got 'er secondhand. She wasn't young, by any means — condemned navy craft, she was — from off the old *Georgia*. But she was handy, and I used 'er to ferry folks from the islands hereabouts into Dockport, and for deep-sea fishin'.

"She was a dutiful craft —" he started, but broke off with a dry chuckle, darting a shrewd sideways look at me, sizing me up. I was listening intently. "Ye'll have to get used to me talkin' of 'er like a human," he explained, apparently satisfied I was not a scoffer, "'cause if ever a boat had a soul, *she* had. Well, anyhow, as I said, she was a dutiful craft — did what she was s'posed to do and never made no fuss about it. She never wanted more'n the rightful amount of oil — I changed 'er from a coal-burner to an oil-burner, soon as I got 'er — and she'd obey 'er helm just like you'd expect a boat to.

"Then I got a call one day over to Quiquimoc. That perfesser feller, Doc Dilbiss, they call him, wanted to have his mail brought, and when I got there, he ast me to take some things ashore for 'im, to the express office. The widder Simpkins' boy was over there helpin' him, and they don't come any more wuthless. The Doc has some kind of labertory over there — crazy place. One time he mixed up a settin' of eggs, and hatched 'em! Made 'em himself, think of that! If you want to see a funny-lookin' lot of chickens, go over there some day."

"I shall," I said. I wanted him to stay with the *Betsy B* account, not digress. His Doc Dilbiss is no other than Dr. Horatio Dilbiss, the great pioneer in vitalizing synthetic organisms. I understand a heated controversy is still raging in the scientific world over his book, "The Secret of Life," but there is no doubt he has performed some extraordinary feats in animating his creations of the test tube. But to keep Abernathy to his theme, I asked, "What did the Simpkins boy do?"

"This here boy comes skippin' down the dock, carryin' a gallon bottle of some green-lookin' stuff, and then what does he do but trip over a cleat on the stringer and fall head over heels into the *Betsy B*. That bottle banged up against the boiler and just busted plumb to pieces. The green stuff in it was sorta oil and stunk like all forty. It spread out all over the insides before you could say Jack Robinson, and no matter how hard I scoured and mopped, I couldn't get up more'n a couple of rags full of it.

"You orter seen the Doc. He jumped up and down and pawed the air — said the work of a lifetime was all shot — I never knew a mild little feller like him could cuss so. The only thing I could see to do was to get outa there and take the Simpkins boy with me — it looked sure like the Doc was a-goin' to kill him.

"Naturally, I was pretty disgusted myself. Anybody can tell you I keep clean boats — I was a deep-sea sailor once upon a time, was brought up right, and it made me durned mad to have that green oil stickin' to everything. I took 'er over to my place, that other little island you see there —" pointing outside the harbor to a small island with a couple of houses and an oil tank on it —"and tried to clean 'er up. I didn't have much luck, so knocked off, and for two — three days I used some other boats I had, thinkin' the stink would blow away.

"When I got time to get back to the *Betsy B,* you coulda knocked me down with a feather when I saw she was full of vines — leastways, I call 'em vines. I don't mean she was full of vines, but they was all over 'er insides, clingin' close to the hull, like ivy, and runnin' up under the thwarts, and all over the cylinders and the boiler. In the cockpit for'ard, where the wheel was, I had a boat compass in a little binnacle. Up on top of it was a lumpy thing — made me think of a gourd — all connected up with the vines.

"I grabbed that thing and tried to pull it off. I tugged and I hauled, but it wouldn't come. But what do you think happened?"

"I haven't the faintest idea," I said, seeing that he expected an answer.

"She rared up and down, like we was outside in a force-six gale, and *whistled!"* Abernathy broke off and glared at me belligerently, as if he half expected me to laugh at him. Of course, I did no such thing. It was not a laughing matter, as the world was to find out a little later.

"And that was stranger than ever," he continued, after a pause, "cause I'd let 'er fires die out when I tied 'er up. Somehow she had steam up. I called to Joe Binks, my fireman, and bawled him out for havin' lit 'er off without me tellin' him to. But he swore up and down that he hadn't touched 'er. But to get back to the gourd thing — as soon as I let it go, she quieted down. I underran those vines to see where they come from. I keep callin' 'em vines, but maybe you'd call 'em wires. They were hard and shiny, like wires, and tough — only they branched every whichaway like vines, or the veins in a maple leaf. There was two sets of 'em, one set runnin' out of the gourd thing on the binnacle was all mixed up with the other set comin' out of the bottom between the boiler and the engine.

"She didn't mind my foolin' with the vines, and didn't cut up except whenever I'd touch the gourd arrangement up for'ard. The vines stuck too close to whatever they lay on to pick up, but I got a

257

pinch-bar and pried. I got some of 'em up about a inch and slipped a wedge under. I worked on 'em with a chisel, and then a hacksaw. I cut a couple of 'em and by the Lord Harry — if they didn't grow back together again whilst I was cuttin' on the third one. I gave up! I just let it go, I was that dogtired.

"Before I left, I took a look into the firebox and saw she had the burner on slow. I turned it off, and saw the water was out of the glass. I secured the boiler, thinkin' how I'd like to get my hands on whoever lit it off.

"Next day, I had a fishin' party to take out in my schooner, and altogether, what with one thing and another, it was a week before I got back to look at the *Betsy B*. Now, over at my place, I have a boathouse and a dock, and behind the boathouse is a fuel oil tank, as you can see. This day, when I went down to the dock, what should I see but a pair of those durned vines runnin' up the dock like 'lectric cables. And the smoke was pourin' out of 'er funnel like everything. I ran on down to 'er and tried to shut off the oil, 'cause I knew the water was low, but the valve was all jammed with the vine wires, and I couldn't do a thing with it.

"I found out those vines led out of 'er bunkers, and mister, believe it or not, but she was a-suckin' oil right out of my big storage tank! Those vines on the dock led straight from the *Betsy B* into the oil tank. When I found out I couldn't shut off the oil, I jumped quick to have a squint at the water gauge, and my eyes nearly run out on stems when I saw it smack at the right level. Do you know, that doggone steam launch had thrown a bunch of them vines around the injector and was a-feedin' herself? Fact! And sproutin' from the gun'le was another bunch of 'em, suckin' water from overside.

"But wouldn't she salt herself?" I asked of him, knowing that salt water is not helpful to marine boilers.

"No, sir-ree! That just goes to show you how smart she was gettin' to be. Between the tank and the injector, durned if she hadn't grown another fruity thing, kinda like a watermelon. It had a hole in one side, and there was a pile of salt by it and more spillin' out. She had rigged 'erself some sorta filter — or distiller. I drew off a little water from a gauge cock, and let it cool down and tasted it. Sweet as you'd want!

"I was kinda up against it. If she was dead set and determined to keep steam up all the time, and had dug right into the big tank, I knew it'd run into money. I might as well be usin' 'er. These vines I've been tellin' you about weren't in the way to speak of; they hung close to the planks like the veins on the back of your hand. Seein' 'er bunkers was full to the brim, I got out the hacksaw and cut the vines to the oil tank, watchin' 'er close all the time to see whether she'd buck again.

"From what I saw of 'er afterward, I think she had a hunch she was gettin' ready to get under way, and she was r'arin' to go. I heard a churnin' commotion in the water, and durned if she wasn't already kicking her screw over! just as I got the second vine cut away, she snaps her lines, and if I hadn't made a flyin' leap, she'd a gone off without me.

"I'm tellin' you, mister, that first ride was a whole lot like gettin' aboard a unbroken colt. At first she wouldn't answer her helm. I mean, I just couldn't put the rudder over, hardly, without lyin' down and pushin' with everything I had on the wheel. And Joe Binks, my fireman, couldn't do nuthin' with 'er neither — said the throttled fly wide open every time he let go of it.

"Comin' outa my place takes careful doin' — there's a lot of sunken ledges and one sandbar to dodge. I says to myself, I've been humorin' this baby too much. I remembered she was tender about that gourd thing, so the next time I puts the wheel over and she resists, I cracks down on the gourd with a big fid I'd been splicin' some five-inch line with. She blurted 'er whistle, and nearly stuck her nose under, but she let go the rudder. Seein' that I was in for something not much diffrunt from bronco bustin', I cruised 'er up and down outside the island, puttin' 'er through all sorts a turns and at various speeds. I only had to hit 'er four or five times. After that, all I had to do was to raise the fid like I was a-goin' to, and she'd behave. She musta had eyes or something in that gourd contraption. I still think that's where her brains were. It had got some bigger, too.

"I didn't have much trouble after that, for a while. I strung some live wires across the dock — I found she wouldn't cross that with 'er feelers — and managed to put 'er on some sort of rations about the oil. But I went down one night, 'round two in the mornin', and found 'er with a full head of steam. I shut everything down, leavin' just enough to keep 'er warm, and went for'ard and whacked 'er on the head, just for luck. It worked, and as soon as we had come to some sorta understanding, as you might say, I was glad she had got the way she was.

"What I mean is, after she was broke, she was a joy. She learned her way over to Dockport, and, after a coupla, trips, I never had to touch wheel or throttle. She'd go back and forth, never makin' a mistake. When you think of the fogs we get around here, that's something. And, o' course, she learned the Rules of the Road in no time. She *knew* which side of a buoy to take — and when it came to passin' other boats, she had a lot better judgment than I have.

"Keepin' 'er warm all the time took some oil, but it didn't really cost me any more, 'cause I was able to let Joe go. She didn't need a regular engineer, nohow — in fact, her and Joe fought so, I figured it'd be better without him. Then I took 'er out and taught 'er how to use charts."

Abernathy stopped and looked at me cautiously. I think this must be the place that some of his other auditors walked out on him, or started joshing, because he had the slightly embarrassed look of a man who feels that perhaps he had gone a little too far. Remembering the uncanny way in which the Wild Ships had stalked the world's main steamer lanes, my mood was one of intense interest.

"Yes," I said, "go on."

"I'd mark the courses in pencil on the chart, without any figures, and prop it up in front of the binnacle. Well, that's all there was to it. She'd shove off, and follow them courses, rain, fog, or shine. In a week or so, it got so I'd just stick a chart up there and go on back and loll in the stern sheets, like any payin' passenger.

"If that'd been all, I'd a felt pretty well off, havin' a trained steam launch that'd fetch and carry like a dog. I didn't trust 'er enough to send 'er off anywhere by herself, but she coulda done it. All my real troubles started when I figured I'd paint 'er. She was pretty rusty-lookin', still had the old navy-gray paint on — what was left of it.

"I dragged 'er up on the marine railway I got over there, scraped 'er down and got ready to doll 'er up. The first jolt I got was when I found she was steel, 'stead of wood. And it was brand, spankin' new plate, not a pit or a rust spot anywhere. She'd been pumpin' sea water through those vines, eatin' away the old rotten plankin' and extractin' steel from the water. Somebody — I've fergotten who 'twas — told me there's every element in sea water if you can get it out. Leastways, that's how I account for it-she was wood when I bought 'er. Later on you'll understand better why I say that-she could do some funny things.

"The next thing that made me sit up and take notice was the amount of paint it took. I've painted hundreds of boats in my time, and know to the pint what's needed. Well I had to send to town for more; I was shy about five gallons. Come to think about it, she did look big for a fortyfooter, so I got out a tape and laid it on 'er. She was fifty-eight feet over all! And she'd done it so gradual I never even noticed!

"But — to get along. I painted 'er nice and white, with a red bottom and a catchy green trim, along the rail and canopy. We polished 'er bright — work and titivated 'er generally. She did look nice, and new as you please — and in a sense she was, with the bottom I was tellin' you about. You'd a died a-laughin' though, if you'd been with me the next day, when we come over here to Dockport. The weather was fine and the pier was full of summer people. As soon as we come up close, they began cheerin' and callin' out to me how swell the *Betsy B* looked in 'er new colors. Well, there was nothin' out of the way about that. I went on uptown and 'tended to my business, came back after a while, and we shoved off.

"But do you think that blamed boat would leave there right away? No, sir! Like I said, lately I'd taken to climbin' in the stern sheets and givin' 'er her head. But that day, we hadn't got much over a hundred yards beyond the end of the pier, when what does she do but put 'er rudder over hard and come around in an admiral's sweep with wide-open throttle, and run back the length of the pier. She traipsed up and down a coupla times before I tumbled to what was goin' on. It was them admirin' people on the dock and the summer tourists cheerin' that went to 'er head.

"All the time, people was yellin' to me to get my wild boat outa there, and the constable threatenin' to arrest me 'cause I must be drunk to charge up and down the harbor thataway. You see, she'd gotten so big and fast she was settin' up plenty of waves with 'er gallivantin', and all the small craft in the place was tearin' at their lines, and bangin' into each other something terrible. I jumped up for'ard and thumped 'er on the skull once or twice, 'fore I could pull 'er away from there.

"From then on, I kept havin' more'n more to worry about. There was two things, mainly — her growin', and the bad habits she took up. When she got to be seventy feet, I come down one mornin' and found a new bulkhead across the stern section. It was paper-thin, but it was steel, and held up by a mesh of vines an each side. In two days more it was as thick, and looked as natural, as any other part of the boat. The funniest part of that bulkhead, though, was that it put out rivet heads — for appearance, I reckon, because it was as solid as solid could be before that.

"Then, as she got to drawin' more water, she begun lengthenin' her ladders. They was a coupla little two-tread ladders — made it easier for the womenfolks gettin' in and out. I noticed the treads gettin' thicker V thicker. Then, one day, they just split. Later on, she separated them, evened 'em up. Those was the kind of little tricks she was up to all the time she was growin'.

"I coulda put up with 'er growin' and all — most any feller would be tickled to death to have a launch that'd grow into a steam yacht — only she took to runnin' away. One mornin' I went down, and the lines was hangin' off the dock, parted like they'd been chafed in two. I cranked my motor dory and started out looking for the *Betsy B*. I sighted 'er after a while, way out to sea, almost to the horizon.

"Didja ever have to go down in the pasture and bridle a wild colt? Well, it was like that. She waited, foxylike, lyin' to, until I got almost alongside, and then, doggone if she didn't take out, hell bent for Halifax, and run until she lost 'er steam! I never woulda caught 'er if she hadn't run out of oil. At that, I had to tow 'er back, and a mean job it was, with her throwing 'er rudder first this way and that. I finally got plumb mad and went alongside and whanged the livin' daylights outa that noodle of hers.

"She was docile enough after that, but sulky, if you can imagine how a sulky steam launch does. I think she was sore over the beatin' I gave 'er. She'd pilot 'erself, all right, but she made

262

some awful bad landin's when we'd come in here, bumpin' into the pier at full speed and throwin' me off my feet when I wasn't lookin' for it. It surprised me a lot, 'cause I knew how proud she was — but I guess she was that anxious to get back at me, she didn't care what the folks on the dock thought.

"After that first time, she ran away again two or three times, but she allus come back of 'er own accord — gettin' in to the dock dead tired, with nothing but a smell of oil in her bunkers. The fuel bill was gettin' to be a pain.

"The next thing that come to plague me was a fool government inspector. Said he'd heard some bad reports and had come to investigate! Well, he had the *Betsy B's* pedigree in a little book, and if you ever saw a worried look on a man, you shoulda seen him while he was comparin' 'er dimensions and specifications with what they was s'posed to be. I tried to explain the thing to him — told him he could come any week and find something new. He was short and snappy — kept writin' in his little book — and said that I was a-goin' to hear from this."

> *"You* can see I couldn't help the way the *Betsy B* was growin'. But what got my goat was that I told him she had only one boiler, and when we went to look, there was two, side by side, neatly cross-connected, with a stop on each one, and another valve in the main line. I felt sorta hacked over that — it was something I didn't know, even. She'd done it overnight.

"The inspector feller said I'd better watch my step, and went off, shakin' his head. He as much as gave me to understand that he thought *my Betsy B* papers was faked and this here vessel stole. The tough part of that idea, for him, was that there never had been anything like 'er built. I forgot to tell you that before he got there, she'd grown a steel deck over everything, and was startin' out in a big way to be a regular ship.

"I was gettin' to the point when I wished she'd run away and stay. She kept on growin', splittin' herself up inside into more and more compartments. That woulda been all right, if there'd been any arrangement I could use, but no human would design such a ship. No doors, or ports, or anything. But the last straw was the lifeboat. That just up and took the cake.

"Don't get me wrong. It's only right and proper for a yacht, or anyway, a vessel as *big* as a yacht, to have a lifeboat. She was a hundred and thirty feet long then, and rated one. But any sailor man would naturally expect it to be a wherry, or a cutter at one outside. But, no, she had to have a steam launch, no less!

"It was a tiny little thing, only about ten feet long, when she let me see it first. She had built a contraption of steel plates on 'er upper deck that I took to be a spud-locker, only I mighta known she wasn't interested in spuds. It didn't have no door, but it did have some louvers for ventilation, looked like. Tell you the truth, I didn't notice the thing much, 'cept to see it was there. Then one night, she rips off the platin', and there, in its skids, was this little steam launch!

"It was all rigged out with the same vine layout that the *Betsy B* had runnin' all over 'er, and had a name on it — the *Susan B*. It was a dead ringer for the big one, if you think back and remember what she looked like when she come outa the navy yard. Well, when the little un was about three weeks old — and close to twenty feet long, I judge — the *Betsy B* shoved off one mornin', in broad daylight, without so much as by-your-leave, and goes around on the outside of my island. She'd tore up so much line gettin' away for 'er night jamborees, I'd quit moorin' 'er. I knew she'd come back, 'count o' my oil tank. She'd hang onto the dock by her own vines.

"I run up to the house and put a glass on 'er. She was steamin' along slow, back and forth. Then she reached down with a sorta crane she'd growed and picked that *Susan B* up, like you'd lift a kitten by the scruff o' the neck, and sets it in the water. Even where I was, I could hear the *Susan B* pipin', shrill-like. Made me think of a peanut-wagon whistle. I could see the steam jumpin' out of 'er little whistle. I s'pose it was scary for 'er, gettin' 'er bottom wet, the first time. But the *Betsy B* kept goin' along, towin' the little one by one of 'er vines.

"She'd do something like that two or three times a week, and if I wasn't too busy, I'd watch 'em, the *Betsy B* steamin' along, and the little un cavortin' around 'er, cuttin' across 'er bows or a-chasin' 'er. One day, the *Susan B* was chargin' around my little cove, by itself, the *Betsy B* quiet at the dock. I think she was watchin' with another gourd thing she'd sprouted in the crow's nest. Anyhow, the

Susan B hit that sandbar pretty hard, and stuck there, whistlin' like all get out. The *Betsy B* cast off and went over there. And, boy, did she whang that little un on the koko!

"I'm gettin' near to the end — now, and it all come about 'count of this *Susan B*. She was awful wild, and no use that I could see as a lifeboat, 'cause she'd roll like hell the minute any human'd try to get in 'er — it'd throw 'em right out into the water! I was gettin' more fed up every day, what with havin' to buy more oil all the time, and not gettin' much use outa my boats.

"One day, I was takin' out a picnic party in my other motorboat, and I put in to my cove to pick up some bait. Just as I was goin' in, that durned *Susan B* began friskin' around in the cove, and comes chargin' over and collides with me, hard. It threw my passengers all down, and the women got their dresses wet and all dirty. I was good and mad. I grabbed the *Susan B* with a boat hook and hauled her alongside, then went to work on her binnacle with a steerin' oar. You never heard such a commotion. I said a while ago she sounded like a peanut whistle — well, this time it was more like a calliope. And to make it worse, the *Betsy B,* over at the dock sounds off with her whistle — a big chimed one, them days. And when I see 'er shove off and start over to us, I knew friendship had ceased!

"That night she ups and leaves me. I was a-sleepin' when the phone rings, 'bout two A.M. It was the night watchman over't the oil company's dock. Said my *Betsy B* was alongside and had hoses into their tanks, but nobody was on board, and how much should he give 'er. I yelled at him to give 'er nuthin' — told him to take an ax and cut 'er durned hoses. I jumped outa my bunk and tore down to the dock. Soon as I could get the danged motor started I was on my way over there. But it didn't do no good. Halfway between here and there, I meets 'er, comin' out, makin' knots. She had 'er runnin' lights on, legal and proper, and sweeps right by me — haughty as you please — headin' straight out, Yarmouth way. If she saw me, she didn't give no sign.

"Next day I got a bill for eight hundred tons of oil — she musta filled up every one of 'er compartments — and it mighty near broke me to pay it. I was so relieved to find 'er gone, I didn't even report it. That little launch was what did it — I figured if they was one, they was bound to be more. I never did know where she got the idea; nothin' that floats around here's big enough to carry lifeboats."

"Did Dr. Dilbiss ever look at her," I asked, "after she started to grow?"

"That Doc was so hoppin' mad over the Simpkins brat spillin' his 'Oil of Life' as he called it, that he packed up and went away right after. Some o' the summer people do say he went to Europe — made a crack about some dictator where he was, and got put in jail over there. I don't know about that, but he's never been back."

"And you've never seen or heard of the *Betsy B* since?" I queried, purposely making it a leading question.

"Seen 'er, no, but heard of 'er plenty. First time was about three months after she left. That was when the Norwegian freighter claimed he passed a big ship and a smaller one with a whale between 'em. Said the whale was half cut up, and held by a lot of cables. They come up close, but the ships didn't answer hails, or put up their numbers. I think that was my *Betsy B,* and the *Susan B,* growed up halfway. That *Betsy* B could make anything she wanted outa sea water, 'cept oil. But she was smart enough, I bet, to make whale oil, if she was hungry enough.

"The next thing I heard was the time the *Ruritania* met 'er. No question about that — they read 'er name. The *Ruritania* was a-goin' along, in the mid-watch it was, and the helmsman kept sayin' it was takin' a lot of starboard helm to hold 'er up. 'Bout that time, somebody down on deck calls up there's a ship alongside, hangin' to the starboard quarter. They kept hollerin' down to the ship, wantin' to know what ship, and all that, and gettin' no answer. You oughta read about that. Then she shoved off in the dark and ran away. The *Ruritania* threw a spot on 'er stern and wrote down the name.

"That mightn't prove it — anybody can paint a name — but after she'd gone, they checked up and found four holes in the side, and more'n a thousand tons of bunker oil gone. That *Betsy B* had doped out these other ships must have oil, and bein' a ship herself, she knew right where they stored it. She just snuck up alongside in the middle of the night, and worked 'er vines in to where the oil was.

"Things like that kept happenin', and the papers began talkin' about the Wild Ships. They sighted dozens of 'em, later, all named

'Something *W* — *Lucy B, Anna B, Trixie B,* oh, any number — which in itself is another mystery. Where would a poor dumb steam launch learn all them names?"

"You said she was ex-navy," I reminded him.

"That may be it," he admitted. "Well, that's what started the newspapers to callin' lern the B-Boats. 'Course, I can't deny that when they ganged up in the Gulf Stream and started in robbin' tankers of their whole cargo, and in broad daylight, too, it was goin' too far. They was all too fast to catch. Commodore What's-his-name just had to sink 'er, I reckon. The papers was ridin' him hard. But I can tell you that there wasn't any real meanness in my *Betsy* B — spoiled maybe — but not mean. That stuff they printed 'bout the octopuses on the bridges, with long danglin' tentacles wasn't nothin' but that gourd brain and vines growed up."

He sighed a deep, reminiscent sigh, and made a gesture indicating he had told all there was to tell.

"You are confident, then," I asked, "that the so-called B-Boats were the children of your *Betsy B?* "

"Must be," he answered, looking down ruefully at his patched overalls and shabby shoes. "'Course, all I know is what I read in the papers, 'bout raidin' them tankers. But that'd be just like their mammy. She sure was a hog for oil!"

THE END

Made in the USA
Middletown, DE
09 June 2022

66923705R00158